CAUTION!
UNICORN CROSSING!

Taken He Cannot Be (Will Shetterly) * *What the Eye Sees, What the Heart Feels* (Robert Devereaux) * *Old One-Antler* (Michael Armstrong) * *Stampede of Light* (Marina Fitch) * *Gilgamesh Recidivus* (P. D. Cacek) * *Big Dogs, Strange Days* (Edward Bryant) * *The Tenth Worthy* (Susan Shwartz) * *Daughter of the Tao* (Lisa Mason) * *The Devil on Myrtle Ave.* (Eric Lustbader) * *Dame à la Licorne* (Judith Tarr) * *Convergence* (Lucy Taylor) * *The Day of Sounding of Josh M'bobwe* (Janet Berliner) * *The Trouble with Unicorns* (Nancy Willard) * *Professor Gottesman and the Indian Rhinoceros* (Peter S. Beagle)

Peter S. Beagle's

IMMORTAL
UNICORN

VOLUME ONE

Edited by

Peter S. Beagle

and

Janet Berliner

HarperPrism
A Division of HarperCollinsPublishers

HarperPrism
A Division of HarperCollinsPublishers
10 East 53rd Street, New York, NY 10022-5299

This is a work of fiction. The characters, incidents, and
dialogues are products of the authors' imagination and are not to
be construed as real. Any resemblance to actual events or
persons, living or dead, is entirely coincidental.

Individual story copyrights appear on pages 397–98.

ISBN 0-06-105480-1

HarperCollins®, ☰ ®, and HarperPrism®
are trademarks of HarperCollins Publishers, Inc.

Cover design © 1998 by Richard Rossiter
Cover illustration © 1998 by Michael Sabanosh

A hardcover edition of this book was published
in 1995 by HarperPrism.

First paperback printing: December 1998

Printed in the United States of America

Visit HarperPrism on the World Wide Web at
http://www.harperprism.com

❖ 10 9 8 7 6 5 4 3 2 1

ACKNOWLEDGMENTS

The editors wish to thank both Harpers—Laurie Harper of Sebastian Agency and HarperPrism—for their support and enthusiasm, and Martin H. Greenberg, arguably the world's most renowned anthologist, for his advice and confidence. And, as always, there's the (mostly) unflappable "Cowboy Bob," Robert L. Fleck, without whose assistance this volume would probably still be in the pipelines. They wish to thank each other for keeping every promise made, the most important one being: "We're going to have fun, stay friends, and create something unique."

Peter sends his special love and gratitude to his wife, Padma Hejmadi.

Yet one more time, Janet Berliner extends unending love, affection, and gratitude to Laurie Harper for all of the long hours she put in, the countless conversations, and her invaluable input; to Bob Fleck, her personal assistant; her feisty mother, Thea Cowan; her daughter, Stefanie Gluckman; and her mentor and friend, Dr. Samuel Draper. You'll love *these* stories, Sam. To paraphrase, methinks that, "Age shall not wither them, nor custom stale their infinite variety."

CONTENTS

Preface
  by Janet Berliner   ix

Foreword
  by Peter S. Beagle   xi

Taken He Cannot Be
  by Will Shetterly   1

*What the Eye Sees,
  What the Heart Feels*
  by Robert Devereaux   15

Old One-Antler
  by Michael Armstrong   35

Stampede of Light
  by Marina Fitch   61

Gilgamesh Recidivus
  by P. D. Cacek   81

Big Dogs, Strange Days
  by Edward Bryant   103

The Tenth Worthy
  by Susan Shwartz   131

Daughter of the Tao
  by Lisa Mason   167

The Devil on Myrtle Ave.
  by Eric Lustbader   195

Dame à la Licorne
  by Judith Tarr   265

Convergence
    by Lucy Taylor   295
The Day of Sounding of
   Josh M'bobwe
    by Janet Berliner   315
The Trouble with Unicorns
    by Nancy Willard   331
Professor Gottesman and
   the Indian Rhinoceros
    by Peter S. Beagle   353

PREFACE

As Peter has written in his foreword to this volume, the range and literacy of the stories we collected is nothing short of mind-boggling. Clearly, the theme of immortality, together with the symbol of the unicorn, tapped a vein in the writers we approached. For that I am extremely grateful.

More clearly, and this is something which Peter-the-modest would never say himself, they would not dare to have given us anything but their very best, their unique efforts. Some of them know him well and are old friends; all of them stand in awe of his modesty and his talent.

I first met Peter more than fifteen years ago, at a writers conference in Los Altos Hills, California. Of course I didn't know it was Peter, as I stood near the campus swimming pool on that hot summer's day, eaveswatching a man who looked like a bearded Jewish magician converse with a shaggy mongrel.

"I talk to dogs, you know," the magician said, when he noticed my presence. "And they answer me." Addressing, I suspect, the skepticism on my face, he said, "Look, I'll prove it. I'll tell the dog to jump in the pool, swim across, get out at the other side, and then walk around the pool back here." He turned to the dog. "What's your name?"

"So you've trained your dog," I said. "Terrific."

"This isn't my dog. I've never seen it before in my life."

The dog obeyed, I became a believer, and Peter S. Beagle—converser with dogs—and I have been friends ever since.

Before I left the campus that Sunday, I had purchased copies of two of Peter's books, *A Fine and Private Place* and *The Last Unicorn*. Those dog-eared, well-read copies have gone with me on every journey. I have long wanted to find a project that would enchant us both. It is my particular joy to have been the instrument that has reunited Peter with the unicorn.

As for the theme of immortality, it too comes directly from Peter's soul. One of the many things I have admired in him over the years is his insistence upon keeping in touch with old, "forgotten" writers. Those who perhaps wrote one opus, and then hid away, thinking themselves unloved and unremembered. It is he who consistently reminds them that, though they may not be immortal in the physical sense, the words they have created are.

I can't tell which I love most, the heart of the man or his incredible talent; I can tell you that it's been a true joy putting this book together with him.

Thank you, Peter.

One more thing: The alphabetical-by-author order of the stories was pure synchronicity. We had no intention of creating an almost-encyclopedia of immortal unicorn stories, but so be it. Whatever works.

—Janet Berliner
Las Vegas, Nevada
April 1, 1995

FOREWORD

—⦅◈⦆—

> . . . and great numbers of unicorns, hardly
> smaller than an elephant in size. Their hair is
> like that of a buffalo, and their feet like those of
> an elephant. In the middle of their forehead is a
> very large black horn. Their head is like that of
> a wild boar, and is always carried bent to the
> ground. They delight in living in mire and mud.
> It is a hideous beast to look at, and in no way
> like what we think and say in our countries,
> namely a beast that lets itself be taken in the lap
> of a virgin. Indeed, I assure you that it is alto-
> gether different from what we fancied . . .
>
> —Marco Polo

In the first place, I blame Janet Berliner for everything. This book was her idea from the beginning: she did
the vast bulk of the editing, the telephoning, and all the
other grunt work; and if you like *Immortal Unicorn,* it's
mostly Janet's doing. If you don't like it, I'm covered.

In the second place, I could happily live out the rest of
my time on the planet without ever having another thing to
do with unicorns. Through what I persist in regarding as no
fault of my own—my children were enjoying the chapters
as I read them aloud, so I just kept going—I've been stuck

with the beasts for some twenty-seven years now. First begun in 1962, published in 1968 (worlds and worlds ago, in a culture that measures time by elections and Super Bowls), *The Last Unicorn* is the book people know who don't know that I ever wrote anything else. Never a best-seller, never so much as a reliable annuity, it's been trans-lated into fourteen languages, made into an animated film, and dramatized in half a dozen versions. People have writ-ten wonderfully kind and moving letters to me about it over the last twenty-seven years. I ran out of shyly sponta-neous replies around 1980, I think it was.

But what amazed me as these stories began to come in is the eternal command the unicorn retains over the human imagination. Whether they turn up in the classic tapestry guises of Susan Shwartz's Arthurian tale, "The Tenth Worthy," or Nancy Willard's poignant variation, "The Trouble with Unicorns"; as dangerously attainable pas-sions, in such works as P. D. Cacek's "Gilgamesh Recidivus" or Michael Armstrong's "Old One-Antler"; or as a source of karmic aggravation and cranky wonder to a rural community in Annie Scarborough's delightful "A Rare Breed," the damn things continue somehow to evoke astonishingly varied visions of soul-restoring beauty, indomitable freedom, and a strange, wild compassion, as well as the uncompromised mystery and elusiveness with-out which no legend can ever survive. Bigfoot, Nessie, Butch and Sundance, the unicorn . . . they leave footprints and dreams, but never their bones.

The title of this book has far less to do with physical immortality than with the unicorn's wondrously enduring presence in some twilight corner of our human DNA.

From the European horned horse or dainty goat/deer hybrid to the ferocious, rhinoceros-like *karkadann* of Persia, India, and North Africa, to the Chinese *k'i-lin,* whose rare appearances either celebrated a just reign or portended the death of a great personage, there are surprisingly few mythologies in which the unicorn, or something very like it, does not turn up. India was the great medieval source of unicorn sightings; but over the centuries there have been accounts out of Japan, Tibet, Siberia, Ethiopia (Pliny the Elder and his contemporaries had a distinct tendency to stash any slightly questionable marvel in Ethiopia), Scandinavia, South Africa, and even Canada and Maine. Entirely regardless of whether they exist or not, something in us, as human beings, seems always to have needed them to be.

(It's worth mentioning that men have for centuries been manipulating the horn buds of cattle, sheep, and goats to produce a one-horned animal—with evident success, if that's your idea of success. Judith Tarr's story, "Dame à la Licorne," deals movingly and realistically with an eminently believable version of this ancient practice. But horns don't make the unicorn; it's the other way around.)

The possibility that unicorns might need humans just as much, in their own way, is well worth a moment's consideration. In *Through the Looking Glass,* after all, Lewis Carroll's unicorn says to Alice, ". . . Now we have seen each other, if you'll believe in me, I'll believe in you. Is that a bargain?" And there is a very old fable which holds that the unicorn was the first animal named by Adam and Eve, and that when they were barred from Paradise the unicorn chose to follow them into the bitter mortal world, to share their suffering there, and their joys as well. You might think about that legend when reading Robert Devereaux's story "What the Eye Sees, What the Heart Feels."

I've indicated earlier that I find the diversity of these stories as exceptional as their quality. What I expected (and after twenty-seven years of being sent cuddly stuffed unicorns, so would you) was an embarrassment of wistfulness, a plethora of dreamy elegies to metaphoric innocence betrayed, and a whole lot of rip-offs equally of *The Glass Menagerie* and the unicorn hunt scene in T. H. White's *The Once and Future King*. I couldn't have been more wrong.

The bulk of the tales in this book focus more on the power, and at times the genuine ferocity and aggressiveness of the unicorn—which is far more in keeping with the mythological record—than on its vulnerability. They range in setting from Lisa Mason's turn-of-the-century San Francisco to Eric Lustbader's all too contemporary Bedford-Stuyvesant district, to Cacek's Siberia, George Guthridge's linked Mongolia and Arctic Circle, Karen Joy Fowler's 1950s Indiana, Will Shetterly's nineteenth-century American Southwest, Janet's own South Africa, and Dave Smeds' scarifying wartime Vietnam. Their tone cuts across a remarkable spectrum of action, style, and emotion, at one end of which we may with confidence place Robert Sheckley's quietly and profoundly flaky "A Plague of Unicorns." Somewhere in the middle we find Melanie Tem's tender and haunting "Half-Grandma," Fowler's "The Brew," Marina Fitch's lovely "Stampede of Light," Kevin Anderson and Rebecca Moesta's "Sea Dreams," Shetterly's "Taken He Cannot Be" (which swept away my grim resistance to reading one more flipping word about Wyatt, Doc, and the O.K. Corral), and Lucy Taylor's "Convergence"—stories less about unicorns per se than about generosity, courage, loneliness, love, and letting go: all immortal realities embodied by those aggravating creatures I appear to be stuck with. A little way along, a splendidly unique fantasy like Mason's "Daughter of the Tao" shades into "Dame à la Licorne," science fiction in the best sense of the term. (Incidentally, no man would have been likely to produce that one, by the way—I speak as the father of two daughters.)

Tad Williams' elegantly original "Three Duets for Virgin and Nosehorn" fits comfortably on the near side of "Daughter of the Tao," as does my own "Professor Gottesman and the Indian Rhinoceros." I'm honored to be in such company, and pleased that we've done our bit to restore the glamour (in the old Celtic sense of enchantment) of a noble beast, maligned and derided from Marco Polo through Hemingway and Ionesco. (Ionesco, by the way, had never seen a rhinoceros when he wrote the play that made the word a synonym for insane conformity. Introduced to two at the Zurich Zoo, I was once told he studied the creatures for a long while, and finally bowed formally, saying, "I have been deceived, and I apologize." Then he shook his walking stick at them and shouted, "But you are not real rhinoceroses!")

At the furthest end of the book's reach stalk Lustbader's "The Devil on Myrtle Ave.," Smeds' "Survivor," Michael Marano's "Winter Requiem," George Guthridge's "Mirror of Lop Nor," and S. P. Somtow's astonishing "A Thief in the Night." These are violent stories, as much or more in tone and vision as in action; and in these, too, unicorns as unicorns are less crucial than the central characters. The unicorn of "Winter Requiem" is a demon, plain and simple; the one literally depicted in "Survivor" is nothing more than a tattoo on a soldier's chest; while Somtow's unicorn is a shadow, a hoofprint, only seen fully for a moonlit moment at the end of this encounter between the Messiah and a strangely sympathetic Antichrist on the boardwalk at California's Venice Beach. For that matter, the unicorns of "Sea Dreams" are narwhals, the steeds of undersea princes in a young girl's fairy tale; in Dave Wolverton's "We Blazed," there is no immortal beast at all, but a rock singer searching for his wife through the universe of her dreams. You won't find these unicorns up at the Cloisters museum, but you may very well recognize them all the same.

Strangers still ask me whether I believe in unicorns, really. I don't, not at all, not in the way they usually mean. But I do believe—still, knowing so much better—in everything the unicorn has always represented to human beings: the vision of deep strength allied to deep wisdom, of pride dwelling side by side with patience and humility, of unspeakable beauty inseparable from the "pity beyond all telling" that Yeats said was hidden at the heart of love. Even in my worst moments, when I am most sickened by the truly limitless bone-bred cruelty and stupidity of the species I belong to, I know these things exist. I have seen them, and once or twice they have laid their heads in my lap. In their very different manners, the stories in this book—altogether different indeed from what we fancied—express this old, foolish, lovely dream of the unicorn.

As I said at the beginning, any praise for *Immortal Unicorn* rightfully belongs to Janet Berliner. Me, I'm happy to be what used to be called, in the New York City garment trade, the "puller-in"—the guy who stood right outside the store and literally yanked people off the sidewalk, you absolutely got to see what we got here for you, fit you like custom-made. Not all of these tales may fit the unicorn of your imagining; but come inside anyway, come in out of the flat, painful sunlight of our time, blink around you for a bit, and see what might almost be moving and shining in the cool shadows.

—Peter S. Beagle
Davis, California
March 25, 1995

WILL SHETTERLY

TAKEN HE CANNOT BE

Peter: I know **Will Shetterly**'s work up to now entirely from the several Liavek collections, which he cocreated and coedited with his wife Emma Bull. Some years ago I had to write a magazine article on shared-world anthologies, and Liavek easily became my favorite of the ones I covered. I'm delighted by the unhurried, understated quality of his prose, the obvious originality of his mind, and the fact that he's the only writer in this anthology who has ever run for governor of a state. Minnesota, it was, and he came in a respectable third in a field of six. I always suspected I'd like Minnesota.

Janet: I confess that I did not know Will's work at all until Peter's request that I solicit a story from him for this anthology. I can now say, happily, that I know Will's voice—on the phone, and insofar as this dandy little story is concerned. Getting to know both voices better promises to be a fun exploration.

Taken He Cannot Be

Things die. This is the lesson that everyone learns. Some do not learn it until the instant before death, but we all learn it. We pass our final exam by dying. Dr. John Henry Holliday earned his diploma from the school of life at a younger age than most. At twenty, he had been told that consumption would kill him in six months, yet at thirty, he still lingered around the campus. He supposed he was a tenured professor of death, which made him laugh, which made him cough, which made him think about the man they had come to meet, and kill.

He rode through the midsummer heat beside his best friend, Wyatt Berry Stapp Earp. They had both grown beards to disguise themselves, and they had dressed like cowboys instead of townsmen. No one who saw them pass at a distance would recognize the dentist-turned-gambler or Tombstone's former deputy sheriff, both wanted in Arizona on charges of murder.

They rode to kill John Ringgold, better known as Johnny Ringo. Wyatt had said that Wells Fargo would pay for Ringo's demise, and Doc had always believed in being paid to do what you would do cheerfully for free.

He did not know or care how much Wells Fargo might pay. He was not sure whether Wells Fargo had made an offer, or Wyatt had merely assumed the coach line would show its gratitude for the death of the last leader of the Clanton gang. Doc knew Wyatt had asked him to come kill Johnny Ringo, and that sufficed. Had anyone asked him why he agreed, he would have said he had no prior engagements. The only person who might have asked would have been Big Nose Kate Elder, and she had left him long ago.

The brown hills stirred frequently as they rode. The two riders always looked at motion—in a land where bandits waited for their piece of wealth from the booming silver mines, you always looked. They never expected more than sunlight on quartz, or dust in a hot puff of wind, or a lizard darting for food or shelter. Vision was simultaneously more powerful and less trustworthy in this dry land. The eye saw far in the parched atmosphere, but it did not always see truthfully.

The unicorn showed itself on a rise. Doc never thought that it might be a wild horse. Though it was the size of a horse, it did not move like a horse, and he had never seen a horse with such white, shaggy fur, and that long, dark spear of its horn left no doubt, at least not in a person who lived by assessing situations instantly, then acting.

Doc acted by not acting: He did not flinch or blink or gasp or look away in order to look back. If this apparition was his private fantasy, he would not trouble Wyatt with its existence. If it was not, Wyatt would say something.

And Wyatt did. "Doc?"

"Eh?"

"What's that critter?"

"Unicorn."

"Eh."

They rode for another minute or two. The unicorn remained on the ridge. Its head moved slightly to follow them as they passed.

Wyatt said, "What's a unicorn?"

"In Araby they call it *cartajan*. Means 'lord of the desert.'"

"I can see that."

"'The cruelest is the unicorn, a monster that belloweth horribly, bodied like a horse, footed like an elephant, tailed like a swine, and headed like a stag. His horn sticketh out of the midst of his forehead, of a wonderful brightness about four foot long, so sharp, that whatsoever he pusheth at, he striketh it through easily. He is never caught alive; killed he may be, but taken he cannot be.'"

"Huh. Shakespeare or the Bible?"

"Some old-time Roman named Solinus, translated by some old-time Englishman who might've supped with Master Will and King Jim."

"I ain't never seen no unicorn before."

"Nor yet. That's a mirage. A will-o'-the-wisp. The product of a fevered brain."

"I reckon you're contagious, then."

Doc laughed, then coughed, then said, "Well, ain't no one known to've seen one before. Not for sure. All that's written down is travelers' tales, 'bout things they heard but never saw."

"We're the first to spot one?"

"In centuries. Far as I know."

"What do you think a circus'd pay for a critter like that?"

Doc laughed and coughed again. "Have to catch it first. It being a bastard of the mind, I reckon it'd race as fleet as a thought."

"Faster 'n horses?"

"S'posed to be."

"We could corner it in a box canyon, maybe."

"That horn ain't s'posed to be for decoration."

"Animal worth anything dead?"

"Depends on the buyer."

"Could stuff and stand it in a penny arcade. I seen a mermaid once. Looked like a monkey and a fish sewed together, but you got to admit, a sight like that's worth a penny."

"At least." Doc was rarely reluctant to tell anything to Wyatt, but he hesitated before he finally said, "Horn's s'posed to cure most sicknesses." He coughed. "Turn the horn into a drinking cup, and it takes the power out of poison. You can smear its blood on a wound, and the wound'll heal right up. Some say its whole body's magical. You're s'posed to eat its liver for something, but I forget what. There's folks who say it can make you young again, or live forever, or raise the dead."

"Any o' that true?"

Doc shrugged. "Three minutes ago, I would'a said it was all proof a lie lives longer than a liar. Now I'm not so sure."

"Let's find out." Wyatt drew on the reins. As his

horse halted, he dropped to the ground and pulled his rifle from its boot on his saddle.

Doc said, "Ain't neither of us sharpshooters. One miss 'd scare it off for good."

Wyatt paused with the rifle butt at his shoulder. "You all right, Doc? Ain't like you to pass on an opportunity set before you."

"I do make some note of the odds, Wyatt. Leastways, when I'm anything like sober."

"Mmm. Your old Roman said they could be killed. There a trick to it?"

Doc considered the answers, and thought of Kate, and said, "We ain't got the means."

"Hell." Wyatt spoke with no particular emphasis. "Then there's no reason not to try what we got, is there?"

"No." Doc whipped his short-barrel Colt from its holster and fired in the general direction of the unicorn. It seemed to study him with disappointment while the sound of the shot hung in the hot, clean air. Then it danced aside as Wyatt's shot followed Doc's, and it tossed its mane and its horn in something uncannily like a laugh before it skipped back behind the rise.

"Damn it, Doc, if you'd'a waited till we could'a both took aim with rifles—"

"Why, sure, Wyatt. I reckon I could'a' taken me a nap, and once you had ever'thing to your liking, I'd'a risen well-rested to shoot ever so nicely, and we'd now be arguing whether unicorn liver'd taste best by itself or with a big plate o' beans."

Wyatt stared at him, then said grimly, "With beans," and slid his rifle back into its boot.

Doc laughed and coughed and holstered his Colt. Then he let his surprise show on his face. The unicorn watched them from the next rise. Wyatt swung back onto his horse, looked toward the unicorn, then looked toward Doc, who said, "It sure is pretty."

He did not expect Wyatt to answer that. Wyatt did not surprise him. The unicorn studied them as they rode by. When they had left sight of it, it appeared again on a farther ridge that paralleled their ride.

Wyatt said, "If we could lure it in close, we'd plug it for sure."

"Mmm," Doc said, and then, "Maybe we should let Ringo live."

"Eh?"

"Ain't like he was one o' the ones who killed Morg."

"He stood by 'em. He planned it with Curly Bill. He was in on the attack on Virge."

"That ain't proven."

"Is to my satisfaction."

Doc laughed, said, "Hell, Wyatt, we'd have to kill half of Tombstone to get everyone who stood by the Clantons," then coughed.

When he lifted his head again, Wyatt was watching him like the unicorn had, with cool speculation. Doc wiped his mouth with the back of his hand and smiled. Wyatt said, "All right."

"All right, what?"

"All right, Ringo don't need to die. 'Less he insists on it."

"How so?"

Wyatt smiled. "Like I said. Depends on him."

Doc nodded, and they rode on. The sands stayed a steady white-hot glare, and the sky continued to leach moisture from their skin and their lungs. The unicorn accompanied them, always at a distance. Each time it disappeared, they thought it had abandoned them, but it always appeared again at a new, improbable vantage where only the most accurate marksman might take it.

Fred Dodge had said Ringo was on a drunk, and camping in a canyon in the Chiricahuas. Both of these things turned out to be true. Near a creek in the shade of a boulder, they found him reading aloud from *The Iliad* with an empty bottle and a pair of boots beside him. His outstretched feet were wrapped in strips of light cotton. He looked up as they rode near and switched from Greek to English to say, "Achilles and Patroclus, welcome."

"Hell, you are drunk if you don't recognize us," said Wyatt.

"Who you think you're playing?" said Doc. "Hardly Odysseus. Poor Hector? Brash Paris? The accommodating Panderus, perhaps?"

Ringo lifted his right arm from beside his body to show them his .45. "Anybody I damn well please. That's a good one, you two whoremasters calling names."

Wyatt said, "Doc, I forget. Why'd you want to warn him?"

"Seemed a fair notion at the time." Doc turned to Ringo. "You began the exchange of pleasantries, my Johnnie-O."

"Oh, all right, all right." Ringo waved the matter away in a broad circle with his Colt, then rose unsteadily to his feet. "So. To what do I owe the honor of this visit?"

Wyatt said, "Wells Fargo wants you dead."

"Wells Fargo?" Ringo drew himself erect and stated, precisely and indignantly, "I am a rustler, not a highwayman."

"It's the price of fame," Doc said. "A few hold-ups, they ask who's like to've masterminded 'em, and your name's sitting at the top of the heap."

Ringo blinked. "So why'd you two come in talkin' instead o' shootin'?"

Wyatt said, "Ask Doc."

Doc worked his lips and wondered at the impulse that had brought them under the gunsight of the man they had hunted. He said simply, "There's been a lot o' killin'. Mind if I water my horse?"

Ringo waved again. The weapon in his hand did not seem to be any more significant to him than a teacher's baton. Doc swung down from his horse, and so did Wyatt. Doc said, "I'll take yours," and led both horses toward the creek.

Ringo said, "So, I'm to infer you take no interest in the blood money?"

Wyatt said, "Why would you do that? We're hardly gonna let that money go to waste, not after we crossed back into Arizona."

"Hmm," said Ringo. He brought the barrel of his pistol to scratch his mustache, and Doc, moving toward the creek with his horse, wondered if the cowboy would shoot off his nose. "So, you're not after me, but you are after the reward on me. Am I to lie very still for several days? If you kept a bottle of good whiskey near my coffin, I might manage."

Doc squatted upstream from the horses to splash a handful of water against his face. As he lifted a second handful to drink, he saw the unicorn walking toward him.

Wyatt and Ringo were only a few yards away, talking about money and death. Boulders and brush gave Doc and the unicorn some privacy. The horses noted the creature, but they continued to drink without a sound of fear or greeting.

The unicorn paused on the far side of the creek. It raised its head to taste the air. Its horn could impale or eviscerate buffalo, but if there was any meaning in the lift of the horn, it was a salute.

Wyatt was telling Ringo, "We'd meet in Colorado after they paid us. We'd give you your third, and you could go to Mexico or hell, for all we cared. Everyone'd be happy. You're gettin' a little too well-known to keep on in these parts as Ringo, you know."

"How would I trust you?"

Wyatt made a sound like a laugh. "How would we trust you? Our reputation with Wells Fargo will hang on you stayin' dead once we said you was."

"Huh," said Ringo, and then he laughed. "Hell, I ain't been dead before. Why not?"

The unicorn, if it heard the speakers, ignored them. It stepped into the creek. At the splash of its hoof, Ringo said, "What's—"

Doc heard them, but he kept his eyes on the unicorn, suspecting that now, if he looked away, he would never see it again. He thought of Big Nose Kate, and how she had cared for him, and he wondered if she had known any man who could not be said to have failed her.

Wyatt said, "Hell, Johnny, ain't you seen a unicorn before? That there's Carty John, the lord of the desert."

"Well, I never," said Ringo.

Doc heard the two men move closer, and saw the unicorn glance toward them. As it stepped sideways, ready to turn and run, Doc said calmly, "Back off. This is my play."

He heard Wyatt and Ringo withdraw a few feet. The unicorn's gaze returned to Doc's face. He extended his left arm, palm upward to show there was nothing in his hand. The unicorn took the last step, and its breath was warm on Doc's skin. He was afraid he would cough and scare it away, then realized he felt no need to cough.

Wyatt called softly, "Want me to fetch a rope?"

Ringo laughed, "Hell, ain't no need of that."

Wyatt said, "What do you mean?"

Ringo said, "Look at that! It'll follow Doc like a lovesick pup now." He laughed again, even more loudly, and Doc heard the sound of a man slapping his knee in delight as Ringo added, "And you know why?"

Wyatt said, "No. Why?"

Ringo said, " 'Cause there's one thing a unicorn'll fall for, and that's—"

Doc heard the pistol shot, then felt the pistol in his right hand. Ringo slumped to his knees and fell forward, hiding the hole in his face and exposing the larger one in the back of his head.

Wyatt went to calm their horses. The unicorn stayed by Doc. It had not spooked at the sound, sight, or smell of death. Doc let the pistol slide back into his holster.

Wyatt said, "Well, it'll be easier to convince Wells Fargo he's dead now."

"Mmm."

Wyatt squatted by Ringo, drew a knife, and cut a piece of scalp from Ringo's hairline. "What you want to do with Carty John there? Start up a unicorn show, or sell him?"

"He won't abide crowds."

Wyatt dropped his hand to the gun at his thigh. "You figure to shoot him then, or should I?"

Both pistols cleared their holsters at the same time. Neither fired. Doc and Wyatt stood still, Wyatt's pistol aimed at Doc's sternum, Doc's pistol aimed more toward Wyatt than anything else.

Time passed, perhaps slowly, perhaps quickly. Wyatt lowered his head, but not his gun, a fraction of an inch in a question. Doc answered by swinging his pistol behind him as he yelled, "Git!" The barrel struck something soft, and he thought it had been easier to send Kate away.

The unicorn did not try to impale him. It spun and ran. As it splashed across the creek and onto the sand, Doc holstered his pistol. He listened to the unicorn's hooves, but he did not turn to watch it go. He stepped forward, then fell coughing to his knees in the creek.

Wyatt took him by the shoulders to lift him and direct him toward the bank. While Doc sat on a boulder in the sun, Wyatt found Ringo's horse, saddled it, rolled Ringo's body in a blanket, then lashed it across the back of the horse. Wyatt said, "You want his boots?"

Doc looked where Ringo had been reading, then shook his head.

Wyatt said, "If they were all that comfortable, he'd'a been wearing 'em."

Doc said, "I'll take the book."

Wyatt picked up *The Iliad*, handed it to Doc, then said, "Ready to ride?"

"At a moment's notice," Doc said, and he stood, wondering if that was true. He tucked the book in his saddlebag, then swung himself onto his horse's back. "Where you taking him?"

Wyatt turned his horse back the way they had come. "I got a plan."

"As good as your last one?"

"I 'xpect."

"That's comforting."

"Killing Stilwell and Curly Bill so publicly just created messes for us. I figure to prop Johnny down by the road into town, which ought to get a story goin' that he up and killed his sorry ass hisself."

Doc considered several flaws in the plan, but said nothing. It would be a last joke on the town that had driven them away. He could hear people arguing why Ringo's boots were missing and whether a self-inflicted wound should be ringed with powder burns. It would be less than a joke, or more. It would be a mystery, and therefore it would be like life.

"Sure," Doc said, and coughed.

They left Ringo near a farmhouse and let his horse go free. Wyatt had hung Ringo's cartridge belts upside down on him, but Doc did not ask whether that was to make it look like Ringo had been extremely drunk, or was another little taunting detail for Sheriff Behan and Tombstone's legal establishment, or was simply a sign that Wyatt's mind was on other things.

When the scene of Ringo's suicide was complete, Wyatt said, "Doc, maybe we ought to split up for a while."

That would be prudent. If anyone decided Ringo had been killed, it would be best if no one could say that two men looking like Wyatt and Doc had been near these parts. Doc nodded.

Wyatt said, "I'll get your share to you."

Doc nodded again.

Wyatt smiled. "Half's better 'n thirds, ain't it?"

Doc coughed, then nodded a third time.

"You'll be all right?"

Doc said, "Sure."

"Well. Be seein' you."

He watched Wyatt ride away. A bullet in Wyatt's back would surprise no one, but Doc did not draw his gun. He loved anything that was simple and forceful and beautiful. Some things should live forever, and some things should die.

Coughing, he rode on alone.

ROBERT DEVEREAUX

—◦≈∭∬∰≈◦—

WHAT THE EYE SEES, WHAT THE HEART FEELS

Peter: **Robert Devereaux**'s story, "What the Eye Sees, What the Heart Feels," deals with the human-unicorn link in a gentle, affecting manner that I'd hardly have expected from a writer who publishes in anthologies like *MetaHorror, Love in Vein, Splatterpunks 2* ("Peter, who *are* these people?"), *Book of the Dead 3,* and *It Came from the Drive-In.* He is the author of the novel *Deadweight,* and has a second, *Walking Wounded,* due out in 1996. Robert lives in Fort Collins, Colorado, ". . . working as a software engineer by day and letting his imagination run wild by dawn . . ." It seems to be having a very nice time.

Janet: This is a very gentle man, Peter, and a damn hard worker at his craft. I herewith thank you, Robert, for your extraordinary patience with my "editorial interference." I hope you agree that the results were worth it; I know the readers will . . . you sentimental slob, you.

What the Eye Sees,
What the Heart Feels

THE DEATH THAT TURNED OUT TO BE THE LAST ONE SHE witnessed belonged to an old woodcutter. And that one, because of her mounting accumulation of ills, she nearly missed out on.

Did the others think her odd? No doubt they did. She saw them infrequently these days, their flashing white bodies glancing through the world, partaking of life. *She* partook of *death*. Or, more precisely, she bore witness to the skimming of life, the final throes, blunting the pain that so often accompanied them. If that was odd, then odd she was and proud to be so.

Her aches made the world seem smaller than it was. Distances, once easy to judge, tended these days to deceive her. As she hastened onward, a hard-packed roadway drove spike after spike into her striking hooves. Her heart, a surging red fury, pounded out of control in her breast. Even so, she pressed at top speed toward the woodcutter's cottage, praying she'd arrive on time.

The wood she entered seemed familiar. That wasn't

surprising. By now, all the world seemed—indeed was— so. Beside the cottage's shadowed east wall, an unassuming grave marker belonging to the woodcutter's wife brought to mind her death years before, a gray sigh in his huddled arms. Without a moment to spare, she burst silently through the thick oak door as a last ray of sunlight faded on his face. Their eyes met. The dying man was a worn husk of wrinkle and bone, his ax idle by the fireplace. Plump misshapen pillows angled him up. Tattered blankets, gray as dust, clung to him. Through one last exhalation, he shivered, his lips thin and dark.

His eyes melted upon hers.

Eons before, when she and the world were young, this witnessing, this absorption of pain, had made her feel superior. She, of all her kind, lived deeper, felt more profoundly, probed life to its roots—or so she had imagined. The others? They drank from far shallower waters, their fluff-white manes tossed carelessly in the wind. They scattered their attention hither and yon, squandering it. Ah, but she—and one other, the one who witnessed births—had chosen, more wisely, to fix on one thing only. For too many millennia, that had been her view. But since her disorders had begun to gather and spread, she'd grown to honor, to envy, the others. Depth, she understood finally, could be gained through sidewise means, glances at experience that seemed superficial but weren't. So they in their way had mined life's riches, and she in hers.

The dying man's eyes widened.

The air about him refused to be drawn into his nostrils, into his gaping mouth. "Accept it," she said, her ribs hurting from how swiftly she'd arrived. Her words took the edge off his panic, softened him, even as lances of pain shot through her, heightening the misery of founder and strangles, the botfly larvae and tapeworms that infested her tract, the colic, the arthritis, the disorders ravaging her lungs. Her coat glowed with the light of immortality. But inside, she harbored accretions of death.

A shiver rose from the woodcutter's body and he lay still. His eyes, dull cuts of emerald, saw no more.

Above him, without tears, she wept.

She understood now what had to be done.

Centuries past, he'd mastered the art of indirection, those quick evasive sidesteps that kept him always a touch beyond their peripheral vision. Eluding detection by one of them was a cakewalk; two were slightly harder, three a tough yet manageable challenge. But escaping notice when four of them were around—particularly if they began to sense your presence—*that* was a major test of one's skills.

Many of his compatriots were retiring sorts, shyly tucked deep in the wild, backing farther into solitude whenever bands of rovers rumbled through the woods. Not he. And not a select few he'd chanced upon, or dallied with, in his long lifetime—those who, like him, had discovered how to hide in plain sight, whose deepest joy lay in witnessing, close up, the strange and wonderful doings of mortal folk.

He stood now in shadow, beyond a roaring hearthfire. These three—the midwife, her scrawny henlike helper, the fat-legged, gap-thighed peasant woman before whose widening vulva the pair soothed and coaxed, waiting in practiced wonder—were much too intent to even *try* to notice the benevolent creature watching over them.

"Come now," the midwife said, her big hands working the woman's flesh like an impatient cook kneading dough. "Just relax into it." Anger sat sharp upon her tongue. He couldn't tell if it was meant for her assistant, for the peasant woman, or for the world at large.

"I can't do it," whined the mother-to-be, her forehead bathed in sweat, wet black curves of hair sweeping like knife blades above it.

"You'll be fine," came the response, muted, mothering. The assistant's head turned in wonder. It was clear she'd never heard the midwife's voice soften that way. Or *any* way. The midwife, too, looked surprised, raising a hint of eyebrow, then resuming more gently her massaging. "That's right," she said. "That's the way. You're doing fine."

"You think so?" A twist of hope fluted up.

"I do." And she was telling the truth.

This part gave him great satisfaction. His presence, like the fire's forgiving light, softened edges, broadcast warmth, infused with blessings everything he gazed upon. Although his immortality derived from wholly other causes, it felt forever linked to the births he witnessed, to the new blazes of life flaring up. It seemed to him too that those amassed witnessings flew out from him as he watched, giving the mortal players in that drama a confidence and strength far beyond their best capacities.

The midwife sculpted an opening—wide, taut, wet with emerging hair and scalp. "That's it," she coaxed, "that's the way."

"Unh," the peasant woman said. "Mmmn."

"It's coming," the midwife's assistant chimed in.

The woman's labia stretched, a wide thin O of taut flesh. Her baby crowned, its head purple and slick with vernix. From the sweep of his tail to the swirled tip of his horn, he knew it was a girl. Mortals didn't know—despite their comical feints at divination—but *he* always knew, the moment he saw a laboring woman's belly, which gender her infant would be.

"Come on, sweetheart," the midwife urged gently. "It's time to be born." One huge palm supported the infant's head; the other worked to help its swiftening passage out. Caught it, an expert catch and swaddle! He thrilled at the sight, the spills of liquid, the squirming of new flesh—a blend of three, then four, bodies. Firelight danced upon fabric and skin. Faintly, like loam, the aromas of blood and life arose. Sounds of delight and relief interwove. Then all was business and love. A bond fixed them to this time and space, a bond never in his memory, nor in theirs, to be broken.

Joy swept along his horn, a rush that filled him to the heart. Tearlessly he wept.

Then abruptly, cutting through his joy, a summons sounded in his head.

The women carried on, oblivious.

He raised his horn to the signal. His ears twitched at its strength.

Before thought could intercede, he sped away,

hurtling silently through earthen walls into the darkness of night. Turning, he galloped at once unerringly east.

As she left the woodcutter's cottage, she heard the moans of the dying, clamoring as ever for her attention. Impossible. For her, the end had come. As much as she owed them her presence, she simply couldn't endure one more death. Time and again, she had relented, taking on her chosen task despite the ills it brought. But her agony had grown so great that words like guilt and selfishness had finally lost their hold.

The world stunned up into her hooves, shoots of pain struck from passing greens and browns, as she hurried back to the purest wood on earth. It was a place no one born of woman would ever reach, a place of trees and moss and generous sun, where night never fell, and where, so long ago, they had all burst forth upon the earth. That memory—how they'd come so swiftly into being, flurrying out of the circle, each of them different yet bound in mind and spirit to the others—emerged in all its beauty whenever she brought this clearing to mind. The wide ring of stones, cozy yet somehow beyond the mind's compass, gleamed with scatterings of mica caught in pure hard white rock, a vast jaw of molars set inevitably, artistically right. They'd been flung from these same stones, and the earth that tracked them before they lifted into the sky remained as soft as on that first day. Hoofprints that had bitten deep then into dirt—each of them unique, not one overlaid or obliterated—shone now with undiminished clarity.

Coming in over the circle of stones, she touched

down on plush grass and found the center, the place of summoning. Her eyes, thick with rheum, cast a film over what she saw; but she felt the power there, the stones equidistant from her like the rim of a wheel brought into true. She stumbled. The parasitic pain had imbalanced her, had knocked her equilibrium askew. It couldn't be shaken off, her horntip making zigzags in the air, her erratic head slowing at last in resignation. Faltering, she lowered herself carefully to the ground (far more dignity was possible from that position) and brought her will entirely to the tip of her rising horn.

As he raced onward, the earth in all its splendor rehearsed itself in his sight. When he idled, when he slept or grazed—these ways of being bestowed their own peculiar grace. But to gallop lightly over the earth, to spin out road and glade and ribbons of sea beneath his hooves, passing through trees and towers, through huts of thatch and sod (their solidity more dream than real)—this movement, this thundering gallop, was a prayer indeed, a perfect blend of beauty and the awareness which affirmed it.

Summonings were seldom. The last one had occurred in the distant past, a celebration of a love the summoner had witnessed and in some way participated in. A svelte young filly had stood in the midst of the clearing, tossing her head and speaking of a rustic couple—how they'd met, how they'd fought, reconciled, found commonalities, nurtured them, all beneath the gaze of the teller. Unbounded happiness had swept through him, had swept through them all, even those who kept shy of humanity. As rare as summonings were, they always taught lessons worth learning, lessons that healed and affirmed.

New vistas rose before him, splitting right and left, joining behind him and vanishing over a rolling horizon. Within them—few at first, then increasing—streaks of white wove through blues and greens and browns. So brilliant and pure were they that they approached silver, liquid shards of mirror, reflecting himself. Random brushstrokes fell closer, quicker, multiplying, resolving into the joyous forms of those he knew so well.

Below, along flanks of thundering white, he watched early comers touch down. At the place of summoning, centered on the greensward, sat the summoner. He felt her in his horn as he had from the first—felt her call, her urgency. Why wasn't she standing, as summoners always stood? Circling with the others, he drifted down, watching those already earthbound draw together in curiosity as latecomers flurried the air behind him. There sat the summoner, majestic, wise. But as she enlarged in his sight, as he saw her more clearly, other feelings arose in him, feelings of sorrow for what her outer majesty could not conceal.

Above her they sailed in, homing on her call. Doves flocking in obedience, they let through cuts of sun, the clearing mottled as those coming down touched hoof to turf. In the mundane world, they let gravity chain them to the earth. But whenever they were summoned here, the skyways afforded them purchase, gave lift and yaw and balance to their airborne bodies.

She'd considered standing. The thought alone shot a fistful of barbs through her breast. A realization stunned her. She would no longer stand, no longer use these four aching legs that had carried her through uncounted eons. They, and she, were finished. Used up. If the others couldn't release her—but surely they could, and would—she'd lie here until the world ended, alone at the place of her birth, beauty surrounding her, torment and suffering within.

As stragglers thinned in the sky, the ones that were earthbound shone with more light than shadow. Innumerable but nearly complete, the host swept from where she lay, across the grass, among wide flat birthstones and the pounded track, and farther out amidst oaks whose tall trunks pierced the heavens. Yet despite their numbers, rounded out by the last-dropped few from the sky, there was no sense whatever of crowding. At all sides, they had ample room to mix and wonder, casting an eye in her direction before settling down to hear what she had to say.

The amber oozings of her eyes had caked like candle wax down her cheeks, but her vision served. She relaxed, letting the signal fall away at last. White bodies swam before her, there, there, sharp, stable—yet impossible, in her dizziness, to fix upon. Every breath she took proved more difficult than the last.

She lowered her eyelids, unrushed, feeling in her heart for the right moment to speak.

He moved among the crowd, each face uniquely beautiful, and familiar as home. "What's it all about?" he asked.

"No idea," they said, or dumbly shook their heads, mane fluff floating like clusters of dandelion.

Wandering nearer to the summoner, he caught an intriguing face, asked again. The wide-flanked mare gazed up and said, "Look at her. You'll find a clue. Settle in beside me, okay? You're not half-bad-looking."

Why not? These gatherings often generated sufficient communal heat that foals joined their ranks eleven months afterward. The planet had plenty of room for more of their kind. None of them ever died, of course. That was strictly the province of men and women and the cyclic life that shared their earth. He and the others had dashed into the world fully grown, and their offspring, over idle centuries, grew to adulthood and stabilized there.

Lowering himself, he felt stiff grass blades brush his belly and soften under his weight. The mare, nuzzling him, smelled of sweet clover. He nuzzled back, a hint at what lay ahead. But his gaze, the mare's, too, fixed on the summoner. Her eyes were inflamed, her throat swollen. Pus lay thick about her nostrils. They called the disease the strangles. He imagined they'd all had brushes with one or another affliction, but they'd thrown them off quickly. Not she. He noted too the outward signs of founder: Around the hoof walls visible to him, and where horn met brow, diverging rings had developed, a crumbling of the laminae. Clearly, from the way she held herself, other ills plagued her as well.

"She's ailing," he said, astonished.

"It's her peculiar ways," said the mare, not judging, just noting, her breath as savory as new-mown hay.

"She's weird. Like you. She's the one who tends to the dying."

"I could never do that." Yet he admired her. Always had. While the others—those not too shy to venture forth—had scattered their talents in many directions, preferring variety, only he and she had lent fierce passion to a single pursuit.

"It can't be healthy, her obsession with the dying, with *being there* for them." Nodding toward the summoner, the mare added, "There's the evidence."

Early in his witnessings, he'd seen mothers die in childbirth. He'd watched infants emerge stillborn or deformed or badly delivered, maimed in removal, deprived of limbs through a midwife's ineptitude. Those witnessings had hurt. Quickly he'd decided to be more selective, a plethora of births to choose from. Sensing the successes, he partook of them alone.

The murmuring started to die down. From this distance—though he suspected those farthest out could hear it, too—labored breathing came to him, wheezes that betrayed lung problems, viruses past any hope of cure.

She craned about, surveying the crowd.

For the first time he understood. They were not here for their usual celebration, not at all.

"My friends," she said, but she had to clear her throat and repeat it. "My friends, seeing you here brings me great joy."

They listened without moving. Yet her eyes refused to hold them still. It was as though the earth and everything upon it had turned liquid in her sight. Whipped white meringue shimmied along withers and loins and horns. Myriad pairs of eyes jittered like cloves in pounded dough.

"You honor me with your presence," she went on. "Why are you here? I see the question in your faces. It's because I'm dying. For years I've been dying. Even so, my life continues. I go on—wrapped, as we all are, in immortality.

"Many deaths have passed before my eyes. Many deaths have pierced me. It's a thing of awe and wonder to witness how men and women abandon the burning houses of their bodies. I've borne witness to nature at her most natural and her most terrible, ugly and beautiful both. But the misery of the dying, and of those who grieve for them, have left an indelible mark on me."

She felt buoyed by the support that came to her from all sides. It assuaged her pain. She wished she could spend an eternity in the presence of these, her kind. But that, she knew, could never be. They had their chosen tasks to be about, their comings and goings upon the earth—and she had one final task to perform.

"I have summoned you to ask a favor." No one had ever told her of the power she wanted them to exercise, but she knew they had it and that they would know it, too. "I want you to grant me release. You alone, in concert, have the power to free me. You alone can let me die. This I now request."

Renewed murmurs caught the crowd. Sunlight plated them in gold, their mouths moving, their great heads swinging in conversation. Inside, she felt parasites crawl and bite, sapping her strength. Fresh wind swept the tree-tops.

One of those seated nearby, a male, rose to speak. Her gaze was untrustworthy, but she recognized the watcher at births, a well-meaning soul whose eyes sparkled with life. He, too, as she, was regarded strangely by the others, the ones not so fiercely focused, not so single-minded, as they.

"Forgive my boldness," he said, trumpeting his words and lofting his head so that all could hear. "You surely don't expect us to kill one of our own kind. We can't possibly do such a thing. Our lives go on without end. I myself celebrate beginnings, as you know. This morning, I watched a woman open herself. She gave new life from her womb and cried at the pain and beauty of what she gave. I cried, too. Each of us in this clearing is a beginning with no end. How can you ask us to close off one such beginning?"

His was a token resistance. She knew that. So did he. A special harmony bound their kind, a oneness of sensibility that had never left them, no matter how scattered the paths they'd taken from their first natal gallop around this ring and off into the world. "Your concern touches me, it honors me," she said. "But in giving what I ask, you won't be killing me. You'll be letting me die. That's the end I want and need. If you hesitate, you'll only prolong my suffering. Be generous. Please. Grant my request."

She knew, without looking at him, that he had resumed his place on the grass. Closing her eyes, she lifted her head toward the sun and offered her immortality to be drawn like dew from the spiraled surface of her horn. It resembled the summoning, but it differed: the focus of her energy—the focus of theirs—shifted, there where the air filled with lilac and the soft breezy lifting of manes.

"Poor thing," said the mare beside him. She had shut her eyes, and her horn pressed upward at a determined angle. The others, too, wherever he looked, had begun to show that same intense readiness-to-charge.

Letting his eyelids fall, he lifted his head.

It wasn't fair. Perhaps there was a way to save her. They might be able to halt her agony, reverse it, take— each of them—a portion of her pain into themselves and so renew her. But even as he maneuvered his horn just so, he knew there was no such way.

They owed her her end.

He imagined he heard a faint high whine, the sort of keening that might issue from a ghostly fiddle strung taut and drawn across with one thin horsehair, so near the threshold between sound and silence as to have been dreamt. Sunlight glowed through his lids. The others, attuned by a commonality of blood, drew closer.

Into his horn's tight twist, the thousandth part of her life's energy drained, an exchange multiplied manifold among the gathered masses.

He felt her eyelids drift open.

Her eyes rested on him.

Him alone.

He sensed her scrutiny but kept his own eyes closed, becoming more giving, more accepting, his ears twitching as he drew off his share of what she offered.

Had any of them held back, she couldn't have yielded what she needed so fiercely to yield. But the hard swirls that twisted from brows, the bold thrust of horns that unified them even in their disparity—these they offered, without exception, to her service.

And serve her they did.

In fancy, her cream-white spiral drew them toward her. The distance separating them shrank, until—haphazardly at first, then uniformly and upon every inch of surface—the blunt tip of each horn touched her horn, siphoning off a tiny part of her life. Her ills, encased until this moment in a shell of immortality, seeped through that crumbling shell. Released from confinement at last, they wracked her as they went.

In her mind's eye, she saw clearly the one who alone had made protest. A handsome steed. Robust. He'd spent his life witnessing births, avoiding the botched ones, the ones that ended badly. Many of those latter she'd seen, many attended. They had cost her much. But in the easing of sorrow, they had returned far more.

She felt herself weaken. No longer did she need to push her gift out. Instead, the others, homed in upon her, reached to embrace it, to accept it.

Slowly her eyelids rose.

There he sat, vibrant, beautiful, shut out from life's bitterness by a choice he'd made long ago. He and the others brought her to tears, shining so firm and heartwhole under daylight. In sorrow, they robbed her of what she'd asked them to steal. She saw it change them, change *him*, seeding riches deep inside him.

His head lifted.

She knew he felt her eyes on him.

The air smelled of sweet apples. Her body was shot through with pain. Through the razored claws of a breeze, sunlight scorched her back.

She watched his eyelids part. Dark pupils gleamed through curd-white slits. Their eyes met. It was *his* horn-tip that touched the tip of her horn, *his* the essence that drank most deeply of hers.

She gave.

He took.

Lightened of her burden, she let herself fly free, rising skyward without liftoff, even as the earth, unbroken, opened to embrace her.

Her weakening, as he witnessed it, happened gradually, a soft easing of the flesh. But her eyelids' last closing caught him unprepared. It began, as the others had, with the lazy downward drift of her lashes. Then, instead of their rise, her neck and head lowered through a slow roll that brought them, as gently as a feather falling through unstirred air, to rest upon the green.

For an eternity they sat there, fascinated by her unmoved corpse. A light breeze toyed with her mane. No other air moved upon her, nor any sign of it—no rib cage expanding, no flare of nostrils.

It seemed utterly wrong.

And nothing less than right.

Shadows passed over him. He glanced up. The ones at the outskirts of the clearing had begun to lift off. He saw their grim-set faces, the broken-stilted waggle of their legs as hooves caught air. His eyes found the summoner's corpse, refusing to believe the stillness that surrounded it.

The sea of white bodies gradually evaporated upward, leaving flat green. Shadows crisscrossed, thinned, and were no more. At one point, he felt the mare nuzzle him. He knew she was speaking words of farewell, but he heard only the kindness of her tone before she, too, was gone.

Another eternity passed.

Reluctantly he rose.

Walking was an effort. Before him lay a pure white ruin, her fallen body. "Please, not me," he tried to say, but no sound escaped his lips. He raised his head, taking in the warmth and comfort of the clearing and the sun's generosity overhead. Already suffering, his heart hurt worse for the beauty of the setting.

Perhaps if he . . .

His neck hung low, a steep white slope which his mane, were it not attached, might curl along like a carpet of snow hurtling downhill. Her horn tilted upward at an odd angle. The tip still pulsed feebly; he found it, by instinct, with his own horntip, a sure solid touch.

The final release of her voice, when it came, was neither sudden nor shocking.

Its warmth entered him and the entirety of his body enclosed it, an infant's mouth meeting its mother's nipple for the first time. "There's no one else," her voice spoke. Then it dimmed and fell silent.

Her flesh turned to granite before him, her horn a twist of white gold. The world had changed in the last hour. The hub at the center of their ring of birthstones, once empty, bore a monument—her transmuted body— to the summoner's devotion. Could he tread lightly in her hoofprints? She'd lived a full long life. *His* life, he felt, was just beginning, on the verge.

He had to try it.

He could always (*he could never!*) change his mind.

He backed away and sprang skyward, catching the air where the summoner's hooves had made their imprint coming in.

On all sides, voices called to him.

Here the births, there the deaths.

With a resolve not solid, but firm enough to see him on his way, he made his choice.

MICHAEL ARMSTRONG

OLD ONE-ANTLER

Peter: As I implied in the foreword, the essence of the unicorn is independent of the form one culture or another may clothe it in. The one-antlered bull caribou of **Michael Armstrong**'s story shares in full the dignity, ferocity, and magical nature of its legendary counterpart, as well as the unicorn's capacity for pity and profound generosity. Michael Armstrong lives in Homer, Alaska, with his wife Jenny Stroyeck. He teaches English through the distance education program of the University of Alaska Anchorage, and has got to be the only writer included in this book who has also taught dog mushing.

Janet: Like so many of the writers in this book, Michael and I go way back. I remain constantly amazed by the breadth of his interests, which doubtless has more than a little to do with the depth of his insights.

Old One-Antler

THROUGH THE OPEN FLY OF THEIR TENT, SAM WATCHED his son peeing in the fresh snow. Malachi had grown about eight inches in the last year, Sam noticed, and some of the growth had been in places Malachi probably hadn't expected. Sam smiled as Malachi gingerly zipped his pants shut. The kid's learning about pubic hairs and the little brass teeth of jeans, he thought. Malachi handled his penis like it was some new toy that he hadn't quite worked all the bugs out of yet. And he probably hadn't, not at thirteen.

As Malachi walked over to the cook tent, Sam savored the warmth of the sleeping bag for a few moments, but then gave in to the same urge that had defeated Malachi minutes earlier: The son had inherited the weak bladder muscles of his dad, but Sam had learned a few things over the years, learned control, a little bit, and not to drink so much the night before.

Standing outside the tent, watching his pee shower down in a gentle arc and steaming in the chill air, Sam laughed at the obscenity Malachi had peed in the snow. That was good, he thought, a kid using urine like ink to express his frustration at waking to five inches of new snow on a late-August morning. A creative lad. Malachi would learn soon enough that snow was a pretty good thing when you were hunting caribou.

Sam finished up and poked his penis back into his pants, nestled it up against his single testicle. It had been fifteen years since he'd lost that nut to cancer. Just when he thought he didn't notice the loss anymore, fondling the lone ball in the floppy scrotum would bring the memory back. Hell with it, he thought. He zipped his fly and stretched, and gazed out at the tundra. They had made it, he realized.

Sam smiled at the sheer conspiracy of the trip. Each summer he got Malachi for exactly five weeks, no more, no less, and he had to connive to make those five weeks last, had to figure out some way to impress upon Malachi that he, Sam, was his father, and that he, Sam, was a swell guy, and that he, Sam, knew a whole lot of things about life that Malachi's mother Roberta could never teach Malachi. Sam was a man and Roberta was a woman and Malachi was a boy becoming a man, and though Roberta insisted that she was teaching Malachi to be a good person, Sam knew that she could never teach Malachi what he had to be before he could be a good person; Roberta could never teach Malachi to be a good man. Although, Sam had to admit, he wasn't sure he could teach Malachi that, that any man could teach a boy how to be a good man. Sometimes only the boy could do that, learn himself.

The conspiracy was that Roberta thought Sam had taken Malachi up to the Arctic to look at birds, Sam having told his ex-wife some imaginative lie about migrating geese and the splendors of the fall tundra. Dumb bitch, he thought. If she knew anything about the Arctic, she would have known that the animal that sucked tanik outsiders up to the ass end of nowhere to Alaska in the fall was not birds, but big game, herds and herds of great animals with rippling muscles and wily minds and hearts and lungs just begging to be ripped to shreds by the sure shot of a 30.06 bullet. But if Sam had said to Malachi's mother, "Robbie, I'm taking our son up to the Arctic to blow away caribou," she would have dreamt up some court order—and he would have paid for it— that would have kept Sam from seeing his son for another year.

So Sam lied. He'd lied even to Malachi, which hurt him most of all. He didn't like the look on Malachi's face the night before when Waldo, their bush pilot, had set them down on a flat gravel bar along the braided Hula Hula River, and they'd set up camp and Sam had pulled out the two Ruger rifles, one new, one old, and gently handed the old one to Malachi.

"My first rifle," he had said. "It's yours now, son."

"Dad," Malachi had said, "it's a gun. I can't shoot it. What would Mom say?"

Sam had smiled, thinking what Mom would say. Robbie would say that guns were horrible things and that Malachi should never, ever, touch one, not even if an eight-hundred-and-fifty pound crazed grizzly was coming at you like a runaway locomotive and you knew the bear was going to rip your face off. But Robbie had never had to face a grizzly like that, and Sam had, and he knew what he would do, because he'd done it: he'd killed the bear, and apologized later, and then cut the bear's heart out and ate it, like Eskimos did.

"Hell, Mal," Sam had said. "You don't have to tell your mom."

Malachi had taken the rifle, held it gently in his soft hands, sighted down the barrel, clicked the trigger a few times, and smiled. Sam felt proud, and hopeful, too, because he knew that the bond was there, a faint spark he'd patiently fanned for all Malachi's life, a bond between father and son that no mother could quench. They were men and there were certain things men said and did to and with each other that women just couldn't understand.

Thinking of all that as he stared at the tundra, Sam breathed in the glory of the Arctic morning. He looked out at the hills dusted—no, covered in deep white snow—imagined the 'boos crawling across the tundra like ants on sugar. He almost went back in the tent to get his binoculars and glass the hills along the river, but shook his head. No hunting today, he thought. Today we throw thunder to the hills. Today we learn about rifles.

Malachi had learned a few things over the summers, and the lesson he'd learned well because Sam had screamed it into him one trip until Sam knew the words were scorched on Malachi's eardrums—the thing Malachi had learned was that the first guy up boiled water. Just like that, no thought, dump some snow in a pot, or walk to a creek, and boil water, even if you hated coffee or tea, because you had to boil water in the wilderness, boiled it unless you liked beaver fever, giardia, ripping your guts out for months after. Sam walked over to the cook tent—really, a tarp suspended over a gas stove on a box of food, the tarp sagging with snow—and smiled to see his son had primed the stove and started water boiling. Maybe he'd learn to drink coffee this summer, too, Sam thought. Maybe.

"Sleep well?" he asked Malachi.

"No," Malachi said. "Damn snow. It sounded like mosquitoes suiciding on the tent."

"Sure snowed a fuck of a lot, didn't it?" Malachi winced at the obscenity and Sam smiled.

"Yeah," Malachi said, punching the underside of the tarp and knocking damp snow off the shelter. "We going to get socked in?"

Sam laughed. "This isn't real snow, son. Not enough to stop Waldo from picking us up." He waved an arm at the expanse of white. "Besides, this will all melt by the afternoon. The serious snow won't come for another month or so."

"What if we get stranded?" Malachi asked. "What if like Waldo forgets us?"

Sam clapped him on the shoulder. "Then I guess we'd have to build an igloo or something, eh?" And Sam grinned at the horrified look on his son's face, at the thought that they might have to spend a winter there on that tundra. Horrors, horrors: a winter with his dad.

They made a quick breakfast—pancakes with blueberries picked the night before—and cleaned the kitchen and then got rifles and shells and went off to shoot. Clouds still covered the hills to the south, but the sun over the Beaufort Sea to the northeast promised to burn off the fog and soon the snow.

Father and son walked to the end of the little bush airstrip Waldo had dropped them off at the day before, away from the spike camp they would hunt from, to a pile of empty fuel drums at the edge of the gravel clearing. The airstrip had been an old military strip, abandoned barrels and stuff the way the military used to just chuck trash on the tundra, but the local Native corporation had picked it up in a land deal. You had to have permission to use it—the locals didn't mind outsiders hunting there, but liked them to pay for the privilege— and since Sam had done some programming work for the village, they let Waldo take him out there gratis.

It disgusted Sam to come here and use the strip, because it didn't seem like real wilderness, but he had to admit the airstrip had its advantages for a good caribou hunt. A few days later it'd be packed with caribou hunters guided by local villagers. For the moment, though, Sam hoped to get some peace with his son. The bulls might not come through for a few days, but that didn't matter, not yet. Today Malachi had to learn to shoot.

Sam dragged an old packing flat out a hundred yards from a drum, tacked a target to the gray wood, and went back to Malachi. The two rifles still lay flat on the top of the drum, still in the open cases, their chambers open. Good, Sam, thought, Malachi hadn't been tempted to touch them. He remembered the first rule Sam had drummed into Malachi four years ago before Robbie got weird about what Sam could do with his son and he could still take Malachi to the shooting range.

Never touch a gun when a person is downrange, leave the gun in its case and with an empty chamber.

He patted his son on the shoulder, took the old Ruger out of the more battered of the two cases, and handed it to Malachi. The Mauser-style bolt had been pulled back, the chamber open and ready to take a cartridge.

"You know how to load it, Malachi?" Sam asked.

Malachi gave his dad a hard look, a little-boy tough-ass glare, said, "Sure," and reached for the box of brass rounds. Handloads, Sam's special mix of bullet and powder. He picked out a shell, held it away from him as if it were a spider, and gingerly slid it into the open chamber. Malachi turned the bolt up, started to slide the bolt forward.

"Son," Sam said, "seems to be a little glare out. You might shoot better with some glasses."

Malachi turned to Sam, and Sam had slipped on a pair of amber shooting glasses, big aviator-style shades that made him look like an evil genius. The boy nodded, reached into his parka pocket, and took out his own pair of glasses, slipped them onto his big nose—a nose like his momma's. He reached for the bolt again.

"And son," Sam said again, "I know you've gone deaf from all those years of being plugged into a Walkman, but if you want to save what hearing you do have left . . ." He held out his hand and opened up a palm in which four little foam earplugs nested.

"Right, Dad," the boy said, taking a pair of plugs and cramming them into his ears. Nice ears, Sam thought, earlobes separate, like his dad's.

"Okay, son," Sam said loudly, and the boy nodded.

Malachi slid the bolt forward and down, locking the shell in, then stepped around to the butt end of the gun, staring at it, looking at it, wondering what to do with it. Sam tapped him on the shoulder, waved him aside. He took the new Ruger down from the drum, laid it on a knapsack on the ground, snapped the old case shut, and put the stock of the old rifle on top of the case. Pulling an earplug out, Sam pointed at Malachi's ear, and the boy took one plug out, too.

"Okay, Malachi," the father said, "the scope's off this rifle, so you have to use the sight. Remember what I taught you years ago? Think of the back sight as a valley, the forward sight as a mountain, and the target as the sun. Put the mountain at the head of the valley, and have the sun setting on the mountain. Not behind the mountain—it's setting on the tip of the mountain."

"Line them up?"

"Line 'em up, one, two, three. You've got good eyes. Let the end of the stock rest on the case, hold the stock with your left hand. Right hand around the grip, index finger hooked slightly against the trigger. Got it?"

"Got it." The boy leaned against the drum, and Sam could see his legs shake slightly. Not good, he thought, the boy would have to get over that.

"Now, remember how you pulled the trigger on your old twenty-two?" Did he even remember his old .22? Sam thought. Did he remember his mother throwing the little pump rifle out the second story window of their house, fully loaded, the rifle discharging and putting a round into their chicken coop? Did he remember his mother unloading the rifle—smart woman, Sam thought—and smashing it with a splitting maul? Probably.

"Yeah, Dad. 'Don't jerk, pull.' One smooth movement."

"Good, son. Pull, then." Malachi put his earplug back in, and Sam smiled at the command. Pull, son. Try. Do it. Put me in front of the rifle and pull the trigger. Put your mother in front of the rifle and pull the trigger. Imagine it, boy. Imagine.

"Trigger won't pull, Dad." Malachi reached up, turned the safety off, and then Sam put his earplug in.

"Good, Malachi," he shouted. "Now try it. Relax. Breathe in, hold the breath, pull, exhale. Relax. Breathe, hold—fire!"

Sam watched the rifle end, always the clue. Watch how the rifle tip moved, watch how the movement of finger translates into eye movement, into focus, into breath, into shot. If the boy is relaxed, the tip will kick up slightly. If the boy is tense, it won't move, his muscles will hold it, fight the discharge, and he'll have a bad shot.

Malachi pulled the trigger. The rifle kicked, smoke rose up around them, and Sam heard the air fold around the bullet, heard the crack and the explosion that propelled the bullet. He always listened for that crack first, that satisfying flight of lead pushing air before it, sound collapsing behind lead. And the tip of the rifle: The tip swayed up, gentle for a 30.06, the boy's left hand riding up with the barrel and not fighting it. Good, boy, good, thought Sam. My son.

"All right, Malachi," Sam said. "How'd that feel? You feel loose?" He looked over at his son, his son sliding the bolt back already, opening the chamber, ejecting the shell.

"Yeah." Malachi looked up at his dad, a little grin on his face. You had to have that grin or you couldn't shoot, Sam thought. You had to feel the power and be in awe of it, not afraid, but in awe, or you wouldn't respect the rifle, respect the death in it. "Yeah. It felt fine, Dad. I felt relaxed, cool, Dad."

"Let's see how you did." Malachi got up, walked around in front of the rifle, glanced back at his dad, at Sam standing still and not moving. "Say the magic word, Mal."

Malachi smiled. "Clear, Dad. All clear." He pointed at the rifle, at the open breech, at the bolt pulled back.

Father and son walked downrange to the target, to the pallet a hundred yards away on the gravel strip. The smoke from the shell hung in the air like the clouds, and the sound of the firing still echoed from the hills. The violence of the firing lingered over the tundra, an unknown sound in a land of roaring winds. Malachi got to the target first, turned—grinning—and pointed at a little hole in the paper between the second and third rings under the bull's-eye.

"Good shot, son," Sam said. He took a pen from his parka and drew an *X* through the hole. "That'd be a lung shot on a 'boo if you had fired at it, if a 'boo would be obliging enough to stand still while we happened to be by that old drum there." Sam smiled. "A good shot, son. Let's keep trying, okay—you and me. We'll sight in the scopes, and then"—he looked out at the rolling tundra, at the hills he imagined treed with the velvet antlers of bulls preparing to rut—"and then maybe tomorrow we can look for some 'boo, maybe get one, okay? Maybe we'll find old One-Antler, huh?"

"Old One-Antler . . ."

Sam smiled at his son, as the memory lit up the boy's face. Years ago, Sam had told Malachi the story of Old One-Antler, a fable he'd made up, a tanik myth told as if it had been an Inupiaq legend. A great bull caribou roamed the Arctic, the story went, its antlers twisted together in one great rack, a single curved horn on its forehead. Legend had it that Old One-Antler could never die, that if you shot it and ate of its flesh or drank its blood before it miraculously healed itself, its immortality would be imparted to you. Even the antlers it shed yearly could serve as an antidote to pain and sickness— or give a tired old man new virility.

"Sure," Malachi said. "Maybe we can get Old One-Antler." And he walked—no, strode, Sam thought— strode back to the barrel and the rifle. He could see the pride in his walk, Sam thought, could see the confidence rippling through the boyish awkwardness, could see the strength firming up his downy legs, his clean cheeks. My son, Sam thought, my son.

They set out the next day to go hunting, the day clear and relatively warm, with a slight breeze blowing down from the north, enough to keep the bugs down. Mal and Sam packed light day packs—rain suit, gloves, lunch, water bottles, emergency blanket—strapped to bare backpack frames, the "torture rack" they'd haul out meat with, if they got a caribou. Sam carried a ground-to-air radio and they both had their rifles, of course, and ammunition.

Sam led the way up the creek valley that flowed into the Hula Hula River, over a small pass, and along another creek and around another mountain, to a set of terraces on the west flank of the mountain, each terrace like giant steps up the mountain—the site. The mountain had no name on the local topographical quad map, only an elevation: 1204 feet. As they hiked through ankle-deep wet bog, Sam counted drainages coming off the sides of the valley, so he'd know which drainage to take coming back if fog came in and hid the more identifiable ridge peaks.

Worst case scenario, Sam thought, if the fog came in so deep and they got totally lost, they could hike up to the ridge tops, and find their way back by the cairns set along the ridge. That's how he had found the site in the first place, found the ancient hunting camp: He'd been hiking over the ridge two summers before, had found the cairns, had followed them down and they led like exit signs to a creek and up to the old Inupiaq Eskimo camp on the lower of the terraces below elevation 1204.

Or, Sam thought, working his way up out of the bog to drier land below the valley ridge to his left, if they really got lost, they could just follow the caribou trails.

Along every hillside, along every creek, over passes and through valleys, generations of caribou, millions of caribou, had etched foot-wide trails in the tundra. Ground through the thin vegetation, through the moss and lichen and willow and grass, muddy trails wound over the country. Nothing guaranteed that the same caribou or the same herd would pass along the same trail year after year, but it was a safe bet, Sam knew, that some caribou at some time that summer would grace this ground with the chevrons of their hooves.

After walking several hours, Sam and Malachi stopped at the head of the creek valley, where it split beneath 1204 and wrapped around the bottom of the terrace. They had a view of the site up on the terrace, and of the tundra beyond. Sam unshucked his pack, brushed away snow from a rock, and sat down. Malachi remained standing.

"Hey, take five, son," Sam said.

Malachi nodded, took off his pack, but remained standing.

"Whatever," Sam grumbled. He pointed down at a clump of droppings, about the size and shape of raisins. With the tip of his hunting knife, he poked at the pellets. "Squishy," Sam said. "Recent, since last night's storm." Sam then noticed tracks, each pair of curved cuts in the snow like two scimitars mirroring each other. Two round dots about the size of a dime were at the base of each set of tracks. The wind had blown over part of the tracks, giving Sam an excuse for not noticing them earlier.

"'Boo, Dad?" Malachi asked.

Sam nodded. "Big one. Maybe Old One-Antler," he joked. The father took out his binoculars and glassed the far terrace, then the hillside across the creek valley, where the tracks had come from. "Just stragglers now, Malachi. The lone bulls coming to meet the ladies as they head back south. The tracks seem to head up to the site." Sam smiled. "Let's follow them up there, set up a watch, and see what comes."

The site hadn't looked like an archaeological site when Sam had first found it: no mounds, no crumbling sod huts or whalebone jaws sticking out of the ground. But if you looked at the bones littering the tundra, their very number indicated something cultural. Someone had killed a lot of caribou in the past there, and not just a pack of wolves or a ruthless grizzly. The middles of longbones had been crushed into unidentifiable fragments, while the ends bore the marks of stone or metal knife cuts. Skulls had been bashed in at the face to get at the delicate brains, and the antlers had been cleanly sawn away. Humans had been there, had hunted many caribou over more than one season, and they had left behind the bones of their butchery.

A more trained eye could detect the depressions of tents, or the rings of stones that held down the tents. Higher up on another terrace, where the grass didn't grow as thick and where the wind swept away soil so that only lichens could take bloom, clear signs of human passing had been more obvious: sled parts, a knife handle made of bone, a steel point, or dozens of blue and turquoise trade beads. And more bones, human bones, the gracile bones of the lower arm and upper leg, or ribs, or the high dome of a skull. None of that remained now, Sam remembered; all the surface artifacts and much of the subsurface stuff had been plotted, excavated, numbered, bagged, and taken away to museums.

Sam had found the site, had led a team of archaeologists back there and helped them dig it, and had developed the computer program to map the locations of bones and beads. Two summers ago he had come out there with one of the archaeologists, and a friend, to do some follow-up testing, and it was then that he had discovered the incredible caribou hunting the ancients had known long ago. Better, he had discovered that the knoll a half-mile across from the site could be used to land a Cessna 185, if the pilot knew his stuff, like Waldo, and if the passengers dared enough. Sam hoped they could get a caribou in the general area, butcher it, and cache the meat on the knoll, then hike back to the airstrip and get Waldo to swing by to recover the meat on the return home.

A side fork of the creek rose up to a little valley to the north, and Sam and Malachi worked their way across the creek and up to the terrace. They spread out, following the tracks, noting the progress of the caribou. There, the bull had stopped to drink from the open creek. Then, it had run for a brief moment, spooked by who knew what. Finally, it traversed the side of the terrace, and over the edge—could still be there. The storm front had broken, and bright sunshine lit up the slope. The bull could be basking in the sun, glad for the respite from flies and mosquitoes, glad for the moderate warmth before the long winter and the longer migration south—or so Sam imagined.

The wind blew into their faces, carrying their scent behind, and the slope hid them as they worked their way up. An old bleached caribou rack lay on the tundra, its tips spotted with orange lichen. Sam picked it up and held it to his head, waggling it. Malachi giggled at Sam's joke, but Sam shook his head. He pointed at his son's rifle, slung across the top of the boy's pack, and then at Malachi. The boy nodded, and took down his rifle. He had the scope on now, sighted in the day before, and five rounds in the magazine, none in the chamber. Sam took his new rifle out, but kept it slung over his shoulder. With his left hand, he held the caribou rack to his head, and then they went up the hill.

At the crest of the terrace, where Sam guessed a caribou might see this rack coming over the top, he motioned to Malachi to stop. Sam had no idea if there even was a caribou above, but he had heard of the trick before. Distract the game with antlers, draw it in at the curiosity of another bull. It would be just before the rut, when any bull would be wary of another bull, and be drawn to the challenge. Or so he hoped. The tracks looked fresher going up the terrace, and even if there was nothing, the 'boo had to be close.

"Ready," Sam whispered, and they went up.

Sam held the old antlers high, brow tines dipped in challenge, and he quickly ran up the slope. Malachi came after him, rifle raised. Father and son came over the crest, to the broad flat slope of the main terrace on the site, and came upon—nothing.

Malachi lowered the rifle, and Sam let the antlers droop down, not holding them as high. The snow still clung to the terrace, white obliterating the bones the archaeologists had not collected. The memory of the site came back to Sam then: the cluster of tents at the far edge of the terrace, the big cook tent surrounded by smaller pup tents, and the mast of the radio antenna central on the site. Lines had been strung up and down the slope, marking the transects, and he could still remember tripping over them in the fog. Now the site was empty, empty but for a plain of snow and a few rocks burning their way to the surface as the snow melted.

Scanning the field, Sam made sure the bull didn't rest in some slight depression, or hadn't bolted away from them. Malachi saw the bull first. He tapped his father on the shoulder and then pointed up. There, on the next ridge, the barren ridge where the archaeologists had found the trade beads and the grave, a massive bull caribou stood. Its off-white coat barely stood out against the bright horizon, but the massive dark rack—still maroon in velvet—revealed its presence. It held its face away from them, the rack most prominent. Even in the glaring light, Sam could count a dozen points. A legal kill, certainly, and a trophy, no doubt. Definitely a trophy.

Sam waved his arm down, back below the ridge, out of sight. Malachi nodded. Sam pointed at the ridge rising up to the base of the higher terrace. His son smiled, understanding: They would work their way along the ridge, staying out of the big bull's vision, and then come up the base of the terrace until they were below where the bull had been. If it didn't move, they would be able to rise up to it, pulling the same antler trick again.

Malachi kept to Sam's right and behind as Sam took the point, skirting the very edge of the ridge, keeping just enough of the higher terrace in view to maintain their bearings. The face of the higher terrace rolled down to the top of the little creek valley, meeting the ridge of the lower terrace. One slab of the upper terrace's face had fallen away, and sheets of purple shale showed the geology of the structure: sandstone and shale topped with soil and tundra. Sam remembered that the terrace had been mostly free of permafrost, the ground too well drained to hold water and freeze.

They walked up to the ridge, up to where the face of the upper terrace had fallen away, to where they would most be hidden. There, Sam paused, adjusting the old antlers. Both of them panted with the exertion, with the excitement. Sam held up a hand, and Malachi nodded, understanding again. Wait. Catch their breath. Don't let the rush of adrenaline spoil what would be a good shot, perhaps an only shot. After a few minutes, Sam jerked his head up the hill, then pointed at Malachi's rifle and mimed jacking a round. Malachi grinned, slid the bolt up and forward, but kept the safety on.

Sam held up five fingers, then slowly let each finger fall down, counting to one. As he raised his index finger, he pointed at the hill above, and they charged. The father stayed to Malachi's left, great rack on his head and leading the way. The son followed Sam, a step behind, and they came up.

The bull held its back to them, head turned away from them and staring at the foothills beyond, the breeze in its face. Its rump faced them, a narrow profile and a hard shot. Sam wiggled the rack, trying to get the bull's attention—to get it to move, a side profile and a clear shot. He wiggled the rack again. Nothing. The bull ignored them. Malachi raised his rifle, clicked off the safety. Sam quickly shook his head, whispered, "Hold." Malachi waited. Sam waved the antlers again, and started to throw them down in disgust at the great bull's disregard of them. He'd throw a rock at it to get its attention. But then the bull turned.

Slowly it turned its head to them, bringing its body around, a clear shot, almost begging for the bullet: low rump, massive hind legs and forelegs and chest, its head nearly the size of a bear's, and its rack four, no five feet high off its head. Sam dropped the old antlers and pulled up his rifle, all the while shouting "Shoot! Shoot!" Malachi held his fire, though, even though Sam had stepped back, even though Malachi now stood in front, rifle held steady and in a perfect firing stance. And he did not shoot.

"Goddamn it," Sam shouted, pulling up his own rifle and jacking a round in, to hell with giving the boy the honor of the first shot. The bull turned to them, and Sam saw what made Malachi hold, why he stood transfixed by the caribou—as the caribou now held Sam in his gaze and he, too, could not move.

The bull caribou's antlers rose from his forehead, the two antlers set a hair's width apart, so that they twisted and grew together, one antler, really—Old One-Antler, Sam now saw. The legend made real. Part of him debunked the mystery of it, calculated how it would be possible for a caribou's antlers to be set close together, so that they grew as one. Enough radiation from atomic testing, from failed nuclear power plants, had dusted the Arctic so that such a mutation could arise. But another part of Sam's intelligence tossed away rationality, and glorified the mystery. Old One-Antler, the immortal single-horned beast, the imaginative tanik's legend that had turned out to be true.

Old One-Antler held them like that, kept them stunned in its gaze, and then it came toward them, a great leap and then a horrible rush. He lowered his horn, the dozen points red with velvet and red, Sam saw, with something else—with blood, its own blood or the blood of others. Even though Sam had faced down a dozen grizzlies, and had the steady nerve to calmly kill them, he found himself trembling at Old One-Antler.

Finally Malachi fired. The bullet cracked in the stillness of the vast tundra, lead flying, and Sam heard a slight thwick as the bullet nicked a point off Old One-Antler's brow tine. A good shot, and had Malachi been an inch lower, a killing shot to the brain.

Sam fired then, but his hands still shook, and the shot went wild, not even passing near the old bull. Old One-Antler turned to the father, his attention distracted. Malachi fired again, getting his range, and he shot off another tine. The bull turned away from Sam, saw the source of danger, and came upon the boy.

"No!" Sam yelled, trying to distract it, seeing what the caribou intended. He took a deep breath, calming himself, aimed, and pulled the trigger again. The feeling came back to him as he pulled, the knowing that he had aimed true and steady, and that the bullet would find home. A hollow click came from the chamber. Sam slid the bolt back, and saw an empty chamber. The next brass round in the magazine hadn't advanced. He worked the bolt, but couldn't get the cartridge to come up. Jammed. Sam cursed at his hand rounds, wondering if he had crimped the bullets properly. He reached into his pocket for another round, inserting it into the open chamber as he looked over at his son.

Malachi kept shooting, the last of his shots hitting, but not killing, breaking off tines but not coming any lower. For a moment Sam wondered if Malachi intended to break the antler and not kill, wondered if he could have pumped every one of his rounds into the bull's head and chest. As the bull bore down on his son, though, Sam saw that Malachi shot to kill, that his last desperate shot had been aimed to kill, but that for some reason the boy just couldn't adjust his aim right. The last shot grazed the bull's forehead, and then the bull came down on Malachi, on his son.

With its massive antler, the bull gored the boy in the stomach, catching the tip of a broken tine on Malachi's rib cage, and throwing the boy up in the air. Old One-Antler held his son—impaled, like a trophy—looked over at Sam, and then dropped the boy. In that moment Sam had a shot, and took it. His son free, the caribou presenting its flank to him, Sam held his breath, let instinct guide him more than thought, pulled the trigger, and heard the satisfying hard-metal click of hammer hitting primer.

A bullet hit finally, its energy hardly shed by the four- or five-yard flight through air; it hit hard on, tearing through lungs and heart and backbone, and the bull toppled to the ground. Malachi writhed on the snowy tundra, his hands bloody and the snow bloody as he clutched at his ruined stomach. Intestines rolled through his fingers, the smell of barely digested food stenching the warming air. And Old One-Antler writhed on the ground, too, legs kicking and a huge hole dappling its skin where the bullet had come out. Sam ignored the dying caribou and walked over to his son.

"Good shooting, Dad," Malachi said, grimacing.

"Shh, boy, shhh." Sam took off his pack and ripped off his parka and shirt, pressing the wadded-up shirt to the boy's stomach. A gut wound, and a hundred miles from a health clinic: The boy was dead. Sam hoped he'd die before he understood that there was no saving him.

The thrashing of the caribou behind him angered Sam. That damn bull should have died by now, he thought. He turned from his son for a moment, and looked at Old One-Antler. The big bull still kicked his legs. Kicked them, Sam saw, not jerking them—not the dying throes of severed nerves. Kicked them. Sam drew his knife to cut the bull's throat, to end its misery as he wished he could end his own son's misery.

Old One-Antler rose.

It rose on good legs and came to them and snorted hot blood into Malachi's face. The boy pulled back at the onslaught of foamy fluid, but the bull's blood streamed down his face. Malachi licked at it, and for a moment quit groaning. Old One-Antler stood, sneezing blood until its lungs ran clear. The wound in its chest closed up, until it was no more than a red stain on white fur. Even the broken tips of its antler seemed to come back.

Malachi groaned again, his stomach still bleeding.

The foamy blood had been only a temporary salve. Sam looked at his son, at the healed caribou, at the knife in his hand. Old One-Antler stood panting. Sam looked at his rifle, still loaded, and at the knife. The caribou couldn't be killed, he saw—not long enough or fast enough. But . . .

Sam raised the knife, held the old bull in his gaze. The bull didn't move or couldn't move, he never did know, but Sam didn't care. Calmly he strode to Old One-Antler, until he was at the caribou's side. Sam stared at the caribou, its eyes almost pleading, and then he quickly hacked off a foot-long hunk of flesh from the caribou's right thigh. The wound closed even as Sam pulled away the steaming meat. Old One-Antler nodded its great rack to them, turned away, and disappeared over the edge of the terrace.

The meat dripped in Sam's hand as he came to his son. Malachi licked at the blood of the steak, and his groans quieted. Sam cut off small chunks of the steak, feeding them to his son. At first, Malachi chewed slowly at the raw flesh. With each bite he chewed harder: greedy, devouring. The boy took the last bit of steak from Sam, but Sam held it back.

It would give immortality, he thought. Some logic of the legend told him, though, that a body had to be nearly whole for the magic to work. It would work on him. For Malachi, it would only heal. Sam dared to look at his son then, wiped away blood from his boy's gaping wound. It had closed up, the intestines had wound back into his abdominal cavity, but the wound still bled. Just a taste, he thought, feeling his age, his stiff bones—the loss of that testicle so long ago.

The loss of his nut still pained, and he realized why: It meant the loss not only of part of his manhood, but of his marriage, of a loving woman. Things had started to go bad with Roberta right after Sam had licked the testicular cancer, as if the sacrifice of a testicle wasn't enough. The empty scrotum seemed to symbolize so many bonds broken. In that moment, Sam realized that what hurt most was that the greatest loss of all might have been of what mattered most: his son.

Just one taste, Sam thought, and perhaps he could be like Old One-Antler, could be whole—and live forever. Perhaps he could recover all that he had lost.

Malachi reached up for the last bit of steak, and Sam held it back, and then he smiled; he knew what he had to do, what fathers did, and he let his son take the last of the meat. He let his son lick Old One-Antler's blood from his hand, let the boy gently clean the blood from Sam's knife blade. Almost every drop went to Malachi. The wound closed up then, Malachi's blood drying up and only the shredded ends of his shirt testimony to the goring.

Sam reached into the bloody snow, the snow where Old One-Antler had lain, and he wadded up the snow and sucked on it. A surge of energy washed through him. The father stood, staring at the blood on the snow, at his son's blood and the caribou's blood. Even as he watched the snow steamed away, the late-summer sun heating the ground. Malachi slept, the sun warming his face.

On a far ridge, Old One-Antler looked down at him,

as if warning him, as if playing with him. Sam understood. He took his rifle, worked the bolt, and the
jammed round and the remaining rounds in the magazine fell to the tundra, more artifacts for the ancients'
site. He left the rifles where they were, then hoisted his
own pack, taking Malachi's day pack off the frame and
lashing it to his own pack. Then with renewed strength,
he lifted Malachi up in a firefighter's carry and took the
boy across the terrace and over to the knoll where Waldo
would land the plane.

On the knoll Sam held his son in his arms, stroking
the boy's hair as he slept. The backpack lay on the
ground, the radio on top of it. Sam waited for the distant
hum of Waldo's plane as he shuttled another load of
hunters onto the tundra. He knew they would find no
trophies that year. Sam smiled, though, for Old One-
Antler had given him something more wonderful than
wild meat or some great set of antlers.

He had given him back his son.

MARINA FITCH

———

STAMPEDE OF LIGHT

Peter: I think of **Marina Fitch** as practically a neighbor, since she resides and works with children in the farming town of Watsonville, California, where I lived for sixteen years. It is therefore a matter of chauvinistic local pride to present her "Stampede of Light" here. But it is also a matter of admiration, since her story is a completely original vision of the nature of unicorns, as well as a genuinely moving view of the terrible kind of loneliness that only children know, and the capacity for friendship and stubborn courage that belongs to the occasional real grown-up. . . .

Janet: Marina is another former member of The Melville Nine. She lived in Santa Cruz in those days, and used to drag herself by train and bus to our monthly meetings. She quit to move to Oregon, came back to California to get married, and, later, moved to Watsonville. Thank heavens she never stopped writing.

Stampede of Light

I DON'T KNOW WHEN I STOPPED BELIEVING I WOULD LIVE
forever.

"Open a child's mind and heart to the world, and you
achieve immortality," my sixth-grade teacher Mrs. Rodriguez once told me. "Whether they remember you or not,
you'll live forever."

I remember Mrs. Rodriguez. I guess that makes her a
saint.

I shaded my eyes with my hand and scanned the kids
racing across the blacktop, smashing tetherballs, clamber-
ing over metal play structures. At the edge of the grass two
boys raised clenched hands. I brought the whistle to my
lips—they tossed dried leaves at each other. I removed the
whistle. Then the boys scooped up more leaves and
dumped them on of one of my second graders.

He ignored them. I frowned, trying to remember his
name: ginger hair, gray eyes, square face, freckled nose.
Alone . . .

Corey Ferris, one of this year's forgotten children.

The one I couldn't place when I saw his name on my roll sheet the first month of school. The one who never caused trouble, never answered questions. The invisible child in a class of thirty-two.

I was a forgotten child, too. Until Mrs. Rodriguez.

Corey stood with his back to me, gazing across the field. I joined him. With a squint, I peered over his head. All I could see was the far corner of the cyclone fence.

"Corey," I said, "what are you looking at?"

He started. Shuffling away from me, he stopped, looked at the corner, then at me. "Don't you see her?" he said.

I looked again. This time I saw her.

The woman sat in the corner, her manzanita-red hair spilling over her shoulders, dark swirls against her turquoise blouse. Her skirt, vibrant with green, raspberry, yellow, and blue, fanned across her knees. She bent over slightly, her hands skimming across her lap.

A child stood beside her. A dark-haired girl, one of Peggy's third graders—Heather Granger. I headed toward them. The woman was probably Heather's mother, but it never hurt to check.

An image flashed through my mind: *Smiling, the woman opened her arms wide. The girl rested her head in the woman's lap—*

The image vanished. A sense of loss touched me. . . .

The bell rang.

I glanced back at the worn, art deco school. My second graders were already lining up near the back stairs. Corey hovered at the end of the line, separated from the others by two paces. I turned a slow circle, searching the far corner, then the playground. Heather and the woman were gone.

I finally caught up to Peggy in the staff room after school. "Peggy, did Heather go home sick?"

Peggy shrugged into her jacket, then took the sheaf of papers out of her mouth. "Heather?"

"Heather Granger. Dark hair, quiet."

Peggy sucked in her cheeks. "I don't have any Heathers this year." She frowned. "I had three last year. No Grangers . . ."

I blinked. "You sure?"

Peggy shook her head. "Nope. No Heathers."

I stared at the toes of my shoes, trying to recall Heather's face. I couldn't.

"Mary," Peggy said, "are you okay?"

"Did you—did you see that woman on the playground at lunch?" I said, looking up. "The one sitting in the corner of the field?"

Peggy's frown deepened. "What woman?"

I left around four. As I clattered down the wide front steps, I saw someone blur out of sight behind the potted rosemary on the landing. I stopped, then walked over and peeked.

Corey Ferris cowered behind the Grecian planter.

I squatted. "Corey, what are you doing here?"

He looked up at me, his mouth twisted in a lip-trembling pout.

I waited, head cocked to one side. Finally, he scuffled from behind the rosemary, dragging his backpack. He mumbled something.

"Say it again?" I said.

He glanced at the curb. "Waiting for Dad."

I stared at him. "Is he late?"

"Is it five yet?" he asked.

"No, not—is that when he picks you up?"

He nodded. I took a deep breath, held it, let it go. Students aren't supposed to be alone on the school grounds after two-forty-five.

"Does he—" I thought a minute. "Is this unusual?"

He shook his head.

I sat on the step. "What do you do?"

He hesitated, then sat beside me. He shrugged.

I glanced at my watch. I was supposed to meet a friend at five-thirty. . . .

So I'd meet her in my school clothes. No big deal. I dug through my school bag and pulled out a book. *The Stone Fox.* I nodded, impressed with myself. Good book. "Listen," I said. "I don't have to be anywhere. Would you like to help me read this?"

Corey stood beside me on the playground the next day, not really talking, just standing nearby. As recess wore on, he slowly inched closer. "Do you think?" he said. "Do you think the Stone Fox gave Willy one of the white dogs?"

I pondered this. "I don't know. What do you think?"

Corey grinned, a sudden, gap-toothed smile. "Yeah, he did. The best one."

"What do you think Willy named—?"

"Teacher!" someone wailed.

I turned. A group of kids ran toward me in geese formation. The girl in the lead scrabbled to a stop. "Teacher," she said, "Kevin threw my softball over the fence!"

Kevin slid to a halt. "Can I help it if Gabby can't catch?"

"First things first," I said. "Where did it go over the fence?"

Kevin and Gabby pointed, then glared at each other. I sighted down their fingers . . . to the far corner and the rainbow woman.

A child stood beside her, a boy with a buzz—Josue Hernandez. I'd had him two years ago. He stood beside her, intent on her hands as they skipped like pebbles across her lap.

An image seared through me: *Josue resting his head in the woman's lap. He dissolved like steam —*

By the time the image faded, I was halfway across the field, the gaggle of students squawking behind me. I froze five feet from Josue and the woman. Josue seemed . . . faded, as if he'd been stonewashed. His eyes were no longer chocolate dark, but faint as a shadow on sun-dried mud. He gazed at the woman's hands.

Long and slender, her hands were crosshatched with tiny nicks. She wore porcelain thimbles on her left thumb and forefinger. She wielded a golden needle with her right, embroidering something onto her skirt with a dark thread. I stepped closer. Her lap glittered as if appliquéd with mirrors. I took another step. No, not mirrors—tiny unicorns that sparkled like distant stars. The newest one, a dull, black unicorn on a field of green, lacked its horn. The woman's hands stopped. I looked up—

"Ms. Scibilin! Ms. Scibilin!" someone yelled. "Gabby threw Kevin's shoe over the fence!"

Little hands dragged me to the fence and pointed out the ball, embedded in a pumpkin, and the shoe, dangling from a bare guide wire. When I turned back to the woman, she and Josue were gone.

I walked onto the playground and scanned the field as I had every day for the past week. There was no sign of the woman. I frowned, disappointed. Juanita Vargas, the principal, had promised to call the police next time the woman set foot on the school grounds.

Even if she couldn't remember Josue or the girl.

Corey fell in step beside me. We'd shared three more books after school—two on dogs and one on magic tricks. He'd taken home the magic book.

"I figured out the Kleenex trick," he said. "How to make it disappear? But I can't get the penny one."

"That's a tough one," I said. "I'll help you with it after school."

He grinned at me. I smiled back, then did a quick survey of the field.

A chill wind whistled across the playground, rearranging the fallen leaves. A string of girls threaded their way between Corey and me, chasing orange and gold maple leaves. I scanned the play structures, lingering on a possible fight, then circled slowly. A football game skirmished along the edge of the field. Beyond the grass-stained players, Corey leaned against the fence, watching the woman.

I snatched at Gabby's wrist as she walked by. "Gabby," I said. "Go to the office and tell Ms. Vargas I need her to make that phone call. *Now.*"

Corey inched closer to the woman.

My chest constricted. I ran toward Corey. I glanced at the woman. She had another child with her, not what's-his-name, Josue, but a blonde second grader, one of Kristy's. Amanda Schuyler. The woman looked up, and even at that distance, I could swear she was looking at me—

"Ms. Scibilin! Watch out!"

Three hurtling bodies tackled me in the end zone. They tumbled over the top of me, then scrambled away. "Teacher, are you all right?" someone said.

I spat out a mouthful of grass. "I'm fine."

I swayed to my feet, then sat down abruptly. I knew if I glanced at the corner, Amanda and the woman would be gone.

I limped into the office an hour after the last bell. Panic muted the pain. The police had found nothing, no bits of thread, no embroidery needles, no matted grass. I'd sent them to Kristy's class to talk to Amanda Schuyler. Kristy told them she didn't have an Amanda Schuyler and never had. . . .

I winced, lowering myself into the secretary's chair. I went through the roll sheets, then the emergency cards. I even hobbled over to the filing cabinet and searched the cumulative folders. According to the Cayuga Elementary School records, Josue Hernandez and Amanda Schuyler did not exist. Not even in their siblings' cum files.

I struck the filing cabinet with my fist.

Juanita poked her head into the office. "You okay?"

"Fine," I muttered. I slipped Jason Schuyler's cum folder back in place, then slammed the filing cabinet.

Juanita studied me. "They hit you pretty hard. You're going to Doctors on Duty."

"I'm fine, Juanita. Really—"

She raised two elegantly penciled eyebrows. "District'll foot the bill if you go now. Something shows up later, you'll need a paper trail."

I hesitated. She was right, but—

"You're going," she said. She jangled her keys. "Come on. I'll drive."

Juanita insisted I drape my arm around her neck as we crept slowly down the front steps. I hunched deeper into my jacket, hoping no one was watching. "Juanita," I said in a low voice, "it's just a bruise. I'll be stiff for a few days, then it'll disappear."

Juanita grunted under my weight. "Could be fractured."

Fractured. I grimaced. "Great."

We passed the potted rosemary. Corey peeked between its branches, his face pale in the shadows. He bit down on his lower lip and withdrew.

I twisted my head to try to catch another glimpse of him. This is where I needed to be. With Corey, not in some clinic. "Juanita, I'm fine, really. It's just a bruise—"

Juanita stopped. She eyed me coolly. "I'm not worried

about your leg. I'm worried about your head."

My cheeks flamed. My head—because no one else remembered Amanda Schuyler.

No fractures, leg or skull, just a bruise the size of a cantaloupe. Between the wait, the exam—complete with X rays—and Juanita's unwillingness to release me unfed, it was almost seven when I made it back to the school. I waited until Juanita sped away, then got out of my car and limped up the steps. I searched behind the rosemary. No Corey, but tucked between the planter and the wall was the book of magic tricks.

Corey veered away from me when he walked into the classroom next morning. Head down, he put his backpack in his cubby and shuffled to his desk.

At one point Lily, the girl seated next to him, opened his desk and took his crayons. "Lily," I said. "Put those back and ask Corey if you may borrow them."

"He's not here—" Lily sat up, startled. Her eyes grew as round as slammers when she saw Corey. Backing away, she dropped his crayons.

Corey sat quietly, hands folded in his lap.

Within an hour, the class had forgotten him again.

It took me several minutes to find Corey when I went out for lunch recess.

He huddled ten feet from the woman. No one stood

beside her this time. Her hands lay still in that colorful expanse of glittering unicorns. I imagined the one she'd been working on while the dark-haired boy hovered over her. I tried to recall the boy's name or face, but all I could remember was that dull, black embroidery amid the stellar unicorns.

I limped toward them. Girls. There had been two girls, too. But I could remember nothing but a sense of them, like perfume lingering in a closed room.

Corey took a step toward the woman. Her face tilted toward him. She seemed to be talking to him, coaxing him—

I gasped at the image: *Corey resting his head in the woman's lap, fading like mist in sunlight to become—*

I stared at Corey and the woman, not daring to shift my gaze. As if by watching them, I could keep that little head from lowering itself to that glittering field.

The woman's hands nested in her lap. Corey leaned into the fence; it bowed behind him like a hammock.

Gritting my teeth, I pushed myself to a lunging jog. The bruise throbbed along my hip. I cupped my hands to my mouth and called.

Corey flinched at the sound of his name, but refused to look at me. He stepped closer to the woman and knelt before her. She reached to pull his head into her lap. . . .

I lumbered toward them, tensing against the pain. Three, four yards and I'd be there. Sucking in a deep breath, I shouted, "Corey, get away from her!"

He snapped upright, swinging to look at me. The woman touched his leg. She murmured something. He glared at me, then bent toward her. The woman ran her fingers through his hair—

I grasped him by the arm. The woman pulled her hand back, plucking a lock of his ginger hair.

"Corey," I said. I dragged him away, reaching out to steady him with my other hand. With a growl, he wrenched away from me and ran toward the buildings. I sagged with relief, then turned on the woman. "Who are you?" I said. "What do you want—?"

She was gone.

I knelt beside the rosemary, parting its branches. "Corey?"

Reaching behind the planter, I patted the landing. I withdrew my dust-covered fingers.

I sat next to the planter. Late afternoon closed around me. "I have a special book for you," I said, hoping he was within hearing. The shadows deepened. I glanced at my watch. Four-fourteen. "It's about dogs," I said. If I stayed too late and he refused to come out of hiding, he'd miss his dad. "Corey, I'm sorry about yesterday," I said. "Ms. Vargas took me to the doctor. By the time I got back, you were gone." I glanced at my watch again. Four-thirty-five. A car pulled up to the curb. I sat up. A teenage couple got out and strolled across the front lawn, arm in arm. "Corey," I said. "I'm going. I don't want you to miss your dad." I pulled the book on Samoyeds from my book bag. "I'll leave this for you," I said. "Behind the planter. I'll see you tomorrow, okay?"

I arrived at school early the next morning, to see if Corey had taken the book. A shoe peeped from the planter's shadow. Puzzled, I squatted beside the rosemary. Corey curled around the planter, his backpack tucked under his head. His mouth hung slack, his eyes were closed. My heart lurched. I reached in and touched him. He murmured, then jerked awake, eyes wide.

I wound my arms around him and pulled him out. I hugged him. The chill of him seeped through my sweater. I smoothed the hair from his face. "Corey, have you been here all night?"

He nodded.

The breath went out of me. "Your father . . . ?"

He looked at me blankly. "Father?"

"My God," I whispered. I held him tight, rocking him. "What has that woman done?"

I had to look up his father in the phone book. Corey's emergency card was gone. So was his cumulative file. When Mr. Ferris answered, he had no idea who I was. "There must be some mistake," he said curtly. "I don't have a son—"

"But Corey—"

"Corey," he said. His voice grew wistful. "That was my grandfather's name." The curtness returned. "Sorry. Wrong Ferris." He hung up.

I weighed the receiver in my hand, then set it down. I went into the nurse's office. Corey huddled under a pile of blankets. I sat next to him. "Hungry?" I said.

He shook his head.

Peggy breezed in, glanced at Corey, yanked open the medicine cabinet. She took out a bottle of lotion. "New student?" she said.

Corey had worked his way to the end of the line by the time I led my students into the classroom. The boy just ahead of him shut the door in his face as if he weren't there. I opened the door and, taking his hand, led him inside.

When I took roll, his name wasn't listed. I flipped through the old roll sheets. According to these, he'd never been listed. I wrote him in and marked him "present."

During independent reading time, I walked over and crouched beside him. "She can't have you," I said. "I won't let her."

I kept him in during morning recess. I read to him; he stared out the window at the field. I moved my chair so that he had to look at me. "What did she promise you?" I said. "Where is she trying to take you?"

He turned away from me.

I touched his knee. "Corey?"

He slumped in his chair, staring at his desk.

The hair tickled along the back of my neck. On a hunch, I opened his desk. It was empty.

I followed him onto the playground at lunchtime. He ran across the field to the fence. I tried to keep up, but the bruise slowed me down. I gritted my teeth, trying to ignore the pain. He spurted ahead. The woman sat in the corner, waiting, her right hand raised slightly. A glint of gold winked between her fingers.

Corey stumbled to a stop in front of her.

"Leave him alone!" I shouted. "Leave them *all* alone!"

Neither Corey nor the woman turned.

I tripped, somehow caught myself. I winced, closing my eyes—

The image swept through me like a flash flood: *Corey, the boy, the two girls, countless other children, resting their heads in the woman's lap. One by one they blazed and disappeared like shooting stars, the only trace of them the bright unicorns on the woman's rainbow skirt—*

I forced my eyes open. Corey inched closer to the woman, his shins brushing her knee. The woman plunged the needle in and out of the cloth like a seabird diving through waves. I limped up to her, clenching and unclenching my hands.

Beneath the woman's needle, the outline of a unicorn was slowly taking shape on a field of blue, stitched in lusterless ginger thread. I searched the constellation of unicorns for the dull, black one, that other boy's, but couldn't find it. I finally located it on its field of green—now as bright as all the others.

Then a dull shape caught my eye. I took a step closer. Amid all the sparkling, prancing unicorns stood one small, brown horse on a field of blue.

Me.

I stood beside the rainbow woman. Her needle

stitched the blue cloth with my hair, filling in the outline of the tiny unicorn. I knelt, my breath quick and shallow as I waited anxiously for her to finish. I would be someone. I would no longer be forgotten. I would become—

Corey dropped to his knees.

I tried to reel the image back, tried to remember. For Corey's sake. For mine.

I would become one of those gleaming unicorns that danced in her eyes.

I looked slowly from the woman's lap.

And trembled, that forgotten longing aching through me. Too frightened to take her in all at once, I started with her hair, that thick, manzanita-red mane that tumbled over her shoulders, then the perfect oval of her chin, the strawberry ripeness of her lips, the gentle slope of her nose. I steeled myself. Her eyes . . .

Her eyes had no color—not even white or black. I gazed into them, knowing what I would find there when my own longing had peeled away the layers of this world: unicorns, tossing their heads, light spiraling down their horns. . . .

I held my breath. They were more beautiful than I remembered. And so many—herds of them, streaking through the woodlands like a meteor shower. My ears rang with the drum of their cloven hooves.

If this is what Corey wanted, to join these magnificent creatures, who was I to stand in his way? I took a step back.

Rage kindled in me. Who had stood in *my* way?

I froze. Mrs. Rodriguez.

Kneeling beside me, she had forced my head up so that I could no longer see the gold needle pierce the blue cloth. "An illusion, Mary," she said. "There is so much in the world, so many things to discover and explore and create. Don't give up everything for an illusion."

I fought her, fought her words and the urging of her hands as she forced me to look. . . .

I swallowed, my throat dry and tight. But if this was what Corey wanted, who was I to deny him?

I am no Mrs. Rodriguez.

I am no saint.

The unicorns wheeled and galloped before me, a stampede of light. Then one of the unicorns stopped and faced me.

It yearned toward me, its eyes overflowing with a terrible loneliness. Another unicorn stopped, and another, until at least a dozen stared back at me. The first unicorn's longing echoed from eye to eye.

Their sadness sickened me. Without looking away, I groped for Corey. My hand clasped his shoulder. I drew him to me, caging him with my elbows and cupping his chin in my hands. I raised his head. "Look, Corey," I said. "Look into her eyes. If this is what you want, I'll let you go. But be sure."

He squirmed. More unicorns stopped to gaze at us.

"I want to be like them!" he said.

"Look *hard* at them, Corey," I said, reluctant to fulfill my promise. "See how lonely they are?"

"And is it any different here?" the woman said, her voice as husky as woodsmoke. "You are lonely here, Corey. There you will have others of your kind."

I wet my lips. "Corey—"

The woman hissed. "Leave us, meddler. You have nothing to offer him."

"Nothing," Corey said. But the word trailed with doubt.

My heart pounded. What had Mrs. Rodriguez said? What had finally reached me?

But I couldn't find the words. Frantic, I lashed out. "What does *she* have to offer you? An illusion, Corey. A lie. It's not real. It's like the Kleenex trick—"

Corey strained against my arms. The unicorns loped away.

"Let him go," the woman said. "He is mine. You have nothing for him. Absolutely nothing."

I loosened my grip slowly. My voice cracked. "Maybe *I* don't, but this world does. I saw you, Corey. I wanted to be your friend. Other people will, too. And they'll want to see that Kleenex trick. They'll want to know what Willy named his new dog."

The unicorns returned, gazing at me intently.

"They'll chase leaves," I said. "They'll throw balls and shoes over the fence. Your father will pick you up and take you out for ice cream. And I can—I can teach you the penny trick."

Corey stood still as my arms fell away. The unicorns crept closer—

Their faces changed. Josue peered back at me, and Amanda and Heather. Jason from Peggy's class last year and Mindy from Kristy's class two years ago. More. Children I had never known . . .

I doubled around the ache in my stomach. I had stopped trying and I had failed them, all of them. I had failed Corey.

The woman blinked. Her eyes became colorless once more.

Corey cried out. He grabbed me, burrowing under my arm, his breath hot and damp through my sweater. I clung to him, resting my cheek on his head. His hair smelled of rosemary. My gaze fell to the woman's hands.

She jerked the needle, snapping the thread. Dull and hornless, the ginger unicorn sank into a fold as she stood. "You've promised him much," she said. "Don't let him down."

She vanished.

Corey choked back a sob. His hands twisted the hem of my sweater. I held him with one arm. With my free hand, I fished a Kleenex from my skirt pocket. Footsteps stampeded toward us. I jerked to look. Unicorns . . . ?

Children.

"Ms. Scibilin! Ms. Scibilin!" a chorus of voices shouted. Small hands pulled at us, some patting me, some patting Corey. "What's wrong with Corey? Is Corey all right? Corey, you okay?"

"He's fine," I said.

Corey's chest shuddered with a deep breath. Tears beaded his lashes. I handed him the Kleenex. He stared at it a minute, then looked up at me. Eagerness and wonder dwelt in those gray eyes. So did Mrs. Rodriguez. So did I.

He held up the Kleenex so that the other children could see it. "Want to see me make it disappear?" he said.

P. D. CACEK

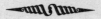

GILGAMESH RECIDIVUS

Peter: **P. D. Cacek**'s work has appeared in a lot of magazines with spooky names, yet most people, I should think, would not call her "Gilgamesh Recidivus" a true horror story—depends on your attitude toward immortality, of course. . . .

Janet: P. D., aka Trish, was a valued member of that same Bay Area writers' workshop I have mentioned before, The Melville Nine. She is a fabulous writer, another one with a unique voice which stems from her bizarre and, in my opinion, all too accurate way of looking at the world. She is also my friend, which is why I took such particular joy in introducing her to Manhattan, to bagels and lox, and—through this book—to a whole new readership.

Gilgamesh Recidivus

~~~~~~

THE COLD WAS A LIVING THING, STALKING HIM FROM the blue shadows, its icy breath encircling his feet as he trudged along the narrow swath of black ice that doubled for a footpath.

He had never liked the cold—once fearing its final embrace, then seeking it out. *For so very long.* But now the cold knew him and teased him like a coy lover, allowing him only the slightest touch before scurrying away.

"My, haven't we gotten poetic in our old age," he chided himself, his breath adding another layer of ice to his mahogany-colored beard. "Fool."

Cresting a small rise, he stopped and looked back over his shoulder. The railway village he had left that morning, huge in comparison to most of the Siberian settlements he'd seen dimly through the train's ice-coated windows, had been swallowed by the cold night. If anyone in the village remembered the tall stranger who had stopped only long enough to ask directions of the station-master, it would be a false memory . . . one that he had fashioned on the spur of the moment. A new identity. A new name. And a manufactured life to go with it.

He had done it so many times before that it was second nature. So *many* times before that if he put his mind to
it, he could almost forget who he really was.

Almost. And never.

Hunching his shoulders beneath the bulky, post–
Afghani War parka he had bought from an enterprising
black-marketeer, he turned back to the path before him.
There was no evidence that another human being had
made the same journey since the first snow. The ancient
stationmaster, once they found a dialect they both could
mutilate just enough to understand, had warned him of
the outpost's intentional isolation. There would be *no one*
to help him if he became lost. *No one* to carry him out.

No one to watch him die.

Finally, to die.

He shook his head and laughed, the sound startling the
cold away from his face. He had become foolish in his old
age. If his journey was successful, he would have more
than enough witnesses to his death.

While the lieutenant studied the documents that
showed a different identity than the one he'd given to the
stationmaster, he studied the men.

There were three others besides the officer—all
identically dressed in the drab brown uniform and
woolen greatcoat of the Home Guard, each wearing a
rabbit-fur hat with the ear-flaps down and tied beneath
cold-reddened chins. Each with a rifle slung over one
shoulder.

A smile tugged at his lips beneath the frost clinging to

his beard. He had witnessed this scene so many times before—the self-important officer, his soldiers, their weapons—that it gave him a comforting sense of déjà vu.

He let the smile fade as the officer looked up. Slumped his shoulders and eased deeper into character. Waited for his cue.

"Biogenetic engineering," the lieutenant said, nodding as if the term were as familiar to him as the small cast-iron stove his men were huddled around.

"Yes," he answered, but gave no further explanation. He could have, of course, gone into the most intricate details of gene-splicing—one of the *benefits* of such a long life was in having the *time* to learn these things—but, as with his total acquiescence during the soldier's rough-handed search, he didn't like to show off.

Unless he had to.

"A very remarkable field. Your papers seem to be in order, however . . ."

The soldier tapped the forged documents with a gnawed pencil stub and cleared his throat. His accent came from the south; perhaps as far as the Caspian or Black seas . . . thousands of kilometers from the Siberian Hell he had been consigned to.

"It must be difficult to be so far from your home, Lieutenant, especially in so inhospitable a place as this."

The soldier looked up through the glare of the kerosene lantern on the desk beside him.

"With such primitive amenities. Don't you miss the sun?"

The narrow face moved away from the light, the almond-shaped eyes going from sea-green to azure. The pencil stub *pinged* when it hit the desk top.

"Why are you here, Doctor . . ."

"Ambrose," he said, filling in the pause. He'd chosen the name as a final jest . . . a pun to defy the gods who had abandoned him so long ago.

He didn't realize he'd been smiling until he felt it stop—at the same instant the lieutenant gathered up the documents and placed them in the desk's center drawer. The sound the lock made when it slid home was still echoing in the chilled air when the soldier stood up, his gloved hand going to the thick gun belt cinched at his waist.

Ambrose took a deep breath and waited. He hadn't planned on killing the men, they were to be his story-tellers. But if their deaths meant that he might finally die . . .

He let his hands slowly ball into fists.

"You will be so kind as to tell me how you knew to come to this place, *Doctor* Ambrose. We are not generally listed in any Intourist publications." The lieutenant's gloved hand moved to the flap on the front of the holster. Ambrose shifted his weight to the balls of his feet. "I suggest you answer now, Doctor. And please . . . the truth."

You wouldn't accept the truth *if I told you, boy.*

Sighing, his breath steaming in the frigid air, Ambrose unclenched the fingers of his right hand and reached toward the parka's inside breast pocket. Matching his movements precisely, three SKS semiautomatic rifles took aim at his heart.

. . . if their deaths mean that I can finally die . . .

No. Not yet.

He lowered the heels of his boots to the wooden floor.

"Peace, friends," he said, more to the lieutenant than to the armed men. "There is an item in my pocket that may explain things to your satisfaction, sir. May I get it?"

A curt nod. "But do so slowly, *Doctor* Ambrose, the boredom of this place has made my men seek diversion where they can find it."

"Boredom?" He forced his hand to stop at the pocket's lip. "*Here?* In the presence of the greatest biological discovery of all time? May God forgive your men, Lieutenant."

The man's eyes flashed and Ambrose pretended not to notice. The ideological wounds the lieutenant must have suffered when first communism and then the Marxist ideal fell were undoubtedly still too fresh for an invocation to *God* to hold much meaning.

But it will, Ambrose promised silently. *By the end of this night it will.*

"I must admit that I heard of . . . this through less than official channels, sir."

Tucking himself deeper into the character of obsessed scientist, Ambrose pulled a five-by-ten-centimeter news article and its corresponding photograph from his pocket and laid it on the desk facing the lieutenant. The picture was overexposed and grainy, showing only the vaguest outline of an elongated neck and flowing mane. But the *horn* was still visible—stark white and pointing straight at heaven like an accusing finger.

"Of course I don't usually *buy* this sort of journalistic trash," he said, urging his voice into breathless wonder, "but the headline . . . and picture. My G— Lieutenant, if this story is true then all I need are just a few cells . . . a

simple scraping of the inside of the animal's mouth and . . .
I . . . I can . . ."

Panting, his breath almost as thick as the frozen mist
outside, Ambrose patted his chest and smiled. Weakly. He
regretted that with the present government in financial
ruin there would be no opportunity to videotape him. It
was the performance of a lifetime. A very *long* lifetime.
And his last performance.

With any luck.

"I apologize, Lieutenant," he said sheepishly, still
feigning vulnerability, "but I'm sure you can understand
my excitement."

The officer grunted as Ambrose leaned forward, com-
pensating for his six feet, three inches, and tapped the article with his finger, drawing the man's attention back to it.

The story had appeared in one of the more "reputable"
American tabloids, the brazen headline

RUSSIAN UNICORN DISCOVERED

piquing Ambrose's interest just enough to buy the paper
and suffer the smirks of an overweight supermarket
cashier. In lifetimes past, he had discovered that truth, like
Edgar Allan Poe's purloined letter, occasionally could
only be found where you didn't look for it.

"I know, I know," he went on, "these papers usually
tend to vie for the record of Elvis Presley sightings and
UFO abduction stories . . . but you have to understand,
Lieutenant. If there is *any* validity to the article—"

His guts twisted over on themselves when the lieutenant looked up.

There was surprise in the man's eyes, yes . . . naturally, considering the publication . . . but there was something else as well. Incomprehension. He didn't recognize the animal in the photograph.

Ambrose forced himself to remain calm as the soldier shook his head. *Are you gods not done with me yet?* It was a lie. Another lie and he should have known better after so many centuries. He almost laughed out loud.

But there was still *something* about the three other soldiers' nervousness . . . the way their eyes kept shifting from his face to the small locked door to his left.

The way sweat kept beading upon their brows despite the coldness of the room.

Something.

He sighed, decided to continue the illusion a while longer.

"So." The pain in his voice sounded so real that even he was moved. "I have come all this way in what is usually referred to as a wild-goose chase."

"I am familiar with the term, Doctor Ambrose," the lieutenant said, moving his hand from the holster, the chair's frozen springs screaming as he leaned back. "I have not been assigned to Siberia all of my life."

Ah.

Go on, Ambrose. *All they can do is shoot at you.*

All illusion faded.

"Then why *are* you here, Lieutenant—if the article is false, that is?" He smiled. "I doubt that even a government in transition would assign men to guard an empty Siberian hovel."

His smile was matched.

"I am but a *humble* officer in the Russian Army, Doctor Ambrose," the lieutenant shrugged, "and I do what I am ordered. Without question . . . even in a transitional government. It is not a lucrative profession, but it keeps food in the bellies of my wife and children."

A man three months in the grave would not have missed the *subtle* hint. A communist he may have been born and bred, but the lieutenant was willing to make the "sacrifice" to capitalism for the sake of his wife and children.

If he even had a wife and children. Not that Ambrose cared. He had never been a moralist.

Pushing up the left sleeve of his parka, Ambrose quickly removed the gold watch he wore. Time, after so many centuries, meant little to him, and gold was still a highly negotiable commodity.

"Of course, I would not ask for the privilege of seeing what may be behind that locked door without . . . showing my appreciation."

"Even if there is nothing there, Doctor?"

"Even so."

The lieutenant shifted in his chair just enough to hide the transaction from his men and slipped the watch into the front pocket of his greatcoat, nodding.

"Then follow me, Doctor Ambrose."

The three soldiers never lowered their rifles as their officer stood up and, taking the kerosene lantern from the desk, led the way across the room. Ambrose imagined the weapons aimed at his back. The sensation reminded him of fleas crawling across his skin; a mild distraction, but of no consequence.

The sound of the hasp opening cracked in the still air . . . still except for the muffled sound of unshod hooves coming from the darkness beyond the door.

"I cannot give you permission to take anything from the animal, doctor," the lieutenant said, blocking the door with his body, the hand holding the ring of keys again resting upon the holster, "not even a picture, and I apologize for the lack of heat. It—it seems to prefer the cold."

The door opened and Ambrose inhaled the scent of fresh dung and musk and hay. *Alive. Whatever was in there was actually alive.*

"Stay away from the horn, Doctor," the lieutenant said, standing to one side. "It has already killed one scientist. A *biologist,* like yourself."

With the light at his back, Ambrose entered the room first.

And froze.

The animal lifted its shaggy head and stared at him through the clouds of steam rising from its nostrils. *Alive.* The light from the lantern turned its dun-colored hide to gold.

The single horn to polished hematite.

It was real.

"I . . ." For the first time in his life Ambrose did not need to pretend wonder. "I thought from your expression when you saw the photograph that . . . that it was just another fairy tale."

"It was the picture that confused me, Doctor Ambrose," the lieutenant said, giving the makeshift wooden corral in the center of the room a wide berth as he walked to a workstation directly opposite the door. "This animal does not look at all like the one in the photograph."

"No," Ambrose said, "it doesn't."

Tiny and compact, ten hands at the shoulder if that, the unicorn resembled a stunted Mongolian pony more than the sleek, alabaster creature of myth. Even the horn, pushing its way through the thick forelock, was different. Where the "mythical" alicorn was supposed to be spiraled like that on a narwhal, the "living" horn resembled the protuberance on a rhinoceros. Black as the heart of a Sumerian whore and curved back toward the tufted ears like a scimitar.

Ambrose took a deep breath and let it out as a laugh. *It was a hoax. And a pathetic one. Some psychotic veterinarian's idea of a joke.* Shifting his eyes, he caught the lieutenant's wide-eyed stare and laughed again.

"My compliments to the designer," he said, tipping his head in a mock bow, "or was this done by committee? That might explain the choice of animal. I'm sure that obtaining an Arab or Lipizzaner, even though it might have looked more like a unicorn, was too much of an expense for the new government to justify. Am I right?"

"You . . . don't *believe* what you see?"

Shaking his head, Ambrose walked to the corral and lifted his hand to the animal. Three things happened simultaneously, only two of which he could understand. One was the lieutenant's sudden shout—something about staying away from the corral—the second was the scream coming from the animal itself as it reared up on its hind legs and struck out at the air between them.

The third was the blinding blue light that knocked him

to the floor and left behind the smell of ozone and singed horsehide.

—tor Ambrose are you

"—all right?"

Ambrose blinked his eyes and for a moment saw only an afterimage of the animal—its color reversed, finally looking like the fantasy creature it was supposed to be.

"What?"

"We put an electrified grid along the inside of the corral. He, the animal kept . . . there was no way of holding him without it. The voltage . . . It isn't capable of hurting him, but he doesn't seem to like it."

I can understand why, Ambrose thought as he allowed the lieutenant to help him to his feet, his own flesh tingling uncomfortably. It was then that he noticed a second gas generator beneath the workstation and the thick cable that ran from it to the corral. A bright red alligator clamp attached the cable to the chicken wire mesh that had been nailed to the inside of the wooden railings. It seemed a makeshift design, but very effective.

Ambrose felt a drop of moisture touch his chin an instant before it refroze and wondered exactly how high the voltage was, even though the lieutenant was right about it not seeming to affect the animal.

The unicorn had settled down, shaking its brushlike mane and pawing at the trampled straw. *That,* at least, Ambrose noticed, concurred with the legend. The hoof, although almost completely covered with thick, black "feathers," was cloven like a goat's.

Like those he had once seen being woven into a tapestry.

So long ago.

"I can understand the need for such security measures, Lieutenant," he said. "You certainly don't want anyone to get near enough to see the suture marks around the horn or study the surgically altered hooves."

Brushing off his sleeve where the man's hand had been, Ambrose turned and began walking to the door. "Thank you for your time. And the sideshow."

"This is no sideshow, Doctor Ambrose."

It was the *way* the lieutenant said those words that made Ambrose stop and walk back to within an inch of the corral. At that distance, he could hear the electricity humming through the wire mesh—could feel it prickle the hair on his arms and legs even through his clothing. His beard and eyebrows felt like they were standing at attention.

"Watch," the lieutenant said.

And Ambrose watched.

Watched the lieutenant remove the sidearm from its holster and take aim at the animal. Watched, with a sensation of compressed time, the bullet leave the muzzle and tear a hole in the quivering chest.

Watched, too, as the shredded flesh curled back in around the wound and closed.

The unicorn snorted and pawed the ground, undisturbed by either the shot or the armed soldiers running into the room.

"It is all right," the lieutenant told his men. "I was just giving the doctor a demonstration. Dismissed."

Ambrose only heard the sounds of their boots striking the wooden flooring as they left. He couldn't take his eyes off the animal. Didn't dare.

"By the gods. How . . . *old* is it?"

He could hear the lieutenant replace the handgun and snap the holster flap back in place.

"The biologist . . . the one who was killed . . . wasn't sure, he never got a chance to collect much data. But he thought it was old. Very old."

"Is it immortal?" Ambrose whispered.

This time it was the lieutenant who laughed.

"Of *course* not, Doctor. No. Nothing is immortal."

"Are you so sure?"

The smile faltered slightly around the edges. "Yes, Doctor, I am. This animal was found in one of the most hostile environments known to man. It's only natural that it would . . . develop certain natural survival skills that our scientists haven't encountered before."

"Yes," Ambrose said, looking again at the animal's barreled chest. Where the bullet had impacted the hair had re-formed in the shape of a star. "I would think that spontaneous tissue repair is not something most scientists deal with on a regular basis. How then do they explain it? Or the animal?"

The lieutenant's grin acquired some of its former glory.

"I'm sorry, Doctor, but the tour is over." Nodding once, he spun on his heels and walked to the worktable. His gloved fingers were closing around the lantern's wire handle when the unicorn suddenly nickered.

Ambrose backed away from the corral and into the lengthening shadows as the lieutenant crossed the room. The cold fingered his throat as he unzipped the parka.

"Ah, do you hear that, Doctor Ambrose?" The lieutenant asked, increasing the lamp's brightness. The shadows slunk back and Ambrose joined them. "That moaning sound? It's only the wind, but sometimes out here a man can imagine . . . many things. A storm is coming and our friend here wants to be out in it. We found him in a storm, did the newspaper mention that? No? Oh, well. It's that sound, I think . . . it's like it calls to him." A shudder passed over the lieutenant's bowed shoulders. "Foolishness. Now, Doctor, if you would be so kind to accompany me back to my desk I can—"

The shock in the lieutenant's eyes bordered on fear when he turned and found himself staring at Ambrose's naked form. Darkness crept closer as the lantern made a shaky decent to the floor. Ambrose followed the dark, closing the gap between them.

Underlit, the lieutenant's face took on the visage of a death mask.

Ambrose nodded his head. It was a good omen.

"It is not so foolish to hear voices in the wind, Lieutenant," he said, feeling the cold wrap itself around him like a lover. "That is how the gods speak to men. And drive them mad."

"*HERE!*" The lieutenant shouted and, like the well-trained dogs they were, the soldiers came running.

Ambrose felt the sensation of fleas tickling his spine once more. And smiled.

Lifting his hands away from his sides, he glanced back over his shoulders, just to make sure his instincts hadn't failed him after so many centuries. They hadn't. The rifles were level and not even a blind man could miss at that distance. The smile grew.

"Get his clothes and handcuff him to one of the chairs out there!" The lieutenant seemed less afraid now, with the men in the room. Or maybe it was the rifles that made him brave. "Then call down to the village and have them send someone to take him off our hands. I don't want this pervert here any longer than he needs to be."

Ambrose lifted his chin, the smile fading as he closed his eyes as one set of boots began moving toward him.

"No," he commanded.

The boots stopped.

He opened his eyes and saw beads of sweat on the lieutenant's face.

The unicorn was prancing nervously within its electrified enclosure—tossing its head, the lantern light flashing across the midnight horn.

It knows.

"Wh-what do you want?" the lieutenant asked, his voice almost lost to the howl of the wind.

Ambrose nodded. "You're direct. I've always appreciated that and will answer in kind. I've come to kill the unicorn."

"NO!" Despite his obvious fear, the officer placed himself between Ambrose and the corral. Gun coming clumsily to his hand. Shaking. One more inch and the back of his greatcoat would brush against the electric mesh. "Are you *mad*? You saw for yourself that it can't be killed. This is the last of its kind . . . you can't kill it. Besides, I'm not afraid of a crazy man. I warn you, *Doctor,* that if you take one more step toward this creature I *will* kill you."

Smiling, Ambrose took that step.

And the room exploded with sound.

He heard and memorized each one: the trumpeting scream of the unicorn, the paper-tearing *rippp* of the assault rifles, the hollow *thump* as bullets punched holes through his body.

The wet sound of retching as the bloodless wounds repaired themselves as fast as the unicorn's had.

Finally, a whisper.

"Who are you?"

Looking down, he ran a hand over his unmarked flesh; brushing away the last remnants of the Ambrose impersonation.

When he looked back up, Gilgamesh smiled at the lieutenant.

"Just an old man who has grown tired of living," he said gently, using the tone he remembered from countless storytellings and lullabies. "If I am successful in killing the unicorn, then I may find the secret of killing myself. Or, perhaps the unicorn will kill me . . ." He took a deep breath and listened to the storm's growing rage. "Either way I shall be dead."

The lieutenant took another step toward the corral, sobbing now, shaking his head.

"No. Y-you can't."

"What do you mean? Kill or be killed? I have done so much of the former that it means nothing. And as for the latter . . ."

Gilgamesh closed his eyes, trying to blot out the memories, but they were still there—as fresh and solid as if he were living through them at that very moment. Again.

"Read the legends, if you want, about a man not much

older than you who *so* feared death that he usurped the powers of the gods.

"See a plant that gave eternal life. You would look for such a thing, wouldn't you?" he asked through the darkness of his closed eyes, not expecting an answer. Getting none. "Of *course* you would. Any man terrified of death would."

When Gilgamesh finally opened his eyes, he didn't look at the man, only watched the animal. The unicorn was calm—neck arched, heavy tail swatting lazily at its golden sides, ears pitched forward as if it, too, were listening.

"Imagine then finding out how much you have given up to become immortal . . . the *last* of your kind . . . to see all that you ever loved wither and fade to dust while you stand forever unchanged."

Smiling as he once had smiled at a precocious carpenter's son in Jerusalem, Gilgamesh reached over and removed the empty gun from the limp hand.

"I will tell you another secret, Lieutenant," he whispered. "That part of the legend where the serpent is supposed to carry off the plant of eternal life is wrong. It never did."

The look on the man's face had shifted from fear to confusion. Gilgamesh chuckled softly.

"Forgive an old man his digressions, Lieutenant," he said, and tossed the gun into the shadows at the far end of the room. When it struck the floor, the unicorn shied and the ends of its tail brushed against the wire. Blue sparks danced across the mesh.

"I'm sorry," Gilgamesh said, not sure whether he

meant to address man or unicorn. "Please, stand aside, Lieutenant, and let me give the story the ending it deserves."

Round eyes the color of broken ice met his.

"You're out of your mind," the lieutenant screamed over the building storm. "Legends can't die."

"Why not?" Gilgamesh asked as the man swung at him.

He hadn't meant to protect himself, there was no need—blows were as meaningless as bullets—but he did. Gilgamesh caught the man's closed fist and pushed. He reacted, and heard the gods laugh.

"NO!"

But it was already too late.

A halo of blue-white flame blossomed around the lieutenant's body as he fell backward into the wire. Steam and sparks, the color of urine in the lantern light, erupted from the generator beneath the worktable as the overloaded circuits shut down.

Silence. For a moment. And then the muffled sound of cloven hooves on straw. Building up speed.

The unicorn's back hoof shattered the lantern as it leapt over its smoldering protector and charged.

Gilgamesh felt the same jolt of energy he had experienced when he had accidentally brushed against the electric barrier, but this was a hundred times worse. It drained him instantly. Collapsing, Gilgamesh rolled into a ball and groaned. It felt as if all the centuries he'd lived through had finally caught up with him.

He was panting, barely able to hear the hysterical shouting of the soldiers above the pounding of his own heart. *No . . . it wasn't his heart . . . his heart hadn't beat in two millennia.* Lifting himself to one elbow, Gilgamesh watched through growing flames as the tiny, dun-colored unicorn cocked its hind legs and kicked out another wall plank.

The building was old, probably constructed in haste against the coming of a long-past winter, its timbers rotted. In less time than it took Gilgamesh to push away from the hungry fire, the unicorn was free.

He thought he heard it once . . . whinnying its triumph to an uncaring sky . . . but it might have been only the storm. The gods laughing at his defeat.

Again.

The flames were already feeding on the dead lieutenant when Gilgamesh was finally able to stand. The clothes he had worn to the outpost had been the fire's first course, but that didn't matter; if there were no extra uniforms in the building he would simply "appropriate" one from its current owner. Being just another faceless soldier in a country still tottering from years of suppression would make it easier to track the unicorn.

To find it and—

He stumbled over a crack in the floor and pitched forward, grabbing the doorframe to keep from falling. *Oh yes, tracking down the unicorn would be child's play compared to simply walking out of the building.*

Then he noticed his hand in the wash of firelight.

It looked *different.*

He raised the second and turned them slowly from back to front. They *were* different.

His hands had always been a source of pride to him—

smooth and strong enough to crack two hard-shelled nuts or a man's skull; but the hands before him now were wrinkled flesh, the fingers knobbed and curled in toward the palm.

Gilgamesh stretched out his fingers as far as they would go and watched them tremble.

They were the hands of an old man.

old

He didn't have to feel his face or look down at the sagging flesh that hung from his limbs. He knew. He had *aged*.

From one brief touch, the unicorn had leeched away centuries.

Throwing back his head, suddenly lighter from its lack of hair, Gilgamesh laughed until the sound caught in his throat and tried to strangle him. *So this was what it felt like to be old.* He didn't care much for it, but it was a start.

Pushing away from the heat-blistered doorframe, Gilgamesh shuffled through the empty outer office and into the howling night. A naked old man wandering through a storm would be a pitiable sight to anyone who saw it, but he knew there would be no one foolish enough to venture out on a night like this. And if one did, he would have clothing and a new identity—either by guile or the knife, which ever was easiest.

He was even less worried about the dead lieutenant's men. They were probably already halfway back to town.

With stories to tell about the unicorn and the stranger who appeared as if by magic and could not be killed.

The stuff of which legends were made.

Bracing himself against the howling cold, Gilgamesh

faced into the worst of the storm. It would be hours . . . days more than likely . . . before any of the townspeople braved the elements . . . and story . . . to come up this far. By then the building would be nothing more than snow-covered ash—whatever truth it held burned away. The tracks left by his bare feet and the unicorn's hooves long since buried beneath the drifts.

Just another story to keep the children from wandering too far into the woods.

Just another joke played on a tired, *old* man.

Gilgamesh raised his fists to the storm just as something moved through the wind-driven snow directly ahead of him, a living shadow—its body the color of old cream, its ebony mane and tail whipping shadows out of the lighter-colored storm . . . the scimitar horn rising into the night as the shadow creature reared.

"WAIT!" he shouted, pleading with it as he opened his arms. "COME BACK!"

The shadow dissolved.

"You aren't finished with me yet," he yelled, looking past the skuttering clouds to the blackness beyond. "Are you?"

Only the wind moaned an answer.

Ignoring the cold, Gilgamesh hunched his bony shoulders and headed north, away from the tiny knot of civilization and into the empty Siberian wastelands.

Following . . . the . . . unicorn.

Back into legend.

EDWARD BRYANT

BIG DOGS, STRANGE DAYS

Peter: **Edward Bryant** is one of those people—Judith Tarr and Octavia Butler are two others—whom I am always running into at fantasy and science fiction conventions, am delighted to see, have a pleasant drink and an intriguing conversation with, and don't see again for several years at a clip, until we run into each other in some other crowded hotel lobby in some other town. I think of Ed as the only cowboy I know, and if he isn't really one, I don't want to hear about it. He was raised in Wyoming and has worked as a stirrup-buckle maker, so there you are. Of his dozen or so books, his *Particle Theory* is one of my favorite short fiction collections, and his *Cinnabar* remains one of the very best novels of the last twenty years. He has adapted his own stories for *The Twilight Zone,* and had others adapted for Lifetime Cable's *The Hidden Room. Flirting With Death,* a major collection of his suspense and horror stories, should be out by the time you read this. See you next time, Ed . . .

Janet: My friendship with Bryant goes back to a small convention in Denver circa 1977, a little piece of forever ago. It was there that I read the first chapter of *Cinnabar* and determined to meet this man whose voice spoke so loudly to me, intellectually and viscerally; there that he taught me about the virtues of drinking Irish coffee out of paper cups; there that I saw first drafts of his stories emerge from his typewriter (yes, *typewriter*) reading better than most final copy I'd ever seen. Edward does this "thing" when he writes. He uses universal buzz buttons to force the reader to bring baggage to his stories, thus adding a dimension that both does and doesn't exist on the actual page. More than that, he once sent me a Valentine that depicted a man lying in the desert, his guts exposed to the world, vultures feasting. Who could resist such a man, who manages to turn even his bloodiest tales into love stories?

Big Dogs, Strange Days

———◆———

HE SAT ALONE IN HIS APARTMENT, AS HE HAD FOR so many days and nights, and painted. It occurred to him that practice was good for his art; he did not consider himself all that accomplished an artist. So he played with various effects and different media.

This year he was amusing himself with acrylics.

Those paints had not existed when he first took up the brush. As best he could recall, that would have been about the year 1810. The man reckoned he was close to 221 years old. One spitting devil of a long while . . .

Never be an old master, he thought, and smiled. An old amateur, probably.

He glanced up above the old wooden desk where he'd hung the first piece he'd ever painted. It was a crude rendering of two men struggling in a fight to the death, rolling over and over in dust and cactus spines. The man in the breechcloth had a knife and the naked man didn't, but the unarmed man had twisted the hand with the knife around so that the blade sank to its hilt in the armed man's belly.

The artist remembered sketching out the scene on a

thin sheet of aspen bark in Manuel Lisa's fort, a rough place that lay in the center of what someday would be Montana.

His artistic media had been berry juice, charcoal, and a little blood. He had used bird feathers as brushes. After this long, the colors had faded, but the artist could fill in their hues in his mind.

He turned back to his current canvas. The artist had only this afternoon begun to sketch the rough figures. This was not a realistic scene. He was attempting to evoke ghostly figures, masked by wind and spitting snow. From different directions, the figures approached a roadhouse. The artist knew—had known—the location well. It lay a mile outside Casper, Wyoming. He believed it had burned to the ground sometime around the turn of the century—the twentieth century, that is. Good riddance. The owner had been a real shit.

The most spectral of the figures was the equine head that overshadowed all else. The human beings approaching the warm sanctuary of the roadhouse included a man in ranching gear, a woman wearing Shoshoni buckskin, an elderly Chinese gentleman in a dark broadcloth suit, and the artist himself.

The image of the artist would be the last executed. The man in the apartment hated self-portraits, but he knew this one was necessary. He had to be true to his materials. And to his memories . . .

Good work as ever, Coyote, said the voice in his head.

"I am not Coyote," he said aloud, irritated, but familiar with this routine.

You're sure *you're not Coyote?*
"Yes."
Well, the hand *of Coyote, then.* Paw *of Coyote . . .*
"Stop bothering me," he said. "I'm trying to concentrate."

Ferret, then. Saved from extinction by dint of extraordinary circumstance.

He ignored the voice and, after a while, it went away.

The artist shook his head, wondered why supernatural beings rarely communicated with him through dreams, as normal gods were supposed to do. He was never quite sure about this business of talking to the divine in broad daylight, right in the middle of his apartment on Patchin Place, just off 10th Street and Sixth Avenue. This was Manhattan, for the love of God, and he was a onetime hunter from the Shenandoah Valley of Virginia who'd had an adventure or two long ago.

Many adventures, he thought, and they continued imposing themselves on his life. He shook his head. Adventures were good. With 221 winters under his belt, it was probably a useful idea not to get bored.

Well, tedium had not yet set in.

The artist glanced up at the row of reference sketches thumbtacked to the edge of the bookshelf just beyond the canvas.

He cocked his head a moment, and stared at the image of the old Chinese man, trying to recapture the detail of the stooped body, the wrinkled face, the sunken eyes that still appeared as dark and shiny as *go* stones.

Dr. Wu's body ached in every one of his atoms.

He sat on one of the hard wooden benches in Denver's cavernous Union Station. The bench was one of a number informally set aside for the use of Chinamen, Negroes, and Mexicans.

He listened for the wail of the locomotive whistle that would herald the arrival of the northbound Union Pacific train to Cheyenne, Wyoming, and then on to Casper. Right now, he heard only the ghost of a whistle's call; it reminded him of being a bit more than a quarter century younger, standing with his quiet fellows at Promontory Point, Utah. It had been May 10, 1869, and Wu had spent a hard year driving spikes and wrestling creosoted ties into place so that the westbound and eastbound tracks could finally meet.

Never mind the stories, there had been no golden spike.

Building a railroad . . . *That* had given him aches. But then so had working on the sluice boxes of the Gold Rush of twenty years earlier, and so had logging and laundering, and performing all manner of other menial tasks. Work had been a blessing. With only one Chinese woman for every hundred Chinese men, marriage had been out of the question.

And now Wu was Dr. Wu. Chinese medicine was what he practiced, and so he added the honorific in the American manner. It seemed to help business. He had learned his art at the feet of a master in his home village back in the Pearl River Delta in the province of Kwangtung. His medicine was that of South China.

Wu's thoughts wandered. They had that right. He was eighty-two years old, after all.

He knew his Western counterparts had a wise saying: physician, heal thyself.

Wu wished he could do that.

His muscles ached, his joints agonized, the pain vibrated in the marrow of his bones.

The worst of it though, the very worst terror of all, was that he feared he was too old to approach the Widow Cho. This beautiful celestial woman had lost her beloved husband a decade before, when their tailoring shop had been set afire by drunken Irish—or perhaps it had been drunken Italians. Wu could no longer remember that specific detail. He simply knew that the Widow had been without male companionship for ten years, certainly long enough to consider introduction to a new potential husband.

At eighty-two, Wu possessed certain apprehensions.

Because of this, he had allowed his colleagues in the six companies to prevail upon him to undertake an important mission. If good fortune smiled, then the Chinese Consolidated Benevolent Association would make a great deal of money, income which Dr. Wu would share.

There was something else the mission might accomplish for him, though, a reward of an acutely personal nature. That was his hope. He already had enough money for the rest of his days. It was his pride that needed a cushion.

The cry of the big steam locomotive shivered the old man's bones as it surely must be shaking the heart and liver of every other human being in this place. Dr. Wu got to his feet and painfully hefted his satchel. He touched the inner pocket of his jacket. He felt the crisp square of paper that instructed him how to find a certain roadhouse a mile or two from the Casper station.

With a little hope and a great deal of pain, Dr. Wu joined the throng straggling toward the waiting train.

The artist brewed himself a cup of coffee. He made it the old way, heating a percolator on the stove burner. Mr. Coffee was not welcome in this home.

No cream for the artist. If there were a few grounds in the cup, so much the better. It gives body, he told himself.

When he returned to the canvas and settled himself in his chair, he critically scrutinized what he had done already. Touch-up could come later. For now, he wanted to rough things in.

He raised his head and glanced at the study of the big man in rancher's garb. The broad brim of his Western hat was creased and stained, certainly weathered for more than a few hard winters. The man's forehead was broad, his eyes wide as though constantly surprised by what he saw. Crow's feet fanned out from the corners of those eyes.

The rancher was dressed for cold weather. His long coat was lined with fleece. He wore gloves. A hint of blowing snow swirled around his exposed face.

The artist couldn't help but shiver.

Barlow Whitaker had come west from Pennsylvania when he was twelve. He was on his own, having no desire to continue reaping his father's harvest of beatings, and more, having no wish to spend the rest of his life working with the hope of inheriting the old man's dirt-poor farm.

Not that Barlow was doing all that much better in southeastern Wyoming. He had worked like a dog for other men, to get enough cash to secure a homestead east of Cheyenne. He had married his nearest neighbor's daughter; that had doubled the size of the spread. Love had come later, but it surely *had* come. Barlow was glad for that. Children had not yet arrived, no heirs, and that bothered him. His wife and he possessed no issue, but it wasn't for lack of trying.

Besides his wife, Barlow's great love was horses. He would rather raise a herd of horseflesh than cattle, any day of the week. He loved watching the stallions breed the mares; he loved helping the mares foal their colts. There was nothing to compare with watching the spindly-legged offspring struggling upright, lurching uncertainly, then tottering off to nurse at their mother's side.

Most of all, Barlow loved breaking the horses to saddle. Every two-year-old was a challenge, each one a tough problem to solve. His neighbors said that Barlow was real good at what he did. He had the reputation for knowing what a bucking horse was going to do the second before it did it. He could ride like the wind.

Maybe he could even ride a tornado the way Pecos Bill could in the old story. He'd never tried that.

His wife said he rode so well, he could be a centaur.

Barlow had to think about that.

Right now, though, he was a little worried. He was a bit apprehensive about leaving the big bay stabled for a week in Cheyenne while he took the U.P. northbound up to Casper. As he stood on the exposed platform of the Cheyenne station, clapping his hands together for warmth, he also thought about the letter from the bank. Last winter hadn't been a good one. Too much snow and cold; too many head of stock had died. That had been the heartbreaker—all those dead horses he'd known and raised, ridden and loved.

All the money he could scrape up in the world was a thin sheaf of greenbacks folded and hidden in the money belt around his waist. He also had a set of directions to find a roadhouse outside Casper.

Barlow was going to buy horses. The Boer War was heating up and suddenly the British Army was combing the U.S. of A. for good horseflesh. The rancher knew the Shoshoni had a wealth of herds right now.

He would buy one. And if they wouldn't sell their horses satisfactorily, well—Barlow didn't want to think about that. He was basically an honest man. He did not wish to use the Colt .45 tucked into his belt beneath the bulky coat.

The man glanced up at the steel-gray sky, which had begun to spit snow. These weren't soft flakes drifting down slowly. The clouds were offering up what was turning into cold sleet.

Barlow heard the distant whistle. Good. The train would be here soon.

The artist stretched; his muscles registered exquisite pain, his joints cracked luxuriously.

This wasn't going all that badly. What looked back at him from the canvas was not as clumsy as he'd anticipated. Still, there was considerable left to evoke with his paints.

He could stop and brew some fresher, hotter coffee. No, he looked up at the working sketch in the center. Coffee could wait. He was on a roll now. He didn't think the woman would be tough to paint at all.

After all, he knew her well.

Her name was Storm Soother and she was a medicine woman of the Wind River band of the Shoshoni. For two days now of increasingly ominous weather signs she had ridden the black stallion called Lightning Tree east toward Casper. She had started out in bright sunshine from Fort Washakie on the Wind River Reservation. She left, not exactly in secret, but still while the Indian Agent was sleeping off his heavy lunch. There was no law that bound her to the reservation, but the whole sorry episode of the dubious prophet Wovoka and the desperate appeal of the Ghost Dance movement was only a handful of years in the past.

Government agents were still nervous; and Storm Soother did not want this spirit errand to be delayed. Thus she left her home under cover of the light. The Indian Agent didn't notice for an entire day.

The journey wore worse on the woman than it did the horse.

Lightning Tree appeared as fresh as he had two days before the woman and he descended from the Rattlesnake

Range, crossed through Emigrant Gap, and saw the dim, distant lights of Casper.

"We will rest in Bar Nunn," she said to Lightning Tree, as much as to herself. "The train must be on its way, but it won't arrive before the afternoon. We'll get some food."

The stallion whickered. She leaned forward and patted the side of his muscled neck.

Storm Soother thought ahead to the coming light, and beyond that, to the afternoon in which she would meet the three men at the roadhouse. She offered up a prayer that an agreement would be reached. The medicine woman had offered up many prayers since dreaming this situation that must be addressed.

It was a knotty problem. It was her task.

The artist frowned. His attempt to fill in the shadings on the medicine woman was dismal.

He would do better. He realized he would have to examine the innermost workings of this painting.

He'd have to go inside.

The man who called himself John Colter was already waiting when the other three arrived. He had ordered a shot of rotgut from the surly proprietor of the nameless roadhouse, and had drunk it down with dispatch. There was no purpose in attempting to savor so foul a brew. Colter suspected the drink was perhaps only hours old.

The manager and he were the only people in the establishment. Colter wondered if the weather was putting travelers off. More likely this place was simply not one that drew passersby through its sterling reputation. Fine, then. Privacy would be useful.

The others arrived. The two men came through the door almost in company with each other. Colter knew the elderly Chinaman must have had to hurry to keep up with the big, bluff cowboy. It was a hike of a mile or more from the station. The two men looked around in the dim interior. Black eyes and blue eyes, both expressions questioning.

The roadhouse proprietor was stacking enough wood in the huge fireplace to burn a witch. He grunted. "No Chinamen."

"I have money," said Dr. Wu.

"Don't need your money," said the proprietor. "*Could* maybe use some laundry done."

Wu said nothing.

"He stays," said Colter. He opened his jacket slightly and let his fingers rest on the hilt of the large Bowie knife lying sheathed against his thigh.

The big rancher laughed. Everyone else turned to stare at him.

"Name's Barlow Whitaker," he said. Barlow gestured at the Bowie knife. "My daddy named me for the knife. Thought it'd be lucky for me. He should have picked that one."

"Barlow knife's got a good blade," said Colter. "Nothing to be ashamed of. Bowie's good, too," he said reflectively.

The proprietor mumbled something and retreated to the bar.

They heard the sound of a horse, hoofbeats approaching, an imperative whinny. A minute later, the woman came through the door.

"No Indians," said the roadhouse proprietor. "'Specially no squaws."

It was the rancher's turn to open his coat slightly. He set his ham-sized hand on the ivory grip of the .45. "She's still a lady," Barlow said. "She stays."

"Then you all better buy something," said the proprietor.

"You stock any sarsparilla?" said the medicine woman.

Dr. Wu had been watching all the goings-on with some curiosity. "I am supposed to meet a person here . . ." he began.

"Me too," said Barlow.

"I think we need names," said the medicine woman.

Colter made the round of introductions without faltering. Barlow and Dr. Wu both stared at him with some evident suspicion. Storm Soother stared at him with frank interest.

He stared back at her. Her hair and eyes were equally dark and lustrous. She was a handsome woman, body soft and capable. "I believe some of us know much more than the rest, Mr. Colter," Storm Soother said.

"Then let's get to it." Colter gestured toward a rough plank table. All four took seats. Barlow chivalrously pulled out the chair for Storm Soother.

Colter took a deep breath. "You all got directions to come here. You all think you're here for a specific reason. Well, you're wrong." He smiled across the table. "Except for maybe Storm Soother, there."

"Please explain," said Dr. Wu.

"Okay," said Colter. "Settle back. Barlow, I think you're a man who wants some sort of future for his family. You want children, right? Heirs?"

Barlow slowly nodded.

"You think you can make a small fortune out of selling off all the horses you can lay your hands on to the British, so's they can ship them to Africa where they're fighting with the Boers." He paused. "I've got to tell you something. What you want to get by hook or by crook from the Shoshoni is more valuable than you could ever pay for. It's too valuable to sell to Mr. John Bull."

"What are you saying?" said Barlow. "What's more valuable than horses?"

"Dr. Wu can tell you that," said Colter. He turned to the small, elderly man. "I think, sir, you and your celestrial brethren have heard some mighty interesting stories about a special breed of horse up here in Wyoming."

Dr. Wu slowly nodded.

"They are, of course, not really horses."

"Wait a minute," Barlow cried.

Colter said to the medicine woman, "You want to bring your steed in here?"

"God *damn* it!" cried the roadhouse proprietor, who had been eavesdropping. "No horses. You're not going to bring that thing in here."

Colter spun something sharp and glittery through the air straight at him. The proprietor reflexively caught it. He stared at the ten-dollar gold piece. He looked up and shrugged.

Colter held the door wide while Storm Soother led Lightning Tree inside. The stallion clopped across the wood floor.

"If he makes a mess . . ." said the proprietor.

"Take it out of the gold eagle," said Colter.

"Fine stallion," said Barlow, "but he looks like a horse to me."

Colter said, "Back to Dr. Wu. Horses that aren't horses; horses with a single horn comin' out of their head. They kindle a real desire in the children of heaven."

"What Mr. Colter is trying to say," said Dr. Wu, "is that we value the powder of that horn for its medicinal properties."

"It's an aphrodisiac," said Colter. He grinned. "I just learned that word. It means any kind of thing that lights up a man's passion." He glanced at Storm Soother. "And I guess a woman's, too."

"Actually," said Dr. Wu, "the value is immense."

"When you find them," said Colter. "And when you poach them."

"I don't get this at all," said Barlow.

"Be patient a moment. 'Long about the sixth century, an Irishman named St. Brendan seems to have landed in the New World. Along with a small crew, he brought over a cargo that just sort of galloped away when they hit the beach. How he ever made it across the Atlantic in a coracle—that's not even a full-sized ship—with a breeding pair, I don't know. But I guess he did, and the beasts bred here."

"Beasts," Barlow said hopelessly. "Irishmen?"

"The critters moved west for about a thousand years. They were pretty lonely. Then in 1600 the Spaniards brought horses to Santa Fe. It was only a matter of time before the Indians got over the belief that the Conquistadores and their horses were one creature. The Indians caught on pretty fast that horses could be used for everything from hunting to war. When the Lakota got them, they called them shun-ka-ka. Shun-ka is dog. Shun-ka-ka is big dog. By about 1690, the Shoshoni had horses, and it wasn't long after that when the horses and the Irish critters met up. Guess you can figure what happened then." He paused. "They bred true, not like mules. They're still around, and slowly growing in numbers." He smiled at Storm Soother. "They seemed to take to the Shoshoni. It was a good match."

"There are some reasons," said Storm Soother. "The reasons go back."

"A long way back," said Colter. "Did you men know there were horses here before the Spaniards came? There were horses here in the New World until about seven thousand years ago. Scientists from the East have found their bones encased in stone. Those horses weren't very big; I guess they were smaller than ponies. But they were part of the family."

Storm Soother looked down at the floor. "This is the part that shames me."

"Not you," said Colter. "Ancestors. All the horses

died out after about eight thousand years of Indians hunting them like deer and eating them."

"So there is a debt," said the medicine woman.

"And every tribe pays on that debt by caring for their horses," said Colter, "and especially caring for the crossbreeds."

"What about you, Mr. Colter," said Dr. Wu. "Where do you enter this tale?"

"Well, a while back I had a bad time with a band of Blackfoot. They were a mite upset that I'd been helping out their enemies, the Mandan. So they stripped me naked and gave me a head start to run across a godawful plain full of rocks and cactus. Then they chased me. One brave caught up, but I killed him. I hid from the rest under a beaver dam in the Madison River. It wasn't too long after that, I found a place I called Colter's Hell. You call it Yellowstone. And when I was there, I found the crossbreed critters. Didn't kill 'em. Didn't eat 'em. I befriended them, and then brought a couple back to the Shoshoni. I didn't know it then, but they decided to give me a gift."

"The Shoshoni?" said Barlow.

"The critters. They're not good just for aphrodisiacs. They can offer other things. Maybe it's a blessing, maybe a curse. I don't know yet."

Dr. Wu quietly, respectfully waited for a pause before speaking. "How will we resolve all this?"

"Poaching and killing are out of the question," said Colter. "So's selling 'em off to the British." He met Barlow's eye. "Here's the deal. You've got the finest horse ranch in the state. The Shoshoni'll give you some breeding mares and a stallion. You just take care of them. Give them space and food, and maybe a little love. Won't take long for you to build up a herd."

"They've got to eat," said Barlow. "So do my wife and me. Should we make it a tent-show and charge admission?"

"Hell no," said Colter. "This is where Dr. Wu comes in. Every other season or so, the critters shed their horns. Just like deer, only not as frequent. Anyhow, the properties are still there. I think Dr. Wu and his friends will buy whatever you supply for a fair price."

Their eyes turned toward the old Chinese man, who slowly nodded. "I could agree to such an arrangement."

"So how can we know if we're all shootin' straight?" said Barlow reasonably enough.

"There's an old belief," said Colter, "from back there in the Dark Ages. Those folks knew that you could use the horn to tell if something was poison. It doesn't have to be just a drink."

"What horn?" said Barlow.

Dr. Wu's eyes narrowed as he stared at Lightning Tree.

Colter said, "Storm Soother?"

The medicine woman nodded solemnly. She pushed back her chair, stood, and slowly walked around the table, passing her hand before each of their eyes.

"Well, I'll be god—" Barlow stopped himself in time.

Dr. Wu said nothing.

"Behold," said Colter.

The horn sprang true and straight from the center of Lightning Tree's forehead. It was at least a yard long.

Black at the base, the shaft was a brilliant white, the tip bright crimson.

"Now," said Colter, "every one of us, grasp the horn with our right hands."

They moved from the table to form an arc around Lightning Tree's head.

"I am left-handed," said Dr. Wu tentatively.

"Then use your left hand." There was only mild exasperation in Colter's voice. "If there is poison in anything one of us has said, then the horn will find it out."

No one hesitated. The four of them reached, twenty fingers curling tightly around the proud horn.

Light exploded.

The four of them staggered back, reeling, electrical fire seeming to shoot from hands and hair. Colter was reminded of the men he'd seen reeling in the generator building down in Telluride. He'd taken a short job working for the crazy, brilliant, European scientist Tesla, helping to build the huge DC power source for the new mine. One of the workers had accidentally shorted one of the motors during a test phase. It was extraordinary fortune that no one had been killed. But the effects had lingered after the electrical dance had ended and the participants scattered across the plank floor. It had taken Colter hours to shake off the effects of the electrical power; much longer to remove all the splinters.

They stared at the aptly named Lightning Tree.

The creature snorted, met their stares, started snuffling in Storm Soother's proffered hand, velvet lips searching for grain. With her free fingers, she dipped into the slung pouch, extracted golden corn, drizzled them into her other palm. Lightning Tree inhaled them, his mane shaking with satisfaction.

"Did it work?" said Dr. Wu.

"Is anyone dead?" Colter smiled.

All stared at one another.

"So," said John Colter, looking straight at each of his companions in turn. "Is each of you satisfied?" He could see the high color in each of their faces, even that of Dr. Wu.

Barlow shook his head wildly for a moment like the motion of a spooked horse, then controlled himself. "Yes," he said.

Dr. Wu nodded slowly.

Storm Soother looked back from her steed, met Colter's gaze, and smiled.

Barlow Whitaker had his long sheepskin coat wrapped around him. He set his Stetson forward on his head, obviously readying it for the stiff winter wind that still howled outside the roadhouse.

"You going on to Wind River?" Colter asked curiously.

Barlow shook his head. "Got things to attend to at home. I believe there is a U.P. steamer heading south later tonight. No snow's heavy enough to stop that train." He hesitated, as though unsure if he wished to continue. "And there's the missus. I've got some business I need to carry out with her."

Colter noted with amusement that the six feet six inches of rancher appeared to be blushing.

"Listen," said Barlow. His voice lowered. "Man to man, I've got to ask you something."

Colter nodded seriously.

"When we all grabbed hold of that critter's horn?" The rancher almost stuttered. "Was that like holding on to the supernatural grandfather of all johnsons, or what?"

"That's about it," said Colter. "The power there's considerable. It's why the Chinamen so value the powder of the horn." He held out his hand. "Good luck to the missus."

Barlow's pause was only momentary. He took Colter's hand in his much larger one and shook it vigorously.

"Oh," the rancher said as he turned toward the door. "I guess maybe I'll share a compartment down to Cheyenne with Dr. Wu."

"He's Chinese," said Colter without inflection.

Barlow smiled. "He's just a man. So long as I don't have to eat his food, it'll be fine."

"Then wait a moment for me to bid my good-byes," said Dr. Wu. The stooped, wizened man took Storm Soother's hand, then Colter's. To the Shoshoni medicine woman, he said, "I thank you for this evening's entertainments. I believe we have reached agreement. Our bargain will be the bargain." As he spoke the last, he looked at Lightning Tree. "The Chinese Consolidated Benevolent Association—and I especially—will be grateful for the shed horn you share with us."

Storm Soother nodded.

Dr. Wu hesitated, then allowed a small smile to creep across his lips. Colter thought he could almost hear a slight sound like stiff papyrus crackling. "Now I will go. Like my compatriot, Mr. Whitaker, I have business to transact at home. I feel it is a good time to attend the Widow Cho." He bowed slightly to woman, horse, and man, and followed Barlow Whitaker out the door.

"And now," said Colter to Storm Soother, "what about you?"

"Yeah." Almost forgotten, the roadhouse manager grumbled from behind the bar. "No horses, no Indians."

"Be silent," Storm Soother told him. He was. She turned back to Colter.

Ferret was snared by the warm, night-black gaze.

"It is my understanding," she said, "that you knew the grandmother of my grandmother."

"Sacajawea?" said Colter. "She was a magnificent and strong woman. She convinced her people—your people—to aid us. Without that help, I fear we wouldn't have prevailed."

"It is my understanding that you knew her very well." Storm Soother's meaning was clear.

"She was one of the two squaws of Toussaint Charbonneau, one of the expedition's interpreters," said Colter. "She brought her papoose. Meriwether Lewis and Bill Clark ran a tight ship."

"You knew her *very* well." Storm Soother's smile did not vary.

The logs shifted in the fireplace. Flames shot up toward the flue. Colter suddenly wondered if he was blushing brighter than the fire. "We had our times, she and I," Colter finally said. "I've never loved anyone more."

Storm Soother's voice and eyes were both level with his. "I'm not minded to start riding back to Wind River at night, in the middle of a December storm."

"There are rooms here," said Colter.

"Now hold on just a damned minute," the roadhouse manager started to say.

"Innkeep, shut up," said Colter. The man shut up.

"We need only one room," said Storm Soother.

"You're young," said Colter. "I'm not."

"Her spirit is with my spirit. It'll do."

He took her hand. Storm Soother's skin seemed hotter than the heat radiating from the conflagration building in the fireplace. "This works out, you realize, there's a chance Lightning Tree won't be resting his head in your lap."

"I'll take my chances," she said.

The artist set down his brushes. The painting was looking pretty darned good, and he was surprised. "You're no Albert Bierstadt," he said aloud to himself. "Not even a Charlie Russell." This would do. Time for a breather.

He went downstairs to get the mail. Rarely did anything more than advertising circulars arrive in the box, but the afternoon was sunny and it would be good to sit on the steps for a while.

But today there was an envelope in the black metal box.

The artist sat on the step below the landing and scrutinized what he'd received. It was a creamy number ten envelope with only his name and address on the outside. He held it up to the light. The postmark told him it had been sent from the Wind River Reservation in Wyoming.

Inside him, a spark flared fiercely.

He carefully ripped open the envelope and took out the piece of folded notepaper. Handwritten, big loops. The ink was blue. He sniffed. No scent. Dated the previous week.

Dear Mr. Colter, it read.

He skipped to the end of the page. It was signed Mallory Storm. He retraced to the beginning.

> *You don't know me, but I believe you have known some members of my family. I have read references to you in the journal of my great-grandmother, Storm Soother. I know you must be getting well along in years now—*

The artist laughed aloud with delight.

> *—but I wondered if I might ask you a favor. I will be coming to New York soon as I have been accepted into graduate school at Columbia University. I'll be seeking a doctorate in American Studies, specializing in political structures of the plains tribes and how they were affected by indigenous religious beliefs. I would very much like to meet and talk with you. I hasten to assure you that I will not take up much of your time*

*or energy. But I would still very much
enjoy the privilege of meeting you.*

He heard the voice in his head. *Hey, Ferret, recall
that last conversation with her great-grandmother?*

Indeed he did. He had said, "You know I'm always
on the move."

She had nodded. "Just keep in touch once in a while.
Safeguarding spiritual concerns shouldn't take up all
your time." The sarcasm was very light, almost playful.
"An occasional card would be nice. A visit would be even
better. Two of the Spoonhunter boys have been showing
signs of tipi-tapping, but I'm not interested."

"I will try," he had said.

He had done that, though Storm Soother and he
never saw each other again. But she had received his
cards, and sometimes they had spoken and held each
other in dreams.

The artist realized the letter was shaking in his fingers, so much so that he could barely read the rest. He
frowned, concentrated.

*If you would be agreeable to seeing
me, my home address and telephone
number are above. My great-grandmother passed on some years ago, but I
know she would have wanted me to
relay her best wishes. I look forward to
doing that.*

> Very Sincerely,
> Mallory Storm

The artist folded the letter, but did not slip it back into the envelope. He could feel the muscles of his face relax from the frown into first a smile, then a broad grin.

The afternoon sunlight burned his face now, hot as fire, and he welcomed it.

He stood, then, and turned to go back to his apartment. He had never really taken to Mr. Bell's invention, though he had learned to use all sorts of newfangled gadgets. His desk held a barely unpacked Macintosh PowerBook loaded with a full graphics package.

Today, he thought, perhaps the telephone would justify its entire miserable existence.

SUSAN SHWARTZ

THE TENTH WORTHY

Peter: **Susan Shwartz** is the only writer in this anthology who chose to draw her story from the Unicorn Tapestries at the Cloisters. Her story is, therefore, more traditional than many of the others in this book. Her take is, however, unique.

Janet: I am sincerely and consistently filled with admiration and not a little envy at Susan's knowledge of medieval history and, in particular, of the Arthurian legend. I tend to store many pieces of knowledge in far-ranging arenas, while Susan is one of those people who takes pleasure in constantly widening her knowledge and understanding in particular ones. I often wish I had that kind of mind, that kind of memory.

The Tenth Worthy

━━◦◦◦━━

M ICHAEL KAYE STOOD ON THE WEST TERRACE. His hands closed on the gray stone, the safe stone, of what was now a parapet, not an ornamental wall. He tried not to think of grapnels and ladders, siege engines wheeled up from the West Side Drive, or missiles flung from the Palisades across the river.

Someone flung a rock up at him. It fell short of the walls, let alone him and the shuttered windows, but he stepped back. He was glad he did not have to look into the whites of the besiegers' eyes. Their soulless eyes. So far, all this lot of Soulless had been able to manage was shouts and stones.

The wasters across the river had more brains. There! Something splashed into the Hudson, disturbing the patterns breathed into it by the wind. Thank God, the Cloisters was still out of range. Thank God, too, that no one had rediscovered artillery.

The wind drove a glowering phalanx of clouds across the horizon, reddened from ground fires. The Wasting that had already destroyed Manhattan burned now on the Palisades. A brazen sort of sunlight forced its way beneath thickening clouds, and thunder growled.

Dimly from outside the Cloisters' walls came the shouts of the latest mob to venture into Fort Tryon Park. Michael heard a shot. One of the guards assigned to the gardeners must have fired. *Waste of a bullet.* Still, what was one bullet wasted if they could scratch the last of the harvest from their tiny fields?

At least, the defenders of Fort Tryon Park had stout walls to be thankful for. If the weather held just a little longer, they would also have rather more food than they had feared. Still, it was problematic whether they could hold out until Thanksgiving, let alone Christmas. Feasts would be fasts. Surviving till next spring seemed past praying for, though they prayed in the Cloisters' chapels anyway.

Michael Kaye's prayers, instead, were for his daughter; but a rising tide of panic swamped them. *Gently, but quite, quite inexorably, the ragged old madman who had forsaken the subway tunnels for the gardens and now worked as orderly to the physicians lifted Michael's little girl from her mother's desperate grasp and carried her into the fresh-air ward that had been St.-Michel-de-Cuxa Cloister before this second, deadlier burning struck. His wife Ari had risen, running after the big, gentle, sorrowing man who bore her child away, perhaps to its death.*

"Tell Jennifer," she called over her shoulder. *"Laurie loves her. She'll come, I know she will! Please!"*

Brassy sunlight struck glints from the gray stone. Michael squeezed his eyes shut, and his tears were not for the brightness of the light. Laurie's eyes had been fevered, but there had been sanity in them. And soul. So many babies these days seemed to lack souls. So did the hollow folk who had devastated the world, caused the Wasting, and ended the world he knew.

Michael had valued his job as a very junior medieval researcher at the Cloisters—when so many elder scholars shuttled hopelessly from junior college to junior college—as a lifesaving chance at even a modest scholarly career. One day, he had brought his family here to visit, but that had been the day the Wasting had begun. As the city burst into flame and Soulless mobs roved the park, they had never dared to leave.

The mighty cables of the George Washington Bridge seemed to jangle in agony; the Brooklyn Bridge collapsed into the caissons that had claimed so many lives. Manhattan was cut off.

The last messenger from the main branch at the Metropolitan Museum of Fine Arts reported a city in flames. Too bad they could not carry some of the arms from Main uptown: spears and halberds, or My Lord Cid's sword. Jennifer was drilling all of them—the guards, scholars, and technicians who had worked here before the Wasting and the refugees who had fought their way to such safety as the Cloisters offered—with what arms any of them could invent.

The heavy, reinforced door banged open. Jennifer walked quickly to his side. "I heard about your little Laurie. I'll visit her this evening."

Like any good chatelaine, she knew what went on in her household without having to be told.

"At least, she's not Soulless." By their eyes, you

knew well which children were the Soulless: infants whose eyes did not track; toddlers who, when their memories began to waken, remembered nothing. God help the world when they grew up. If they grew up. They might do such things as made the Wasting look like child's play. Having no memory and little mind, they saw no reason why they should not—or any reason at all.

He . . . but he remembered. Not just the memories of this current life, but fragments of what had to be another life. Today's Michael would have been happy as a minor academic or librarian. But serving the leader of this keep had waked his oldest memories: It was a dark guilt that, here at the end of his world, to know he had been fulfilled.

He turned toward his chatelaine, and she held up a hand.

"I wish," her voice was cool at his side, "I remembered more about siege engines. I remember staring out over the walls, watching the armies and hoping I had thought to lay in the supplies I needed most. Of course, I hadn't." The voice turned wry.

Jennifer had turned up here in the earliest days of the Wasting, stick in one hand, knife in the other, serviceable pistol tucked into her belt, and, in her pack, a box of jewelry, some of it ancient, as what she called her "dowry." When they had opened it, they had found in it torques, rings, and the Red Dragon of Britain.

It was mad, impossible—but it had to be true. He *remembered*. So Michael had shut the box, bowed to her in homage, and brought her before the Museum's Head. She had approved the Main Hall for its defensive capabilities and charmed the Head with the courtliness Michael remembered from the days he had been a sharp-tongued steward and foster brother to a king. At least, he thought he remembered.

He soon got proof, as the Head insisted on taking his newest refugee on a tour of his domain.

"Here," the Head's dry voice ripened into warmth, "are our tapestries. The Nine Worthies, or Heroes, though not all nine tapestries survived the Revolution. Three pagan—Alexander, Caesar, and Hector. Three Hebrew—David, Joshua, and Judah Maccabee. And three Christian—Godfrey of Bouillon, Charlemagne . . ."

Jennifer looked long at the tapestries of the pagans and Hebrews. They were in remarkable condition, considering that they had been used to store vegetables. But then she came face to face with the remaining tapestry.

"Arthur of Britain," said the Head.

She turned on her heel and followed her guides into the room that housed the Unicorn Tapestries, her back almost too straight. It was the most dignified retreat Michael had ever imagined: or Kaye, as he had been in the life when they had bowed to each other across Arthur's hall.

Got you, Your Majesty, Michael thought her. Not Jennifer, but Guenevere. The Queen. Drawn here, no doubt, by the King—and the tapestry—she would not face.

Michael, still in attendance, suppressed another chuckle. Taking the director's arm, Jennifer had strolled the wide, pegged planks past the huge fireplace as if she were at home in Camelodunum, agreeing in the way she had agreed with so many equally long-winded lords that Mr. Rockefeller had been absolutely right to love the tapestries so and nodding as he pointed out violets, peri-winkles, and cherry trees in the rich backgrounds of the huge weavings.

Out in the Cloister beyond the paneled room, the madman saw Jennifer and started, shocked from his usual round of digging and fetching and carrying and murmuring to himself. The old street person tugged at his forelock and dipped his head. Jennifer blanched at the sight of him. Michael looked at him more closely, so used to seeing the familiar madman that he had never recog-nized his older guise. *Oh, I know you too, half-mad, wise in the ways of forests, devoted to your King.*

The Head pointed to the unicorn that dipped his horn into a fountain.

"Unicorn's horn was said to draw a serpent's poison from the water. It could even bring the dying back to life. I daresay we could use one about now."

But the age of wonders was past. Or was it? Why else had these old figures from Michael's past assembled here? Why was he here, hiding his old knighthood at the end of his world? *To serve my Queen,* he told himself, more Kaye than Michael in that thought.

Lacking unicorn's horn, some among the Cloisters' staff and refugees sickened. The Head collapsed, dying between one breath and the next. No one was surprised when Jennifer took over his responsibilities. She was, after all, trained for them.

A rattle of stones barraged the Terrace, given strength by a fresh gust of wind. They both ducked.

Michael saw his hands flexing. Michael knew to duck. His former self had been a champion once and would gladly have snatched up one of the rocks and hurled it back. His skin prickled as lightning stitched itself across the sky. It was leaden now, though sunlight still pierced the edges of the clouds.

Jennifer put out a capable hand. "No point in goading them."

Abruptly, twilight replaced the day. Beneath them, the Soulless howled. A gust of wind howled louder.

"The madman said the cold's coming," Michael told the Queen.

"He'd know," she said.

The wind pressed against the thick door, reinforced with black iron. As the first squall hit, Michael motioned for the chatelaine to precede him into the safe long vault of the corridor up toward the paneled galleries.

She stalked past the tapestries of the Nine Worthies—Caesar presenting arms eternally in the faded weave—as if she were furious at them all.

The madman had carried the children from the Chapter House into the room housing the Unicorn Tapestries. How much he had changed from the homeless man who had staggered in here, sat, watching the gardeners, and then, like Jennifer, in the grips of his memories, taken charge. Even the trained horticulturists and doctors deferred to him. Did they know why? Maybe some of them, too, remembered stories of Merlin, wise in the ways of herbs.

The children sensed his love and needed no more. If the magician moved them, it was to a place where, at least, he could watch them as he went about his business in the various gardens. And the rain washed away the reek of smoke that wafted even this far uptown.

Michael watched him from the windows separating galleries from Cloister. The old man's hands were very sure, the three middle fingers almost of one length: such hands might well have belonged to a healer or scientist, not a gardener or grubber in trash cans.

Merlin had been right. The cold was coming in, even piercing what delicate equilibrium of heat, dryness, and air circulation that the engineers could force from the ever-crankier climate-control system. The tapestries had survived revolutions and decades in barns; the children were not so durable.

Jennifer threw herself down in the thronelike chair between two of the great tapestries, glancing from time to time into the next room or toward the Worthies of the pagan world.

Her eyes went to the doorway beyond which the children, the sick and dying children, huddled in winter coats harvested from the Lost and Found.

"They're so cold," she murmured. "And they'll get colder." She straightened. "That much I can cure right now."

Stalking over to the Arthur Tapestry, she looked the woven king in the eye for the first time. Seizing hold of the tapestry, she tugged one corner free of the frame that held it. The heavy cloth resisted.

"Damn you," she muttered. Then she yanked with all the strength of her body, her love, her anger, and her fear. The frame buckled, and, with a ripping sound, the ancient cloth tore free.

"Lady," Michael protested. Torn, after all those centuries, and by a hand that should have cherished it.

"For pity's sake," she told him, as if protesting the sorrow in his eyes, "you know their history. These things were used to cover vegetables for years. I wish we had the vegetables, too, to help get us through the winter. We'll be lucky if we don't lose half the children to starvation. At least, they'll be warm."

She tugged the heavy weaving up into her arms. Arthur's face looked up. The way the cloth was bundled up, his face seemed to grimace.

"He's of no use reigning from the wall. Let him protect *these* children." She began to drag the cloth into the next room.

"Are you going to help me or are you going to complain like you always do?" He followed her.

Waked by the noise, the children huddled together for reassurance, even more than warmth.

"We've brought you something nice," Jennifer reassured them.

Together, they spread the tapestry over five little bodies. Jennifer tucked it in at their feet. A ring from her trove gleamed on her hand in the candlelight. Michael looked down at the children. How quickly their shivering had stopped.

"Let's take the rest of them down and shake the dust out of them. Then we can start on the tapestries in this room," Jennifer said. "Michael?"

But Michael had hastened to the corner where his wife Ari restrained their daughter's hands—so hot that she, surely, had no need of tapestries. "Her fever's so high

I'm afraid she'll have a seizure," Ari said. "I'd take her outside, but that's worse. The old man says we can cool her off in the fountain."

"I'll help you carry her," he offered. Thank God for ribs. Otherwise, his heart would burst out of his chest with fear. He heard Jennifer's footsteps, leaving the room, followed by the tugging and victorious crash as she pulled down another tapestry, the faint ripping sound (he winced) as she separated it from its frame, and the swish and drag as she dragged it along the floor, shook it, and piled it in a corner against need for it.

"Michael? Ohhhh . . ." she was at their side in an instant, her hands going out to the little girl.

"Laurie . . . Laurie . . ." A minor miracle: the child's eyes opened and recognized her. Her lips parted on Jennifer's name. Ari leaned forward, urging the child to drink, and Michael raised his daughter on his shoulder. In his past life, he had never been so gentle with children: well, live and learn—and Kaye had a lot to learn.

The child drank, sighed, then reached out with a free hand, attracted by the gleam of Jennifer's ring. She stripped it off and put it in the child's hand.

"Get better, sweetheart," Jennifer murmured. "We need you."

Laurie's smile almost stopped her father's heart. Acquiescent, she let herself be settled back into the nest of pillows and blankets.

"You don't think she'll swallow it, do you?" the chatelaine asked Ari, practical again.

"When she falls back to sleep, I'll take it and give it

back to you." Ari reached up and clasped the older woman's hand. "Thanks."

"She's going to make it. She's got to. You want to get her under covers? I brought something warm."

Ari's eyes followed Jennifer's gesture toward the folds of tapestry.

"Not now; she's too hot. If we can bring her fever down, thank you."

"Good luck." Jennifer touched the child's forehead, then sped away.

Michael knelt beside his daughter. She murmured in a troubled sleep. Even in the dim candlelight, her face and hands were so pale, almost translucent, that it terrified him. But her fingers clutched the ring tightly, resisting his attempts to pull it free. He patted the little hand, then dared to meet his wife's eyes.

My gracious silence, he thought. Before the world changed, he had classmates and colleagues who had married, almost, as a form of professional advancement: doctors, lawyers, bankers. He had married not for income, but for peace: he for the library, she for the garden; both of them content to let the outer world flow around them as long as they could share their private sanctuary.

"What does Jennifer think she can do?" Ari's voice trembled.

I don't know, Michael wanted to say, but dared not. "Hold out, as long as we can," he said instead.

She looked at him. *Make it right again.*

I am not a leader, he protested silently. *I am an attendant lord!*

Dear Lord, was he going to fail Ari and Laurie in

what he was as well as what he did?

Seeing his confusion, Ari took his hand. "It's all right," she said.

But he had only to look down at their daughter to know that it was not all right at all.

They sponged Laurie for hours in the courtyard's fountain, until her fever had broken. Shivering in his shirtsleeves—Ari had accepted his sweater as much because it was *his* as because it was warm and now slept beside their child wearing it for reassurance—Michael slowly entered the Nine Heroes' Room. The tapestry frames lay tumbled on the floor.

Footsteps and his shadow brought Jennifer's head up, and the candlelight cast her silhouette onto the emptiness where the Arthur Tapestry had hung.

She turned to face him. He hoped it was only the lamplight that made them too bright.

"It's not going to be enough, you know."

"We'll make it right." He offered her what reassurance he could.

"Ah God, my back." Her voice was the merest breath, and she twisted her shoulders as if she could shrug off some of her burden. It was presumption to touch her and cowardice to flee. Michael drew up one of the few chairs that had not been sacrificed yet to reinforce the shutters. He was glad of those shutters: It was witch weather out there tonight.

"You should sleep."

He shrugged.

Wax sputtered and fell to the base of the tarnished polycandelon standing on the table by the wall. They heard footsteps: a guard, no doubt, making the circuit of the halls and corridors, checking shutters and doors. The emergency generator hummed, powering the floodlights, keeping the Wasting at bay for one more night.

The guard stepped into the room, nodded, and went on. *All's well.* Only it wasn't. The guard's footsteps subsided as he padded down the hall.

"You should sleep, too," he told her. "Let me tend to things."

She shook her head. Michael settled his hand on his cheek and fell into an uneasy doze.

A door banged open. He leapt up, but not as quickly as Jennifer.

"That's the West Terrace door," she said. "We've got a three-inch bar on it. And an armed guard."

That guard not only had one of their rare guns, but one of the last mobile phones that worked. He should have called out. They should have heard him. In the last extremity, he should have shot anyone who scaled the wall. *He should have died before letting anyone pass.* The words, older than he and darker by far, thrust themselves into Michael's consciousness. Those had been his instructions at Camelodunum.

The footsteps echoed, sure and measured. Up the dark corridor from the Terrace. Through the Pontaut Chapter House and into the Cloister, they *clicked* upon the stone.

"Do you hear? He's wearing spurs." Jennifer's words were almost a sob. Her hand came up to cover her mouth.

Michael reached within his pocket for his Swiss Army knife. *What an absurd toy*, the ancient memories protested. *You need a sword.*

I cannot use a sword! the mind of the graduate student, the urbanite, the survivor of the Wasting cried.

In the end, only the scholar's ravenous curiosity from his current life held him in his place. *You may indeed die in the next moment,* it told him, *but you will die* knowing.

Jennifer rose. She forced her hands to her side and stood before the thronelike chair, waiting as the stranger's armored feet drew nearer.

The intruder paused on the threshold. The candlelight flared. It illuminated his bright hair, brighter for the gold circlet with its Gothic trefoils that crowned it. It picked out the rich bullion of the three golden crowns—England, Scotland, and Brittany—woven upon his surcoat and drew a winelike glow from the great amethyst upon the pommel of his sword Excalibur.

Michael's chair toppled and he fell to his knees on the uneven floor.

"Sir," he whispered. "Beyond all our hopes, you've come back to us."

Maybe his King knew no English, the thought occurred to him. How would you translate that into Latin? He forced his voice to stay level. His King would not want him to weep.

Arthur spared him a glance, humor flickering in it for the briefest instant. "What happened to my Kaye's sharp tongue?" he murmured.

Then the King's attention was caught and held by Jennifer.

How not? If the tapestry had drawn his Queen to this place, she had drawn him and, in tearing down the tapestry, somehow released him. But then, she had always been his lure, trap, and beloved destruction of his hopes.

In this life, she might be Jennifer, refugee, then chatelaine of this pathetic fortress. But in her memories and the King's, she was his Queen.

She met Arthur's eyes without flinching. They were very much of a height.

"Well, and so you have called me to your side again. How may I serve you?"

Jennifer's shoulders relaxed as if a burden had been lifted from them.

She gestured at Michael, past him at the tapestried room beyond, the whole embattled fortress that had once been a museum. "These people are mine, and thus your charge. I beg you, save them."

The King smiled at her. Then, with a bow, he withdrew.

They found the door to the West Terrace untouched, its guard asleep. With nothing more to do until dawn, they went to the children's infirmary and helped the nurses with tucking in, washing down, soothing, and reassuring the sick children. Their numbers had grown during the night.

Jennifer tucked one last fold of tapestry in at the side of an eight-year-old boy, then sat and watched the children twitch and whimper in fevered dreams. If some slept, muttering, others lay awake, if you could call it that, their eyes vacant. It might be that, when their fever broke, they would be restored—but to what? Soullessness? Better that they die. Above them, the unicorn dipped his horn into the fountain, draining it of poison, before the hunt began. Later, they would have to take these tapestries down, too.

At least, Laurie still slept. *If the King returns, I shall wake her. I want her to see him. They used to say that the King's touch . . .*

Jennifer had taken over the task of trying to feed Laurie when Michael heard the clang and click of the King's footsteps outside. Through the leaded windowpanes, he could see the tall figure pace across the cloister. It stopped for a moment and gazed up at the sky. As if feeling Michael's eyes upon him, Arthur nodded greetings and moved on.

"Majesty . . ." New ceremony filled Michael's voice, and he bowed his head to her.

"Don't call me that," Jennifer said. "Don't *dare*."

The King stood poised on the threshold. His vitality filled the sickroom. Laurie opened her eyes, then opened them even wider at the sight of the splendid figure. She even managed a broad smile.

The King smiled. He had no children who had lived save the one, as soulless as those who yammered now outside. It had been a grief to him. Michael remembered talks of "Kaye, *my* son will grow up to be . . ." from when they'd been scarcely more than boys themselves, over much, much of the best wine in the cellars.

A beaker stood upon the table by the window.

Wrought of a narwhal's horn, it was part of the furnishings of this room when it still had been an exhibition hall. With its special properties of healing—at least, if you believed it to be a unicorn's horn, not a narwhal's, it would do for Arthur. He filled it with wine and ventured forward. Arthur drank, returned the beaker, then beckoned his Queen and her seneschal out of the room.

"Your walls are sturdy," said the King. "You have done well to shield your windows . . . a foolishness, those wide panes of glass. I gather you are short on food?"

"We will be very thin by spring," the Queen replied. "Next year, I plan to clear more fields. Meanwhile, we can send out foragers under guard . . ."

Arthur frowned. "You have no horses. No weapons to speak of beyond what you have made and your guards' arms, though—my lady, you can hardly call those soldiers! While outside, in their tens of thousands . . ." He paused, looking at the place where his tapestry had hung. "It is like Camlann. Very like."

"So you counsel us to despair?" Jennifer's voice arched upward, haughty as her eyebrows.

"Lady, lady, lady, with *your* valiant heart? You invested Londinium against my son, and now you rule this keep. Surely, both times, you did not expect quick victory, or victory at all. I counsel you to hold off the long defeat. That is what kings are for. Why else did you summon me?"

"The world has better weapons now," Michael ventured, his voice faint.

"So it has. So tell me, my lord Seneschal, did you procure them, or do you take the darkest view of things as you always did since Merlin taught us both?"

In the next room, children, waking, began to cry and fret. The madman emerged from whatever shed he occupied at night. He had to bend to enter the room. Seeing the King, he blinked. Michael watched as he sloughed off his familiar guises of madman, gardener, children's nurse to bow to the King. It was the bow of one used to courts rather than city dumps; and that, too, no longer surprised Michael.

"So my old friend Merlin found his way to you, too," murmured the King.

"Can you take down the tapestries in the Unicorn Room?" Jennifer asked the old man. "We can probably use them for blankets, if nothing else."

The madman bowed again and slipped away, moving as the leaves move. Michael thought he heard him mutter, "All shall be well and all manner of things shall be well."

It was good that someone felt optimistic.

"And you always thought he mistrusted you," Arthur the King told Jennifer.

"Well, wasn't he right to think I'd be the ruin of you?" For a moment, they glared at each other. Then, she made herself shrug. "What would you have me do now?"

"You shall send your guards to me," he said. "I shall review them. And then we shall see what we can see."

It was no answer at all, really.

"You should rest while you can," she told the King. "Michael will see that you have food. I shall call the guards."

She gestured to the chair. As he seated himself, she bowed. The courtesy had nothing of humility about it, as if a wave or a ridge of stone had bowed, a line of such sudden grace that Michael gasped. Arthur smiled as at a beloved memory.

That day, Michael helped take down the Unicorn Tapestries. Then he worked in their woodshop until every muscle ached as if the Soulless beat him with clubs. When he grew too tired to work, he wrapped himself in fabric that he rather thought had been a Spanish bishop's cope and curled up in a paneled corner. Perhaps Ari would call to him from the other room with something he could do for their child. When the sunlight faded, he stared at the candlelight for warmth. If only he could shut his eyes for a few moments before the evening meal.

When he awoke, they were talking, the chatelaine and his King. As Michael Kaye, he knew how long it had been since he had last walked the earth as Kaye, the knight. Here was his brother, and here his Queen. Perhaps the age of miracles was *not* past.

"It is no use. Of course, I honor you; of course, I am grateful," said the Queen. "But the stain is set, the vessel defiled, the gem cracked at its core."

The King bent forward. He caught her hand and kissed it, then her brow. "I, too, am a great sinner. But even if this time looks like the end of all things, I see it indeed as a new dispensation. Of grace, not law. Of forgiveness, even in the teeth of bitterest remembrance."

Arthur stood very close to the Queen, but she turned her head away from any comfort he might offer.

She shook her head. "So, here at the end of all things, you come to forgive me?"

"I tell you, this may not be the end. I say we march

out and grasp what all we can, and thus hold off the long defeat . . ."

"And turn thief? If we do that, what becomes of *us?*"

"We fight. We heal. We rebuild, please God. Not just in body, but in soul. For I tell you, my heart, I have lived this long while with the heart cut out of me."

"Where have you lived?" the Queen asked. "And how?" Involuntarily, she held out her hands, then pulled them back before he could clasp them.

"Healing my wounds."

"Ah!" She turned away. It was not just the wounds to Arthur's body that he meant, but to his heart and soul. She had helped cause those wounds, and memory of that would haunt her till Doomsday.

"*I* have healed, my lady. Have you?"

Hearing armored footsteps and a rustle of cloth, Michael dared look up. Too often, Kaye's tongue had been harsher than his heart would have liked.

His brother and the Queen stood, stubbornly apart, facing each other. She whirled, her ringless hands flashing up to cover her face. Michael held his breath. For a moment, even the sheltered candle flames ceased their dance. Arthur leaned forward, bending over his wife's bright hair.

Were they embracing now, his brother and his errant wife? Did he kiss her hair? It was not a moment that brother or foster brother should witness.

That night, the frost clamped down upon Fort Tryon Park. Outside, fires danced. The fevered children woke, coughing out what strength they had left, then lapsed into listlessness and sleep, from which feebler coughing woke them. They were always cold, even through the protective warmth of the Unicorn Tapestries.

In the days that followed, the King sent out foragers. They ventured into Washington Heights and below it into Harlem, fought their way back within the stone bridge that guarded the park from the highway and back behind the Cloisters' walls with treasures of cough drops, OTC remedies that were now as rare as the roc's egg, and even (from an office from which the doctor had long since fled) a few precious antibiotics, and news of fires on every block, of Central Park stripped of its withered trees.

It was fine for the madman to speak of retreat in terms of a sick beast returning to its lair to eat herbs, lick its wounds, and wait for a healing spring; but what healing could there be when the whole world was poisoned?

They might as well expect what Arthur had suffered at Camlann: to line up knights against knights, soldiers against soldiers, in hope of treaty—and have a serpent strike from behind, shattering the truce.

Michael Kaye, helping nurse the furnace as well as sick children, watched Arthur fight. This time, he managed not to press for decisive battle; and the battle against his nature was perhaps the hardest he had fought. Day after day, he fought it and won. But Michael knew his foster brother: As they ran out of food, out of healing, out of time, he would order one last sortie. Already, he had begun to drill the guards for assault, not for defense.

It was too cold now to meet in the Pontaut Chapter

House, too dark to meet in the Gothic Chapel now that the shutters guarded the windows. They were holding council of war in the Nine Heroes' Room. One of the Nine sat in the great carved chair, Jennifer standing beside the throne from where she had once ruled.

Came a crash, a shuddering of walls, and a scream from outside—the highway between the Terrace and the Hudson, Michael thought. He must run and check for damages.

"What's that?" asked the head of Arthur's guard, also poised to run, but obedient to Arthur's hand-slashed order: *stay*.

"You know," the madman said, "I tended those foragers who returned.

"They brought back news, which we need as much as we need medicines," the old man continued. "Even if the news is grave. Prepare yourself: The Soulless have learned to hurl fire."

"My shutters," Michael worried. "Please God they hold."

Again, the wall shuddered. Dust trickled from the ceiling of the apse. Outside, a shout went up.

The King cocked his head. "Too close," he judged. "Even if your shutters hold, brother, they mean to pen us within or keep us fighting fires until they're strong enough to overrun our walls."

He paused, looking toward the next room. This time of day, the children were at their best. None of them raved with fever, and one or two even could laugh.

The words came from him as if under torture. "Call out the guards."

"Oh no," said Jennifer. "No. At least, let us try to treat with them first."

Arthur raised his head. "I tried that last time, at Camlann," he told her. "And you know how it ended. One adder-strike in the foot, and another deep into the heart of all Britain."

"We have to try. You told me, we have to try!" She was gone before the King could forestall her, her footsteps ringing on the stone. They heard her struggle with the new bars on the door to the West Terrace. It crashed open . . .

"God, no," whispered the King.

Again the catapult wound and struck. Something whistled through the air, smashing against the parapet. Air rushed in, and stinking of smoke.

"No!" screamed Arthur. "NO!" He had screamed thus at Camlann.

Armored though he was, no man ever moved faster. He dashed into the next room. The sick children scarcely had time to whimper as he snatched up the first tapestry he saw, then raced toward the West Terrace.

He flung open the door, sending Jennifer reeling away from it across the scorched stone, her hands beating at her burning clothes. Arthur pounced. He wrapped her in the heavy wool of the tapestry, snuffing out the fire. The stinks of singed hair and flesh rose as the fire died. Drawing his dagger, he cut free Jennifer's burnt locks and tossed them aside. Her knees sagged, and he caught her. For a long moment, they held each other. Then he snatched her back through the door and kicked it closed.

"Merlin!" he shouted for the madman. "Merlin! Get in here!"

He swept her up into his arms, bearing her back into the room where he had sat such a short time ago and lowering her onto the table. She clung to him with her burnt hands, tears of pain running down the ash on her face, leaving clean streaks.

The tapestry, much charred, fell away from her body. The Unicorn at the Fountain, the creature imprisoned in a garden, had survived all those centuries. Now, in an instant, the fire had consumed the dry wool that had housed it.

They were all the losers for its death; but at least they had not lost Jennifer. The madman appeared loaded with supplies of bandage and aloe and water.

"Tell the children . . . oh, tell them something!" Michael snapped when his wife came to the door, demanding information. He could hear the wails of sickly children. They would all die, God help them. But with Jennifer alive, they had a chance to live a little longer.

The captain of the guard watched the King for orders. Still, Arthur stared at Jennifer's streaked face.

"This time," she whispered, "you *saved* me from the pyre."

Arthur shut his eyes. "I would rather have cut my heart out than send you to it last time."

Jennifer put out a hand to touch the ruined tapestry.

"The poor unicorn," she mourned. "Like the sly girl in the weaving, I was its death." Then she wept as she had not done in all the days of terror, all the years of betrayal, war, and the long, long hallowed silences of her old convent at Amesbury.

"It's gone," she wept. "Destroyed. I was not fit to look upon the unicorn, and so it's gone."

"No, lady," said the magus. "Fire purifies. The pattern is complete. You wrought its first links, and you are its heart." He wound fragrant linen bandages about her hands and wrists, washed the soot from her face, then lovingly completed the hair trim that her husband had begun and botched.

And still she wept. Merlin gestured to the King to hold her. He moved with his powders toward the wine . . .

. . . A tapping sounded up the stairs, across the Cuxa Cloister, and toward them. A tapping of delicate, immortal hooves.

Released by the destruction of the tapestry that had imprisoned it, the unicorn appeared in the door of the Room of the Nine Worthies. This was not the tamed pet of fantasy, but a majestic white creature, at least sixteen hands high. No wonder they said the touch of a unicorn's horn could restore life to the dying. There was eternal joy, Michael thought, and grace in every flourish of its tail, strength in its bearing, and splendor as the candlelight played upon its horn.

"Lord," whispered Merlin, "shall these bones live? Shall these bones live?"

Jennifer gasped, tore free of Arthur, and fled into the hall where the listless children lay. The unicorn followed. It stood poised upon the threshold, as if announcing itself, until the children saw it. They exclaimed in joy as it paced within the room. Ceremoniously, it touched each sick child with its horn, leaving health in its path where fever had stalked. When it had touched them all, it turned to stand before the Queen, who stood with her back against the wall, her bandaged hands held to her mouth.

Queen and unicorn faced each other. Light filtered in and glinted off the unicorn's horn, held at the level of her heart. Jennifer pressed back against the mellow wood. Michael could see how she forced her gray eyes to remain open, in the high arches of their sockets. Behind her, he heard the unfamiliar buoyant gurgle of his daughter's laughter. He ran to sweep her up in his arms. Who would have thought the age of miracles was *now?*

"Go ahead," said the Queen. "Pierce my heart. After all these years, I'll be relieved."

Bending its stately maned head with its rakish goat's beard until the horn clicked upon the floor, the unicorn stretched its forelegs out and bowed. It raised itself, then stepped closer. When the Queen reached out and took its face between her hands, its horn blazed aloft in benediction.

The bandages dropped off her hands. The burst blisters shrank, then disappeared. Even the pink of tight-drawn new-healed skin subsided. Her hair, the color of an autumn leaf, flourished, waving down her back. The Queen sank down and wept as if she were a child that had been forgiven.

Arthur the King ran his hand along the unicorn's flank as if it were a favorite war-horse. The beast rested its head against his shoulder.

"Now," said the King, "we go forth. To the sea."

Jennifer rose. Arthur held out his hand to his Queen.

Shabby though she was, she placed fingertips upon its back. The two of them walked from the room. The children, tended by the madman, followed then into the Great Hall, down the stairs, and into the park. Laurie broke out of Michael's arms, ran to the unicorn, and—before she could be stopped—clambered onto its back.

Outside, the Soulless yammered. Seeing the fortress door open, they abandoned their catapults and pressed forward hungrily. Arthur's drawn steel restrained them. Then the sight of the unicorn forced them into a silence that was oddly reverent.

It started forward—and there was Michael's daughter riding on its back! He lunged forward to protect her. The unicorn lowered its crowned head at him in warning, and Arthur held up a hand.

"Do you think I would let harm come to her?" asked the King. "Or that *he* would?"

Two of the Soulless stole up to the unicorn and held out shaking dirty hands. The mighty head bent, sniffing those hands, then nudging against them. The unicorn's horn gleamed. No longer soulless, the pair fell to their knees. They were a woman and a boy. Jennifer came forth to comfort them and guide them into line.

"Now," said the King, "to reclaim our world."

Arthur raised Excalibur. The amethyst on its pommel gleamed in the winter sunlight as he brought the blade to his lips, saluting the unicorn that led down the twisting road and out toward the city.

Shadows followed at their backs. Kings and princes guarded them. A man bearing the Cross of God upon his back sang a Crusader's hymn as a Hebrew king harped.

An aged paladin with a mighty beard marched alongside, holding the fragments of his kinsman's horn. One or two people had seized food and blankets. Ari, Michael noticed, had caught up a piece of tapestry, now empty of figures.

South through Washington Heights, where even the timid oldest emerged from the older buildings and fell into step, they marched, and into Harlem. Vacant lots in the 120s, where untidy camps had been set up teemed as people raced toward the unicorn. The blocked-up houses disgorged squatters as if the last trump had been sounded and the dead were raised. The unicorn reared in greeting, and the little girl upon its back laughed with joy.

"What a rider we'll make of her, brother!" Arthur called to Michael where he marched with his wife.

The newcomers clustered around, petting the unicorn. Two adults carried a pallet out into the street and laid it at the unicorn's hooves. With a gentle touch of its horn, the unicorn released the old man on it from mortal sickness. He rose and walked alongside, steadying himself against the unicorn's flanks until he was strong enough to walk on his own. In another time, Michael would have recoiled at the stinks of sickness and fever that rose from the old man, but he pressed forward toward his daughter.

Her head was not so high above his now, and Michael, sharp-eyed as a seneschal must be, understood. With every touch of a child's hand, with every life-giving touch of the unicorn's horn, the creature's light and substance seemed to diminish. The unicorn was *dwindling*. No longer was it the size of a war-horse, but only the size of, well, the unicorn of legend, more delicate and vulnerable now than it had been.

Jennifer came over to him. "Do you see how small it's getting?" he asked her.

"We both saw, my lord and I," she whispered.

"Can't we stop it?"

"Only if we retreat," she said.

"We'll drain it," Michael warned.

Arthur had gone over to the unicorn, had laid his arm over its shoulders, and walked beside it. The unicorn arched its neck and caracoled for a moment, taking heart and strength from the King.

"It is the unicorn's privilege to spend its strength for the good of its world," said Jennifer. "It is very like a king in that respect."

Michael found himself laughing and weeping, both. "I thought King's Touch, surely, was for other things."

Jennifer shook her head. "All he can do is comfort the poor beast." She blinked once, then proudly raised her head. The King spent his life for the country; the unicorn for the world; and the chatelaine must look as if all were well.

Past 125th Street, they marched. Now the wasteland of Central Park gaped before them. Men and women, even a few sad beasts that survived from the zoo in the West 60s, thronged out to greet it. At the sight of the unicorn and its company, some fell to their knees. Others shuddered, stretched, and yawned, as if soullessness were a sleep from which they finally had waked. They watched as people in New York had watched parades long, long before the Wasting, but they watched in silence.

The silence drew out, becoming oppressive. Michael's little girl leaned forward, smoothing her cheek in the silk of the unicorn's mane, somewhat dingy now. Had she whispered something?

Again, the unicorn began to caracole. Arthur stepped away from it, again drawing Excalibur. He saluted the crowd, which responded with a cheer. Downtown they marched, toward the ruins that jutted like ruined teeth from what had once been called the Canyon of Heroes. Leading the parade was another Hero, the tenth—a unicorn now fragile, with a translucent brittle horn. Each time it touched someone, it lost more light and strength. Oh, it was so tired!

Its head swung toward the King, dark eyes imploring. Arthur signaled a halt. Michael lifted his little girl from the unicorn's back, winning thankful looks from King and beast. The creature's back was lathered. Michael laid his own coat upon it. Someone brought it water, warmed against his body. Arthur talked gently to it, walking with it up and down.

When the procession again moved, the sky had turned darker with clouds and the waning sun. There was no smoke—another miracle in a day full of them.

Murmuring rose from the throng, as if they were children who only now realized what they had done in a burst of temper and were now sorry. And down farther, past the welters of twisting streets that each released its own survivors, eyes feasting on the unicorn walking beside the King and dwindling more and more swiftly. Arthur beckoned to the Queen. When she approached, the unicorn pushed against her outstretched hand, then leaned its head against her. Arms linked across its back, King and chatelaine urged it forward. It was no larger now than a pony. A sickly pony.

The walls guarding the tip of the island from the rest of the world opened its gates to let the unicorn and the former Soulless pass. One man threw down his gun, and then they all did. A woman in a tattered suit sobbed, then joined the line of march through the fortress that no longer saw the need to protect itself, eastward toward the Seaport with its ancient reek of salt and fish, where stubs of the masts of sunken ships protruded from the dark water, and so to the tip of Manhattan Island.

The sun was only the merest coal of warmth in a gray sky above where the East and the Hudson rivers flowed together when they reached Battery Park. The last flicker of sunlight and the first campfires sparked off the unicorn's horn one last time. With a groan, the unicorn sank to its knees. It shivered in the evening winds, chill from the water. Michael's coat was drenched; Arthur covered it with his own cloak. Some of the former Soulless, expert from far too much practice, kindled fires from the dried-out stumps of trees near where cannons had guarded New Amsterdam and then New York in its early days, trying to make their camp as comfortable as they might.

As if in response, the tiny islands across from the park set out lights of their own. Bonfires sprang from about the feet of the statue, its torch fallen, on the island across the bay.

Toward midnight, rain doused the remnants of the

fires. Michael crept away from his wife and child to make certain that the unicorn was covered. Arthur's cloak was soaked through.

"Do you want water, friend?" Michael asked. "Grain?" There must be something he could do for it. When he had charge of Arthur's hall, he had always had a way with horses. Still, he wished he could call for Merlin. He remembered: The madman had a way of turning up when he was needed. If he were not here, it must be because he could do nothing. So, Michael must rely on hands and voice to comfort at least the unicorn's heart.

The unicorn snuffled once at Michael's hand.

"You don't want me to leave you, boy? Well then, I won't."

Arthur appeared, handlinked with Jennifer, blankets pulled like hoods over their heads. They, too, sank down beside the unicorn.

Near dawn, the rain subsided. A wind blew across the tip of the island, bracingly chill and salty. It seemed to cleanse whatever it touched. The unicorn's head turned; the dulled eyes brightened, and it looked up. Its body barely made a mound beneath the King's sodden cloak.

The wind scoured away the clouds, revealing the morning star. Light began to tremble where the sky touched the East River. The unicorn stirred beneath the heavy woolen folds.

Arthur pulled the cloak away. Michael's eyes filled. Was this ancient creature that struggled up onto unsteady legs the triumphant unicorn that had broken a siege and transformed its besiegers?

It was drained, dying, surely. But it shied away from Arthur's sustaining hands. The King nodded, then knelt before the beast. Together, they waited. The first rays of the rising sun struck the unicorn's horn, kindling fire along its whorls and ridges. The unicorn whickered welcome. It sounded stronger—didn't it?

And then, with a speed astonishing for a creature so withered and drained, it raced straight toward the shore, toward the barriers, vaulting them in a leap that did not end in the river, but soared instead into the gleaming sky. A mist shaped like a giant horse with a gleaming horn formed before the sun, then dissipated in the morning wind.

Sunlight struck the ground, kindling light like an ember in a dying fire. Michael's daughter raced over to it, pounced, and, a look of awe on her face, held up her hand.

On it gleamed a stone large enough to cover her palm. A gem of adamant, Michael thought. They would have to revise the folklore, wouldn't they, when they could spare the time from rebuilding their world.

"Give it to the King," he heard his wife urge the little girl.

She held it aloft like a torch, but brought it to Jennifer instead. The woman bent to take the stone. It shone pink through their joined hands.

"For your new crown," the lady told the King.

"No," he said, "for yours."

He leaned forward. Their kiss was almost a passage of arms.

Hand on his Queen's shoulder, Arthur started forward. "Well, brother Kaye," he called to Michael, "I have a mind to turn gardener."

He always could count on Arthur to come up with good ideas. Unlike the gardens on the Unicorn Tapestries, Arthur's gardens would reclaim a world.

LISA MASON

DAUGHTER
OF THE TAO

Peter: All I know about **Lisa Mason** is that she lives in Marin County, California, and that her story "Daughter of the Tao," besides being lovely and sad and fluidly inventive, is one of only two stories in this collection ("Mirror of Lop Nor" is the other) to deal with the *k'i-lin*, the unicorn of China and Japan, which is more like an element, a force of nature, than it is like the European horned horse. I wish there had been more such tales, but I'll gladly settle for these two.

Janet: I, on the other hand, know Lisa well. Aside from being gorgeous, talented, an attorney, and another sometime member of The Melville Nine workshop, she's a prolific novelist and short story writer. She is also, I am happy to say, my friend. We talk at length on the phone, of shoes and sealing wax, cabbages, kings, and publishing. I wish she lived around the corner.

Daughter of the Tao

1. DRAGON

SING CHOY DARTS THROUGH FISH ALLEY SEEKING fresh shrimp for her master. She swings her basket joyfully, savoring ripe odors of raw sea creatures, ginger root, peanut oil smoking in someone's wok.

A *mooie jai* does not skip along the streets of Tangrenbu, not on most days. Certainly not on a day as crisp and sunny as this, which her master's cook would have savored for himself. But Cook injured his leg. Ankle swollen from Cook's misstep into a pothole on Dupont Street. Cook seized Sing Choy's skinny arm as she knelt on the kitchen floor scrubbing with her soap and brush, flung her to her feet, and said, "Here, stupid girl, go get two pound shrimp and make quick."

"Yes, Cook," she said.

Sing Choy carefully washed her hands and face, retied her queue, smoothed wrinkles from her *sahm*. And set out with coins and basket, joy bobbing in her heart. Shrimp good luck. Perhaps her master will permit Cook to give her one fried shrimp for supper along with boiled rice and greens. "You shrimp girl," Cook joked. "Master buy you for two hundred dollars gold, plus five pound shrimp."

Sing Choy pauses among the fish peddlers in Fish Alley. Peasants in denim *sahms*, that's what the peddlers are, with felt slouch hats or embroidered caps, the crudest ones in the flat straw cone of the coolie. Her master employs men like this. She can feel their eyes. After all, a *mooie jai* does not skip along the streets of Tangrenbu.

Fish Alley is not even a street but a narrow, mean passage between forty-niner shacks long abandoned to slum landlords, crowded with bachelors who shift in and out with the fickle tides of opportunity and poverty. Weathered clapboard walls are plastered with vermilion bulletins, black calligraphy announcing news near and afar. A gilt *t'ai chi* adorns a lintel. A potted star lily mournfully turns to what sunlight it can glean before shadows close over its corner.

Huge baskets bulge with the bay's bounty: black-speckled oysters; green and pink crabs with slow-pinching claws; shrimp, of course, of palest celadon before they go to the wok; silvery salmon, some flopping still, tepid water streaming into the gutter. Sing Choy's heart catches at the sight of their dying. She pauses, struck with sudden nameless shame.

"Hey, you girl, why such a sad face?"

Sing Choy turns. Another girl! Who ever sees a girl in Tangrenbu? Yet it's true, another girl stands beside her. Black cotton *sahm*, basket slung upon her arm, queue wound around her head. She is taller than Sing Choy by a handspan and very skinny. Face like the moon, a laughing mouth. Around her neck a black silk cord and a tiny gilt *t'ai chi*. Little shadows beneath the bones in her cheeks, little shadows beneath the gentle swells of her breasts. The fish peddlers gape at her as if she were a two-headed pig.

"I . . . I sorry pretty fish must die."

"Your heart too soft. Salmon delicious! Your master so cruel he never let you taste salmon?"

Sing Choy stares at her big bony toes. Peasant feet made for walking, standing in fields planting peas, carrying loads of millet. She is nothing. She is no one to taste salmon. "Sometimes my master give me one fried shrimp with rice and greens."

The girl throws back her head and laughs like the tinkling of a bell. The fish peddlers murmur. Sing Choy is only too aware of their eyes now. "Don't laugh like that," she mutters to the girl. "They all looking."

The girl takes her arm, draws her beneath a balcony with curved railings painted the color of an egg yolk. "Who you?"

"I Sing Choy."

"I Kwai Ying. You *mooie jai?*"

"Yes."

"Me, too. Cook sick?"

The beautiful language of Cantonese embraces so many dialects that Sing Choy, a girl from the north, can barely understand this girl from the south. They both must twist their tongues around the language of Gold Mountain.

"Cook step into hole!" Sing Choy suppresses laughter. A little awed. This bold girl, *mooie jai*, too? And her master let her taste salmon?

The balcony shades them from sun and the fish peddlers' eyes but affords no relief from the stench rising
from a spattered bin groaning with all manner of offal.
Fish heads and fins and guts, husked shrimp shells, the
small flat mitt of a manta that wandered into someone's
net. Sing Choy wrinkles her nose. Kwai Ying peers in
curiously.

"Look," she says.

There, amid the garbage next to the manta, is
another small dead creature, mottled gray in color, ser-
pentine like an eel. But the creature is not an eel. Four
fragile legs lie slack, each tipped with delicate fingers
and long curved claws as fine as needles. The dead face
resembles a tiny ox. A tuft of dark scarlet bristles
sprouts from its pate. Its jaws hang open, miniature roar
silenced forever.

"Poor thing," Sing Choy murmurs. "What is it?"

"Your heart too soft," Kwai Ying says, voice thick
with contempt. "That just *lung*; a dragon."

"A dragon!" Sing Choy's eyes widen.

"Sure." Kwai Ying says, a frown tugging at her
mouth. "It one of the four fabulous creatures, but look at
it. Caught in fisherman's net like worthless manta,
thrown away like fish guts. No better than garbage."

"But a dragon!"

"Stupid girl, you know the four fabulous creatures?"

Sing Choy shakes her head, humiliated.

"Dragon, phoenix, unicorn, tortoise," Kwai Ying dutifully recites. "My teacher say. I have teacher once, you
know. Teacher say each very good creature. Supposed to
bring good luck. Supposed to show harmony with the Tao.

Supposed to"—raising her eyebrows significantly—"bring magic."

Sing Choy's mouth falls open. "Magic!"

"But I see no harmony in Tangrenbu," Kwai Ying says. "I see no Tao. I see no magic for *mooie jai*."

Sing Choy could cry at the bitterness in Kwai Ying's voice.

Kwai Ying only shrugs. "When you come to Tangrenbu?"

"In Year of Golden Tiger. *Swallow* take me."

Sing Choy gulps. Still fills her heart with grief how her father sold her to a man in Shanghai, the ship's master of a clipper with three sails named for a pretty bird. The *Swallow,* a coolie clipper carrying illegal human cargo. They stowed her belowdeck for so many miserable days she lost count after tying two bits of string on each finger of her hands. Was grateful when they carried her up into the cold sunshine of San Francisco. Was grateful when they shimmied off the stinking rags she'd huddled in. Was grateful when she stood naked and shivering on a block beneath gaslights and an auctioneer opened her mouth, spread her skinny legs. Was grateful to go to her master for two hundred dollars, plus five pounds of shrimp. She was *mooie jai*, destined to scrub floors, polish pots, clean night soil from the water closet. Is grateful for one fried shrimp with her rice and greens. This Tangrenbu, City of the People of Tan.

"Golden Tiger," says Kwai Ying. Her pretty black eyes gleam. Her tone is as tart as new oranges. "And how many celestial creatures you see before Year of Golden Tiger?"

Sing Choy grins. Likes this game. Cook asks her this,

too, so she will know how old she is. "I remember Year of Dog, but only a little because *I* little." The girls giggle together. "Then came Boar, then Rat, then Ox. And at last Tiger, all in gold."

"I know more animals than you," Kwai Ying says. "I know Cock and Monkey." Stern, quizzing. "And after Year of Golden Tiger?"

Sing Choy thinks carefully. Cook only asks her year by year, not all at once. "After Tiger came Hare."

"Yes."

"After Hare came Dragon." Doesn't want to look at the little dead dragon anymore. Stares into Kwai Ying's eyes. "After Dragon came Snake. I don't like Snake."

"Yes, yes."

"After Snake came Horse. Now is Year of Ram."

"And new year coming?"

"New year coming is Monkey!"

"Good." Kwai Ying rewards her with a squeeze of her hand. "I born in Year of Monkey."

"Then new year coming is your lucky year," Sing Choy says. "Another Year of Monkey!"

"Yes," Kwai Ying says. A small wry smile like she has swallowed something sour. "I see twelve celestial animals come and go. That is why my master make me eat salmon till my belly can hold no more."

Sing Choy should be glad Kwai Ying can eat so well but her heart catches as painfully as when she saw the flopping salmon, the little dead dragon. "Why make you eat?"

Kwai Ying takes her arm, pulls her away from the reeking bin. Flies land on the dragon in a buzzing tribe.

"Because I am woman now."

2. PHOENIX

Sing Choy sprints back to her master's house with two pounds of fresh shrimp and change. Taking his ease, ankle propped on a cushion, Cook counts out the silver coins carefully. Glances up at her, smiling his black-toothed smile. "Very good, girl. I tell Master you not so stupid, after all."

"Thank you, Cook. Any other thing you want?"

"No." Cook studies her, calculating. Doles out a silver coin. The sun angles over Russian Hill, casting shadows over Tangrenbu. But the day is not yet old. "Yes. You go get salted plums for Master. He like plums. And a coconut candy for you. But just one. And bring change."

"Yes, Cook."

"And put jacket over *sahm*." Cook produces one of his, throws it roughly over her shoulders. "Wrap hair, take hat." Jostles her around, coils the queue into a bun at the nape of her neck. Jams a slouch hat over her skull. Hat much too big, she looks like a little old man. Giggles. Cook whirls her to face him, shakes his finger in her face. "No laugh. You must look like boy. I cannot send girl into Tangrenbu. Since *lo fahn,* the white devils, say we cannot bring our families from China to Gold Mountain, there no women, no girls in Tangrenbu. Only *mooie jai* and . . ."

"And who, Cook?"

"And daughters of joy." Cook shakes his finger again. "Listen, girl. Never go to Bartlett Alley. Never go to Spofford Alley. Never go to Waverly Place. I hear someone see you there, I thrash you till you cry no more. You *sabe?*"

There was a time when Sing Choy would have cringed before Cook's finger. She has passed by Bartlett Alley, Spofford Alley, Waverly Place. Forbidden places, always. Recalls the strange birdlike cries she hears whenever she passes by those places. And another recollection: the time in Year of Snake when she walked with Cook through Waverly Place and saw men dragging something out of a shack. Something small and dark, which they tossed in the back of a wagon like trash. Cook had made her hurry.

But Sing Choy is bold after her foray into Fish Alley. She does not cringe. She says, without blinking, "I *sabe*."

And sets out for salted plums, one coconut candy for herself. Brings back change, shows Cook the candy, which he splits in half and eats. No matter. Half a coconut candy is well worth freedom she never had before.

And this is how Sing Choy sees Kwai Ying again: darting down Stockton Street, turning the corner at Broadway, disappearing into a pottery shop on Dupont. Every now and then they meet and pause, dart beneath a balcony, talk in breathless whispers.

"I never had teacher," Sing Choy says as they lean against two bales of rags bound with thick straw cords. Ashamed of her ignorance, but curious. "What is the Tao?"

"My teacher say Tao is the Way," Kwai Ying says. "Tao is eternal female, mysterious and mutable. Tao is chasm *and* mountain. Tao is light *and* dark. You see?" She takes her tiny gilt *tài chi* in her fingertips, shows Sing Choy the disk, half light, half dark. And within each half, a dot of the opposite.

They both giggle, unsure if they understand what Kwai Ying's teacher meant.

"And what is harmony with the Tao?" Sing Choy asks, thrilled with her friend's wisdom.

"Harmony with the Tao means all is well." Kwai Ying muses. "Tao means peace and prosperity. Tao means good luck and magic. The four fabulous creatures appear in the world when the world is in harmony with the Tao. The four fabulous creatures cannot live when there is evil. The four fabulous creatures die or disappear when the world is not in harmony with the Tao."

A dark look passes over Kwai Ying's face that makes Sing Choy's breath snag in her throat.

They can never talk for very long. Bachelors' eyes are everywhere in Tangrenbu. Perhaps Sing Choy may look like a boy, but Kwai Ying cannot conceal her burgeoning femininity. Worse, she does not even try. Her master has given her black silk to wear. The luminous fabric clings to every hill and valley in the changing landscape of Kwai Ying's body.

"You so pretty, Kwai Ying," Sing Choy says. Envious; also admiring. The sight of Kwai Ying makes her heart bob with joy.

"Master say 'eat, eat, you skinny girl,'" Kwai Ying says, and produces a coconut candy for Sing Choy. "For you, little Sing. I cannot eat cheap sweets. I am stuffed with shrimp."

One day Sing Choy is carrying a basket of new lettuce from the farms in Cow Hollow when she finds Kwai Ying standing on the corner of Sullivan Alley.

A knot of bachelors crouches on the cobblestones

surrounded by a crowd of onlookers. The men grin and
spit, the mood is tense and ugly, but no one cheers too
loudly. Some illicit gambling game. The bachelors love
to gamble. No one wants to attract the bulls of the
Chinatown Squad. Dreadful squawking noises arise from
inside the circle like the tumult of an unhappy barnyard.

"Hi," Sing Choy says.

"Hi, you little girl," Kwai Ying says. She has grown
haughty lately.

"What is it?" Sing Choy says, putting down her basket. Standing beside Kwai Ying's beauty, she feels sweaty,
unkempt. Annoyed, too, at Kwai Ying's aloof mood.
Perhaps Sing Choy is just a peasant girl and once Kwai
Ying held some higher station, but they were both sold by
their families. They both sailed belowdeck in coolie clip-
pers, both stood naked and shivering on a block beneath
gaslights. Both *mooie jai* in Tangrenbu.

Perhaps aware of her friend's annoyance, Kwai Ying
turns with a sunny smile. A beguiling smile as though she
wishes to make Sing Choy do something she would not
want to do. "It's a cockfight. Want to see?"

Sing Choy backs away. "No . . . no . . ."

"Come on! Leave your basket. No one will bother
your stupid lettuce. I said, come on!" She seizes Sing
Choy's hand, won't let go.

They slip through the crowd to the knot of crouching
men. It is a horrible sight! In a makeshift plywood pen
two blood-spattered birds confront each other in a struggle to the death. A rooster with a scarlet comb, dark scarlet feathers, huge vicious spurs struts around the other
bird, which staggers pitifully. The gamblers toss gold

coins at a croupier, a man who holds the money and calculates odds in a low monotone.

The rooster pecks and kicks. "Oh," Sing Choy groans but Kwai Ying squeezes her hand so tightly she does not dare cry out. The other bird is a beautiful thing with variegated crest, tail, and wings. The long swooping feathers drag in mud and blood, but Sing Choy sees cerulean blue, golden yellow, cinnamon red, ivory white, ebony black. The rooster kicks again, spur connecting with the bird's breast, and the bird shudders in agony. The men yell, gold coins clatter. As Sing Choy blinks away tears, the bird cocks its head at her and Kwai Ying. For a moment its bright suffering eye looks right at them.

The bird bursts into a ball of fire! Flames of blue, gold, red, white, black shoot as high as a house. The crouching men fall back on their heels. The onlookers press forward. The croupier scrambles for his collection of coins. A rending cry rises up, inhuman, ghastly.

Kwai Ying drags Sing Choy through the crowd.

Now men jostle and push. A thin boy tumbles to the cobblestones, his face and *sahm* dappled with blood. Little blue flames spring from the blood like sparks catching and ebbing in cooking oil. Shriek of the bulls' whistle and the bachelors scatter, footsteps ringing down the alley.

Faces drained, eyes wide, the girls press up against the window of a sweetmeat shop. As still as feral creatures, as quiet as shadows, they wait till the Chinatown Squad has rousted everyone out of Sullivan Alley. Kwai Ying's hand in Sing Choy's is as cold as Cook's iron pot on mornings when fog curls through Tangrenbu.

3. UNICORN

Since the phoenix burned, Sing Choy has not seen Kwai Ying. She searches Stockton and Dupont, jogs down Broadway and up Fish Alley, even goes back to Sullivan Alley though she does not stay there long. Year of Monkey passes by, Year of Cock comes, and suddenly Sing Choy is taller than Cook. Her rough cotton *sahm* dangles above her ankles and wrists. The slouch hat she wears while running errands fits her skull perfectly now. Her thick queue hangs to the backs of her knees.

One evening Cook comes into the pantry behind the kitchen where Sing Choy sleeps on a cot and eats her meals. He brings in her bowl of supper, bangs it down on the little side table. "Master say you too skinny," Cook says. Baleful glance. "Eat."

Sing Choy takes the steaming bowl. Rice and greens, as usual. To her astonishment, she sees the bowl is also heaped with steamed salmon, chunks of fragrant pink meat more enticing than coconut candy. She takes the bowl, digs in chopsticks, greedily devouring. She is always hungry these days. Delicious salmon!

But she pauses in her gluttony, struck with sudden guilt.

Kwai Ying, where are you?

Kwai Ying could have left Tangrenbu, of course. Her master could have moved to San Rafael, Sacramento, Salinas, Russian River. A *mooie jai* could disappear anywhere in Gold Mountain.

But when Sing Choy turns the corner at Pacific

Avenue, she sees a tall, pretty girl turn the corner onto Broadway. In Fish Alley, she hears the tinkling of a bell and is certain she hears Kwai Ying laughing. When she pauses before a gilt *t'ai chi* tacked to a lintel, she remembers the *t'ai chi* Kwai Ying wore around her neck on a black silk cord.

Kwai Ying is still in Tangrenbu.

Sing Choy finishes her supper. Making a show of gratitude, she steals a half glass of whiskey from Master's bottle in the pantry, brings it into Cook's room.

Cook smiles his black-toothed smile. "Smart girl. You pour a little water in bottle, Master never notice." Sucks whiskey from the glass. "You good girl." Cook's eyes blur. He wipes a tear.

"I lock up, okay?" she says, annoyed. Sad old man, a little whiskey makes him cry.

"You good girl," Cook says again. Sorrow tugs at his mouth.

Sing Choy locks up the house for the night the way Cook would have done. But she leaves the pantry door open, leaves the back door to the kitchen open. Reties her queue, jams her slouch hat over her forehead, fastens the frogs of her padded jacket. And creeps into the fog-shrouded night, seeking the places she has always been forbidden to go.

She walks down Bartlett Alley, Spofford Alley, Waverly Place. Recalls the small, dark thing thrown like trash by men into the back of a wagon. Recalls how Cook made her hurry, how Cook tried to turn her face away, but she saw anyway. Saw the corpse of a woman. Hears the same strange birdlike cries she has heard whenever she passes by, "Two bittee lookee, four bittee touchee, six bittee doee."

Forty-niner shacks in these alleys have long been abandoned to brothels. The procurers have subdivided the shacks into cubbyholes with locked doors, windows without glass set with sturdy iron bars. Cubbyholes called cribs. In every crib beneath gaslights, at every barred window, stands a girl in black silk calling, "Two bittee lookee, four bittee touchee, six bittee doee."

Sing Choy carefully tours each alley, peering in at the faces. Sees a northern girl, her broad flat cheeks dappled with bruises. A mountain peasant, her thick wide mouth crusted with lip paint and sores. A crone, withered and hacking, death etched in her eyes, yet she cannot be more than seventeen years old. And at last a moon face, a laughing mouth, little shadows beneath cheekbones. Charm always charms no matter how dark the shadows.

Sing Choy has bargained with merchants over the time Cook has let her run errands. She has carefully saved change from shrewder bargains than even Cook would have expected. She gives the procurer six bits. The procurer, a buffalo of a man with a butterfly knife stuck conspicuously in his belt, lets her into Kwai Ying's crib.

Sing Choy takes off her hat and sits while Kwai Ying bustles about, not noticing who the visitor is. Dirt floor and clapboard walls. A tiny cot, a chamber pot, a pitcher of water, some cotton cloths. A pipe, the bowl gray with opium ash. Candles, incense, a bottle of expensive whiskey, another bottle filled with some other astringent smelling fluid. If Sing Choy spread her arms straight out, her fingertips could just about reach

each wall. The crib is freezing cold. Shrine on a side table, a spray of brown star lilies. Tacked on the wall by its black silk cord, the tiny gilt *t'ai chi*.

"Oh, Kwai Ying, don't you wear it anymore?" Sing Choy says.

Kwai Ying whirls, a snarl disfiguring her face, a knife in her fist. Then her mouth drops at the sight of Sing Choy. "Little Sing," she cries. Runs to her friend, embraces her. Then flings Sing Choy away. Pretty girl deeply shamed. Covers her pale cheeks with her hands. Dark circles rim her eyes. "Your heart too soft. I am no longer *mooie jai*."

"You what the bachelors call a daughter of joy."

"Daughter of joy." Kwai Ying's voice is as bitter as lye soap. "Master sell me to Chee Song Tong."

Sing Choy nods. She knows now. Chee Song Tong runs most of the cribs in Tangrenbu. Smuggles girls from China, buys *mooie jai* when they are old enough to become daughters of joy. Sing Choy says at once, "I buy you back. How much?"

"What money have you?"

"Cook send me on errands for a long time now. I save fifty dollars in gold and silver." This is a great fortune for a *mooie jai*. Sing Choy has never had so much money in her life. Carefully hoards it in a hidey-hole beneath her cot in the pantry.

"*Stupid* girl. Chee Song Tong pay my master a thousand gold coins for me."

"A thousand . . ." Sing Choy's heart catches.

Kwai Ying scornful. "Fifty dollars." Unfastens the frogs on Sing Choy's jacket, poking, probing with her hands. "You still like boy, but your time coming."

"No!"

Haughty Kwai Ying again, beautiful and imperious, as tart as new oranges. "You will be daughter of joy, too."

Sing Choy is incredulous. "You like this, then?"

"Oh, little Sing!" Kwai Ying shakes her head. Tears squeeze from her eyes. Her mouth falls slack in a mask of grief. "How bachelors come and go. Dozens, dozens, and dozens more. All day long, all night long."

"No, no!"

Cruel Kwai Ying. "How they come at you, one after the other." Rubs her belly. "How they hurt. How they numb. How they steal your soul."

"I run away!"

"You are *mooie jai*. Where can you go? There is nowhere you can go. Except my teacher once say . . ."

But Kwai Ying clamps her lips shut. Bows her head.

"Please tell me," Sing Choy says. "I never had teacher. *You* my only teacher. I know nothing."

Sharp knock on the door. "Time up," the procurer says.

Sing Choy hands another six bits through the bars. "More time, please."

"Okay," he says, taking the money.

But another sharp knock batters the door.

Kwai Ying springs up beside Sing Choy, leaning out the window. Mutters, "The lousy . . ."

A creature thrusts its snout through the window. The horn on its forehead strikes the bars with a resounding *clang*. The creature opens its mouth and speaks, a tumultuous sound like many bells ringing. Two cinnamon red tendrils hang down below its nostrils like a man's mustache. Bushy hair wreathing long pointed ears is cerulean blue. Its scaly skin glows golden yellow. The long swishing tail and dancing hooves are as black as ebony. It stares at them with eyes like ivory marbles.

The girls shrink back before the blind-white gaze.

"Go away!" Kwai Ying says. Tremulous; then firmer, "Go away!"

The creature pulls back. Sing Choy expects the clatter of hooves on cobblestones, but there is only silence, the distant singsong, "Two bittee lookee, four bittee . . ." Sing Choy dares to peek out. There is nothing but the fog and night and Spofford Alley.

The girls sit on the cot, stunned and trembling with fear.

At last Kwai Ying stands, gets down her whiskey bottle, tips a sip. Stern, quizzing. "And what was that, little Sing?"

"That was unicorn," Sing Choy says dutifully, but her heart still cannot contain her bewilderment. "Third of the four fabulous creatures. But, Kwai Ying. We saw dragon dead. We saw phoenix die. The unicorn; he . . ."

"He very much *alive?*" Kwai Ying tosses her head, offers the bottle.

Sing Choy refuses. She has only seen eleven celestial animals. Next year, Year of Dog, is *her* lucky year. She does not drink foul liquor of *lo fahn*.

"What you really want to know," Kwai Ying says, "is why unicorn has come for *me*."

Little shivers of shock pop all over Sing Choy's spine

like the first time she saw and heard firecrackers. "Why does unicorn come for you?"

"Because I can be daughter of joy; I can allow bachelors of Tangrenbu to numb me, steal my soul; I can allow procurer and landlord to steal my gold. Or I can be daughter of the Tao. I can embrace the Way." Kwai Ying sips more whiskey. Sulky girl. "I can choose. My teacher say."

Sing Choy is appalled. "Then why you choose *this*?"

Kwai Ying whirls on her like a striking snake. "My father did not sell me. My mother did not sell me. I am orphan. I am raised by the Daughters of the Tao. You know Daughters of the Tao?"

Sing Choy shrinks back on the cot. "No. I never hear of this."

"Daughters of the Tao," Kwai Ying says, "are immortal sisters. They embrace the Way. They practice *magic*. How we lived, oh my! On a beautiful island off shore of Hong Kong. Small island with a curved back, forests and clear streams. Lovely houses, balconies and pools, flowers and shrubbery. Not like ugly streets of Tangrenbu. And shrimp and salmon to eat, all you want, little Sing! Fried rice and pretty greens such as you have never seen."

Sing Choy does not know. Glances at the opium pipe, the whiskey bottle, the awful crib. Surreptitiously takes the knife from the cot where Kwai Ying left it. Perhaps Kwai Ying has gone mad in her slavery.

"You think I gone mad?" Kwai Ying says, laughing at Sing Choy's astonished look. "Gone mad, yes. Daughters of the Tao gone mad, too. They do not accept dynasty, do not accept patriarchy. Do not accept bound feet or concubines or dictators or daughters of joy. Or *mooie jai*."

"Then why they sell you?" Sing Choy says. Blunt girl, learning how to be hard, too.

"Daughters of the Tao did not sell me," Kwai Ying says. The bitter voice fairly tears Sing Choy's heart from her breast. "Daughters of the Tao could not themselves withstand the evil of the world. The opium; the slave girls; the coolies; the oppression. One day our island swam away."

"Swam away?"

"Our island," Kwai Ying says impatiently, "has a head, four legs, a tail. One day our island swam away into the Tao, fleeing from the evil of the world. No one could have foreseen the whims of tortoise, I suppose. My teacher and I had gone on errands in Hong Kong. We were left behind. Just like that."

Sing Choy considers her friend's wild story. Very sad, how addled pretty Kwai Ying has become in so short a time. This will not happen to Sing Choy. No. Never. But she asks because she must, "And what happened to your teacher?"

"My teacher waited for omens," Kwai Ying answers at once, though her voice is low and slurred. "Omens came. The four fabulous creatures: *lung* the dragon, *feng huang* the phoenix, *ch'i lin* the unicorn, *wang pa* the tortoise. They crept through the gutter, swam in cesspools. And when the time was right, my teacher allowed the unicorn to pierce her and take her back to the Tao. It was horrible, little Sing!"

"Kwai, what do you mean?"

"They found her. In an alley. Blood pooled on her breast, blood everywhere. And I had no one. I was sold to slavers. I came to Gold Mountain as *mooie jai*. And now I am here, daughter of joy. The Tao is lost to me."

Sharp knock at the door. The procurer growls, "Time up. You go."

Sing Choy jams her slouch hat over her face. "Okay," she calls to the procurer. To Kwai Ying, "Then your teacher die? She took her own life? That what you mean?"

"No," Kwai Ying says. Takes a final slug of whiskey, caps the bottle, wipes her mouth. "No, I mean unicorn sought her, unicorn came for her, unicorn pierced her breast. Unicorn took her back to the Tao. To the island of immortal sisters. Yet . . . immortality look very much like death to me."

"You make no sense," Sing Choy says harshly. "Once I love you, Kwai Ying. Now I see you weak. Mad; deluded. I *never* be like you." Fastens the frogs of her jacket. Turns to go.

"Fine, I am weak," Kwai Ying says, touching Sing Choy's hand as the procurer lets in another bachelor. She yanks the black silk cord from the wall, takes down the little gilt *t'ai chi*. Slings the cord over Sing Choy's neck. "I fear the unicorn more than I fear my fate in Tangrenbu."

4. TORTOISE

And this is how Sing Choy comes to meet her womanhood.

First, Cook finds Sing Choy's hidey-hole beneath the

cot, takes the fifty dollars in gold and silver coins. "Thief! Thief!" His black-toothed scowl, baleful glare. "You think you smart? Too smart for girl!"

Next, Cook and Master strip her of her black cotton *sahm*. She fights till Master whips his knuckles across the back of her head. She wriggles, shamed and naked as a frog. She is frightened Master will take her *t'ai chi*, fingers the black silk cord of the amulet Kwai Ying gave her. But Master does not seem to see the amulet at all, though it burns upon her breast like a hot coal. Master shimmies the tunic of a black silk *sahm* over her head, sliding the luminous fabric over the changing landscape of her body. She reaches for the trousers, but Master bunches them in his fist. No trousers.

A man is there to see Sing Choy. What they call a highbinder, a man who buys and sells girls like Kwai Ying. Like Sing Choy, too.

"Smart girl," Master says to the man, a weary graybeard with deep wrinkles and one eye. "Pretty girl." Master takes the hem of Sing Choy's black silk tunic, lifts the fabric up, showing her burgeoning breasts. The rest of her, too; curved waist, lanky hipbones, thighs sturdy from walking errands. She is not like boy anymore.

The graybeard pokes her ribs, her hipbones. "Too skinny."

"We fatten her up before you take," Master says. "Two thousand in gold."

"One thousand for this skinny one," says the graybeard. He laughs, a barking sound. Hard fingers, poking everywhere. Poking in places no one has been since Sing Choy stood on the auctioneer's block.

"*Very* pretty," Master says. "*Very* smart. One thousand seven."

"One thousand five," the graybeard says.

Sing Choy says nothing. What can she say? She has no voice in this transaction. She is *mooie jai*. Kwai Ying said *I see no magic for* mooie jai. Oh, Kwai Ying, Sing Choy cries in her heart. Cook has taken Sing Choy's scrimped money, taken all her things. She has nothing. She has no one.

"Done," Master says to the graybeard. To Cook, "Fry shrimp and salmon for this girl. Fry rice and greens, too." To Sing Choy, "You good girl. Make Master happy."

Master and Cook lock her in the pantry that night with bowls of greasy food. Master is so excited at the prospect of one thousand five hundred dollars in gold for his little servant girl who has grown up so beautifully that he forgets to take his whiskey. He probably has whiskey in his own bedroom, anyway. Master is old. Master has been old since Sing Choy came to his house in Year of Golden Tiger. Master came to Tangrenbu before the railroads, before the Silver Kings. Master does not care about a young girl. He has suffered much himself in Tangrenbu though now he has a house, a business, gold, coolies, and *mooie jai*. Master can let Sing Choy go. He can buy another *mooie jai* for two hundred dollars, plus five pounds shrimp.

Sing Choy tries the pantry door again, desperate to escape. She has been sold to the graybeard, she understands this now. Bound where, for what crib? She does not know but can guess. Bartlett Alley, Spofford Alley, Waverly Place? The pantry door is locked up tight. There is no window, no other way out. The clapboard wall abuts Hangah Alley, a mean cobblestoned passage slick with trampled offal and the waste of Tangrenbu.

Desolate, Sing Choy sits back down on her cot, sips a bit of Master's whiskey in the bottle he left behind. Wonders if she should get drunk and forget. Wonders if she should get drunk and kill herself. Kill . . . *They numb you, steal your soul.* Kwai Ying, Sing Choy thinks, I so sorry. I understand at last.

But with what can Sing Choy do this deed?

The knife she took from Kwai Ying, of course. Not a big knife, not a jagged knife. A very small knife but sharp enough to make blood flow from the little blue branches in the stems of a young woman's wrists. Sing Choy finds the knife where she hid it behind a jar of pickled onions in the pantry. A small knife but powerful enough to defy the cruelty of Tangrenbu.

Suddenly Sing Choy hears the clatter of hooves in Hangah Alley, the cacophony of a galloping creature.

Boom!

The horn of the unicorn slices through clapboard and cheap plaster, tearing a gap clear through the wall above her cot. The unicorn's head thrusts through the dusty aperture. Plaster dust spills off the tip of its horn in a fine cloud like her breath on a chill morning. The creature stares at her, snorting. Blind eyes like ivory marbles. Variegated colors—cinnamon red, cerulean blue, gold—stream from its wild mane. The mustache, the horn, the golden scales, stomping hooves of glossy ebony.

A dream? A nightmare? A reality Sing Choy cannot accept?

"What you want?" Sing Choy whispers to the unicorn.

Immortal sisters do not accept dynasty, do not accept patriarchy. Do not accept bound feet or concubines or dictators. Daughters of joy or mooie jai.

Is this the secret voice of the unicorn or only the desperation of her own heart?

Sing Choy does not care anymore. "All right," she says, heedless with despair and a sip of whiskey. Bold girl, haughty and disdainful of death. She tears open her black silk *sahm*. Presents her breast to the unicorn.

The unicorn bows its head at once and pierces her. The horn slides in easily. A tiny prick, then nothing. Sing Choy looks down, expecting the bloodbath Kwai Ying saw of her teacher in the alley. But there is nothing. Nothing but a gentle throbbing like grief ebbing away. Nothing but the unicorn's forehead cradled against her like a suckling baby.

Suddenly the unicorn flings its head up.

Sing Choy gasps as the horn impaling her lifts her from the cot and hurls her through the ragged gap in the wall. *Now* she feels the stab of immortality! Like the flaying of skin, like burning. Is she screaming?

Dizzy, tumbling through the air like a circus acrobat, she slides off the horn and lands astride the unicorn's back. The scaly skin of the creature is as coarse as burlap and freezing cold. Yet in an instant, leaning over the creature's neck and heaving for breath, she regains her balance. Looks up; there, the ragged gap in the wall, the pantry, her cot. Only she is outside now! There is a small, dark thing on the cot, too, a wet red stain on the sheets.

She turns her head, does not want to see.

The unicorn shifts beneath her, backs away from the torn wall of Master's house, and slowly turns. Straddling the unicorn, Sing Choy feels immense power, like the one time she rode on a horse's back and felt the power of the creature beneath her. But this is not the mundane power of Horse. This a power unlike anything Sing Choy has ever felt before.

Riding the unicorn now, not merely straddling, Sing Choy trots out of Hangah Alley. Proud girl; she regards the familiar sights of Tangrenbu like the passing of a dream and feels no regret, no clinging to this place.

The unicorn knows the way. They gallop up Dupont Street, up the long angle of Columbus Avenue to the northern docks where fishermen drink and gamble the night away. Salty sea air smells like life and like death and very much like the Tao. The unicorn gallops past the piers to a place where the land tilts down to the bay. The unicorn picks its way through rocks and debris till it stands upon the shore and paws at the sand with its gleaming ebony hoof.

The bay shifts and sighs beneath the full moon. Sing Choy sees breakers curl like snippets of lace merging into dark velvet. Far off, she can see islands, huddled and black in the roiling bay. Platters of rock, immutable, placed into the deep waters of the world long before humanity ever made its mark.

Dark shapes move beneath the breakers around one of these islands. An ancient face on a leathery neck lifts in a spray of foam. Huge fins flap around this island, a tail as long as a clipper ship whips the waves. A pearlescent mist hovers. Sing Choy sees women gathered on the distant shore. Pale hands wave at her like the wings of moths. Beautiful faces peer anxiously from afar. Voices call. Is Kwai Ying's teacher there? Sing Choy spies her at once, a woman in silk as red as blood with a braid to the backs of her knees.

Sing Choy waves back, heart bobbing with joy. Perhaps she will have teacher now.

The unicorn does not hesitate. It paws at the waves. The unicorn steps upon the water without sinking and takes Sing Choy home.

ERIC LUSTBADER

THE DEVIL ON MYRTLE AVE.

Peter: **Eric Lustbader**, best known to a general audience as the author of bestselling novels that include *Black Heart, The Ninja,* and *Second Skin,* is another one of those people who somehow pack several other people's careers into their résumés. He spent fifteen years in the music industry in various capacities, including working for both Elektra and CBS Records, as well as Cash Box Magazine, and running his own independent production company. Somewhere in there, amazingly, he also taught in the All-Day Neighborhood School Division of the New York City public school system, developing curriculum enrichment for third and fourth grade children. He has also taught preschoolers in special early childhood programs. He lives in Southampton, New York, with his wife Victoria, who works for the Nature Conservancy.

Janet: When Victoria Schochet—onetime editor-in-chief of science fiction and fantasy at Berkley Books—announced some years ago that she was marrying someone talented, handsome, and famous, I was impressed. Little did I imagine that it was *the* Eric Lustbader, or that down the road I would be asking him to write a story for this volume. The story is a standout. It will, I believe, surprise many and shock others with its theme. As for working with you, Mr. Lustbader, Suh, I can hardly wait for the next project.

The Devil on Myrtle Ave.

IT WAS RAINING CHILL NEEDLES THAT KNIFED TO THE bone when Garland Montgomery found his mother. She was curled up like a baby on the threadbare rug of their Bedford-Stuyvesant housing project apartment. She was cool and still and there was a ball of bubbly froth at the corner of her mouth. The used syringe lay, milky and evil as whitey's face, at her side.

Garbage was heaped helter-skelter every which way and the room had that too familiar smell of old grease, rotting food, and rank human flesh. In the weeks since he had been here rats had begun to rustle in the shadows.

Without a second thought, Garland turned and ran out of the filthy apartment, down the bare concrete stairs, almost tripping over old Mrs. Blank, who slept on the landing between the second and third floors, wrapped in grease-smeared newspaper. Mrs. Blank was nuts, raving about little pink men from Mars when she was awake, so no one paid her any mind. They were sure she was dreaming of whitey. Her breath smelled of lighter fluid.

Out in the rain, Garland ran as fast as he could. He

slipped in a gutter filled with all kinds of shit and slammed hip-first into a wildly braking car. Lights flared and an angry horn blared. Then he had vaulted across the car's hood, crossed Myrtle Ave. as a truck coming the other way veered away from him, and was racing around the corner. He ducked down a side street and into a back alley, filled with vermin and not much else.

Garland, who was fifteen, had seen his brother shot dead in this alley, because he was trying to sell a bag of cocaine. Garland had two other family members he knew about. His oldest brother, Derryl, was in Attica, in prison for three counts of manslaughter. His sister, who was seventeen, lived in Pittsburgh with two squally children and a common-law husband who most nights beat her. Garland, who was the man of the family, had wanted to go down to Pittsburgh and pistol-whip the man into shape but his sister had said no. "My life ain't so bad," she had said to him by phone. "At least he ain't run out on me."

A bitter comment about a father neither had known.

Garland found the building, reached up through the pouring rain for the iron fire escape ladder. He scrabbled upward, a familiar journey, until he reached the roof. He broke through the skylight without much trouble, cut through the wire mesh beneath the glass with cutters, and dropped to the floor. He was in Dr. Gupta's office, the Indian, who he and his pals from the Bloods made fun of every time they saw him. The doc and his fat wife lived in the two-bedroom on the ground floor. The place always stank from curry and weird spices.

The building was important because it was in a kind

of no-man's land between Blood turf and Crip turf. The two gangs were mortal enemies, and there wasn't a man alive Garland hated worse than Levar, the rival gang's leader. He'd bludgeoned to death two Bloods single-handed. For Blood or Crip, coming here was an act of heroism.

Garland knew Dr. Gupta's office like the palm of his hand; it'd been here he'd made his initiation into the gang, breaking and entering, stealing some shit—opium and morphine—to prove his feat. In celebration they'd pierced the soft bony stuff between his nostrils and stuck through a thick silver chain. He'd been nine; three weeks before, he'd been given a gun by his mother, who'd wanted him to have protection in a neighborhood filled with danger and death.

He was strapped; he never went outside without his gun. He touched it now, then fingered the unicorn charm that hung from his nose chain like it was a sacred talis-man that could keep away harm. Within minutes, he had gathered up the things he needed. Then he vaulted back up through the skylight, ran across the rooftop, and climbed back down the fire escape.

He made his way through the courtyards of the pro-ject. Looking at the graffiti-covered brick buildings, you'd never know they hid a whole other world inside. Old Mrs. Blank heard him coming full tilt and pulled her head into her shoulders like a tortoise. More than once there'd been gunplay in her stairwell.

Back at his mother's apartment, he knelt down beside her. She hadn't moved. Water dripped from him onto the carpet as he got to work. He ripped the paper off the disposable syringe, broke out the vial of epinephrine, drew it into the syringe. He turned his mother onto her back, pounded her rib cage with his fist, slapped her cheeks hard. Her head lolled loosely from side to side but she didn't open her eyes.

He felt for the soft places between her ribs, counted, was so nervous he had to start all over again. Counted, *three, four, there!,* got the spot where her heart was, and jabbed the needle through the skin. He moved the needle very slowly between her ribs. He'd once seen this done with a sharp jab and the needle had broken off as it struck bone.

When he was into the spongy layer beneath, he drove home the needle. He made the injection. Had he got the heart? His mother's eyelids fluttered and he heard a rattling in her chest. He put his ear against her breast, heard her heartbeat thundering like a runaway chopper. It was much too fast, out of control.

He jumped up. In the kitchen, he took down a canister of salt, mixed it with warm water until the crystals were dissolved. He poured half the liquid into another glass, filled the syringe with the salt water, making sure there were no crystals in the syringe. Then he opened the freezer, put a tray of old, smelly ice under his arm.

He found the vein into which she'd injected the heroin and pumped in the salt water. Then he jammed the ice against her crotch. Her eyes flew open.

"Mama?" he said, shaking her. "Mama?"

She stared wide-eyed at him. Did she know who he was? Her mouth gaped open, foam dripping onto her chin.

"Mama, yo' gotsta get on yo' feet."

A sudden seizure gripped her and she began to quiver.

"Mama!" Garland cried, holding her tighter.

Another spasm made her teeth clack together, and her breathing became labored, ragged. She pulled a shuddering breath and never released it.

Garland began to cry. He knew it was definitely not the kind of thing the man of the family did. But he was also a kid, and he was so scared. He wiped the chain through his nose with the back of a hand made clumsy by fear. The silver unicorn that hung from it jingled lightly. For a long time, he couldn't move. He stared into his mother's wasted face. Just thirty-three and she looked as old as Mrs. Blank. That seemed so sad, he began to cry all over again.

He knew she was dead, but he was reluctant to leave her. He clung to whatever was left of her warmth and thought of how she had sung him to sleep when he'd been young. He tried to remember the song she sang to him, but he couldn't. It was gone with her. All he could remember was the moment she had given him the gun.

He had thought that being strapped made him a man, but the members of his gang had wasted no time telling him uh-uh, he'd have to do much more than just carry a gun. He'd have to shoot someone before he'd be a man in their eyes. He'd have to prove his courage by being master of life and death. This he had done most willingly during a gang scuffle, firing off two shots and wounding two of the enemy. He'd been cut off from the rest of the

Bloods, all alone without backup. From that incident, he'd gotten the street name of Unicorn.

But he'd never killed anyone.

On the morning after his mother's OD, Garland lay in wait on Myrtle Ave. It was a wide street used by maybe a hundred trucks a day servicing the independent supermarkets and corner groceries from Fort Greene to Bushwick. Because they weren't part of big chain stores, they had to pay cash for their deliveries. That meant more often than not the truck drivers were holding big bucks. But not always. One of Garland's gang homeboys had shot a driver in the neck for twenty-three dollars. It seemed stupid, except that his status in the gang had skyrocketed.

The trucks had certain set routes and schedules, so they were easy marks. All the gang members had memorized the routes and times of deliveries. Garland turned his head as a black Camaro jounced down the street spewing rap from its speakers. It paused for a light, then cruised through it, leaving a cloud of blue exhaust in its wake. Just down the block from where Garland crouched in hard morning shadow, colored plastic pennants cracked in the stiff breeze. They were strung from nylon lines in front of the Associated market and wound around a lamppost. A nasty-looking yellow mutt with a damaged leg limped in the gutter, rooting for breakfast. Old Moses, a grizzled black man in a tattered mackinaw, was doing his thing, selling hijacked gloves out of a Dumpster. But he was chilled; he wouldn't make a move. As Garland waited for the potato chip truck to come by, his mind was completely blank. It was like he didn't want to think.

A blue-and-white squad car from the 79th Precinct cruised by and Garland smiled. The cops were under mounting pressure from the papers and TV to do something about the hijackings and killings along Myrtle Ave. Too bad the cops didn't have a fucking clue.

The potato chip truck swung into view, slowing as it passed Garland. It stopped in front of the market, the big beefy white man swung down from the cab and rolled up the back door. Garland watched him as he began to unload the cartons of potato chips. The time to take him was after he'd made delivery, and, his pocket bulging with bills, he was just getting back into the truck.

Garland was patient, his mind filled with nothing, a red nothing that took his breath away. He was waiting to hear again that song his mother used to sing to him, but all he heard was an ambulance siren on Lafayette Ave. It screeched against his eardrums. The yellow mutt began to bark at Old Moses selling his stolen gloves.

Old Moses kicked at it. The mutt yelped in pain and loped clumsily away. Garland tried not to think of his three-month-old son, whom he'd never seen. His name was Marcus; Garland never even saw the mother, a thin, inky dark girl he'd fucked in the back of a friend's car. Once. It meant nothing to Garland, just another way to get off. The last thing he needed was to be burdened with a girl he barely knew and a squally kid. He'd be damned if he was going to end up like his sister.

Cool, Garland thought. Let's be cool.

In front of the Associated, the driver was wheeling his loaded-down hand truck across the sidewalk and into the market. He was inside maybe ten minutes, then he came out, more nervous now. He rushed back to his truck, stowed the hand truck, banged down the rolling back door. As he went around the far side of the truck to the cab, Garland made his move.

By the time the driver slid behind the wheel, Garland, clinging with one hand to the outside of the curbside door, had his gun pointed into the cab.

"Oh, shit," the driver said. He was one of those big, flush-faced Irishmen, who drank too much and then went out looking for trouble.

"Here be trouble," Garland said.

The driver's hands were on the wheel. Garland was thrilled to see them trembling.

"I don't want none of that," the driver said. He was trying, unsuccessfully, to ignore the gun pointed at him. "Go ahead. Take my money."

His words might have been Russian for all Garland made sense of them. His mind, so recently drained of everything, was now seething with a fury he could not name. He saw his mother, dying. He saw himself helpless to save her. Helpless because he was not yet a man, for all the mannish pretense of his young life. Deprived of youth, he yearned for something beyond it, an adulthood for which he was wholly unprepared. But his thought was this: If he had been a man, he could have saved his mother. The red rage gathered around this thought and, given form, demanded an immediate and explosive outlet.

Garland stared hard into whitey's eyes and pulled the trigger.

When Tony Valenti heard the gunshot, he was on Myrtle Ave. just east of Bedford. He stamped on the accelerator of the truck and ran a red light. His pulse was running hard and it felt as if his heart was sitting in his throat. He wanted to gag with the apprehension.

He saw Jack Halloran's truck in front of the Associated. Halloran was known as the potato chip man, just as Tony was the pie man. The drivers' real names weren't used on the street. A small group was gathering while a grizzled old man scrabbled through a Dumpster, his back to the commotion. Tony hit the brakes, swerving to the curb. He grabbed the baseball bat he kept in the cab in case of trouble and, without turning off the ignition, banged the door open and swung down into the street.

Vehicles were stopping or slowing down, their occupants rubbernecking as they crept past Halloran's truck. Tony ran through the thickening crowd. He knew Halloran well. Besides working for the same wholesaler, they were friends. They had dinner once a week, their wives exchanged gossip, their kids played together. They'd even spent this Thanksgiving together.

He reached the cab and, for an instant, hesitated. Then he climbed up and stared in.

"Oh, Christ," he whispered, and ducked his head back out. He closed his eyes but he could not block out the inside of the cab, splattered with blood and bits of bone and brain. Jack Halloran's face had been blown away. Tony felt a pressure in his chest. Maybe he was having a heart attack. His face was flushed and his hands shook as he held on to the outside of the truck.

"Someone call the police?" he asked.

He felt a firm hand on his shoulder, and a voice say, "The police're here, bud."

He turned to see a pair of uniforms, their squad car behind them, lights flashing. A black and white duo, very PC, he thought.

"Yeah?" he said, addressing the white one. "Where were you when my buddy got his face shot off?"

"Easy does it," the white cop said. Then, "Would you mind standing down from there?" When Tony had complied, the black one, eyeing the baseball bat he gripped with white knuckles, said, "You better put that weapon away before someone confiscates it."

"This?" Tony hefted the bat. "A Christmas present for my boy. He's in Little League."

"You witness the shooting?" the white cop broke in.

"No," Tony said. "I heard the shot, though. I was just passing Bedford."

The white cop nodded. "Well, stick around, anyway."

The black cop, on his way past Tony, said, "And all you could afford was a used one? Tsk, tsk."

Tony went back to his truck, stowed the bat in its spot behind the seat. As he did so, he watched the black cop systematically going through the crowd, looking for witnesses. Tony saw him saunter over to the grizzled man beside the Dumpster. Even then, the old guy kept his back to the street and Jack Halloran's truck. The black cop kept asking questions and the old guy kept shaking his head from side to side, no, I ain't seen nothing. But Tony suspected that he was lying. Something in the way he refused to turn around, look at the scene of the murder, like he'd already seen more than he wanted of it.

Tony waited patiently until the black cop got around to him, was reassured that Tony did not, in fact, witness the shooting.

"What is it?" The black cop stared right into Tony's eyes. "Do I smell bad or something?"

"What?"

"You got this look on your face, like you smell a bad smell, you know, like rotten meat."

"Hey, just a minute," Tony said, trying to recover. He had, in fact, been wanting to speak to the white cop, who he assumed was in charge. "My buddy's been shot to death on a route we both use. I gotta right to be upset."

The black cop told him he could go.

Tony watched him walk away, then said, "That old guy at the Dumpster, he see anything?"

The black cop paused, folding away his notepad. "What's it to you?"

"Jack Halloran was a pal," Tony said. "We had Thanksgiving together not two weeks ago."

The black cop looked at him deadpan. "That a fact?" He glanced over at the grizzled old man, bent over his Dumpster. "Nah, he's so out of it I doubt he remembers what day it is. He's useless."

Tony nodded. "Listen. There's a photo in Jack's cab. Him and the family. I'd like to take it back to his wife."

The black cop sighed. "I understand, Mr. Valenti, but right now it's evidence. Soon as it's dusted for prints and we can release it, it'll go to the next of kin."

"But that's just it," Jack protested. "I don't want it to come to her from the police. It'll kill her."

"Sorry. It's regs."

Tony took a step toward the black cop. "Maybe I should speak to your partner."

The black cop gave him a dark and menacing look. "Take my advice, Mr. Valenti. Go home, get on with your work, whatever. But leave the scene now."

It was after six when Tony returned to the warehouse. Because of the incident, he'd been late delivering his packaged pies and cakes. Also, because he'd taken time out to call Katie to reassure her he was all right and to tell her to get over to Eileen Halloran's and give her what moral support she could. God knew Eileen was going to need it.

Tony's boss was waiting for him. "I want to see you in my office," he said as he turned his back. "Now."

Mr. Tolan's office was one of those old dusty spaces marked out by metal walls and frosted glass. Tony guessed it must date back to the turn of the century. Inside, it didn't look as if much had changed since it was built. Ancient file cabinets lined the walls, there were two metal and vinyl chairs and a chewed wooden desk on bare wooden floorboards so worn they had lost all color.

"So," Tolan said as soon as Tony walked in, "I heard about Halloran."

"Yeah." Tony shook his head sadly. "A helluva thing."

Tolan, balding, burly, in shirtsleeves and toting a massive cigar, advanced on him. "I also heard from the cops that you're toting a baseball bat."

That black bastard ratted me out, Tony thought. "Well, whadaya expect, Mr. Tolan, it's a fuckin' jungle out there. Look what happened today."

"Listen to me, Valenti. You chose this job, it didn't choose you. The situation on Myrtle Ave., it's part of the job, nothing more. What makes you different than the other drivers on my payroll? You know the rules. You're expressly forbidden to carry weapons of any kind. And if you want to keep your job, you'll get rid of yours immediately."

"But what about Jack Halloran? For Christ's sake, look what happened to him. If he'd been armed—"

Tolan shouted down Tony's protest. "What happened to Halloran is tragic, no doubt. But it's over. The police'll do their job—"

"The police, that's a laugh," Tony grunted. "The police can't catch these gangsta kids. They melt into the jungle of the projects and the police come up with zilch every time. One of these days they're just gonna forget about trying."

Tolan went back behind his desk. "None of this is your problem, Valenti. You gotta forget about Halloran, forget your anger. You gotta think about yourself—and all the other drivers who work here." Tolan shook his head. "Look, I explain this to every rookie who signs on. You been here, what, twelve years? By now you know it as well as I do. I got a whole company to think about. My guys start holding and what happens? They get carried away, bust up some citizen by mistake, and who gets sued? This company gets sued, that's who. With liability insurance what it is I can't afford that, Valenti. None of us can. That kinda suit would put this place out of business, then where would you an' all the other drivers be?"

Tony clocked out and went home. But he couldn't forget Jack Halloran and he couldn't let go of his anger. He came from a poor background. His father had worked hard—fourteen hours a day to feed his family and put them through school. College for all of them, had been his motto. Whether they had wanted it or not. Tony hadn't, had hated all four years of it. In fact, he'd spent most of his senior year working in a gas station, which was where he developed his love for big engines and trucks.

Tony had never told his father; the old man would never have understood. But that basic gulf between him and his children hadn't stopped Tony's father from loving them, providing for them. He'd been an honest man, a man who'd lived by his ideals. And he'd passed those ideals down to his sons and daughters. Tony did not believe in environment excusing behavior. His father had taught him to fight against adversity, not use it as an excuse to sin.

Katie and the kids were over at the Hallorans'. She had left him dinner in the oven but he had no appetite. He nearly choked on a beer, poured himself some whiskey instead. That didn't taste good, either, but at least he could get it down. He had another. Then, he climbed the stairs and went into his kids' bedroom. He remembered waking up at night to the sound of his father's heavy boots striking the floorboards downstairs and, secure, drifting back off to sleep. As a father now, he recalled so many nights tiptoeing upstairs to look in on the peacefully sleeping faces of his children and feeling a warm glow inside knowing that they, too, slept in the security of his tread.

On Amanda's side of the room, he picked up her stuffed animals one after another: a penguin, a panda, a manatee, a unicorn with a rainbow-colored horn, three different kinds of bears. Each one had a place in the pantheon of her beloved pals. When she was frightened at night she'd call out to him and he'd hear her no matter how deeply he was sleeping. He'd pad in and, without her seeing, pick one animal in the dark, animating it. Pitching his voice high, he'd speak to her through it. Often, he'd tell her stories of his own father's life or fantasies he'd make up on the spot. Amanda loved them all. She never giggled, always took the playacting seriously, and soon she'd calm down, snuggling back down under the covers. Then, he'd put the animal in her arms, her eyes would close, and she would sleep.

On Kevin's side of the room, he saw the book of Maxfield Parrish paintings he'd given to his son last Christmas. On his day off, he'd trekked all the way to the Metropolitan Museum of Art in Manhattan to get it. He'd only meant to run into the gift shop but, dazzled, he'd drifted through the galleries the whole day. Picking up the book, he leafed from one gorgeously tinted page to another. If only the world were full of light and peace like the scenes Parrish painted. But it wasn't.

He had become afraid, not for himself or for Katie so much as for the kids. What kind of world had he brought them into? And if one of them should be killed, what then? This is what Jack's murder had shown him: He'd be unable to go on. Guilt burned him like inhaled acid. At the moment of Jack Halloran's death everything changed for him. He'd had enough of the chaos of his neighborhood. He was bound and determined to bring some form of order to a world gone completely mad. It was the best—the only lasting—legacy he could give his children.

He put the picture book on Kevin's bed, stroking it one last time. Then, he got up and, without looking back, went into the master bedroom. From the top shelf of his closet behind his winter boots, he dragged out an olive WW II metal ammo case. He took out the .38 and loaded it. Then he carefully put the case back, put the gun inside his waistband and zipped his plaid jacket over it.

The Hallorans' smelled of macaroni and gravy; Katie's doing, no doubt. He remembered Thanksgiving dinner. The old table around which they had joyously sung songs was draped in black crepe. An Irish ballad was playing on the stereo. He made the rounds. Eileen cried on his shoulder, he gave a pep talk to Jack's thirteen-year-old son, he felt tongue-tied around Jack's daughter, whom Katie held in her arms, and he got thoroughly depressed.

He talked to Amanda first, doing his best to reassure her, but he could see she was frightened.

"Willie was a little upset when we left the house," she whispered with her head in the crook of his shoulder. Willie was her stuffed penguin. "I didn't know whether to leave him but I didn't want to bring him here." No, she wanted to seem more grown-up than that.

"Is Willie scared?" Tony asked her.

She nodded. "A little."

"I'll speak to Willie." He snuggled her in his arms. "He's got nothing to worry about." He turned her face so she could see him smiling at her. "He'll believe me, won't he?"

She nodded, and an answering smile spread over her face. She threw her arms around him and his heart came close to breaking. He held her tight, feeling more certain than ever that his children's future was all that mattered.

"How you doin', buddy?" he asked Kevin when he'd let his daughter run off to the kitchen for some more cookies and milk.

"Okay, I guess."

Tony looked deep into his son's eyes and saw what he didn't want to see. "It's getting a little freaky out there, that what you're thinking?"

Kevin shrugged, not meeting his gaze.

"I mean, last week we were having Thanksgiving with Jack and now he's gone." He put his elbows on his knees, leaning forward. "I think that's kind of scary."

Kevin's gaze slid toward him. "You do?"

"Listen, son, any time someone we know dies it reminds us that bad things can happen." He struggled to think rationally, to keep his children secure in mind, body, and soul. The words came so easily he had no time to dwell on their hollow ring. "It's part of life, and even if we can't understand it, we have to accept it."

"Mom said she doesn't want us out after dark for two weeks."

"She's right. Because of what happened to Jack, we have to be extra careful for a while." He ruffled Kevin's hair. "But, I'll tell ya what, we do that and everything'll be cool."

Kevin seemed to mull this over for some time. At last, he said, "I heard it was you who found Uncle Jack."

"We had the same route, y'know, so . . ." His voice

trailed off. He knew he had to be careful here, say something Kevin would understand. "I held his hand."

Kevin nodded. "I would have liked to say good-bye to Uncle Jack."

Tony put his arm around his son's shoulders. "Yeah. Me, too."

He watched as Kevin got up and went over to the TV to watch *Ren & Stimpy*.

Then he got up and dragged Katie away from Eileen Halloran's mother. Because of worry, his wife's dark eyes seemed more deep-set than usual. Tony thought she looked very sexy.

"Come on," he whispered in her ear. "Let's get outta here."

She shook her head. "No way. I can't leave Eileen yet."

He put his arm around her and rolled his eyes heavenward.

Katie almost burst out laughing and her face got red. "Are you nuts? *Here? Now?*"

"Sure," he whispered. "Why not?" He was already leading her through the crowded living room and up the stairs to the deserted second floor.

"Sweetheart, this isn't the time—"

From just behind her on the stairs he reached around to cup one breast. "This is *just* the time."

Katie hesitated. She did not yet understand what finding Jack had done to her husband; she suspected he didn't know himself, but she knew he needed to find out. She turned back to stare into his eyes, and she saw a pain there that struck her through the heart. He needed to heal, and right now he needed her. She put her hand over his, squeezing her breast harder. She could not refuse him. Besides, there was something needful in it for her as well. So close to death she could feel its cold breath on her cheek, there was a kind of pressure from deep inside, an urge to prove that she and Tony were still very much alive.

When Tony felt her lean back against him, he scooped her up in his arms like he used to do when they were just married. He'd carry her everywhere through their tiny apartment. They'd both be naked and laughing like loons until the heat of their bodies impelled them into another round of feverish lovemaking.

As he carried her into a back bathroom and kicked the door closed, Tony felt feverish. It had begun when he'd walked into the Hallorans' with the .38 digging into his hipbone and had seen his wife across the bustling room. She'd looked as radiant as a rose in full bloom, her dark eyes dancing beneath the solemnity of her expression. In their long relationship Katie had always been the optimist; it was that eternal sunshine that got him through his darkest days of unemployment, bad jobs, and worse hours.

He needed a full dose of her now.

Without releasing her, he set her down on the edge of the porcelain sink. They kissed as long and passionately as they had in their teens. Tony felt familiar hands at his belt, and had to quickly take over so the .38 wouldn't go crashing to the tiles.

"Do you think we'll go to hell for this?" Katie's lips took on this bruised and bee-stung look when they'd been kissing. The sight inflamed him all the more.

"We're husband and wife," he said as he pushed up her dress. "We can do what we like."

"But isn't it a sin? This is a time of mourning. It's disrespectful of the dead." Her eyes fluttered closed as his hands closed over her breasts.

"There's no disrespect." Tony licked her ear as he entered her with a powerful rush. "It's life, baby. It's life. And there's no sin in that."

Afterward, they hung onto one another, even though the position was vaguely uncomfortable. It was like that moment when you awake, remembering a good dream, Tony thought, and you don't want to move, don't want to open your eyes for fear that the real world will come crashing in.

At last, Katie gave a little shudder, as if against a chill wind. She looked into his face as she smoothed down her dress as best she could, and he could see tears standing in the corners of her eyes. "I know I have to be strong," she said, "but I'm scared." She gripped him suddenly. "I'm scared for you."

"There's no need," Tony said. "I'll never end up like Jack."

Katie searched his face. "How do the kids seem to you?"

"They'll be fine," he reassured her as he dressed. "Don't worry."

He stepped back so Katie could hop down off the sink. She said, "There's got to be a better way."

"When you find it, let me know."

She turned around, examined herself in the mirror.

"Look at me. Everyone will know what we were up to."

"Not everyone," he chuckled, kissing her neck. "Not the kids."

She began to wash up. "Maybe we could move."

He laughed mirthlessly. "Yeah? Like where?"

She looked at him in the mirror. "Florida, maybe." Her voice sounded hopeful. "Marjorie—"

"No offense to your cousin, hon, but she's not the most realistic person in the world. Look who she married, some used car hustler, who's been indicted twice. Besides, what could I do down there, be his assistant?"

She patted her face dry with a *Mighty Morphin Power Rangers* towel. "Drive a truck, same as you do here."

"But, hon, here's where I have a job. It may not be much, but it's all we've got. I've got seniority, which means I don't have to be driving nights or weekends. We got pretty good benefits. The kids're comfortable in school. They got their friends. Besides, we haven't got anything to fall back on. What if I can't find a job for three months, six, a year?" He shook his head. "Not to mention, all our close family's here. You want to leave them?"

Katie had no answer for that. Here's where they had made their life, and for good or ill, here's where they stayed.

Together, they went quietly down the stairs into the riot of the house. On the TV, *Ren & Stimpy* had been replaced by nonstop music videos.

He squeezed her hand. "Hon, I've got to get outta here for a while."

Katie nodded. Obviously, he needed more than her body to get his head straightened out. That was okay; she'd expected as much. But as she walked him to the front door, she was filled with a deep sadness she could not explain. She was struck dumb, tears rolling down her cheeks. There was so much she wanted to say, but she could not find the right words.

"It's going to be all right," he said. They both had to believe that now, or they'd have nothing. But in his heart of hearts he knew that his version of all right wasn't anything like hers. He moved as gently as he could out of her arms, and out the door into the cold, clear night.

Tony followed the sound of rap music as if it were a glowing ribbon. It led him inevitably to Myrtle Ave. A bunch of black kids seemed to be having an impromptu party outside the Associated. It looked to Tony as if it were on the spot where Jack Halloran had been shot to death. Rage gripped him anew and he fingered the .38 hidden beneath his coat.

He forced himself to look away. To rap's hard-edged beat he saw the grizzled old man dozing at his post by the Dumpster. Tony knew he'd find him here. People like that marked out their territory and rarely left it.

Like all street people, he smelled. Tony tried not to concentrate on it. The man had his back to Tony until the very last minute. Then, as Tony approached, he whirled around, an unfortunate move, since it sent out a wave of garlic, alcohol, and rank body odor that made Tony dizzy.

"Hey, old man," Tony said.

"Hey, whitey." The old man laughed. "This here's my turf. Get yo' white ass outta my face."

"Now listen—"

"No, *yo'* listen." The old man whipped the blade of a long knife at Tony's throat. "Yo' don't count fo' shit here, motherfucker. So why don't yo' split 'fore yo' gets hurt."

Tony felt the pulse pounding in his temples as if it were screaming to get out. "My pal got shot to death today." His voice was none too steady. "Just over there, where the party's going on."

"Doan' mean shit t' me." The old man pushed the blade an inch forward. "Doan' change nuthin' 'tween yo an' me."

"You saw who did it, didn't you, old man?"

It was a question the grizzled man wasn't expecting. For just an instant Tony saw the light of a mute answer in his eyes. Then a kind of curtain came down. The old man spat. He had good aim for an alky; he hit the toe of Tony's workboot. "I didn't see shit. I'se a businessman; tha's all I see. Business."

"No." Tony shook his head. "You saw the murder. You know who pulled the trigger." He took a lurching step back. "Well, I got a message for you to deliver to this rat punk. You tell 'im Tony's lookin' for 'im." Very carefully, he reached inside his coat, drew out the gun. He held it at his side, the muzzle pointing at the pavement.

The old alky's eyes opened wide at the sight of the weapon. "What yo' got in mind's plain crazy," he said. "Sho' as I'm standin' here it'll get yo' dead."

Tony ignored him. He was playing to the balcony: the group of partying kids in front of the Associated. More than one of them must know who had shot Jack in cold blood. "You tell the murdering bastard that he won't get away with it. Enough's enough. When he gunned Jack Halloran down he stepped over the line. He's a dead man. You tell 'im that, old man. You fuckin' tell 'im that."

Then he turned and melted into the shadows of the shuttered stores lining Myrtle Ave.

For a time, the grizzled old man did nothing. He put away the knife and mumbled something to himself. He rooted through his Dumpster, still talking to himself. He withdrew a pint bottle of cheap booze, finished it off. Then he grabbed out a bottle of electric blue after-shave and drank that as well. He closed his eyes as his whole body shuddered. If Tony didn't have the red rage running through him, he might have felt a twinge of pity for the alky. But he didn't have time for that now; not with Jack Halloran's bloody, unrecognizable face looming up on the stage of his mind.

After what seemed a long time, one of the kids detached himself from the dancing, drinking crowd, and sidled up to the grizzled old alky. He looked about fourteen. Everything he wore was grossly oversized; his sneakers looked like they were size twelves. His black face shone in the glare of the streetlight and Tony could see his features were still unformed. The kid shuffled anxiously from one foot to another while he screamed at the old alky. Tony thought he heard the word "unicorn." Then the kid's face got mean and he barked something, drawing a gun. The old alky's face went white and he began to babble, pointing and gesticulating wildly. Now Tony did feel for him; adults in this neighborhood were at the mercy of teenagers with guns, knives, and the kind of unreasoning savagery that put them beyond any hope of redemption. What they lacked was any sense of conscience; their amorality was harder to penetrate than tank armor.

At length, the kid nodded, then with a casual flick of his wrist, sent the old alky staggering back against the Dumpster. With a contemptuous look on his face, the kid waved the gun threateningly in the old alky's bloodied face before he began to lope away.

Keeping to the deepest shadows, Tony followed him. His moment of compassion for the old alky vanished. Now he gave him not a thought; his mind was filled with the image of Jack Halloran's mutilated head.

Not surprisingly, the kid led Tony into the projects. The Marcy complex stretched from Myrtle Ave. to Flushing Ave., a warren of shadowed brickwork that housed a whole other world. Tony felt a moment's hesitation. He'd heard so many horror stories about what went on here at night—had read about them in the safety of his own home over coffee and a Drake's cake—he knew he was entering uncharted waters. Terrible danger lurked here, but so did Jack Halloran's killer.

As he pressed on, sprinting from shadow to shadow, he felt Jack's presence at his side, urging him on, confirming that what he was doing was right. Justice had many faces, Tony thought. Who was to say which one would show itself tonight?

A chill wind dragged soot and grit up from the concrete sidewalk, swirling it like black sleet as Tony crossed a courtyard eerily deserted. He felt a twinge of nervousness now; he was totally vulnerable, a white face in a black continent where everyone was either strapped or stoned or both. That made each person he saw a potential paranoid. He hurried past stringy plane trees eking out a mean existence from small squares of packed earth piled with candy wrappers, broken bottles, used syringes, and dogshit. Gangsta rap music drifted from a window, then was abruptly cut short. A gap between buildings revealed a group of kids smoking, hanging out. There were distant sounds of scuffling, and one brief shout. A car peeled out, roaring down Myrtle Ave.

The outer door of the building the kid went into should have been locked, but the lock was broken. Tony pushed through the door, watched the elevator rise to the fifth floor. He waited. It sat on five until he pressed the button. It returned to the lobby empty. He took it up.

He thought of Jack Halloran, the potato chip man, and the family he'd left behind: a son whose life would be scarred forever, a daughter who might never remember who her father was. Again, he felt a wave of red rage sweep over him. He reached for his .38 as the door opened on five.

He just had time to register a young black face with eyes that seemed to hold no emotion.

"Excuse me, I'm getting off—"

He saw the charm hanging from the thick nose chain and he remembered the old alky's word he'd overheard. *Unicorn*. This was the kid who'd blown Jack's face off. Then he saw the gun the kid was pointing at him.

"You sonuvab—" Tony began.

The explosion rocked him back, slamming him against the rear wall of the elevator. He felt no pain, nothing. His numb legs gave out and he slid down. He smelled something sickly sweet: his own blood.

"I hear yo' lookin' fo' me. Well, heah I is." The kid pointed the gun at him. There was a roaring in Tony's ears. "So long, sucka."

A second explosion sent Tony rocketing down a black hole so deep it seemed to have no end.

Tony opened his eyes. Blood pumped out of two holes in his chest. *Whoosh, whoosh*, rhythmic as a metronome. Tony, disembodied, looked down at his own bloody form and saw it in two separate places at once. Terrified, he looked around. In one scene, he could see himself with Katie beside him. His vantage point was dizzying, as if he were a fly on the ceiling of a green and stainless steel room. She was crying. Two—no four— people hovered over his body, gloved hands manipulating instruments. With a start, he realized they were doctors, that he was looking at a scene in a hospital emergency room. He saw a nurse lead Katie out. The doctors got back to work, operating on him.

Sickened, his mind half-numb, he turned his gaze in the direction of the second scene. There, he saw something entirely different.

He saw himself in a pastoral setting—Prospect Park, he thought at first. But no, it couldn't be, there were no familiar landmarks and all the trees were green in the lushness of midsummer. But this was December! What was he looking at?

As he watched, he felt himself drawing closer. This was the discorporate self. The self that saw and thought and moved, as opposed to the body of flesh lying in a Brooklyn hospital emergency room. And, as he stretched out his arms and looked down the length of his body—yes, he had a body—he saw himself as he had been when he was twenty-one, in his senior year of college.

He could feel a soft breeze on his face, hear the rustling of the ancient oaks that girdled the sun-dappled glade. High above the canopies of the trees, puffy white clouds drifted lazily in a luminescent blue sky right out of Kevin's Maxfield Parrish picture book. This scene reminded him of that kind of perfect, idealized world. Except for one thing. Though there was plenty of daylight, Tony could not find its source. No sun or any celestial body for that matter was visible. And the light itself was curiously flat, shadowless, as if it emanated from all directions at once.

Returning his gaze to the glade, Tony became aware of a great shadow where no shadows should exist. It dominated the far end of the glade, jumping and flickering like a flame in the wind, waxing and waning, its outline blurred and indistinct. It seemed humanoid, but its head was wreathed by a pair of what appeared to be huge curling horns, like a broken crown of thorns. It was large, almost as tall as the oaks. Before it, was a white horse. It was the most beautiful creature Tony had ever seen. The sheen of its snow-white coat was so pure it almost made him weep. This astonishing creature knelt in front of the shadow as if in obeisance.

Now, as Tony drew closer still, he could see that the great shadow had placed the knuckles of one hand hard against the horse's forehead, as if it were pressing the horse downward. Then, as if alerted that they were not alone, the horned head turned in Tony's direction. Perhaps the shadow spoke, because all the oak leaves began to tremble at once. The knuckles were removed from the horse and Tony saw that the animal had a spiral horn growing out of the center of its forehead. This horn was as black as pitch and gleamed and refracted light as if it were a faceted jewel just polished.

The shadow came toward him. As it did so, it became smaller, more clearly seen with each stride it took. It stood before him, a man, old but robust, with flowing white hair, a full beard, and apple-pink cheeks. The mouth was a cupid's bow and the eyes that fixed him in their gaze were ice blue.

"Do I know you?" the silver-haired man said.

"Who are you?" Tony asked. "God?"

"Close," the man said. "But not close enough."

Tony blinked. The scene seemed to have changed a bit. Behind where the unicorn knelt was a split-log fence and, to one side, a clapboard house with a wood-shingle roof. A wide wraparound porch held rough-cut cypress furniture with the bark still on. A shingle by the porch steps read: FRANCHISER. Tony sniffed. The tangy, luscious scent of barbecue was in the air. He'd once driven down to Florida with some buddies, what was it, twenty years ago. Along the way, they'd stopped in Georgia, turning off I-95 to find some mouthwatering pulled pork smothered in hot sauce.

"Look familiar, huh?" the man said, only he was no longer a man with flowing white hair, but a fat black woman with a red-and-white bandanna tied around her forehead, a greasy apron over a cheap calico dress.

"I met you," Tony said. "A long time ago."

He was remembering how during spring break in their senior year of college he and his buddies had trussed her up, put the pig's snout they'd carved off the smoked beast into her mouth while they stuffed their faces with its rich, fragrant meat. Then, laughing like loons, they'd painted, "Howdy, Nigger," across the front of her apron and, hopping into their car, had sped all the way across the border to Florida. Except for gassing up, they didn't stop until they reached Ft. Lauderdale. Even when Pete got sick from eating too much pulled pig, they hadn't slackened speed. Laughing, they'd rolled down the window and stuck Pete's head outside while he barfed his lungs out. But they hadn't meant anything by what they'd done; it was just a stupid prank. No one got hurt, not really. But Tony, seeing the fat black woman reincarnated in front of him, remembered the sinking feeling in his gut as he'd watched his buddy writing that phrase. *Howdy, Nigger.* Which one had actually done it, Billy, Pete? He found he could not remember, as if in some time past he'd tried to wipe his memory clean. What idiots they'd been, wanting so badly to be big shots by throwing their weight around. Against an old black woman? Unfortunately, she had presented the best target. But what could he do? He'd had to go along with them, otherwise they would have ostracized him.

"Time's got no meanin' heah-bouts." The fat black woman cut in on his thoughts. She had a curious look about her as if she knew what he was thinking. "That bein' the case, I thinks we should gets reacquainted."

She waved her arms, the loose flesh of their undersides flapping like startled chickens, and Tony could see the barbecue pit where she'd been smoking the pig. She waddled over to the pit, lifted up the corrugated metal lid, just as he had so many years before. But instead of a pig smoking on the rack, there was a human being.

Tony gagged, his mind frozen in disbelief.

Then the fat black woman took up a long-handled brush and painted the carcass with thick, tomato-red sauce. She turned back to Tony, her face wreathed in a grin. "Almos' time fo' lunch."

He let out a little moan. He could see what was scrawled across her apron, those two words, "Howdy, Nigger." She glanced down at herself and a look of profound sadness crossed her face.

"Yo 'an' yo' friens' did this to me, put th' tattoo t' me." She pointed to the one word that meant far more to her than it ever would to him. "Yo' know this here's the filthiest, most hateful word I can think of." She shook her head. "No, I don't s'pose yo' do."

She brushed her calico dress with knobby-knuckled hands as if it were the only one she possessed. "Yo' go' any idea what hurts the mos'? Fact yo' didn't even ask my name. But why should yo', sugah? I was no more 'n' a piece of meat to yo'. Barely human." The grin flitted across her face again, fugitive as a butterfly. "Din' stop yo' from gorgin' yo'self on my food, did it, sugah?"

Tony shivered. "What is this? Where the hell am I?"

The fat woman shrugged her meaty shoulders. "Why ask when yo' already knows?"

"How would I know?" And then it hit him like a shotgun blast. He was in hell.

"But I can't be!" He looked around frantically. Down there, as if seen through the wrong end of a telescope, he could still make out the doctors working over his body. Was it his imagination, or had their efforts become more frenzied?

"Is he going to die?" Katie's voice echoed as if through a mountain pass. So filled with sorrow and terror it sent a shiver through him. "Why won't you tell me whether he's going to live or die?"

"Because they don't know," the fat woman answered softly. "It's not up to them."

"Who *is* it up to?" Tony shouted. "You?"

The fat woman looked at him with profound pity. "I'm goin' show yo' the position yo' in, sugah."

At that moment, the unicorn made a sound. It was like a choir singing, a gorgeous blend of melody and harmonies, but as the fat woman turned toward it, the sound turned dissonant and a hard, unpleasant edge drove like a spike through Tony's ears. Its head bucked and its hindquarters rippled. Its back legs scrabbled against dirt and grass as it strove to rise from its bondage.

Without a word to Tony, the black woman strode toward the still-kneeling beast. With each step, her outline became less defined, darkening like a storm cloud, growing in size until it approached impossible proportions. A black hand reached out, sharp knuckles staining the unicorn's trembling white forehead until its head bowed and, trembling terribly, it settled back into the grass.

Tony almost cried out, for the moment the unicorn lowered its head he felt a sharp pain in his chest.

"Now where was I?" The fat black woman was back. "Oh, yas. It occurred to me that yo' needs a graphic illustration o' the position yo' find yo'self in."

The fat woman vanished. In her place was a man's head and torso. Without arms or legs it fit neatly into a handsome gilt frame of mitered wood.

"Does this give you the picture?" The man was dark-haired, with severe features, penetrating eyes, and an old-fashioned goatee that Tony had never seen except in films.

Tony looked from the strange limbless figure to the unicorn.

"What are *you* looking at?" The man seemed annoyed.

"What are you doing to that unicorn?" Tony could not help staring at the unicorn. "It looks so unhappy."

"I'm sure it *is* unhappy," the man said. "It is my job to make it so."

"Why don't you let it go?"

The limbless man smirked. "You haven't earned the right to ask, my friend." The smirk became a leering grin. "You have murder in your heart. That makes you my meat." He nodded toward the sign that swung from its post on the side of the porch steps. "I'm the original Franchiser. But what I franchise is damned hard work. You can't take shortcuts."

Tony made himself look at the quadriplegic in his fancy gilt frame. "Just what is it you franchise?"

That smirk was becoming irritating. "Oh, come on. You can't fool me. You're not thick as a brick. Look at what's smoking in the barbecue pit."

"I can't," Tony said. "It turns my stomach."

"You are a weak and wimpy boy."

As if a powerful hand flung him forward, Tony was pitched to the lip of the pit. He tried to avert his head but he couldn't. It was as if it were held in a vise. His eyes opened and he stared into the pit, at the body slowly smoking on the grill. It was the fat black woman. He blinked and it was the old black alky from Myrtle Ave. He blinked again and saw the kid from the Marcy projects, the one who had shot Jack Halloran. The thick chain through his nose was dark with soot and the unicorn charm had burned its imprint into his upper lip.

Tony groaned.

"That's your own mind you're looking into, my friend," the boxed man said. "Still feeling queasy?"

Tony tried, unsuccessfully, to look away from the horrific pit. Being pushed around by the quadriplegic, this lack of control was like a killing pressure, squeezing all the life out of him. He didn't like it one bit. But perhaps, given this creature's disposition, that was the point.

"That's what I franchise, my friend. Evil."

Tony stared. "Then you must be—"

"An angel." The quadriplegic smiled benignly. "Only an angel."

Tony smelled the fragrant grease dripping from the grill and he gagged. "Take it away. Please. I can't stand the stench."

"How hard it must be to live with yourself." Contempt turned the quadriplegic's voice to acid. "You mealy-mouthed—I can't franchise anything to the likes of you."

Abruptly, the killing pressure vanished and he was released. In his newfound freedom, Tony risked another glance downward at his life on Myrtle Ave.

"That's right," the quadriplegic said. "There's the place for you. Everything you love or have ever loved is right there in the O.R."

Awareness of Katie and the kids was overpowering. It was pulling him downward, back toward the operating room far, far below. He took a last look around. Surely this couldn't be death. A place where time had no meaning. What was it?

"Go on back where you came from," the quadriplegic said, "while you have the chance."

Tony turned to him. "What do you mean?"

"Hey! You need a road map? You're dyin' down there. That little sonuvabitch got you good, brother. Blood's pumping out of you like well water. You wait too long up here you won't be able to go back. Ever."

Tony wanted to cry. He thought of Katie; he thought of Amanda and Kevin, conjuring their faces one by one. His heart was breaking. He saw Katie's face as if it were veiled by tears. Just outside the O.R. she gripped the kids' shoulders with fingers of iron. *I know I have to be strong,* she had said to him, and she was.

It was at that moment that he heard again the exquisite music of the unicorn. It held within its subtle harmonics the pain of imprisonment that pulled at Tony's heartstrings. It spoke to him on a deeper level than he had imagined possible, and it seemed to break the spell he was under. Though he still felt the pull from below, it was no longer overpowering. More like an old toothache, he thought, dulled to a background throb.

Tony knew he should be concerned about what was happening to his body, but this new world—wherever it was and whatever it might be—was at the moment so astonishing, so compelling that he could not bear to leave yet.

As if reading his thoughts, the voice of the quadriplegic broke through the unicorn's melody in a kind of music hall parody of an Irish accent: "It's a siren's song you're hearing now, m' boy. Best skedaddle 'fore it eats you for lunch."

Tony turned to look at the unicorn, which still lay in the same spot, gazing at him with eyes the color of clear, deep gemstones—emeralds he and Katie had once goggled over in the corner window of Tiffany's. He wondered if the unicorn could move at all or whether it was spellbound to the spot. He stared at it for a very long time, and suddenly a thought popped into his head. How could he be running out of time here where in this place time had no meaning? He was being lied to.

When he turned back to confront the quadriplegic, there was no sign of him or of the fat black woman or the amorphous crowned shadow. He-she-it had vanished.

Tony needed some answers and the only other creature here was the unicorn. As he walked toward it, he passed the huge, dreadful smoker, the front steps of the clapboard house, with its mocking sign: FRANCHISER. The frayed and scarred cowboy boots he'd worn all through college crunched on the blue-gray gravel drive. The noise, sharp as needles pinging against glass, caused the unicorn to look up. Its great horn swung around so that it was leveled at Tony. He paused in mid-stride. Until that moment he hadn't realized how menacing it could be. Now that he was this close he could see that the edges of the spirals were razor-sharp. Even a glancing swipe could flay skin and flesh from sinew and bone.

He took a step forward and the unicorn rose on its forelegs. He had never thought of the creature as being menacing. When he thought of unicorns it was in the context of a fairy tale; they were creatures of goodness and light, weren't they? Amanda's surely was. Like teddy bears, they were synonymous with comfort and warmth.

And purity of spirit.

He took another step toward the unicorn and it rose on four legs, backing away. The black and shining horn was aimed at the center of his chest. *Think*, Tony told himself. *What are you missing?*

Then he thought of something the Devil had said to him, for he was now convinced the creature of shadow and changeable substance he had encountered was, indeed, the Devil: *You have murder in your heart.* He did not want to be the Devil's meat; the thought sent shivers down his spine, assuming he still had one. Clearly, the Devil didn't think so.

He moved closer to the unicorn, who now stood alert and clearly restless. The powerful muscles along its flank jumped and spasmed as it bucked a little, backing up against the split-log fence. Its black horn lowered and it shook its head, clearly uneasy.

"I'm not going to hurt you." Tony took another step. "Don't be afraid."

Suddenly, the unicorn's forelegs collapsed under it,

and it genuflected as it had earlier. Its eyes rolled in terror and its mouth opened.

"I'm not afraid, stupid. You are unclean. Unfit to touch me."

The voice, familiar in its mocking contempt, brought Tony up short. It seemed shocking and obscene coming from the unicorn's mouth. "Who . . . who are you?"

"You know me," said the voice emanating from the apparently stunned unicorn.

"What do you want from me?" Tony asked.

"Climb aboard and we'll get things in gear," the Devil said.

Tony stood, transfixed until the Devil said, "Come on, don't be more of a wuss than you already are."

Slowly, hesitantly, Tony approached the unicorn. Its head was lowered, the tip of the long, black horn gouging a furrow in the grass. Tony climbed upon its back and, immediately, the unicorn rose.

"Hang onto your hat," the Devil advised.

Lacking one, Tony just had time to clutch the thick, white mane before the unicorn took off, paralleling the fence, heading away from the house. It soon came to a section badly in need of repair and, gathering its strength, leapt over the cracked top split log.

With a stiff breeze in his face, Tony was obliged to bend over the arched neck as the unicorn galloped at full speed across the vast expanse of undulating grasslands beyond the fence. Galloping was the wrong word, however, since it appeared as if the unicorn's hooves never touched the ground. Instead, it was flying, and not just flying but bursting through the air like a jet. Tony looked around, gaping, until they came to rest on the flat, dusty top of a mesa. Shards of glittering stone sparked beneath the unicorn's dancing hooves as its head came up.

"You know what I want," the Devil said, still speaking through the poor enslaved beast. "But you've got to give it to me willingly. It's the one thing I'm enjoined from taking."

It's my immortal soul he covets. Tony jumped as if bitten. "Never."

"We'll see," the Devil said.

Though the light in the sky had not waned, there was a sharp crack of thunder, accompanied by the unmistakable smell of buttered popcorn. Lights danced in front of Tony's dazzled eyes. When they cleared, he saw a small, stunted creature, dark-skinned, with a barrel chest and immense muscles. He had wild, black hair, matted and strewn with shards of bark and leaf. Into his forehead was tattooed a curious set of symbols. By the tools he held in each massive fist Tony could tell he was a metalworker of some sort. As Tony watched, dumbfounded, a pillar of fire flashed down from the heavens, enveloping the tattooed man. Flames crackled and licked greedily, feeding like a voracious animal. The tattooed man burned until all that was left was a pile of bones lying atop the blackened implements. With a spine-chilling rustle, the bones stirred, rising until they arranged themselves into a human pattern. The naked jaws clacked open and shut.

"Let's talk about you for a minute so we know where we stand," the skeleton said. "Why are you here? I'm certain you'd like to know."

Tony, who was already learning not to question the

curious transformations of this place, said, "You bet I would."

Wind moaned eerily between the bones of the skeleton. "Evil stalks you, that's why."

"Are you another medium? Is the Devil using you like he did the unicorn?"

The skeleton shook his head, setting off a round of rattling. "Not a bit of it, though I suppose you could say I'm one of his many defeated incarnations. But you could look at yourself in the mirror just as well."

"Who defeated you?"

The skeleton deflected this question. "Irrelevant. This interview is about you." One bony hand lifted, pointing in Tony's general direction. "Take the incident that may very possibly lead to your death. All you thought about was taking revenge on Jack's murder. You didn't think about your job, your wife, your family."

"You didn't see what the . . . the animal did to Jack." Tony slid off the unicorn's back to ease the ache in his inner thighs. "He had absolutely no regard for human life."

The skeleton continued, unperturbed. "In fact, all of the responsibilities that made you a man, that defined life and your place in it were eradicated by the one bestial urge to take vengeance."

Though Tony refused to utter this admission, he knew what the skeleton said was true. It was as if one tiny but powerful part of his brain left over from a distant and primitive age had taken control, overriding any sense of prudence or conscience.

At Tony's side, the unicorn's tail flicked nervously,

then was still. "At this moment," the skeleton said, "you are closer to the boy who killed Jack than you are to Jack himself."

Tony felt a surge of panic and he curled his hand into a fist. "That can't be."

"Oh, but it is. You have only to take a hard look inside yourself."

Something was stinking, like meat long gone rotten, and Tony turned this way and that, trying to locate its source. He finally realized it was coming from the spot where he'd secreted the gun. Its taint was on him like the mark of Cain.

"Christ, no."

The skeleton laughed. With a dry rattle, it collapsed into ash, which was quickly borne aloft by the wind. Soon there was no trace of it on the mesa beyond an insignificant charcoal smudge.

Tony looked at the unicorn. Its eyes were clear; the terror that had caused them to roll was gone. It snorted as it bucked in its newfound freedom.

Tony felt a great surge of empathy toward it. Filled with fear and self-loathing, he reached out. "Help me!" he cried. "You can save me! You have the power!"

The unicorn stamped its powerful forelegs. It stared at Tony with a pain beyond human comprehension. Music poured forth from its mouth like golden radiance. These most beautiful harmonies resolved themselves into words Tony could understand. "Once, perhaps," it said, "but no more. I am held spellbound; you have met my master." The great head bobbed up and down. "He has stripped me of most of my power. And he has put you beyond the possibility of redemption."

"I refuse to accept that!" Tony shouted.

"Give it all you've got, boy!" the Devil crowed in a peal of almost-deafening thunder that threatened to split open the sky. *"Fight on even under the most crippling of odds. I applaud you!"*

Tony covered his head as if he could hide himself away from the mocking voice. "It's not fair," he whispered, after the last echo had died away.

"I disagree," the unicorn sang in the myriad voices of a choir. "You had no compunction about using the old man. What did you feel for him when he was being beaten? Compassion? Did you go to his aid? No, you simply watched. Did you even think of him? What regard did *you* have for human life?"

"But that was different," Tony protested.

"Tell me how."

Tony opened his mouth to reply, but too late he realized that he had no answer. Except . . .

"I was frightened," he said softly. "That's what life on Myrtle Ave. did to me—to everyone in the neighborhood. We all lived in fear."

"Even the children."

Tony nodded at the unicorn. "Especially my children. I was going to do it for them."

"Better and better," the Devil cackled. *"Blood legacy's an eight-course banquet in itself."*

"I was speaking of *all* the children," the unicorn sang.

"You mean those teenage gangsters who rule the streets with their guns and their attitude."

"It's do or die for them, isn't it?"

Tony did not want to think about that. "If I'm really beyond redemption, at least let me help you," he pleaded. "Maybe that's why I was put here. Maybe we can heal each other."

"Look at you; you're a pathetic sight." The unlovely notes made Tony cringe. The unicorn snorted, steam rising from its velvet nostrils. "You can't even help yourself, let alone anyone else." The head waggled from side to side as it stirred up more dissonance with its restless hooves. "Here's my gift to you. It's all that's left of my power."

Suddenly dizzied, Tony put a hand to his eyes. There was a bright flare of greenish-white light and he blacked out. When he awoke he was looking at a cockroach the size of his thumb. He tried to react but his body wouldn't move. In desperation, he swatted at it with the back of his hand. A black hand. In fact, all of him was black. He saw his reflection in a windowpane. What was he, all of fourteen years old? Then he strained forward as he caught sight of the thick nose chain and the unicorn that hung from it, stinging his upper lip with half-frozen metal.

He looked around, saw that he was huddled in the corner of a ramshackle apartment. It was winter and the apartment was freezing. He wondered why the heat wasn't on, then remembered his mother didn't have the money to pay for it or for the electricity.

He started as the gloom was shattered by headlights on the street outside blazing through the cracked windows. That's when he saw his mother lying on the floor in a pool of frothy vomit. That's when he remembered trying to revive her after her OD, working on her, the cold sweat of desperation drenching his clothes. Her dead eyes stared at him like the blank windows of the project. He began to whimper. His mother was dead. What kind of life had she ever had beyond shooting heroin and being slapped around by a succession of boyfriends who acted as her sometimes pimp. Often as not, though it wasn't her fault, she forgot to have food for him and he'd have to scavenge around the neighborhood. His father he could remember not at all. In fact, the faces of all the men ran into one another like paint in the gutter. Where his father might be now was anyone's guess, but the simple truth was he had no interest in his son. In fact, none of the adults in this world did. They had no power. Kids with knives, guns, and a belief in their own immortality had all of it. At least, that was what his two brothers had thought. One had been shot to death during a drug deal gone bad, the other was serving twenty-to-life in Attica for carrying out a blood vendetta. He also had a sister who seemed good for nothing but having babies. In fact, he had his own baby boy, but the very thought of it sent icicles of terror flashing through him. He'd fucked a girl, nothing more. It was a harmless night in the back of a car. Just a quick fuck. It should have been without consequence, right?

Vanished because they had never existed.

Tony never felt such terror in his life. He tried to cry out, but he was again overcome by vertigo. Another flash of greenish-white light crashed through his senses, stunning him. When he opened his eyes again, he was back on the eerie dark mesa top, confronting the unicorn.

Tony still saw torn bits of Unicorn's life, echoing in his mind as if the vision he'd been shown had somehow become part of him. This was a world without limits, without law, without anyone in authority to say this is the line across which you will not walk. There were no such lines for these new children of the street, armed, orphaned, pockets filled with drug money, and dangerous because none of the defining rules parents create for their children existed. Defining rules that a child might, at times, rebel against, but which, after all, allowed him the comfort and security of a dreamless sleep at night.

"You felt the fear."

"Yes." Tony squeezed his eyes shut. "It's terrible."

"This is not your fear," the unicorn sang. "It is *his*."

"Am I supposed to feel sorry for him now?" Tony asked, incredulous. "He's a *murderer*. He leveled a gun at my friend's head and calmly shot three-quarters of it away." Saying it still took his breath away, nothing had changed. "I still feel it. I can't stand it but I still have murder in my heart." He clenched his hands and raised them over his head. "I want to be healed! But you ask too much. You want forgiveness but there is none inside me."

"I said nothing of forgiveness," the unicorn sang.

"Don't listen to its honeyed song," the Devil thundered overhead. *"Of course it wants you to forgive the little savage. What else was it created for? But you know as well as I do that forgiveness is its own lie. It lets evil live on, untouched."*

Something burned hard and bright in the deepest part

of Tony's heart. He looked at the unicorn and said, "I can't forgive him."

The echoes silenced the unicorn. It hung its head as if defeated.

"That's the kind of spirit I can sink my teeth into!" the Devil's voice exulted in a storm of cracked lightning.

The unicorn stamped its hooves as it trotted to the edge of the mesa. Beyond, Tony could see a rock-strewn plain without end. It was studded with gnarled cottonwood and mature weeping willows, their cascades of leaves looking like bursts of spring rain. Streams rippled like liquid silver, here and there bubbling over rock-strewn rapids. But beyond, dimly seen, a set of dark, low hills chilled his bones.

"How cold and deserted the sky above my home looks," the unicorn lamented. "Once it was filled with stars, and the starlight bathed all of us in its brilliance. Once this place was filled with my brethren. Now all are gone."

An icy ball was forming in Tony's stomach. "What happened to them?" he asked.

The unicorn lowered its head, and its harmonies turned dark and nearly ugly, so that they caused a kind of pain that was almost physical. "As belief in them died, so did the stars. They began to migrate toward what stars remained until they approached the edge of the land of shadow. There they came under the spell of—what did *you* call him?"

"The Devil," Tony said.

"The Devil," the unicorn sang in a series of notes that hurt Tony's ears. "My people could not long live beneath his yoke, and, gradually, they perished."

"But what killed them?" Tony asked.

"A growing evil."

"Like kids with guns killing each other and people like me."

"Forget about a plague of locusts. This here's a fucking cancer," came the Devil's fierce rumble across the sky. *"You know all about that, doncha?"*

"I sure do," Tony said.

"Don't be so sure. It's more than that," the unicorn sang. "That form of evil has been around for centuries. This evil's different: a pervading sense of helplessness, an inability to act, to make the one, single selfless gesture that could begin again the chain of salvation. This is what killed us off."

"What d'you say?" the Devil chuckled. *"This beast is too much, ain't it? Some stinking nigger kid whacks you and all it wants you to do is forgive the sonuvabitch. That kinda shit doesn't cut it with me—and I can see it doesn't cut it with you, either."*

"Shut up!" Tony shouted. "You're manipulators, both of you. I refuse to be a soldier in this war."

Tony looked up into a sky filled with billowing clouds but no acid comments or cheap shots were forthcoming. Tony's gaze lowered to the unicorn. For the moment its song was stilled. Could he trust any being in this eerie world? Why would it have shown him Unicorn's painfully squalid life if not so he could find forgiveness in his heart?

And yet it had told him that it was not his fate to be redeemed.

"But the darkness didn't kill you," Tony said.

The unicorn snorted. "It will, eventually," it sang. "For now, I am waiting."

"For what?"

"For someone to bring back the stars."

"Don't look at me," Tony said. "It isn't going to be me. I don't have it in me to forgive Unicorn. He had a choice and he made it. There were so many other paths he could have taken."

The unicorn's head bobbed up and down. "There's no denying it. But the one who brings back the stars will see that it doesn't matter. Forgiveness doesn't matter. Beginning the process of change, the chain of salvation that will save us all, is the only thing that matters."

"Git on outta heah. Yo' mama's callin' yo'."

Tony started, saw the fat black woman had reappeared. She stood with tree-stump legs spread, her balled-up fists on hips wide as Myrtle Ave. There was a fierce scowl on her face. "Git back t' where yo' belong," she said. "Ain't no use yo' bein' heah, thas fo' *damn* sho'."

Far away, he could hear Katie sobbing, calling his name over and over, but her voice sounded odd, like an old 78, flattened and dusty, and filed away in some forgotten back room.

"Go on now, sugah," the fat woman urged. "Yo' ain't but got seconds left. Seems as if yo' dyin'." She took a step toward him, and Tony had the distinct notion that she was about to spit flames. "What chew waitin' fo'? Lissen to yo' po' missus. Boo-hoo. How she misses yo' sorry ass." She lifted an arthritic forefinger. "Then thas yo' children t' think of. 'Manda an' Kevin, right? Yo' doan' wanna up an' leave 'em now, do yo', sugah?"

There seemed to be a riddle here that had been posed in different ways by both the unicorn and the Devil. It was up to him to figure it out. He could chuck all this talk of chains of salvation and bringing back the stars. That was what the Devil wanted; judging by the persistent wheedling, he wanted it very badly. That meant Tony was a real threat to him.

Why? Could Tony really be the one to bring back the stars, to begin again the chain of salvation that would redeem the unicorn from eternal night? Yet, even if it were so, it meant leaving Katie behind—Katie and Amanda and Kevin. Leaving them to the jungle that Myrtle Ave. had become.

As Tony stared down onto the scene in the operating room far below he was struck by an odd thought. He had been able to fool himself that he'd been on a mission to provide a legacy for his children. How deluded could he have been? When he had set out to stalk the kid who'd murdered Jack Halloran what he'd really been about to do was to give up Katie and his family. Dismaying at it might seem, going back to them now meant returning to the man he had been. No wonder the Devil was so eager for him to do just that. *You've got murder in your heart. That makes you my meat.*

He'd be damned if he would let himself be the Devil's meat. Far better to become a soldier in this as yet unknown war, to brave the unicorn's challenge, whatever it might ask of him. And with that knowledge came the realization that he could not return to his old life—he'd been changed in some fundamental way. Even Katie would not recognize this Tony as her husband. He'd made his choice without knowing it.

There was a spark of blue lightning, and he staggered momentarily as if in response to an earthquake. In that instant of hollow silence after the last echo rolled away, he heard Katie's wail of grief. But when he turned, he found that he could no longer peer through the doorway into the operating room. It was gone, and Katie, the kids with it.

Thunder rumbled from a sky turned yellow. It resolved itself into a voice filled with spite: *"You'll be sorry. Immortality isn't all it's cracked up to be."*

But Tony knew he'd dealt the Devil more than a glancing blow, and he was glad of it. "Now what?" he said to the unicorn.

"That's entirely up to you," the creature sang.

"I am here, for good or ill," Tony said. He threw his arms wide. "My heart is my heart, but my spirit is delivered up to you."

"Oh, certainly not to me." The unicorn sang like a massed choir. "I am but one link in the chain."

It looked upward and, following its gaze, Tony saw a sky now devoid of all cloud. Clear and pellucid, the starless, indigo firmament seemed to contain the infinite.

Tony heard a chord struck deep in the core of him, and he was dazzled by the essential truth flooding through him like celestial light. "That was why I was brought here." He turned to the unicorn. "That's what this struggle has been about. I am to become one of you."

"Too long beneath the yoke of darkness, I am dying," the unicorn sang. "But you shall take my place. You are the one I have been waiting for, the one who will return the stars to my sky."

He supposed in a way he'd known it all along. "But how?"

The unicorn dipped its head. "Forgiveness was never the issue, can you understand that now?"

"I do," Tony acknowledged.

"Neither is redemption," the unicorn warned. "This transformation is not about you; it's about everything else."

"I am a book waiting for words to fill it."

"In a moment, they will come flooding." The unicorn raised its head and, with a clip-clop of its hooves, came toward him. The long, black spiral horn was aimed at the center of his chest.

Overhead, the sky roiled. *"It's a trick!"* the Devil shouted. *"Don't just stand there! Run! Run or you'll be changed forever!"*

Tony knew better than to listen. Yet his muscles jumped and spasmed and a certain terror filled his belly.

The tip of the unicorn's horn touched Tony's chest. "Are you frightened?" it asked in a welter of fluting harmonies.

Tony nodded. "Yes."

And the unicorn sang him a glorious song as it impaled him. The gleaming black spiral went clear through him until he began to vibrate in response to a pulse, ancient of ancients.

Garland Montgomery and an entourage of four strapped teen gangstas were picking their way through the littered streets of Bedford-Stuyvesant when the winter rain changed to snow. In an instant, the hard, almost icy pellets were transformed into a dazzle of spiraling white flakes. The change broke in on Garland's thoughts, dark as night-time shadows. Garland looked up, past the grimy brick-work, the blinking Christmas lights taped around window frames, the spiderweb of iron fire escapes draped with messages of whitey's Christmas, over the rooftops to watch the snow swirl down, pure as a bride's dress. He thought of nothing as he looked, unaware that merely being out in the snow might feel good.

He was late for a gang meet, a rally from which they'd get to the meat of tonight's entertainment: a street fight between them and Crips along one flank of the Marcy Projects.

But the snow just kept on falling until it was like curtains so thick they seemed suspended in the night. It was an amazing sight, even for Garland, and he stopped to keep the moment alive.

Through the snow he saw a spark of light. At first, he assumed that it was a low-flying plane on its way into La Guardia. Except that it did not move, did not blink. A star, then. Except how could starlight be seen through the snow and the nighttime city glow? Garland contemplated this question without success.

When he looked back down at the street he saw that he was alone. Where had his entourage got to? He whipped around and saw a shape moving toward him. Instinctively, Garland went into a semicrouch behind a row of galvanized steel garbage cans as he reached for his gun. He had two guns now—the one his mother had given him and the one he'd taken off the white man he'd killed in the elevator. With two shooting deaths to his name, he'd vaulted in status, leapfrogging others older than him, to become one of the leaders of his gang and a big man in the 'hood. People feared him; he could see it in their eyes. If they were smart, they feared him. Otherwise, he knew how to teach them fear.

Now, as the shape came toward him through the fast-falling snow, he clicked off the gun's safety. "I'll fuckin' clean yo' out, yo' take anutha step," he shouted. His voice sounded weirdly loud. He refused to believe that he might be scared; the leader of the Bloods couldn't be scared. So he shouted all the harder to cover his fear.

He took aim at the large shape approaching through the thick snow. He would have pulled the trigger, too, had he not been frozen in place by the sight. A big horse, whiter even than the snow, came toward him. Mist blew from its nostrils, icicles clung to the tufts above each ankle, and the water of melted snow ran down its spiral horn, black as the closet where Garland had once been imprisoned by one of his mother's pimps as he had his way with her. Not a horse, then: a unicorn. Unconsciously, he touched the cold silver pendant hanging from his nose chain.

As the huge snow-white animal loomed out of the night, Garland could see pinpoints of light sparkling like diamonds along the edges of that horn. He thought, *I'll kill this motherfucker and take its horn. Nobody else has a horn like that. What a weapon it would make! A symbol of power no one else's got!* He rushed from behind the trash cans and, aiming his gun at the unicorn's neck, pulled the trigger.

At least, he wanted to pull the trigger. In fact, nothing moved. It was like he was frozen in time, except that he could feel his heart fluttering in his chest as the snow swirled wildly between the buildings. The snow blotted out everything, leaving him alone with the white animal in a white world. Then he saw someone step out from behind the unicorn.

Wide-eyed, Garland watched his brother Derryl walk toward him. But something was wrong with him. He was leaning to one side like he'd been shot or his leg was broken. Then Garland saw that Derryl was dragging a body along behind him.

"Derryl," he breathed, "what chew doin' here. Yo' break outta Attica?"

Derryl, still in his dull prison overalls, spread his arms. "Check it out, bro'. I ain't never gon' get outta that hellhole." Then he pointed to the gun. "Wass up? Yo' gon' t' shoot yo' own blood?"

Suddenly self-conscious, Garland put the gun away, pointed to the body at Derryl's side. "Who yo' got there?"

"Don't you recognize him?" Derryl hauled the body in front of him. "Thas our brother Jovan."

Garland started as if slashed with a blade. "That ain't Jovan. Jovan be long dead."

"Look at his face, Garland." Derryl reached down, pulled the body up by its shoulders. "Jus' look at him."

Garland took a step toward his brother despite himself. But one look at Jovan's bloody face made his stomach turn over. "How this be happenin'?" he asked of no one in particular. "Jovan be dead, man. Dead an' buried."

Derryl was looking from Jovan to Garland. "Yo, I never noticed this before but yo' and Jovan could be mistaken for one 'nother." He let go of the body, which sprawled awkwardly at his feet.

Garland could see the point his brother was trying to make. But he knew Derryl was dead wrong. He'd never end up like either of his brothers. He shook his head vigorously. "Uh-uh, that ain't me," he said vehemently. "I gots the power now, bro.' I gots all the power I need."

"You a willful boy," Derryl said. "Yo' always was."

"Ain't no boy," Garland screamed into the howling wind. "I'se a man now, Derryl. A *man!*"

But the surging snow had already wiped out all trace of his brothers. In their stead he found himself in a tiny cramped cubicle in a crowded ward in Community Hospital. It was a dark place, dreary with the groans of the hurt and dying. He stood beside a bed on which lay a man so bony thin it was hard to believe he was human. In fact, judging by the size of his thick brow and his bull nose, this man must once have been big and robust. No more. His skin, scarred by bleeding sores, was so unhealthy it was charcoal gray.

As Garland watched, a white nurse entered through a gap in the curtain that hung from a stainless steel track in the low ceiling. She was wearing all kinds of protective shit: a mask and those thin rubber gloves. She checked the man's vital signs, checked on the fluids slowly dripping into his veins, shook her head. As she left the cubicle, Garland saw she stripped off not one, but two pairs of gloves. Just before she disappeared, he caught a glimpse of a sign pinned to the outside of the curtain: CAUTION. AIDS PATIENT WITHIN. EXTREME BIO-HAZARD.

Garland was wondering what he was doing here when he noticed two tattered photos on a ledge beside a stack of boxes containing sterile cotton gauze. When he looked closer, he saw a shot of his mother and, beside it, a photo of himself as a small child.

Garland stood still for what seemed an eternity. In his mind were two questions. Could this be his father? Could this be the man who broke his mama's arm in three places?

Garland's heart skipped a beat and he drew his gun, aiming it at the bony man's chest. "Yo' did that to her, I'll blast your sorry ass to Kingdom Come."

The bony man, of course, said nothing.

Something dark and terrible seemed to fill Garland's chest, making it so hard to breathe he sobbed with the awful weight of it. "Motherfucker. You broke my mama's arm and you walked out on me." He put down the gun. "A quick death's too good for yo'. Yo' gettin' what yo' deserve."

Then the snow came swirling back and, momentarily lost within that chilling fog, Garland had a vision that terrified him. It was years from now. He was an old man, forty or so, dying of some unnamed disease. Visited in a mean hospital bed by a young man, handsome, strong, vital. It was his son, Marcus.

"Marcus," Garland said in this vision. "I'm dyin'."

Bending over him, Marcus looked him in the eye and spat on him.

The snow came roaring back, hitting Garland full in the face, momentarily blinding him.

"Marcus!" he cried into the howl of the storm. "Marcus!"

As if he had been summoned by Garland's heightened emotions, a squally three-month-old boy-child appeared. Garland looked at his face through the falling snow and saw with a start that it was his own face.

Marcus.

Something inside him broke like a bowstring too tightly strung. It echoed through him like a gunshot. He took a halting step toward his son, if only maybe to get a better look. But, no, he had to get closer, take him in his arms, hold the baby tight. His terrible vision of the future lay before him like a smoking ruin. The thought of it made him sick to his stomach.

In fact, now he thought of it, ever since he'd seen that weird star pulsing electric white in the sky just before the unicorn appeared, he'd had a liquid feeling in his gut like he'd eaten something that was going to make him real sick. But now he realized that it was something he'd eaten a long time ago, a kind of poison that had been seeping through his veins like rainwater someone had pissed into. It was something that was making him do to his own son what had been done to him.

He could not let that happen. He could not abandon Marcus.

Garland reached out for his son. He could almost touch him now. In a moment, he'd set things right. He'd make sure that vision of the future never came to pass.

That was when the bullet spun him around. He never really heard the report, just the echo of it, half-muffled by the snow, as it ricocheted off the project walls. He was falling. His left knee struck the snow-covered pavement, jarring his spine, making his teeth clack together. He felt the blood spurting from his chest but, oddly, he felt no pain.

Lying on his side on the icy pavement, he saw the evil moon face of that fucker Levar striding toward him. Levar, the leader of the Crips, who'd been out for vengeance on the Bloods ever since Garland extended his gang's crack-dealing territory. Levar had sworn to kill Garland and now he was going to make good his promise.

Snow pattered onto Garland's cheek, cooling the feverish rush of blood. Something convulsed inside him and his legs drew up. He was coughing blood and Levar was laughing.

Levar leveled the 9mm at Garland's head and laughed. "Yo, it's the end, motherfucker." He moved closer, keeping the muzzle of the gun trained on Garland's head. "There's bets you'll crap yo' pants when the time comes. Here's where we gets to find out."

Garland looked up then, his heart beating fast as he watched the big old unicorn come prancing at him through the snow.

"Jesus," Garland muttered as, through pain-filled eyes, he saw the unicorn lower its head, bearing down on Levar. Levar, high on crack cocaine, had eyes for no one but his intended prey.

Then Garland heard this sound that made the small hairs at the base of his neck stand straight up. Levar heard it, too, because his attention wavered. A kind of singing like a choir of angels in full voice was coming from the unicorn's open mouth. Levar's gaze flickered once, the muzzle of the 9mm moving a little off its mark. The unicorn was almost upon Levar and, out of time, he pulled the trigger.

Garland screamed at the second explosion. Something slammed into the side of his head and, for a time, he passed out.

When his eyes fluttered open, he saw the unicorn at his side. It stood there for a moment, pawing the ground like it was undecided or something. Then it knelt, its huge forelegs folding in on themselves.

Garland had trouble seeing; all the blood running down the side of his head, he supposed. Pain overcame him and he cried aloud. He was very frightened as he looked into the unicorn's left eye. He thought of his brothers, one dead, the other locked away, and remembered what Derryl had said to him. He thought of his father, dying of AIDS. But, in the end, neither of them mattered. Only Marcus mattered. More than Garland could have imagined; more than he could say. His sole thought was this: to live another day so that he could hold his son in his arms; to live another week, another month, if possible, years, so that his son could have what he himself had never had and wanted more than anything else.

With his last ounce of strength, Garland climbed with terrible agony onto the unicorn's back. He steadied himself, but his thoughts kept running away from him. For sure if the pain kept up he'd be dead in no time.

He was already insensate when the unicorn rose and, snorting smoke, trotted through the thick and unnatural snow. It cantered down the eerily deserted streets of

Bedford-Stuyvesant; it crossed Myrtle Ave. where, as Tony Valenti, it had witnessed the death of the potato chip man, Jack Halloran; it trotted past the quiet courtyard of the Marcy Projects where, with murder in his heart, Tony had stalked Garland to his lair; it passed the fire escape Garland so often climbed on his way up to the vulnerable skylight that led to the doctor's office. The unicorn clip-clopped soundlessly up the rutted stoop of the brown-stone. No clods of snow were thrown up in its wake; no hoofprints appeared at all in the snowfall.

With Garland stretched out on its back, it passed through the closed front door as if it did not exist. In the hallway, the complex aroma of Indian spices could not quite hide the stench of rotting meat and stale grease. It walked down the meanly lighted tiles, chipped and color-less with age and neglect. With the tip of its black, shin-ing horn it rang Dr. Gupta's bell. Then it knelt, lowering its burden carefully in front of the door.

Dr. Gupta's wife, a round, jolly Indian woman gave a little shout as she opened the door. Garland's dark, hand-some head fell against her slippered feet and a touch of blood smeared her sari. Her husband, a very large, very dark Indian, appeared with a cigarette in one hand and a forkful of curry in the other.

"My God," he said, kneeling down beside the boy. His wife took his cigarette and fork from him as deftly as a surgical nurse plucks used implements from her doc-tor's grasp. His hands explored the areas around the gun-shot wounds in chest and skull, widening in concentric circles until his preliminary examination was complete.

"I'll call the hospital," his wife said.

"Save your time," Dr. Gupta said. "He'll be dead by the time an ambulance arrives."

Without another word, he hoisted Garland over his shoulder in an expert fireman's lift and took him upstairs to his office.

"It's fate this snowstorm," the doctor's wife called up after him as he ascended. "If the weather hadn't changed, we'd be at your sister's in White Plains."

Once in his office, Dr. Gupta placed Garland in the back room—the surgery where, from time to time, he performed abortions as well as other minor operations.

Garland, very near death, kept watch over his son. He held that image close to him, clinging to it even when the snowstorm became terribly fierce, the howling winds threatening to rip the vision from him. He fought the snow, the wind, and the bone-chilling cold, desperate to keep Marcus close to him. Everything else slipped away: guns, crack, Bloods, Crips, power—all were cauterized, reduced to ash before his determination to hold on to the image of his son. It meant a great deal to him whether he lived or died; more than he could ever say. Life was suddenly precious, and he had seen so little of it.

Marcus even less.

He fought and fought until he was utterly exhausted. What was it Derryl had told him? Only a child is willful; a man lets go of his willfulness to live in the world. Now Garland understood. He wanted so much to live in the world beyond Bed-Stuy.

He had fought. He had done all he could. It was time to give up being willful. It was time to put himself in the hands of something larger, something in which he could believe and, if he lived, teach his son to believe in. He felt the comforting weight of the silver pendant on his upper lip. He willed the image of the unicorn into his mind.

I am yours, he whispered in his mind, delivering himself into the care of that extraordinary beast.

When he woke, hours later, he felt sunlight streaming onto his face. It was dark and he could not see, but, sniffing, he smelled the combined odors of antiseptics and Indian spices and knew without looking around where he was. It will be clear tonight, he thought. There will be starlight.

He must have stirred because, a moment later, he caught an intense whiff of curry, and felt a presence at his side.

"You had me very worried, young man," Dr. Gupta said. "You are exceptionally lucky to be alive. But you'll be all right now. Do you understand me?"

"I can't see," Garland said in a voice that seemed throttled by cotton wadding.

"There are bandages over your eyes," Dr. Gupta said. "It cannot be helped."

Memory flooded back and he saw Levar standing over him, aiming at his head, about to pull the trigger. He heard again the terrifying explosion and he must have spasmed off the table because the next thing he knew, he felt hands on him and Dr. Gupta's voice saying, "Easy does it."

Then a needle slipped into the meat of his upper arm and he felt a soothing warmth seep through him.

"I got shot in the chest," he managed to get out. "And in the head."

"One bullet could have torn your heart to shreds," Dr. Gupta affirmed. "As I said, very lucky." There was a small hesitation. "The other creased your skull, nothing more. The bandages are a precaution only. Tomorrow, when I take them off, you will see as well as you ever could."

"Yo' mean I'm not blind?"

"No." Dr. Gupta said. "But your body has taken a nasty beating and you've lost a lot of blood. That's why you're so weak. Not to worry." He chuckled. "You know, my wife is already cooking you soup and curry, even though I told her oh so many times that I'll be feeding you intravenously for a while."

"Yo, doc, why'd you save me? Yo' shoulda let me die."

"Life is precious," Dr. Gupta said. "My profession preaches that, but it is my children who have taught me the real meaning. No matter how difficult life seems, it is still worth living."

Garland felt dark despair threaten to overwhelm him. "What yo' know, 'bout it? Yo' may be brown but yo' ain't no nigger."

"One of my children is autistic. Do you know what that means? There's something wrong with her brain. Chemicals missing or all messed-up. Chemicals you have and take for granted. She can't think right, can't develop or learn past the age of six, but she struggles on. She's almost twenty now."

Garland thought of his son. He sure didn't want anything like that to happen to Marcus. Thinking of Marcus, he forgot about himself and his despair subsided.

Dr. Gupta said. "You know, I've had my eye on you.

Yes. 'There's a willful boy,' I told my wife many times. 'Once he learns to let go of that willfulness, to give himself over to life, he'll be okay.'" He tapped Garland's shoulder. "And now, here you are. Karma, as we Hindus say. Fate. You understand?"

And somehow Garland did. He reached up and fingered the pendant that hung from his nose chain. His fingertips traced the full outline of the unicorn and, in doing so, he was able to keep its image in his mind. Somehow this calmed him. In a very real way, he needed to know that it was still with him, for he felt a deep conviction that in the days and weeks to come, when he might be at low ebb, the unicorn or his memory of it would give him strength.

Clutching the pendant made him want to tell Dr. Gupta that it had been he who had broken in and stolen the doctor's opiates, that he had done far worse, killed as Levar had meant to kill him, but he was so weak, so full of drugs that made him feel weird and floaty that when he opened his mouth all that came out was a tiny, dry croak.

He remembered his brother Derryl calling him willful. At the time, he only dug in his heels and shut his ears. Now he could see that only children were willful. It was cool to be willful, he could see that as well. The gangs were cool, breaking rules and laws as they saw fit. Being willful. But the gangs' willfulness only extended so far. Death took some of the gangstas—as it had taken Jovan, as it had almost taken him. The cops took others, sometimes, like Derryl.

In a moment of sharp and painful insight, Garland saw just how limited willfulness could be. Because it was that spiteful willfulness that was cutting him off from his son, from all the days of a future he could not as yet imagine. And yet, with the unicorn's help, he knew it existed.

That was a step. Such a big step that he was suddenly terrified of what lay ahead of him. It was a new world where everything was unknown and, therefore, would be a terrible struggle. His new life would be far harder than it had been working his way up the gangsta hierarchy. And, in many ways, more dangerous. Would Levar or a gangsta from the Crips wanting to make a name for himself come after him? But he knew he had no other choice; he was committed now.

Committed. That word had a good sound in his mind, like music that stirred his soul.

Dr. Gupta said, "I must confess I've taken your weapons. I've never stolen a single thing from anyone in my life, but in this case . . ." He paused and Garland supposed he was debating with himself. "I propose a deal. You let me keep the guns and I promise not to report this incident to the police." He tapped Garland's shoulder again, and, this time, Garland had a vision of the unicorn pawing the snowy pavement with a white hoof. "Like I said, I recognize you from the neighborhood. You threw in with a bad lot but, as I tell my wife often enough, every child needs a chance at life, eh? Eh?"

Garland felt Dr. Gupta close beside him. "What do you say to my proposal?" Dr. Gupta asked.

Garland, thinking of Marcus, nodded as best he could. *Every child needs a chance at life.*

"Ah, delicious," Dr. Gupta said. "There's no going

back on your word once it's given. That's the mark of a man, you know."

Garland wanted to tell Dr. Gupta he was not going to go back on his word. It was odd. Just as it was a chain that held the unicorn pendant close to him, he felt part of a chain now, one link in a long line that stretched so far away in either direction he couldn't see the end. Where this vision came from he had no idea, but he was certain that the chain existed and that he was part of it. This was what gave him the determination to be the right kind of man for Marcus no matter how hard it would be to walk away from the gangs, from Myrtle Ave., from everything he had known. When he thought about it that way, it seemed overwhelming, impossible even. He wanted to cry, feeling no older than his fifteen years.

He nodded again, and Dr. Gupta made more noises of delight.

Garland blinked beneath the tightly wrapped bandages. He was gripped by a peculiar kind of warmth that had nothing to do with the shit floating around in his veins. It was so strong he felt terrified. It must have shown on his face because Dr. Gupta slipped his fingers through Garland's. His hand squeezed gently but forcefully until Garland felt Dr. Gupta's warmth running through him like a river.

It was a feeling wholly unfamiliar to him, but he knew it felt good. He knew it made him feel calm and protected. It made him feel like however scary and uncontrollable the world might seem, he'd be able to handle it. And he knew it was the feeling he must give to Marcus, because Marcus, too, was part of the chain.

And then something happened inside of him, as strange and magical as the star in the snow-swept sky or the appearance of the unicorn.

"I remember," he whispered in a dry and cracked voice.

"But what is it you remember?"

"I remember the song my mother usedta sing me."

From this, Dr. Gupta deduced that Garland's mother was gone. "That's good. Memories like that are what keep us going. To my mind it means you're over the worst." He kept a firm hold on Garland's hand. "In any case, I'm here now. I won't let anything bad happen to you."

All of a sudden, Garland began to cry.

JUDITH TARR

━━◦⊸⊷❍⊶⊶❍⊷⊶◦━━

DAME À LA LICORNE

Peter: When I first put **Judith Tarr** on my wish-list of possible contributors to *Immortal Unicorn,* I knew her as the author of seventeen historical and fantasy novels, and as the holder of a doctorate in medieval studies from Yale. Reading "Dame à la Licorne" made it obvious that she lived with, loved, and understood horses. But I didn't know about the Lipizzan who owns her, out there in Tucson. . . .

Janet: Before the birth of this anthology, my only (semi) personal contact with Judith was through the occasional dialogue on GEnie. Though I have still never met her in person, this story makes me feel as if I know her just a wee bit better. The story is one of the few SF tales we received; it says something about the writer and her love of horses, and shows us a future where, though much changes, much that is human nature stays the same.

Dame à la Licorne

I.

THEY TURNED OFF THE RAIN AT DAWN THAT DAY. By early feeding the sun was on, the filters at their most transparent, and the sky so blue it hurt. The grass was all washed clean, new spring green.

Some of the broodmares had taken advantage of the wet to have a good, solid roll in their pasture. Old Novinha, pure white when she was clean, had a map of Africa on her side, and a green haunch. She was oblivious to it, watching with interest as the stallions came out for their morning exercise.

Novinha was thinking about coming into season. Some of the other mares were more than thinking about it. They paced the fence as the stallions danced past, flagging their tails and squealing at any who so much as flicked an ear.

The stallions knew better than to be presumptuous. Young Rahman snorted and skittered, but his rider brought him lightly back in hand. The others arched their necks, that was all, and put on a bit of prance for the ladies. Because they were dancers and this was Dancer's Rest, they pranced with art and grace, a shimmer of white manes and white necks and here and there a black or a bay or a chestnut.

There were horses already in the training rings, the great ones, the masters of the art that the others were still learning. They had gone through the steps of the dance, and for duty and reward were dancing in the air: levade, courbette, capriole; croupade and passade and ballotade. The names were as archaic and beautiful as the dance.

Marina should have been riding one of the young stallions, dappled silver Pluto Amena or coal-black Doloroso or fierce blood-bay Rahman who was fretting and tossing his head under Cousin Tomas' hand. Tomas had less patience than Rahman liked, and stronger hands.

But Marina was up on the hill beyond the broodmares' pasture, where she could see the whole of Dancer's Rest like an image in a screen. She had gone up there to watch the sun come out, and stayed longer than she should, because of the flyer that was coming from the west. West was City and Dome. West was the Hippodrome, where things raced and exhibited themselves and even tried to dance, that were called horses but were not horses at all. Not in the least. Not like the ones that danced and grazed and called to one another in spring yearning below and all around her.

She had seen the horse-things. Everyone at Dancer's Rest had, because Papa Morgan let no one in the family ride or train or handle the horses unless he or she had seen what had been done in the name of fashion and function and plain unmotivated modernity. Horses in the Hippodrome looked very little like horses at Dancer's Rest—and very little like one another. Those that ran were lean whippy greyhound-bodied things, all legs and speed. Those that exhibited could not walk, could not trot, could not canter or gallop, could only flail the air in the movement called "show gait." It was a little like a prance and a little like a piaffe and a great deal like the snap and ratchet of a mechanical toy. And those that were there simply to be beautiful, could stand, that was all, and pose, and arch their extraordinarily long necks. They could carry no rider; their backs were grown too long and frail. They could walk, but with difficulty, since their hindlegs were so very long and so very delicate. But they were lovely, like living art, pure form divorced from function.

After a long day in the Hippodrome, Marina had come home to shock and a kind of grief. The family's horses were old stock—raw unmodified equine. They looked small and thick-legged, short-bodied, heavy and primitive. Their movements were strange, too varied and almost too heavy, all power and none of the oiled glide of the racers or the flashing knee-action of the exhibition stock. They were atavisms. The world had passed them by. All that was new and bold and reckoned beautiful was engineered, designed, calculated to the last curve of ear and flick of tail.

"That's why," Papa Morgan had said when she came back too cold of heart to cry and too angry to be wise. "That's what you needed to see. What they've made, and what we keep."

"But why keep it?" Marina had demanded. "Why bother with old stock at all? Nobody wants it. Nobody likes the way it looks or moves or handles. It can't run, it can't show, it can't stand up and look correctly beautiful."

"And worse than that," said Papa Morgan, "it has a mind of its own." He sighed. "That's why. Because it's not what people want. It's what it is."

She had understood, as she should, because she was family and she had learned the lesson from infancy. But her understanding was a shallow thing. She thought too often of going away as so many of the cousins and the siblings did, leaving Dancer's Rest to live in the world of cities and domes and gengineered equines. Only the strongest-minded stayed, and the ones who loved the horses above anything in the greater world, and those like Marina who were too weak-willed to leave.

Weak-willed, and bound to the horses, however primitive or unfashionable they might be. She was family. She was bred to this as surely as racers to the track and show stock to the ring.

The flyer was close enough now to see. She scrambled up from the damp grass, brushing at blades that clung, and knowing but not caring that her breeches were stained as green as Novinha's haunch. She ran down the hill toward the road, to the delight of the yearlings whose pasture it was. They swirled about her, a storm of hoofs and tails and tossing heads, parting and streaming along the forcefence as she ran through. She felt the tingle of the field, though the gate-chip was supposed to make it invisible and imperceptible. But she always knew where the fence was, and in much the same way the horses did.

Horse-instincts, Papa Morgan said, had been in the family since long before gengineering.

And why, she wondered, did she want to rear and shy and run away from the flyer that was coming to rest on the family's pad? It was only the inspector from the Hippodrome, come as she did every year at the start of breeding season, to inspect the stock and approve the roster of breedings-to-be and enjoy a long and convivial visit with Papa Morgan and the rest of the family. Marina had honed and polished Pluto Amena's levade for the exhibition that would crown the afternoon—she should be in the stable now, seeing that he was clean and ready to be shown.

But instead of turning toward the stable she kept going toward the house. She was not the only one. Papa Morgan and the elders were waiting, of course, as was polite, but there were others about as well, who should have been in the stables or in the house. Tante Concetta was standing near the pad, and Cousin Wilhelm, and Tante Estrella in breeches and boots with a long whip in her hand. Tante Estrella was a wild one, as wild as the young mares she preferred to train and handle, and as beautiful as they were, too. She looked a little frightening now, as if her ears were laid back and her tail lashing, threatening to kick or strike at the person who had emerged from the flyer.

It was not round smiling gray-haired Shanna Chen-Howard, nor any of the people who had always come with her to Dancer's Rest. This was a stranger. No human person came with him; only a mechanical, a mute and blank-faced metal bodyguard and recording device. It looked slightly more human than the stranger did, to Marina's eye.

Pity, too. He was young and not bad-looking. Gengineered, of course, but not so as to be obvious. That was the fashion these days. His parents would have designed him to emerge au naturel, with any serious flaws or inconveniences carefully and unobtrusively smoothed away.

They did not seem to have included a module for good humor. He looked as if he never smiled. His eyes as they scanned the people and the place were cold, and grew colder as they passed Cousin Wilhelm. Cousin Wilhelm stayed at home mostly, not for shame or shyness but because he was more comfortable there, where he did not need eyes to know where everything was. Implants had never taken, and mechanicals, he said, were worse than nothing at all. Marina thought he preferred the dark he had been born to, as rich as it was in sounds and smells. He was a better rider than most men who could see, and a wonderful trainer of horses.

This stranger in the inspector's tabard saw none of that. He saw a blind man in antique riding breeches, leaning on the arm of a graying and unnecessarily plump woman. Marina could read him as clearly as if he had spoken. *Primitive,* he was thinking. *Atavistic. Outdated.* Like the house in front of him, and the stables and the pastures beyond, and the horses in them, crude unmodified creatures without even the grace to be clean.

He was at least polite to Papa Morgan. It was a frigid politeness, with a bare minimum of words. Papa Morgan, who was never flustered, moved smoothly through the formulae of introduction, and took no notice of the brevity of the responses. It was briefest of all in front of Cousin Wilhelm: a sharp dip of the head that Cousin Wilhelm could not see, thoughtless maybe, but to Marina's mind as rude as an outright insult.

Papa Morgan noticed. He showed no sign of offense, but Marina saw how he led the inspector into the house without offering the greeting-cup, the wine and the bread and salt that sealed a friendship. Shanna Chen-Howard would have known what that signified. This person, this Hendrick Manygoats Watanabe, did not even seem to realize that he had been slighted.

Marina trailed after them. She was not invited, but neither was she shut out. There was a smell in the air, a little like hot iron, a great deal like fear.

"Yes," Papa Morgan said. "We do unregulated breeding here. We have a license to do so—a dispensation under the Mandate, for the preservation of rootstock."

He should not have had to explain to an inspector who administered the Mandate. The inspector knew exactly how much and how far Dancer's Rest was permitted to depart from the laws that governed gengineering. But he was insisting on being obtuse.

There was nothing convivial about the meeting. He had refused refreshment, which meant that no one with him could have it, either: distressing as the day wore on and they all went hungry. He had also refused the tour of the stables, and declined the pleasure of the exhibition. He had come, he said, to investigate the breeding practices at Dancer's Rest. They would present the records, please, and explain the entries, and be quick about it.

Papa Morgan was the most patient person Marina knew. He had to be, to be the head of the family. She had never seen him lose patience. Nor did he now with this stranger who would not look at his horses, but there was a glitter in his eyes that she had not seen before. It made her shiver.

She could have left long ago. But she stayed, and the others stayed, too, unnoticed and unreprimanded. They were like a bodyguard, she thought, though what they were guarding against, except bureaucratic niggling, she did not know.

Hendrick Manygoats Watanabe was not a patient man. He would never make a trainer of horses, she thought as she watched him scan the records. She wondered if he knew anything about horses at all, or if he cared. Shanna Chen-Howard had been one of those unfortunates who lack both the balance and the talent to do more than haul themselves into a saddle and sit more or less in the middle, but she had loved to watch the horses, ridden and free, and she had known many of them by name.

This man who had come in her place, who had not troubled to explain why, would never know Novinha and Selene and Bellamira and Sayyida, nor care that Maestoso Miranda liked sugar but Rigoletto preferred apples. His whole world was a scroll of data, columns of numbers, files labeled by genetic type. The living flesh, the animal that was the sum of its genes, was an irrelevance.

He frowned as the files scrolled behind his eyes.

"Random," he said to himself, but not as if he cared who heard. "Untidy. This string—" He called it to the wall-screen in the family's meeting room, which was an insult of sorts: They all had implants, they were not primitives or atavists who refused the seductions of the net. The pure flow of data resolved into an image, a helix of stars, each with its distinctive color and form.

Marina recognized the shape of it. One of the elders, Mama Tania, said what they all knew. "That's the Skowronek gene-line. Very old, very illustrious. Prepotent."

"And severely flawed," said Hendrick Manygoats Watanabe. "You see here, here, here." Light-pointers flashed. "This is worse than untidy. This is a possible lethal recessive."

"So it is," Papa Morgan said mildly.

"And you make no effort to remove it?"

Papa Morgan seemed to grow calmer, the more agitated the inspector became. "Of course you do understand, Ser Watanabe. It was explained to you. We preserve the old stock, the rootstock. Unaltered. Unrefined. Flaws and all."

"But that is against the Mandate," said Watanabe.

"We are exempt from the Mandate," Papa Morgan said.

"That," said Watanabe, "is a matter of debate."

There was a silence. Someone drew a long, slow breath. It was as loud as a rushing of wind.

Marina was too young to remember how the exemption had been granted, but everyone knew the story. Someone, the family had argued, should preserve the old stock—for antiquarian reasons, or sentimental ones, or for scholars and scientists who might find new modifications based on the old genetic materials. There had been a movement then in favor of such curiosities; the exemption had passed, and no one had challenged it.

Papa Morgan was not surprised to meet a challenge now. Nor were the other elders. They had expected this, then. They might even have expected the stranger who came in Shanna Chen-Howard's place.

She felt a flicker of anger. No one had told her. And how many of the others knew, who had kept it quiet because it could only upset the young and disturb the horses?

Elders' prerogative. She did not have to like it. She was here, when she could perfectly well have been told to leave—she had no place or position, and no authority beyond that of an assistant trainer.

So. She knew what this stranger was here for. Why he had been sent, and how he had gained authority for it—and also, within the rest, why Shanna Chen-Howard had not come. Her faction must have lost power in the Hippodrome. This was the new faction, and the new law.

"Your exemption is revoked," said Hendrick Manygoats Watanabe. "Your breeding patterns are invalid. You will be receiving instructions, which you will follow. This complex, for example," he said, tilting his head toward the wallscreen, "will be removed. There will be no further random breeding of live male to live female. You will conduct your program in accordance with the rules and regulations of the Mandate."

Papa Morgan did not bother to contend that there was

nothing random about the family's choices. He only said, "The Mandate has no provision for the preservation of rootstock."

"The whole of the Mandate encompasses such a provision. Your stock has been allowed to proliferate without rule or regulation. It has no specific function—"

"On the contrary," said Papa Morgan. "It is the most purely functional of all the equids. It lives to dance."

Watanabe's mouth opened, then closed again. Marina wondered if he had ever been interrupted in his life.

"We will appeal the decision," said Papa Morgan.

Watanabe recovered himself with an air almost of pleasure. "Your appeal is denied."

"We have to fight them."

The family was gathered where the elders had been since morning, all of them down to the toddlers from the crèches. There had been food earlier, and there was drink going around, intoxicant and stimulant and even plain water. The inspector was gone. He had taken his mechanical and his flyer and flown back to the Hippodrome without ever once looking at the horses.

"We should have dragged him out there," some of the younger trainers were insisting. "If he could see—"

"He saw all he needed to see." Marina surprised herself by speaking out—usually she kept quiet and let the others do the talking. "He looked at the helices, he saw how untidy and unregulated they were, and he knew they couldn't be allowed to continue."

Up among the elders, the same argument was going on, at nearly the same volume. Papa Morgan said in his deep voice that carried without effort, "We've been fighting the Mandate since it was made. We've been appealing this decision at every level. The answer is always no. We can keep our rootstock—by which they mean the type we breed and raise here. But we have to clean up its helices."

"But if we do that," Cousin Bernardin pointed out, "it's not rootstock anymore. It's modified. You know— we all know—that the helices are untidy because they need to be. That's where the strength is. That's what makes our horses what they are."

"The Mandate believes otherwise," said Papa Morgan. He sounded tired.

Papa Morgan was never tired or impatient or, all divinities forbid, defeated. But now he was close to all of them. He looked as if he wanted to turn and walk away, but the press of people hemmed him in. He had to stay and listen to all this fruitless babble.

Marina was freer than he was, but she could not leave, either. Whatever had brought her here in the morning was not letting her go. Family intuition, Tante Estrella would call it. Tante Estrella had more than her fair share of it herself.

As if the thought had invoked her, she came quietly to stand by Marina, not doing anything, watching people argue. She was still wearing her breeches, but her long whip was gone, laid aside somewhere. She did not seem agitated at all. If anything she was amused.

"Wait," she said to Marina out of nowhere in particular. "See what happens."

II.

Nothing happened, that Marina could see. The gathering ended in disarray. The Mandate left no choice and no debate. Its rules were strict and its regulations precise. Genetic codes would be corrected according to its guidelines, animals bred without the untidiness of stallion courting mare in the breeding pen or the pasture, pregnancies monitored and embryos transferred with clean mechanical precision.

There was none of the usual springtime excitement, the pleasure of matching this stallion to that mare, the waiting for her to come into season and accept him, the beautiful randomness of conception in a living womb. It was all done in the laboratory, as coldly meticulous as a chemical equation.

One thing at least the Mandate did not forbid, though it did not encourage it, either. It could not keep mares from carrying their own foals. Their clean, derandomized, genetically perfected foals, each set of helices prescribed by the authorities in the Hippodrome. Hendrick Manygoats Watanabe himself, according to the signature, reviewed and approved each one. The family's breeding managers were not permitted to select the matches. Not this season. They would be shown, he had informed them, what they were to do; then in other seasons they would know what was correct and what was permitted.

In much older days an insult of that proportion would have led to a duel at least, and maybe to a war. This season, with their greatest power stripped from them and handed to strangers, the elders in the breeding pens said nothing whatsoever.

They did as they were told. They collected specimens, handed them to the inspectors who flew in from the west, stood by unspeaking while those same inspectors returned from the laboratory with technicians and racks of labeled vials. When the horses objected, they made no move and spoke no word. More than one inspector or technician discovered that these undersized, primitive creatures were remarkably strong and self-willed—and utterly unforgiving of insults from strangers.

When the tech who had tried to collect a specimen from Favory Ancona went home with a broken femur, Papa Vladimir, who looked only to Papa Morgan for authority in the breeding pens, was seen to smile slightly and observe, "He should have asked first."

There was only one mercy in all of it. Once breeding season was over, the inspectors and technicians went away. They had done all they needed to do. The rest they left to the mares, and to the family. In the spring there would be foals, genetically purified and officially sanctioned, each with the Mandate's signature in its cells.

Marina did not know why, but after the first shock she stopped being upset. Angry, yes. The family had been trampled on. Its horses had been relegated to the status of a disease in need of a cure, its beautiful old bloodlines condemned as unsanitary. She could sit in the library with the books scrolling behind her eyes, telling over the names. The breeds that they kept pure here, the old breeds, the horses of princes: Arabian, Andalusian, Lipizzan. The lines preserved in each. Skowronek whose helices Watanabe had sneered at, Celoso whose sons were all kings and whose daughters were all queens, Favory and Conversano and Siglavy who had danced before kings. Ghazala, Princesa, Presciana; Moniet and Mariposa and Deflorata. They were woven in the helices, flaws as well as perfection, a memory as deep as the bone and more lasting.

It was immortality, not of the single creature but of the species itself. And the Mandate wanted to kill it in the guise of perfecting it.

Novinha was the first to come into heat and the first to get in foal. On a day of early spring when snow had been allowed to fall, she showed signs that she would foal in the night. Marina had foal watch in the broodmares' barn, blankets spread on straw next to the foaling stall. In the Hippodrome she did not doubt that they left such things to monitors and mechanicals. Here it was reckoned that foals of the old stock grew and thrived best if they were born the old way, with human hands ready if the mare faltered.

As the old mare began to pace her stall, Tante Estrella slipped in past Marina. She always knew when it was time, and she always came, no matter how late the hour. In fact it was early for a foaling, not quite midnight.

The long waiting, close on a year from breeding to birth, ended as it always did, with astonishing speed. As Novinha went down, Estrella was there, Marina close behind her, moving in concert as they had so often before.

There was little actually to do till the foal had slipped free of its mother. Novinha knew her business. This was her seventh foal, her luck-foal as family superstition had it, and she gave birth easily and quickly, from the first sight of the hoof wrapped in glimmering caul to the wet tangle of limbs sorting itself out in the straw.

Marina and Estrella stared at the foal, the perfect foal, designed and conceived under the Mandate. It was struggling to its feet already, lifting its head with its delicate curled ears.

Novinha was a Lipizzan, and so was the sire of record, Favory Ancona who had left so lasting a mark on the technician from the Hippodrome. They were all born dark, and turned glimmering white as they grew.

This foal of theirs under the Mandate had bypassed the dark phase. It was silvery white already, though it was no albino: Its skin was dark under the pallor of the coat.

It was a colt. He was a big one, substantial for one so young, with a big square shoulder and a solid rump. In that he was just as he should be. There was even a hint of an arch to his profile, the noble nose that distinguished his breed and his line.

And yet there was something odd . . .

Estrella was quicker than Marina, and maybe less unwilling to acknowledge what she saw. She inspected the small hoofs as the colt wobbled up on them, marking that each was the same and each preposterous, cloven like a goat's or a deer's. And the tail, not the brush of a normal foal but a tasseled monstrosity, and on the forehead where the silver-white hair whorled to its center—

Marina laughed with unalloyed delight. "Didn't we warn them? Didn't we, then? And they meddled with our beauties regardless."

All the mares were foaling unicorns. Every one. Colt or filly, Lipizzan or Andalusian or Arabian, each was the same: silver-white, cloven-hooved, with the bud of a horn on its brow. The Mandate had outsmarted itself.

"There was a reason," said Papa Morgan, "for the untidiness in the helices."

"We did try to tell them," Tante Concetta said. She kept to the house and seldom went among the horses, but she had gone down to the barn that first morning to look at Novinha's colt. She laughed as Estrella had, with the same high amusement.

None of the elders was at all surprised, no more than they had been by the lowering of the Mandate. They had expected this. It must be something one learned when one became an elder, a secret that had stopped being a secret when Novinha's foal was born.

He had a name from before birth in the ancient tradition of his breed. Favory Novinha: Favory for the ancestor of his line, Novinha for his dam who inspected him with as little surprise as the elders had shown, and a quietly luminous pride. If it disconcerted her to be mother to such strange offspring, she did not show it.

Marina was beyond surprise when they got him out into the light and she had her first clear sight of his eyes. They were not brown at all, not even the near-black of his heritage, but a deep and luminous blue. Nor did they change as he grew. They were part of him, like the goat-feet on which he walked and the horn that sprouted on his forehead.

She was more or less in charge of him. It was usual for whoever had foal watch on a particular night to inherit, in a manner of speaking, the foal who was born on that watch. There was not much to do when the foal's dam was as experienced as Novinha. Mostly Marina watched him. She never quite admitted that she was waiting for him to do something unusual, something magical.

But he never did, unless it was magic that he grew so fast and moved so light. Lipizzans grew into their grace. When they were young they were awkward, gangling, often heavy on their feet. This colt was graceful from birth. He was born knowing how to move, how best to dance.

That was his magic, she supposed. He knew what other foals had to learn.

The Mandate had no provision for such an eventuality as this. It had not intended to create a new—or recreate a very old—species. It had been meddling, that was all. Asserting its sense of order on a disordered breed.

Hendrick Manygoats Watanabe came back as the last of the mares waited to deliver their foals. This time he was accompanied by Shanna Chen-Howard. She, for once, was not smiling. He was looking remarkably humble.

"They retired me," she said to Papa Morgan as they walked away from the flyer that had brought her. She was direct as always, though Watanabe looked sourly disapproving. "They tossed me out on my ear, told me to take myself a vacation, gengineer some roses, take up locust-keeping in the Sahel—anything but get in their way when they decided to lay the Mandate on everybody who was exempt. I gather they did much the same to you."

Papa Morgan spread his hands, eloquent of resignation. "What could we do? We're subject to the law. If the law says we have to give in to the Mandate . . ."

Shanna Chen-Howard slanted a glance at him. Marina, following at a discreet distance, thought she saw laughter in it. "You were always law-abiding citizens," she said blandly.

They had turned the mares out in the wide green pasture that rolled down to the river. Two sides of it were fenced in water, with a forcefence to remind the bolder foals that they were not to go exploring. All the mares with foals at side, as it happened, were grays; none of the dark mares had been bred this year, again under the Mandate.

It was a pretty picture from a distance, white horse-shapes on green, the larger grazing peacefully, the smaller playing or nursing or lying flat on the grass in the sun. Closer in, one realized that the mares were ordinary enough, but the foals were odd.

Marina found herself walking just behind Watanabe. He stepped gingerly, as if he had never walked on a dirt road before. The glances he shot at the pasture almost made her laugh aloud. He must be having dreadful visions of hip-deep mud, reeking manure, creatures crawling up the grassblades to devour him whole.

The fence along the road was an atavism, a real post-and-rail fence, though there was a forcefence just behind it to keep it secure. One of Papa Morgan's predecessors had thought it worthwhile to have at least one old-fashioned fence for leaning on and watching the horses. Papa Morgan did just that now, and Shanna Chen-Howard kept him company. Watanabe hung back, with Marina still behind him.

The mares had been aware of them all along, but most were busy cropping the new grass. It was Novinha's colt who came forward first, curious to see who these visitors were. He took a circuitous way about it, showing off his floating gait, spiraling in toward the fence till he stood just inside of it, nostrils flared, head up, bright eye fixed on them all.

Shanna Chen-Howard took a while to find her voice. When she did, it wobbled a little, but then it was its forthright self again. "Well. You weren't exaggerating."

"Neither were the holorecords we sent you," Papa Morgan said.

"No," said Shanna Chen-Howard, "but somehow, in the flesh, it's more effective."

She stretched a hand over the fence. The colt sniffed it, thought about nipping, caught Marina's eye and behaved himself. He let Shanna Chen-Howard stroke his nose, and stood still for her to run her hand up it till it touched the base of the horn. She almost recoiled then: Marina saw how she tensed. But he leaned into her, encouraging her to scratch where it was always itching.

"It is real," she said as he obliged him. "It really is." She began to laugh.

The only one who seemed to need an explanation was Watanabe. He was not about to get one. She kept laughing when Papa Morgan let her into the pasture, the same way Tante Estrella had when the colt was born, and Tante Concetta. It was a grand joke on the Mandate.

"The trouble," she said as they lingered over dinner that evening, "is that the Mandate has no sense of humor whatsoever. You're exonerated—there's no sign of tampering, and every breeding was administered entirely by technicians from the Hippodrome—but you know how the law works. It has to cast blame on somebody."

No one looked at Hendrick Manygoats Watanabe. He had a plate in front of him as they all did, the elders and the trainers who had been admitted to the meeting, the senior trainers and the younger ones like Marina who were in charge of this year's foals. He had eaten nothing and said nothing. It was probably excruciating for him to have to dally like this, being endlessly inefficient, eating and drinking and hanging about instead of working on the problem at hand.

"I'd ask, Why not blame the Mandate?" said Tante Estrella, "except I'm not that foolish. We did warn you— them—of what might happen if they tried to meddle with old stock."

"So you did," said Shanna Chen-Howard, "but after all, the horses bred under the Mandate were meddled with, too, in the beginning. Why would these be any different?"

"Because they're old stock," Tante Estrella said. "The others had already been meddled with till they forgot where they came from. These never did. The Arabian is the oldest and purest of all. The others were bred from it by masters who knew better than any Mandate how to make perfection in the form of a horse. It's dangerous to meddle with perfection."

Shanna Chen-Howard shook her head. She was not arguing, at least not with Tante Estrella. "So. We tampered with something that was already finished. We turned it into something else altogether."

"Exactly," said Papa Morgan.

Shanna Chen-Howard sighed heavily. "This is not going to go over well with the committee in the Hippodrome. There's that clause in the Mandate, you see, that your predecessors helped write. The one that draws the line between modification and complete transformation. We can tidy up your horses' helices. We can't turn their offspring into something other than horses."

Papa Morgan smiled. There was nothing smug about it, but Hendrick Manygoats Watanabe got up abruptly, kicked back his chair, and stalked out.

III.

None of it was really about the Mandate, or about the Hippodrome's mistake. Marina's, too, for thinking that it was so simple. She had not been paying attention. That was a bad fault in a horse trainer.

It was a long summer. The weather was on a random cycle, which meant heat and sun and a daily explosion of thunder. The nights were steamily warm, with a crackle of lightning near the horizon.

Marina liked to walk the pastures at night. The horses were quiet then, grazing or drowsing. There were monitors set to catch anything out of the ordinary, but they were part of the forcefence, invisible and almost imperceptible.

She went out on a night when the moon was full and the lightning had sunk almost out of sight over the world's rim, and wandered from pasture to pasture. There were mares in foal again, bred the old way, without the Mandate to interfere. They were standing together at the far corner of their pasture, looking out into the next, where their sisters were, and the foals.

Novinha's colt had a horn now as long as Marina's hand. It was ivory, densely spiral-grained and keenly pointed. The elders had been talking about blunting the foals' horns or capping them like an elephant's tusks or removing them altogether, for their own and their mothers' safety.

While the elders failed to agree on what to do, the foals did each other no damage, though they loved to spar like swordsmen. They seemed to have an instinct, a sense of just how far it was wise to go. It held even with humans. And that, thought Marina, was the most unfoal-like thing about them. Young horses were reckless of their strength, but these were remarkably careful, for babies. It was as if they were born knowing how to conduct themselves in the world.

Novinha's foal called to Marina as she came down to the pasture, running along the fence with head and tail high, tossing his head with its moon-bright gleam of horn. The others followed more slowly. They had their own chosen humans; they acknowledged Marina but did not welcome her as the colt did. In that they were Lipizzans, but again they were young for it.

She slipped through the gate in the wooden fence. The colt was waiting for her. He followed her as she walked to the river, with the others trailing behind, and even a few of the mares.

She stopped as she always did at her favorite place, a stone like a chair, where she could sit and watch the water flow by. The colt lay down as he liked to do and laid his head in her lap. The moon glowed in his coat. She stroked it. It was the softest thing in the world, and warm, and it smelled of flowers. He closed his eyes and sighed.

He was not asleep, not quite. His ears flicked as the other foals and their mothers found things to do nearby. A pair of shadows moved softly through them, stroking a neck here, a nose there.

Tante Estrella and Tante Concetta sat on the grass near Marina's stone. Some of the foals circled, curious, even came to be petted, but none came as close as the colt had, or laid his head in a welcoming lap. Maybe it was Novinha who prevented it: She had come to stand over Tante Concetta, huge and white and quiet.

Marina's head was full of questions. There were too many of them; they crowded each other. They silenced her.

Tante Estrella only sat for a moment before she was on her feet again, stroking and talking softly to one of the younger mares. That one had a filly, who came to investigate Estrella, nibbling boldly on the hem of her coat.

"Look," Estrella said abruptly. Marina started. The

colt opened an eye but closed it again, refusing to wake for anything as trivial as human chatter.

"Look around you," Estrella said. "Do you know what you see?"

She was expecting an answer. Marina groped for one. "A mistake," she said. "The Mandate carried too far."

"No," said Estrella. "You don't see."

Marina frowned. She had come here to be alone in the quiet, not to be put in the training ring and set on a circle.

"Estrella is saying," said Concetta from Novinha's shadow, "that you need to look harder. What do you see?"

"Twelve baby unicorns," Marina said sharply, though she tried to be light. "Next you're going to tell me you planned this."

"We did expect that it would happen, yes," Concetta said. "We thought the Hippodrome needed a lesson."

"It could have blown up in your faces," Marina said. "We could have been shut down. If they get angry enough, we could still—"

"No," said Estrella. She was smiling. It was the same smile Papa Morgan had had, that had driven away Hendrick Manygoats Watanabe.

Marina was not as easily routed, and she had a unicorn in her lap. She looked around as she had been told to, in the moon's bright light. The mares were all around them, and the foals, watching as if what she said could matter to them. And how could it? She had nothing wise or intelligent to say.

She had to say something. She said, "We're old stock, too. Aren't we? What happens if they put us under the Mandate?"

Estrella laughed. It was a silvery sound, but very human. "Not what you're afraid of! We turn into what we were to start with. Gypsies. Tinkers. Tamers of horses from Old Troy onward. No more and no less than we always were."

"But," said Marina. "I don't—" She stopped herself, started again. "I'm not seeing what I obviously should see."

"We're all blind when we're young," Concetta said. "We have to learn to see. Like foals."

"Not these," Marina said, ruffling the colt's mane. "We're custodians, aren't we? We were given them, and they us. We protect them."

"That's part of what we do," Concetta said. "We watch over the old arts, too, and the old lines."

"Which happen to go back to the old stories," said Estrella. She seemed to find the fact delightful. So would Marina, if she had time to think about it—if she were not so afraid. She had grown up under the Mandate. She could not imagine it giving way so easily. The family could not be that strong. No one was.

She said that last aloud. Estrella shook her head at Marina's foolishness. "We don't need to be. We have our horses. And," she said, "their children. Haven't you wondered what will become of them?"

"Often," Marina said.

"In an older world," said Concetta, "there would be no place for them. This world, that makes new species out of the rags of the old . . . there's room in it for a myth."

Marina looked at the colt asleep in her lap. He did not feel like a myth. He was warm and solid and inescapably real.

"Is he going to live forever?" she asked.

She had no idea where the question came from. It simply was, hanging out there in front of them.

One of the mares snorted and stamped. The sound swelled to fill the silence.

Estrella spoke softly, almost too soft to hear. "We don't know."

Marina widened her eyes. "You don't know? But you know everything!"

Estrella said nothing. Concetta sighed. "We only know what all the elders know. What we teach the young ones when they're ready. What we preserve here, as far as the world ever knew, is the old way of training horses, and the old lines. Now it knows what the old lines are, and what they come from. But what else we've let the Mandate make here . . . we don't know. They may just be very long-lived."

"How? Like their mothers, still strong at thirty? Or like us with our hundred years? Or more than that?"

They did not answer.

The colt stirred suddenly and scrambled to his feet. He shook himself all over. He scratched an ear with a hind hoof; scratched his rump with his horn. He nudged against Novinha and, with a careful twist of the head that kept the horn from her belly, began vigorously to nurse.

Miranda could see how he would grow, from the way the moonlight struck him: not tall but broad and sturdy, built to carry a rider, to pull a carriage, to stand in marble on a monument. He was not the delicate goat-creature of the myth. None of them was, even the ones who had been bred from Arabians. They were all as real as the stone she sat on.

"And they said," she said, "that the rootstock was a rhinoceros."

"That was a diversion," said Estrella, "to keep the secret safe till people were ready to know it. It's not how long one of them lives, do you see? It's that the line lives. Just as with us. One person dies, gives way to another, but the species goes on and on. Eventually it changes. Or if people meddle with its helices, it discovers what it would have been."

Marina nodded slowly. "I wonder," she said. "Will they breed true?"

"We don't know that, either," said Concetta, but not as if she were deeply troubled by it.

Marina thought of finding answers. Of breeding under the Mandate; of being exempt from it. Of discovering what they had, and what it would turn into.

Shanna Chen-Howard would come back. Others would come with her. They would try to meddle. They could not help it. Somehow under the moon it did not matter. The world was so much wider than it had been, the day the Mandate lowered itself on Dancer's Rest.

"It did better than it knew," she said.

"Oh, it knew," said Concetta. "It just didn't know how much it knew." She pushed herself up, shaking out her skirts. "It was meant, after all, to make the imperfect perfect."

"And when it found something that was exactly as it ought to be," Estrella said over the back of her favorite mare, "it made something completely new, that was as old as memory."

And they said the magic had gone out of the world. Marina shook her head and found herself smiling. It was hard not to smile, with mares and foals all around her, and one coming to rest his horn gently over her heart.

"I wonder," she said, "how you'll take to the training ring." He snorted and raised his head and stamped. And went up, smooth and sure, all silver in the moonlight: a levade as polished as any in the arena.

She laughed. His eye seemed to laugh with her. She had an answer to that question at least. It was quite enough to go on with.

LUCY TAYLOR

CONVERGENCE

Peter: **Lucy Taylor**, like P. D. Cacek, is another one whose stories appear in anthologies with names like *Hot Blood 4: Hotter Blood,* and *The Mammoth Book of Erotic Horror.* She lives in the hills outside Boulder, Colorado, with her five cats—which, speaking as a person who has lived with a lot of cats over the years—could quite easily account for a propensity to write horror fiction. But her "Convergence" is no horror story at all: It's a love story with a wonderfully happy/sad ending. . . .

Janet: Lucy is attractive, bright, and ballsy. She's also a terrific writer and a consummate professional. Sometimes I fantasize that up-and-coming writers like Lucy—and Lisa Mason, P. D. Cacek, Marina Fitch, Robert Devereaux, Dave Smeds—all of them close to a generation younger than I, are the new breed of authors. In these fantasies, they dedicate themselves to the development of an intravenous which is plugged into young writers and pumps into their veins a solution containing equal measures of work ethic, respect for deadlines, willingness to pay their dues, modesty, vision, determination, and talent.

Convergence

ALITTLE AFTER ONE A.M., THE WORLD TEETERED AND tipped onto its side like a badly spun top. Sable Finley jerked awake with a cry of pain and surprise. She found herself lying on the floor, disoriented and confused, still half-asleep. Where was she? For a moment, she thought she was in Dan's bed back in Charlotte, North Carolina, and somehow, maybe thrashing about in a dream, he had shoved her out of bed. Or that she and Dan were visiting her daughter Miriam and granddaughter Elise in Oakland and an earthquake—the Big One that everyone always talked about—had hit.

Then she opened her eyes and saw, by the light she'd left on in the tiny bathroom, that the room was canted crazily to one side. Her suitcases had tumbled down from the overhead rack—she'd barely missed being bashed by falling Samsonite. The things she'd left out on the desk the night before—her journal, a copy of *Redbook* turned to a page on exercise for women over fifty, the necklace Elise had given her and the photo of her and Dan taken at their wedding the month before—had all slid off onto the floor.

From outside came a great commotion, doors being slammed, voices clamoring. The thunk and scuffle of panicked feet, objects crashing, a man shouting "What's going on?" and a woman's voice, razor-edged with fear, "Oh my God, where are the life vests?"

Then Sable was more awake than she'd ever been in her life, because she remembered now where she was—somewhere between Harwich, England, and Hamburg, Germany, on the Dutch ferry the *Nieuw Amsterdam*.

Going to meet Dan at the software convention in Hamburg before they took off for a few weeks to explore Europe together.

With their first stop in Paris to pick out their new apartment.

To start their new life together as husband and wife. *Dear God*.

She shucked off her pajamas, got into a pair of slacks and a shirt. She wanted to take the photo of her family with her, but that was impractical under the circumstances, so instead she snatched up the necklace Elise had given her, just a child's trinket really, a small silver unicorn with a red rhinestone eye and glittery horn on a cheap metal chain ("To protect you, Grandma," Elise had said). Sable put it around her neck and then stumbled out of the cabin into the chaos of the corridor, up the stairs past the car deck. From where the vehicles had been loaded on board the ferry, she heard what sounded like a demolition derby, metal crashing and crunching against metal and—*no, it couldn't be, wasn't possible*—the roar of water rushing in.

She was pushed from behind and fell forward, banging her knee on the stair. A foot crushed her hand. She yelped, pulled herself to her feet, and made it the rest of the way to the upper deck and then outside into the black, steel-cold night.

The boat felt like it was taking roller coaster plunges off huge cliffs of water, crashing down into jagged crevasses of obsidian sea. More and more listing to starboard. Sable skidded on the slippery deck. Her feet were bare—in her panic, she'd been unable to find the pair of Reeboks she'd left by the bed.

No matter, she told herself, she wasn't going to need shoes. The sea would calm down, the ferry would right itself, and she'd go back to bed. And soon she'd be in Hamburg and Dan would pull her into his big arms and she'd tell him about this terrible night, how afraid she had been, and he'd comfort her, hold her, make it all right.

It was all a bad dream. They weren't sinking. They *couldn't* be sinking.

Someone—a crew member with a bright shock of blood in his hair—thrust a life vest at her.

"Put this on!"

She stared at him, not comprehending.

"What's happening?"

He didn't answer. He was too busy forcing her arms through the holes in the vest, buckling it in the front. He was a small man, dark complected, his eyes cartoonishly big, like an electroshocked owl. She tried to ask him again what was happening, but the ferry lurched violently and water crashed over their heads in a long icy spill. A man and woman, pale lumps of doughy white flesh in little more than their underwear, pushed past her, jabbering in German. Sable followed them, clutching at whatever she could to stay on her feet.

The crew and able-bodied passengers were lowering life rafts into coal-colored waves that bucked and writhed like the back of a sea monster.

Someone shoved Sable from behind. "Go, lady, go!"

She slipped in her bare feet and skidded, arms flailing wildly. She saw the rail coming up—the same rail where just yesterday morning she'd leaned over and tossed bits of brioche into the sun-dazzled sky for the seagulls to catch, daydreaming of Dan and their future—and she screamed as she almost plummeted headfirst into the water, but then hands gripped her and she was lowered, swung really, into a wildly rocking, pitifully small rubber raft with eight other drenched, terrified-looking people.

"Get away, get away before the ferry goes down!" a long-haired man yelled.

Those closest shoved the raft away from the *Nieuw Amsterdam*, which was almost completely capsized now, the starboard deck partially underwater. Many of those left behind dived into the sea. Sable thought she heard seagulls shrieking out words in a Babel of tongues and then realized it was the screams of women who'd jumped or fallen into the sea.

She reached up, fingered the unicorn charm at her throat, where she could feel her pulse beating.

I'll be all right. I'll make it. I have to make it. Dan's waiting for me in Hamburg.

The sinking *Nieuw Amsterdam* went suddenly dark as the electricity failed. Whoever was left aboard now, Sable thought, would be fighting their way through the maze of the luxury ferry's corridors, through its bars and restaurants and casinos, in tomblike blackness. Anyone who hadn't gotten off the ferry by now . . .

But I'm all right, she thought. *I got off the boat and I'm not in the water.*

She clutched at the unicorn charm with numb fingers.

Then a wave the size of a three-story building struck the raft broadside, flipping it over and dumping Sable and all the others on board into the churning North Sea.

"You sure you don't want to fly over with me?" Dan had said. "We can take an extra couple of days before the convention starts to see Hamburg."

Sable had laughed, shook her head. "Sure you don't want to sail over with me instead of flying?"

She and Dan were sitting out in the backyard of her town house in Charlotte, enjoying the benign bake of an Indian summer. They were taking a break from the gardening, snipping back the errant branches of Sable's roses and clipping the weeds, the better to impress potential buyers when the Realtor started showing Sable's property the next week. A pitcher of iced tea and a small plate of lemon bars sat on the table between them. Sable's hands smelled of planting and soil, the loamy tang of turned earth.

"I'd love to come on the boat with you," Dan said, biting into a lemon bar, "but then I'd miss most of the software convention. MacroBite isn't hiring me to head up the Paris office so I can miss out on their international trade shows."

Sable was grateful he didn't offer his oft-repeated lecture on the safety of flying versus the take-your-life-in-your-hands risk of the freeway drive to the airport. She already knew the statistics proving air travel was safer than almost anything you could do besides sitting at home in an armchair, but that didn't change how she felt about it. She was terrified of flying, of rising into the seamless bowl of sky held aloft only by principles of aerodynamics she had little faith in and no understanding of.

"I'll leave the cruise ship at Southampton and take the train to Harwich," she'd said, thumbing the well-worn travel brochure. "There's a ferry between Harwich and Hamburg every three days."

"I'll meet you," said Dan. "The convention will be winding up then. There's so much I want to show you in Hamburg—the Fish Market and the Old Town Hall and the Rapierbahn, bless its scurrilous heart." He squeezed her hand. "Then we'll drive to Paris and start looking for an apartment."

He'd leaned over and kissed her, and she'd marveled at it all over again, the miracle of meeting the right person this late in life. His lips tasted of lemon and honey and she could feel the desire rising in her as she hadn't felt it since she was a young girl. Sixty-one and in love. In lust as well—to hell with all that platonic, companionate stuff the magazines touted for couples their age—in the bedroom, she felt like a teenager. She felt absurdly lucky.

Sable snapped back to full consciousness in the water. She could hear moans and cries for help and there

were things floating—people, objects—all around her.
The air tingled with the terror of people in the water. Even
for those who wore life vests, thought Sable, how long
could they stay alive in water this cold?

How long could *she?* All her life she had been a
strong swimmer. She still swam two or three times a
week at the health club near her home, but this wasn't
about swimming. This was about keeping her head above
water and not dying of cold.

The dark, lozenge shape of a lifeboat loomed near
her. Sable reached out as it passed, but there was no way
she could haul herself into it—the raft was upside down.
A wave lifted her up and heaved her away like a bathtub
toy in the hand of a child, sending her skidding down its
steep slope into a trough. Her head went under. Her
mouth filled with brine. The vest shot her to the surface,
gagging and gulping for air.

And she was cold, so bone-jarringly cold, every pore
quaking with the sensation of being stabbed with tiny
hypodermics of ice.

There was no sign of the *Nieuw Amsterdam.* Just the
screams and the thrashing of those alive and still in the
water.

Oh, Dan, Dan, what should I do?

Cries came to her. She turned and saw another
lifeboat approaching her, this one right side up. Someone
leaned far out, reaching for her.

"Help me, please help!"

A wave came between them, slapped her away.

"Help!"

The hands reached again and got her this time, hauling her up into the raft, where she collapsed in a shuddering heap against the wet rubber.

In the boat was a man with a well-trimmed goatee wearing a sodden jacket and slacks. Beside him huddled a young woman wearing only a pullover sweater and a pair of underpants, clutching her sides and shivering so hard she looked as if a huge vibrator throbbed at her core.

"The ferry?" asked Sable.

"Gone," said the man.

"What happened?"

"I don't know. Somebody said there was a leak through the doors on the car deck . . . who knows, it all happened so fast."

The girl moaned and clutched her knees, rocking back and forth like an autistic child. Her wet hair, stringy and kelp-like, was plastered around her colorless face.

"Only the two of you made it into the lifeboat?"

"The others fell out," the goateed man said. "A wave hit and turned us over. The other people . . . I don't know what became of them."

"But the *Nieuw Amsterdam*," said Sable, "they must have had time to radio for help. They'll send ships, helicopters. They'll find us."

"They've got to . . . or the cold . . . even if we don't drown, the cold will . . ."

A wave bunted them high, smashed them down. Sable was almost dislodged. She clutched at the ropes crisscrossing the raft.

The girl cried out in French, invoking the names of the saints.

Sable laid a hand on the girl's quaking shoulder.

"We'll make it," she said, not knowing if the girl understood her or not, but wanting to offer comfort. "They'll send searchers for us. They'll divert all the boats in the area to look for survivors. We'll be all right."

But what she thought was: *I can't die. Not now, not here. Let someone else die, please God, not me. Dan's waiting for me in Hamburg.*

She reached up and fingered the unicorn charm, wishing it were a crucifix. To distract herself from her terror, she tried to recall what she knew about unicorns. Only that they were partial to virgins, that they were immortal and ancient, and that her eight-year-old granddaughter was fiercely enamored of their mythical species.

And that, like all things miraculous, splendid, and deeply yearned for, Sable knew they didn't exist.

Please God, don't let me die.

"To protect you, Grandma."

Sable had sat with Elise in San Francisco's Golden Gate Park. Dan and Miriam had stayed at home, ostensibly to watch a baseball game but really to allow Sable some private time with her grandchild, a consideration she deeply appreciated. It was Saturday and the green was confettied with bright rectangles of picnic cloths, the blue sky a shifting geometry of Frisbees and kites. Children scampered and dogs raced after balls. A pair of teenage lovers, androgynous with their nose rings and tie-dyed tee shirts that looked like they'd been gleaned from a sixties' rummage sale, cuddled and smooched.

Elise had scowled at the lovers and snorted with disapproval.

At her age, she was still blithely contemptuous of boys and blessedly indifferent to sex, something for which Sable was grateful. She played shortstop on an all girls' softball team, wore her blond hair waifishly short, and populated her room, not with the culture of Barbie and posters of sexless young pop stars, but with unicorns—stuffed unicorns, books about unicorns, coy, bendable unicorns with curly latex manes meant to be combed out and styled. Around her neck she wore a silver unicorn with a ruby-colored eye.

"I wish you wouldn't move to Paris," Elise said. "It's too far away."

"Dan's new job is there," Sable said. "And don't forget, your mom promised to let you come over and spend next summer with us. So you'll be seeing me again in no time at all. And you'll like Paris. Dan says it's a wonderful city."

From the way Elise's lip pouted out, Sable knew she found the idea of Paris about as exciting as the stewed prunes that she'd rejected at breakfast.

"I tell you what," Sable said. "When you come to Paris, I'll take you to see a unicorn. How would you like that?"

Elise perked up. "A unicorn in Paris? Where?"

"A very famous unicorn, in fact. It's in a tapestry in the Musée de Cluny in the Latin Quarter. Dan says that—"

"Oh. I thought you meant a *real* unicorn."

"Honey, there are no real unicorns."

"You mean they're extinct? Like the dinosaurs?"

"I don't know. Maybe there were unicorns at one time or another, but not anymore."

Tears gleamed in Elise's eyes.

Sable said, "Oh, honey, I suppose anything's possible. Just don't cry because I said that there aren't any unicorns."

"I'm not crying about that," said Elise, close to sobbing. "I'm crying because you have to move so far away. I wish you hadn't gotten married. Do you think you'll ever get divorced and come back home?"

"No," said Sable firmly, "Dan and I won't get divorced."

"But Mom says you aren't even going to Europe on the plane together. You're going on a boat by yourself."

"That's because I've got a silly phobia about flying. It's why Dan and I had to take the train out here."

"Why are you afraid?"

"I'm not sure," Sable had answered. "Something to do with the fear that I'll fall. That it's not really possible for the plane to be up there in the first place and that it has to fall down."

And I'll die and that will be all there is, she had thought. *The end of my being, end of love, end of life, everything.*

"You won't fall," Elise had said. She reached up, removed the unicorn locket from around her neck and handed it to Sable.

"Here you go, Grandma. To protect you."

"I can't take this. It's your favorite."

"It's okay," Elise said. "You can keep it for me and

give it back next summer, when I come to visit." She looked suddenly uneasy. "You won't change your mind, will you?"

"Of course not, sweetie," Sable had said. "And until you come visit, I'll hang on to the unicorn."

The young woman in the pullover sweater was dead. Sable knew even before the man checked her pulse. The girl's face had the gelid, boneless quality of aspic, like you could scoop out her flesh with a dessert spoon and it would quiver and sparkle with ice crystals.

The goateed man looked at her, shook his head. "Dead."

"But . . . what?" Sable said. "Was she hurt?"

"She was wet," the man said. He could barely get the words out for his teeth's savage clacking. "The cold killed her."

A wave one-two punched the raft, spewing brine into Sable's face, over her sodden clothes. She clutched the ropes as the raft skidded down the side of a wave and partway up another. It was all she could do to hold on. She could not feel her fingers, her toes.

In the distance, like a beam from some hovering spacecraft, a cone of greenish-white light angled down, illuminating the water.

Sable pointed and shrieked, "There! There they are! I told you they'd come! There they are!"

And she thought of the dead girl's family and how they'd have to be told that she died right before help arrived, that if she'd only hung on a few more minutes, just a little while longer, she'd have made it like the other two people in the raft. Sable found herself overcome with gratitude. *I'm going to be rescued.*

The light was joined by another. The two lights criss-crossed and zigzagged. They wove patterns of pearl on the crests and the swells. They cleaved rents in the great, towering black of the sky. Brighter than moonglow, more dazzling than a skyful of northern lights, quicksilver carving the night into ebony hexagons.

Then they moved away in the other direction.

Away from the raft.

"No!"

Sable opened her mouth and banshee-wailed into the night like a madwoman, moonstruck and feral.

"They've gone," said the man, as though the enormity of the horror must be articulated.

"But . . . they can't . . ."

Sable found herself barely able to speak. She sat mutely, staring into the black sky and the fierce, blacker sea, watching the lights of salvation grow thinner and smaller and finally disappear.

They floated.

At one point Sable closed her eyes and either slept or lost consciousness. When she woke up, the French girl wasn't there anymore. Sable didn't know if a wave had washed her out or if the bearded man, not wishing to share their lifeboat with a corpse, had tossed her overboard.

She hoped it wasn't the latter. If she died, she would want someone to find her, send her body home, bury her. Not leave her to rot in the sea.

Don't think like that. Don't.

She shut her eyes and prayed, although she was not a praying person—had grown away from the Faith of her childhood decades ago—but it was as much a bitter rebuke as a plea for mercy. She was angry at this God she did not believe in. How dare he or she! How dare he let her meet Dan, the love of her life, the first man who'd ever held her hand when they went out in public, the first man who'd ever kissed her down *there,* who'd ever moved inside her, slowly, slowly, and made her believe in the power of sexual love for the first time in her life, and let her meet him this late, and then—when they hadn't even had a chance to enjoy a few years together, a few months—take her away.

Unfair.

And Elise.

She must live to see Elise finish high school, finish college, get married or maybe stay single, but become a young woman with all the promise and passion of youth.

Unfair.

She touched her neck. For a second, she thought the unicorn wasn't there anymore, but it was only because her fingers were so cold that she could barely feel the dimpled curves of the metal flank, the tiny sharp point of the horn. She scraped her nails over its surface to assure herself it was still there.

Then white noise and cold night filled her head again. The raft and its other occupant disappeared, and she was clinging to the mane of a powerful unicorn whose jutting horn opened a path through the waves. Wonder and gratitude filled her, but the creature began to melt out from under her, its snowy withers and flanks liquefying into meringue-colored foam. "No!" she cried out as the unicorn's neck dissolved into a high, glistening wave and she was swept under the water.

When she awoke this time, the goateed man was sleeping, and a pale light shone in her eyes. Not the light of the rescue helicopters but the thin, salmon-gold streak of dawn.

The sunlight. The sunlight will warm me.

She felt strait-jacketed by the cold. It was hard to move and harder to think clearly, hard even to remember her exact situation. She'd read that was one of the signs of the last stages of hypothermia.

The sun nudged up into the clouds a bit, like an infected eye squinting up into grey brows, and Sable saw something else.

"My God, look!" she shouted to the goateed man. "Wake up, look!"

Land, a whole verdant shore of it. She tried to remember her geography, the map in the atlas back home. The *Nieuw Amsterdam* had been halfway through the journey when it went down. If the current was sweeping her eastward, then she might be near the Frisian Islands, a narrow necklace of land off the coast of West Germany and the Netherlands. She could see the waves breaking on what looked like a smooth, barrierless shore. The beach appeared deserted, but on the hillsides, she made out dark, rectangular shapes that might have been houses.

"Look!"

She tried to shake the goateed man awake. He slumped forward. Vomit and water ran out of his mouth, and he flopped facedown into the pool of water collected in the bottom of the raft.

"No!" Sable tried to turn the man over, but he was too heavy. She tried holding his head up in her lap and rubbing his head—*there, Dan, does that feel any better? It's late and I'm so tired. Let's go up to bed. Dan, please, help me upstairs*—but after a while Sable realized the man wasn't Dan, but some stranger who wasn't breathing, who hadn't, in fact, been breathing for a very long time, and she let his head slide off her lap and plop back into the water.

Alone now, she gazed toward the land. It didn't look far away. If she were rested and fresh, she could make it. As cold and exhausted as she was, though . . .

She waited to see if the land grew closer, but the current seemed to be sweeping the raft farther out into the sea, bypassing the shore that appeared so tantalizingly near.

I can do it, she thought. *I can make it.*

The life vest would keep her afloat, but prevent her from swimming efficiently. She squirmed out of it and did a few stretches to loosen her stiff limbs. Then she dove into the sea.

Dan is waiting. Waiting for me.

She plowed into the waves, forcing herself to deny the exhaustion and numbness in her muscles, fighting the urge to give up and let herself sink, to rest her weary limbs on the sea bottom. She wasn't going to be like the girl who had died in the raft last night or the man who had died this morning. She could stay alive a little longer. Long enough to get to the shore. To get help.

I can do it for Dan.
For Miriam and Elise.

For once, the sea seemed to side with her, the waves behind her now as she got nearer the beach, pushing her on. The water grew warmer. It felt almost springy and soft now, like a plush carpet, and it was filled with small speckled fish, bright, bug-eyed fish like calico clowns, and Sable knew they were just dots fizzing behind her eyes, rainbow-hued illusions, but that didn't matter—they were beautiful—and she swam with the beaded and calico fish and with hordes of nimble, pinwheeling starfish, she swam with the shimmering schools of them toward the land.

Her knee scraped something hard, a layer of pebbles along a gently inclined beach. She crawled through the surf, then collapsed in the shallows, coughing and spitting up water.

Thank God.

With her eyes still shut, she reached up to touch the unicorn charm. Somehow it had stayed around her neck throughout the ordeal. Maybe Elise had been right, she thought, dizzy with gratitude. Maybe she had been protected.

Surely that she had survived this nightmare, thought Sable, was as miraculous as the powers of any unicorn.

She opened her eyes.

And stared around her, blinking, because something wasn't right, was not as it should be.

The beach she had dragged herself onto appeared to be covered with a vast shallow lake. The smooth vista which, at a distance, she'd thought to be sand was actually the sleek, glassine surface of a huge tidal pool. What she'd taken for houses, she saw now, was really light playing off the facets of rocks on the distant hillsides.

But the water . . . the water was comforting as a bath. Rumpled skeins of velvet flowed around her hips, her wrists. Schools of the wonderful fish swarmed around her fingers, minuscule pinpoints of light in colors she'd never seen, thousands of iridescent fish in what amounted to a cup of seawater. Liquid fish rippling and pulsing beneath the water's sleek skin, around her skin.

Through her skin.

She gasped and stared at this marvel.

The sea of fish eddied and whirled, creating tracer-like patterns. She sat mesmerized by this resplendent geometry and felt a subtle unfurling of memory taking place, a re-weaving of time into one seamless coil.

And all the while the miraculous flood swirled around her, as though the entire lake, ocean, and galaxy were a single drop of semen swarming with sperm.

A pointillist painting created from billions of droplets of life.

Life commingling, reforming, resurrecting itself.

Resurrecting.

She was part of this now, she thought, had always been part of it, and realized with a kind of horrified awe that the solidity of her body was already in question. The world and her physical self were blurring at the edges, bleeding into each other like coloring book pictures crayoned in by a child with no regard for boundaries or lines.

The bright fish, these marvelous dollops and squiggles of life, now pulsed through her bloodstream, her bone marrow, her brain, pulling her into the ebb and flow of the tide, the life that continued, survived, even though it had no right in the world of logic and reason to do so, even though she had never believed such a thing could be possible, any more than she had believed a unicorn charm might keep her safe.

Yet she was safe, she knew, here on the edge of this vast sea of souls.

And she would wait.

As Dan must be waiting for her, even now, through the long, awful morning at the dock in Hamburg. As Miriam and Elise, when they learned what had happened, would wait for news.

She would wait on this strange, benevolent shore for her loved ones to join her.

Knowing, in time, they would come to her.

JANET BERLINER

THE DAY OF SOUNDING OF JOSH M'BOBWE:

A READ-ALOUD TALE

Peter: My buddy Janet is South African Jewish. I'm Bronx Jewish. There's a difference.

What I've always envied in Janet's work is her ability to extract from her background and from a truly dizzying jumble of influences and experiences exactly the tone and exactly the soul she needs to inform a particular story. We all do our best with what we have, certainly; but only Janet Berliner could have come up with a tale of a Jewish-Zulu adolescent in great need of a rite of passage of some sort, and a guardian animal spirit in need of a decent night's sleep. Trust me on this one. Only Janet.

Incidentally, if you happen to notice the cameo references, as it were, to a certain Professor Gottesman and a rather odd rhinoceros—well, in the immortal words of Lena Horne, "A little nepotism never hurt *nobody,* honey."

The Day of Sounding
of Josh M'bobwe:
A Read-Aloud Tale

⸺⸺

ARE YOU AWAKE DOWN THERE, MR. GEMSBOK?"

Gemsie groaned and rolled over. Hours of trying to fall asleep and when he's finally at that point where he's managed to set aside his problems and drowse, he has to be really alert. "Awake, now, Sir, and listening," he said. "Your voice has a certain resonance—Saint Peter, Sir."

Peter gave a low chuckle. "I suppose it does," he said. "I thought I'd remind you that it's almost dawn. Act as your alarm clock, in a manner of speaking. Sleep on by all means, if you are ready to join us up here."

"Not yet, Sir."

"Well, then, Mr. Gemsbok—did I pronounce it right this time?—I suggest that you forego sleep and take some action."

"Almost right," Gemsie said, wanting nothing more than to be left alone.

"Almost right, *Sir*."

"Try deep in your throat. Like L'Chaim . . . Sir." Damn, but it was annoying having St. Peter as his supervisor, Gemsie thought. So was being on the thirteen year installment immortality plan. He'd have had a far easier life if they'd assigned him to Aristotle, with his particular fondness for cloven-hooved creatures, and his deep regard for the oryx of the species.

"As I recall, when we spoke thirteen years ago you reprimanded me. You said that you were anything but a jewel. I took note."

"Last time I looked at my reflection in the river, I was as pleasingly plain as ever. Nor do I like the image of myself with wings any more now than I did then. I'll leave that to the heaven-bound unicorns and the chi-lin, Sir."

"All right then, Gemsie. Over and out. I'll be watching you."

I'll just bet you will, Gemsie thought.

"You there, Gemsie?"

"I'm here, Rhino. What's up?"

"Thought I'd remind you that this is the day. I know that you are . . . forgetful, shall we say. Don't want to lose you, you know."

"Forgetful? Say what you mean friend. Lazy's the word."

His friend chuckled in a manner all too reminiscent of St. Peter's. "For all I know, you've had enough and want to don wings and go up there to the big place."

"I don't think so," Gemsie said. "Much as I'm anxious to meet your Professor Gottesman and some of the others you've told me about, I'd just as well try a thousand years or so more down here first."

"Well, then, get on with it, my friend. Over and out."

Over and out! Give me a break, Gemsie thought, wide awake now, after the two calls, and feeling himself going into a renewed bout of panic over Josh M'bobwe. *Over and out!* Both of them were getting mod on him, even Rhino, for all of his erudition. If only there were a way to monitor thought-calls, like that caller ID system people were using these days. Not that it mattered, because Peter could circumvent any system. Heaven knows, he'd had enough practice adjusting to new technologies over the millennia.

While he, on the other hand, was increasingly confounded by the changes. First the new morality, then AIDS and back to old morality; first the Dutch in South Africa, then the British, then apartheid. Then the new South Africa, with its mix-and-match society and mores. How was a Gemsbok expected to keep up without a manual of new rules?

He rehearsed the speech he would make to St. Peter. "This mix-and-match stuff is complicated, Sir. This is the New South Africa, Sir. I did my best, Sir."

Which, he knew, would do him no good at all.

Giving up on his pleasant, drowsy procrastination, he left the cave and went out into the dawn of Josh M'bobwe's thirteenth birthday. His day of entering manhood, had the boy's parents cared a whit about anything except their own sensibilities.

Barbara M'bobwe, nee Rosen, and Denis M'bobwe.

What grand plans they had made before Josh's birth. He would have the best of both worlds, the best of both traditions.

A piece of cake for Gemsie. Or so he'd thought. Denis would teach the boy about finding his spirit guide. He'd take him out into the Karoo the night before his thirteenth birthday and leave him there till dawn. He'd see Gemsie, they'd dance together, and the boy, thoroughly initiated, would be home in good time to get on with his birthday party and his Bar Mitzvah. *Sikelel'i Afrika* in the morning; *Hatikvah* in the evening.

A piece of cake.

Life should only be that simple.

Gemsie couldn't figure it out. Barbara was a nice Jewish girl from Johannesburg. Had a Bat Mitzvah and everything. Was a Bar Mitzvah right for *her* son? No, of course not. She was too contemporary for that. Too self-involved was more like it, leaving the boy's grandfather to teach him the traditions and, finally, leaving the boy himself to go off and search for herself. Anything to avoid taking responsibility for her own creation.

Was Denis M'bobwe any better? Not at all. If you don't care, I don't care, he'd said. And off he went in the opposite direction, giving no thought at all to the boy who had been Gemsie's charge since the day of Josh's birth.

What was a Gemsbok supposed to do?

His first stroke of luck had come when Barbara and Denis decided to leave their son in the care of his grandfather who, fortunately, lived outside Pretoria, close enough to Gemsie that he did not have to cope with going into Johannesburg to try to get Josh's attention. When he was younger, he'd loved city assignments; now all he wanted to do was hang around the desert where the only dangers he had to think about were snakes. Carbon monoxide was no longer perfume to his nostrils.

The point was, Gemsie thought, that none of this was his fault. He had watched over Josh conscientiously, which had not been all that much of a chore since he kind of liked the kid. Josh's parents, now they were something else. At the point of divorce, leaving Josh to his own devices—neither Jewish nor Zulu, neither black nor white. Small wonder the boy was interested in nothing except playing the trumpet, like he was the son of Wynton Marsalis or something.

Which thought, after thirteen years of being at a loss, gave Gemsie the idea he needed . . .

Josh took apart his new trumpet, tucked it in its case, and took out the notebook Grandpa Rosen had given him, along with a fountain pen which he'd said was a traditional gift to give on a boy's thirteenth birthday. "You're a clever boy. Write down my stories for me, Joshie," his grandpa had said.

Of course Josh had to pay for both of the gifts by listening to one of his grandfather's stories about his own boyhood in Berlin, but he didn't mind. He loved the old man, which was a good thing, since he was living with his grandpa while his parents decided, as Mom put it, what they wanted to be when they grew up.

"I could use a glass tea," his grandfather said. "Want one, Joshie?"

Josh shook his head and stroked the notebook lovingly. He always did that with a notebook before he disturbed its pristine cleanliness. Then he took out the new pen, filled it with radiant blue ink, and wrote, "I do not want to be a Jewish boy. I want to play the horn."

"You could do both, Joshie. Be Jewish and be a horn player."

Josh shook his head at his grandfather, who was reading over his shoulder. "I just want to be me, Grandpa," he said.

"That reminds me of a story."

Already it was the second story of the day, but Josh didn't mind. Everything reminded grandpa of a story, and in a way that was cool. Like everything made Josh think of music.

"It happened in Berlin, on the day *I* turned thirteen. I can hear the echo of my mama's voice, as she gave me a small wheelbarrow loaded with paper money. 'Your little sister needs milk and butter, Izzie,' she said. 'You will have to stand and wait, maybe all day to get it. They will keep pushing you to the end of the line. Don't let anyone take your money, and don't drop the milk. Whatever is left over I will use to make you a birthday cake.'

"So I waited in line. I was so proud when at last I had the milk in my hands and the butter in my pocket, you can't imagine. I walked carefully out of the shop, looking only down at the street so I shouldn't trip and fall. And what did I see? Right away a black boot, tapping impatiently on the sidewalk. Like so." He tapped his foot. "I stared at the boots, dusty they were, not shiny like I would have expected, and gripped the bottle.

"'Say Heil, little Jew boy. Come. Salute. It's not hard. Lift that arm,' the man said.

"I lifted my left arm. My free arm.

"'You Jews. So stupid, you can't do anything right. The other arm. Like this.'

"The man took my sister's milk and flung it through a plate-glass window—Herr Freund's cigar shop, it was. Then he grasped my arm and lifted it. I could feel the butter squish in my right pocket. I started to cry.

"'I should shoot you before you grow horns,' the man said. 'Next time, do it right, or I will put a bullet through that thick head.'

"I was so angry, Joshie. You cannot imagine how angry. I was still in a fury after we escaped Berlin. I remember how I huddled at the rail of the *Julius Caesar*— such a fine ship—watching Bremerhaven disappear. I listened to the smoke stack and it sounded to me like the unbroken sound of the shofar wailing *tek'iah* on Rosh Hashanah. I clapped my hands over my ears and whispered over and over, 'I am not a Jew, I am not a Jew.'"

"Yes, but—"

"Yes, but, nothing, Joshie. Think about it. Where is it written that you cannot be a Jew and a Zulu and yourself, the famous trumpet player, all at the same time? Show me where it is written, and I will not bother you with this again. I will even stop plaguing you with my stories."

He put his hand on Josh's shoulder. "Now, don't you have anything better to do on this beautiful Saturday spring morning of your birthday than to sit around listening to an old man? I thought we were driving some of your pals to the Cango Caves. I hope they'll all fit into the car."

Josh closed his notebook. "Just me, Gramps," he

said. "I didn't feel like inviting anyone else. The caves open at ten." He glanced at the fancy luminous watch his father had sent to him.

"Just the two of us, Joshie?" His grandfather looked sad. "All right, but shouldn't we be leaving about now? We wanted to get there before the crowds."

On impulse, Josh kissed his grandfather. "I love your stories, Grandpa, but it's not a beautiful spring morning. Look out of the window. The wind is blowing gales. Maybe we should stay home—"

"We'll go." His grandfather gave him a gentle push. "As my old friend from Grenada used to say, God rest his soul, 'We'll go to come back.' Which reminds me of a story . . ."

Josh grinned and grabbed his parka and his trumpet. "Later, Grandpa," he said. "Let's go to come back."

With as much energy as he could muster, Gemsie headed toward the caves. Nothing like a storm over the Karroo to clear the old head, he told himself, holding his horn steady against the wind. He had the sudden awful feeling that the inclement weather might cause Josh's birthday trip to be canceled, but not being one to take pleasure in crossing needless bridges, he set the very idea aside. He ate a few berries off a bush or two, stopped at the watering hole for a drink, and admired his reflection in the water. In all modesty, he thought, he was a rather glorious creature. What he lacked in the porcelain delicacy of his unicorn cousins and the regal stance of the chi-lin, he made up for in size and agility. Four hundred pounds, a single black-and-white spiraled horn almost four feet long, muscles strong enough to defeat any lion who came along.

Josh should be proud to have him as his guide, proud to dance to his music.

It occurred to Gemsie that maybe Peter would consider it enough if Josh interpreted his guide's music on the trumpet. He should have asked the Boss about that one, he thought. A new wrinkle for a new age.

"Sorry, Gemsie. No deal," Peter said. "This is an all-or-nothing game. No compromises."

"Always there, aren't you, Sir," Gemsie said. Eavesdropping, he thought, but did not say. Peter could hear it of course, but fortunately did not comment.

As always, breakfast made Gemsie feel a whole lot better. So did the knowledge that under normal circumstances—though God only knew what was normal any more—humans could not usually see him, except for his charge, and that only during one twenty-four hour period. If they could, someone would have popped him off long ago and he'd be looking down from somebody's wall, wishing he could be up there with Peter, wings or no wings.

Somewhat comforted, he marched past security at the caves and went inside. Because the serendipity of it pleased him, and because it was the one place Josh always liked to visit—as if somehow he knew there was a link to Gemsie there—the Gemsbok chose the area of the ancient wall drawings of him as the place to put his plan into motion.

"Hi, gorgeous," he said, waving his horn at the crude

prehistoric picture of himself. "You're going to see a little something different today from the usual run of
tourists."

It took Gemsie no more than a few minutes to set
things up. Praying that Josh and his friends would be the
first to visit that area of the caves, he went back outside to
wait for their arrival. There would be a car full of them,
no doubt—just to complicate matters—he thought, parking himself under a tree. He closed his eyes and relaxed.
Even if he fell asleep, he would be awakened by a noisy
group of teenagers.

Since there was no noisy arrival, he considered it a
stroke of uncommon good fortune when a stray horsefly
bit him on the nose at the very moment that Josh and his
grandfather drove into the parking area.

"Happy birthday, Josh," he said quietly. In gratitude,
he shook off the fly and did not squish it underhoof. He
watched the boy tumble from the car, horn case tucked
under his arm, and heaved a rumbling sigh of relief. The
horn was a major part of the plan, and he hadn't figured
out what he would do if the boy did not bring it along.
"Just keep your head, kid," he said, "and we'll both be
fine."

Provided, he thought, that the kid did not get carried
away like some of his charges. He was in top form for an
old Gemsbok, but that was not good enough to dance for
hours, like in the salad days of his youth.

"It's twelve o'clock, Joshie. We've been in here for
two hours. Isn't it, maybe, time for lunch?"

"In a moment, Gramps. I still want to visit the oryx on the wall."

"You haven't seen it before?"

"I have to see it again."

"You have to see it? Who understands children these days." His grandfather smiled. "All right. It's *your* birthday. But this is one tired old man." He perched on a ledge and waved the boy on. "Since I do not *have* to see your friend on the wall, I will wait here for you."

Josh crouched next to his grandfather. "Sure you'll be all right alone?"

His grandfather laughed. "I think I am supposed to be asking you that question. Alone I'm used to. I'll live, I assure you."

Josh hesitated, not quite sure why but all at once reluctant to move on.

"Go on," his grandfather said. "Get on with it, so I don't starve to death before you're back. If I don't turn into a block of ice first." He looked around at the stalagmites and stalactites in crystal formation around him. "It's so pretty in here. You want I should call your parents to join us for lunch?"

"Both of them? Together?"

"And why not? They had you together, did they not?"

Josh laughed and shook his head. "I don't think that's a good idea, Gramps. If they wanted to be together, they'd be here with us now."

"If you're not back in half an hour, I'm calling them anyway to tell them you're torturing an old man. You want I should hold that precious horn of yours?"

"Yes. No." Josh drew back the horn. "I won't be long. Why don't you go to the restaurant and warm up. Order me a hamburger and fries—"

"Always the same. A hamburger and fries. The oryx drawings. Your horn. You should know a little matzoh ball soup every now and then wouldn't do you any harm."

"You eat the matzoh, Grampa."

"And get constipated?"

Josh laughed out loud and took off in the direction of the labyrinth of smaller caves, one of which held the wall painting that drew him back again and again. In some funny way, he thought of the antelope as his own personal unicorn. One day, he would write a song about it, he thought, standing in front of the drawings and running his fingers across the curves of the oryx horn. Maybe Wynton Marsalis would hear it and play it and Josh would become famous and go to America—

His fantasy was interrupted by a rumbling which he assumed to be thunder. Must be awfully close to penetrate all the way in here, he thought. The sound came again, louder this time. Josh looked up, wondering if the stalactites ever dropped from the roof of the cave.

The idea had no sooner occurred to him before a final loud roar and a tumbling of rocks sealed him inside.

He leaned against the rock wall and, trying not to panic, contemplated his fate in the absolute darkness that surrounded him. Almost lethargically, he wondered what would come first—rescue, freezing to death, starvation.

He zippered up his parka and slid his way down to the cold earth. Sitting, he wondered about all of the things he had hoped to do with his life.

"God, it's cold," he said out loud, mostly for the comfort of hearing a voice, even if it was his own.

He could hear nothing out there, no sounds of people digging him out, nothing but cold and silence and the dripping of water from the stalactites. He remembered the story he had heard about an Arctic explorer trapped in an igloo which got smaller and smaller as ice was formed by his breath.

He tried not breathing, timing himself by his new watch.

Shivering, deciding that anything was better than inactivity, he stood up and felt his way to where he thought the rockslide was. He pushed at it gently, then with all his might. Nothing budged. He wanted to jump up and down to keep warm, but fear of causing more rocks to fall kept him still.

It seemed to him that hours passed.

Finally, growing scared at last, he made a few random promises to himself and his grandfather, since his parents didn't seem to care. "I'll do the dance thing. I'll look for my spirit guide. I'll do the Bar Mitzvah thing."

Still nothing happened. "Help," he yelled. "It's Josh. I'm in here."

He stopped. "It's no use, Oryx," he said, figuring it was better to speak to the drawing than to continue to talk to himself. "We're stuck with each other. Might as well accept the fact that I'm going to freeze to death right here, in front of your eyes."

Cold and miserable and at the point of tears, he opened the catch on his trumpet case and took out the instrument. There was only one more thing left to try; if it started a new rockslide, so what. A bash on the head was better than freezing to death.

Slowly, he began to compose his ode to the oryx antelope. The music came to him easily, African and bittersweet.

Without realizing what he was doing, experimenting with the reprise, Joshua found himself segueing into familiar notes. He played the music of a black man's plaint and a Jewish battle.

And the wall came tumbling down.

"You had better know what you're doing, Mr. Gemsbok," Peter said.

Gemsie stared at the gathering outside the caves. The old man had contacted Josh's parents. They stood together, the three of them, pressed against the wind.

"Anything I can do to help?" Rhino asked.

Gemsie answered neither St. Peter nor his friend, Rhino. He was listening to a soft melody that seemed to be coming to him from a world away.

Old and hardened as he was, Gemsie was not totally inured to sentiment. The boy's melody had gone straight to his heart.

He let the tears flow, as he listened to the reprise. The boy was playing the right song, now, the one that combined the soul of the African slave with the determination of the Jews.

"Well done, Josh," Gemsie whispered into the wind, as the wall came tumbling down. He stood to his full height and watched Joshua move out of the cave.

Taking the horn from his lips, Josh hugged his grandfather and kissed each of his parents in turn. Then, staring straight at Gemsie, he smiled and once more raised the horn to his lips.

Keeping the first of his promises, he began to dance.

Gemsie danced with him. From somewhere above him, around him, he thought he heard Peter sigh with relief.

"Glad for me, or for you, Sir?" he asked, his moment of sentimentality already a thing of the past.

"Close call," Rhino said.

Light on his feet despite his bulk, Gemsie kept on dancing. He did not stop until Josh began to play *Hatikvah.*

Holding hands, old man Rosen and his daughter and son-in-law formed a tiny circle. As they, too, began to dance, Gemsie turned and headed for home.

"See that you don't cut it so fine next time," Peter said. "Your next charge will be born shortly."

Gemsie groaned. "One night's sleep," he begged.

"One night's sleep, *Sir.* You may have one hour."

"What I only have to do for another thirteen years," Gemsie said, lying down at once.

He had hardly heard the "What I only have to do, *Sir,*" before he was fast asleep.

NANCY WILLARD

THE TROUBLE WITH UNICORNS

Peter and Janet: Nancy didn't want anything said about her, beyond giving her biographical data. We don't think, however, that she'll object to us saying that we are extremely pleased that she wrote a story for this anthology.

The Trouble with Unicorns

THE LAST WEEKEND SARAH CAME TO VISIT HER father before she left for Europe, Mack the white cat crawled under the upstairs bathroom sink to die. The sink in Toby's apartment leaked and was stained with purple streaks; the previous tenant had been a painter. Mack neither ate nor drank. He had spread himself flat on the blue towel, like an island about to be submerged. Sarah sat on the edge of the bathtub and wept. The week she was born, seventeen years ago when they were still a family, a white kitten had mewed at the door and stayed. Now on an ordinary Friday in April he was dying.

Tk tk tk.

The faucet dripped slowly and steadily.

Toby lifted Mack into the cardboard carrier. He gave a thin cry deep in his throat, and Sarah tucked the towel around him. On his honeymoon Toby had stolen that towel from a hotel in Venice because he loved the winged lion in the center, and Sarah's mother had said, "If you're going to steal from a hotel, steal an ashtray. It'll last longer." They'd ended up fighting about it.

Sarah sat rigidly beside her father in the car, embracing the carrier, her long blond hair falling across her cheeks.

"Comfort him," said Toby. "Talk to him."

Though he did not care much for cats, Toby had learned to love this one. After the divorce Sarah's mother suddenly discovered she was allergic to all fur-bearing animals. Toby got complete custody of Mack and custody of Sarah every other weekend.

He drove into the parking lot of the Hudson Valley Animal Hospital with a feeling of dread.

"I'll take the carrier," he said.

"No, let me," said Sarah and jumped out of the car and walked ahead of him to the door of the animal hospital.

Toby was astonished to find the waiting room empty. The plump receptionist was sitting with her back to him, and he had to lean across the counter and call out, "We're here with Mack."

"Take room five," the receptionist said, and continued typing.

When Sarah tipped the carrier to coax Mack out, he looked as though he'd been poured onto the examination table. Dr. Wu bustled in, felt the cat's back, and peered into his yellow eyes, which gazed past all of them as if at a distant horizon.

"You've had this old fellow a mighty long time," he remarked.

"That's right," said Toby and wanted to weep.

"I know this is tough on both of you. Take your time saying good-bye."

Dr. Wu left them alone in the treatment room. Mack

kept his eyes open as Sarah stroked him, but he did not purr or rub his face against her palm, and Sarah said, "Is he going to die?"

"I think so," said Toby. "Yes. He is going to die."

No point in telling her about the lethal injection, he thought.

"Can we bury him?" asked Sarah. She had stopped crying.

"Of course we can," said Toby, "Did you think we'd just leave him here? When they call me to come, I'll pick up his ashes—"

"Oh," said Sarah, "ashes."

"I think that's how they usually do it. When you go back to your mother's house, you can scatter them in the garden. Or wherever you want."

Sarah said nothing for a long time.

"Dad, when Mack dies, can we get a baby ferret?"

Toby was shocked.

"Sure we could get a ferret, but not right away. I mean, don't you think we should have a period of mourning?"

"Oh, sure," she said. "I didn't mean right away."

He knew she was only saying that to placate him. Still, he'd made his point, that someone who has watched over you since you were born deserves a few tears, a warm bed by the fire in your broken heart.

Saturday morning when he went to his job at the piano store, he saw the old cat's face in every gleaming surface, heard his faint mew behind every note he played to show customers why they should buy a Yamaha spinnet and not a Steinway grand. He left work early and drove to pick up the ashes.

"Name?" asked the receptionist.

"Toby Martinson."

A different day. The office was filled with elderly people and cats in cages. There were two poodles on leashes and a black spaniel inert on his mistress' lap. Today's receptionist was thin, blond, and efficient. She tipped her face up to him.

"And when did you bring Toby in?"

The vision of his own ashes being carried out in a cardboard box sent chills through him.

"I didn't bring Toby in," he heard himself shouting. "*I'm* Toby. I've come for Mack's ashes."

The receptionist stared at him. "You should have said so right off."

She disappeared through a room directly behind the desk. She was gone so long he wondered if she'd lost Mack or given him to the wrong person. God knows, he told himself, it would be easy to get ashes mixed up. What was that poem he'd had to memorize in freshman English? He'd forgotten the author, the title, the poem. All he could remember was a single line.

A bracelet of bright hair about the bone.

Turning his back on the waiting room full of beasts and their masters, he read and reread the notices on the bulletin board beside the receptionist's desk.

BROWN HUSKY, 12 weeks old, all shots, loves children, needs good home. Owner moving and can't keep her.

TWO CATS FREE to good homes. Neutered, declawed, 1 male, 1 female.

Must give away my baby male enrocinul. Call evenings.

Toby reread the third notice more carefully, a pale green index card. *Enrocinul.* A computer glitch, probably, for something as ordinary as a parakeet. But were parakeets ordinary or merely familiar? Nothing in the universe was ordinary if you really thought about it.

An interesting computer glitch. Then he realized the notice was handprinted.

He heard his name called and went forward to receive the plain brown box that held Mack's mortal remains. On his way out, he pulled the green card from the board, tucked it inside his coat pocket, and walked out into the May morning.

To his relief, Sarah was not home when he arrived. He left the box on the backseat of the car—Mack had always loved riding in the backseat—and hurried into the kitchen and put water on for spaghetti. Well, why not get another pet? he asked himself. Another reason for Sarah to spend time with you, said a voice in his head, but he dismissed it. But not a ferret. Another cat, maybe. Unless she has her heart set on a ferret.

He locked the box of ashes in the trunk of the car.

Sarah was in the kitchen, talking on the phone. "Gotta go," she said. " 'Bye, Mom."

"Honey, I've got Mack's ashes."

She stood very still.

"Can I see them?"

"There's not much to see," said Toby. "If you want the key to the trunk, you're welcome to look. But the real Mack isn't in that box."

He could not tell how she was taking it.

"Can we go to Wendy's for supper?" she asked.

On the way, he talked about school and about the trip to Europe. Suddenly she said, "Were there pieces of bone?"

"What?" exclaimed Toby, startled.

"Were there pieces of bone in Mack's ashes?"

"No," he said. "I don't think so."

"I read that sometimes there are," said Sarah.

After supper while Sarah was watching TV, he pulled out the green index card, kicked off his shoes, and standing in the kitchen full of dirty dishes, he dialed the number. He counted the rings, four, five.

I'll give it ten, Toby told himself.

On the seventh ring, a woman's voice broke in.

"Hello?"

"I'm calling about the enrocinul."

"Oh, yeah," said the voice. "You want it?"

"I don't know. Could you give me a little more information?"

"What kind of information?" The woman's voice was veiled with suspicion.

"I've never heard of an enrocinul. Could you tell me—"

"It's a horse," she replied. "A small horse."

"A horse is out of the question," he said. "I live in an apartment."

"So do I," said the woman. "Two Triangle Court. When will you be coming?"

"How about two o'clock on Sunday?"

She answered him with a long silence.

"How will I know it's you?" she whispered.

"I beg your pardon?"

"When you come on Sunday, how will I know it's you? What do you look like?"

"I have blue eyes and short brown hair, and I'll be wearing a faded denim jacket. My daughter will be coming with me."

"And your wife?"

"No, that's over," he laughed. "Just my daughter."

He hung up the phone and padded barefoot into the living room. Instantly his daughter lifted the remote control and switched off the TV. He pretended not to notice.

"Honey, I've got a lead on a new pet," he said. "Not a replacement for Mack, of course. Nothing can ever replace Mack."

"A ferret? "she asked.

"An enrocinul," he said. "It's a small horse."

She stared at him, wide-eyed.

"The owner is keeping it in her apartment," he added. "I thought we could just drive over to Clintonville and take a look at it."

Though he'd grown up in Clintonville, Toby had never heard of Triangle Court. Probably one of those new suburban developments, he thought. But when he stopped at his favorite Mobil station and asked for directions, there it was, on the map on the wall in the office, a tiny road in the old downtown, behind the public library.

His heart sank. Half the murders in Clintonville happened within a three-block radius of the library. The evening hours had been canceled. Two weeks ago, a man was found shot dead on the library steps clutching a book on how to raise bonsai.

As he climbed back into the car, Sarah said, "Dad, when are you going to teach me to drive?"

"I thought your mom was going to teach you."

"No, she says it makes her nervous."

"Well, I guess we could go out on one of these country roads and get you started some evening," said Toby, hoping she wouldn't pin him down to a time. He had a recurring image of her climbing back into the car after the first lesson and driving away from him for good. "Lock your door."

They passed the Daily Treat Deli and the library and turned into the empty parking lot behind the library. On the far side of the lot stood a row of old apartment buildings, three of them boarded up. Someone had pinned a handwritten note to the PARKING FOR PATRONS ONLY sign:

This is Triangle Court.

"We're here," said Toby.

Sarah squinted out of the window.

"Dad, this can't be the place."

"Two Triangle Court. It's got to be that one."

The neighborhood looked almost benign with the sunlight gleaming on the budding branches of ascanthus, sumac, and honeysuckle, tangled in the small backyards behind the buildings. Toby searched for a buzzer.

"I don't see how we can ever locate—"

"Dad," said Sarah, "the door is open."

There were six mailboxes in the dark hall. The names had fallen off all but one of them.

"Number Two, Betty Belinsky," read Toby, "It must be that one at the end of the hall."

The corridor smelled of mildew; Toby had a brief but intense image of *National Geographic*s piled to the ceiling in the basement of the house where he'd grown up. Beyond the door of number two droned a voice, just below the level of comprehension. Toby knocked. Nobody answered.

"She can't hear me over the TV."

"She'll hear *me*," said Sarah and pounded the door with her fist.

The voice stopped droning.

The door opened.

Oh, my Lord, thought Toby, what a homely woman.

He was used to attractive women, like his daughter, who had the bloom of youth on her, and his ex-wife, who had short red hair and had dieted herself down to a size 8. Betty Belinsky was fortyish, tall, and chunky about the hips, and she wore her straight brown hair pulled back in a blue plastic barette. Both her Led Zeppelin sweatshirt and her jeans looked a size too small for her.

"I've come about the enrocinul," said Toby.

She squinted at him.

"Who are you?"

"My name is Toby Martinson." He slid a card out of

his wallet and handed it to. "I sell pianos for Yamaha."

"Um." She did not take the card, and she did not close the door.

"Sometimes I tune them," he added.

"Come in," said Betty Belinsky. "Make yourselves at home."

She pointed to an overstuffed sofa that had long ago given up on the good life and was dragging its belly on the floor; the red plush cushions had bald spots. It rose forlornly above the open boxes of books that covered the floor. Toby could not resist glancing at the titles in the box nearest him: *The Joy of Cooking, The Collected Works of Plato, Selected Songs of Thomas Campion*. Perhaps they weren't her books at all. Perhaps she was organizing a sale of the public library discards. But who would discard *The Joy of Cooking*?

Stepping over the cartons, Toby and Sarah sat down gingerly on the sofa, which smelled of cat urine.

As Betty Belinsky disappeared behind the red velvet curtain that separated her living room from all that lay beyond, Toby had the odd feeling they were about to see the first act of a play.

"Sorry about the mess," she called out. "I'm moving."

In a few minutes she stepped back into the room, holding the enrocinul in her arms.

A faint pang of disappointment filled Toby; he looked more like a goat than a horse.

Until she set him down, and then he saw the animal as he really was: a small white horse with a knob in the center of his forehead. No goat had hair this fine, with the sheen of loosened milkweed on it. Toby reached out and stroked the animal's back. It was soft as the fur under a cat's chin. The enrocinul's tail was long but stringy, a dull ivory; the exact shade of my great grandmother's hair, thought Toby, when she let me braid it before she went to bed.

Sarah sank to her knees beside him and stroked his bristly mane.

"Oh, he's adorable," she cooed. "Where did you get him?"

"He was standing on the center strip along Route 55, trying to cross," replied Betty Belinsky. "So many animals get hit crossing that road, I figured he wouldn't have a chance. I pulled over and went back and got him."

"He let you pick him up?" exclaimed Toby.

"Maybe he was somebody's pet," said Sarah.

"Well, of course he was somebody's pet. He was wearing a collar with his name on it. Enrocinul."

"Is that his name or the name for what he is?" asked Toby.

"Oh, who knows what he is?" said Betty Belinksy. "I figured if I ran an ad for a small horse, nobody would answer it. This building's due to be knocked down next month. Did you bring a pet carrier?"

"A carrier?" inquired Toby.

"I thought maybe you'd have one."

"He doesn't need a carrier," said Sarah. "He has me."

She led the way into the parking lot. The enrocinul shivered a little, though the air was not cold, and buried his head in the crook of Sarah's arm. Very carefully she climbed into the backseat.

"Well, good-bye, Miss Belinsky," said Toby.

In the rearview mirror, Toby saw the animal lay its head on his daughter's lap. He watched her hands stroke the creature's milky ears and fiddle with the golden collar. The sun caught the letters on the animal's golden collar; they were deeply engraved and easy to read: *L'Unicorne*.

Toby nearly hit a parked car.

"Dad!" cried Sarah.

"Honey, we have a unicorn!" he shouted. "Look at the writing in the mirror! We have a unicorn—a French unicorn!"

They decided not to tell anyone.

"Especially not Mom," said Sarah. "She'd let the whole world know. I wish I weren't going away for the summer."

Before they got out of the car, Sarah unbuckled the unicorn's collar. The unicorn whickered and scratched his incipient horn against Sarah's hand, as if it itched. Toby remarked that a golden collar was far too valuable to leave lying around the house. At his suggestion, they hid it in the icebox, behind a saucer on which sat one rancid chunk of butter.

"Not much of a hiding place," said Sarah. "I mean, your icebox is so empty."

Since the divorce Toby had gotten into the habit of ordering takeout, mostly pizza and Chinese.

The unicorn licked its lips.

"What does the unicorn eat?" asked Sarah.

Toby felt a little stab of guilt.

"I don't know. We could try him on granola." He took a soup bowl from the cupboard, filled it with water, and set it in a corner of the kitchen. "I need to stop by the A & P and pick up a few things," he added.

"I'll stay here," said Sarah, "with the unicorn."

He left them in the living room watching *Sesame Street.*

The A & P was thronged. Toby grabbed a cart and dodged his way first down one aisle, then another, hoping inspiration would strike him. The array of cereals daunted him: bright boxes emblazoned with children grinning over bowls that foamed with cornflakes or Wheaties, and waving their spoons for joy. What if the unicorn didn't like granola? What if it preferred Cheerios or Quaker Oats?

He passed the fruit juice aisle. The pet food. Kiblets for the Older Cat. Chow for Seniors: twenty-five percent less fat.

What if the unicorn ate hay? "Christ," he muttered, "I don't know a damn thing about unicorns."

He remembered the pay phone just outside by the rack of shopping carts, and when his hand found the green card in his jacket pocket, he left his empty cart in the pet food aisle, hurried out of the store and dialed Betty Belinsky's number. She picked it up on the first ring.

"Hello," said a soft voice.

"Is this Betty?"

"Who is this?" demanded the voice.

"Toby. I'm the man who came by your place today and picked up the unicorn."

"I gave you an enrocinul," said the voice. It sounded like Betty trying to disguise her voice by holding her nose.

A truck stopped at the curb, its gears screeching.

"What does he eat?" shouted Toby. "I forgot to ask you."

"Where are you? I can't hear a thing."

"I'm at the A & P."

"Hot milk with honey is good," said Betty dreamily. "That's what I'm having."

"Thanks," said Toby. "Sorry to bother you."

When he opened the front door, clutching his bottle of milk and jar of honey, the TV was on but there was no sign of Sarah or the unicorn.

"Sarah?"

"I'm in the bathroom."

The door was open. Sarah was sitting in the middle of the floor, with the unicorn beside her. He had tucked his legs neatly under himself and was watching a faint reflection of himself in the full-length mirror on the back of the door. How murky the glass had become! The three of them might have been gazing into a pool of dark water for all the clarity it gave them.

"He's lonely," she said. "Dad, your mirror is so dirty I can hardly see myself."

Toby left the unicorn looking for its reflection while he drove Sarah back to her mother's house. It was a custom they all accepted, that he said good-bye to Sarah at the curb and never entered the house. He felt sure her mother was at the upstairs window, watching them hug each other.

"Take real good care of the unicorn for me," said Sarah. "God, I wish I weren't going. He'll be all grown up next time I see him," she added in mournful tones.

"Maybe he's a toy unicorn," said Toby. "Betty said he could live in an apartment."

Maybe she was lying a voice very much like Betty's whispered from deep inside his head.

As he turned into his own street, he remembered Mack's ashes, locked in the trunk.

He unlocked the door of his apartment and headed straight for the bathroom. The unicorn was still gazing into the mirror on the back of the door. The glass looked less murky, now, or perhaps he was getting used to it.

"What do you see, little fella?"

Toby sat down on the tile floor next to the unicorn and scratched it between the ears, glanced up at the mirror, and gave a whistle of surprise. The sink, toilet, and bathtub had vanished, and in their place he found himself staring at a porphyry pedestal, an alabaster urn, and a marble pool ringed at the top with gold, sunk in a lush bed of violets and columbine and bleeding hearts. Seated cross-legged in the violets was a young man with snappy blue eyes and short brown hair and a jacket that might have been cut from the sky on a spring morning.

What right does that guy have to be so goddamn happy? thought Toby.

Then with a shock he realized the man in the mirror was himself.

He spun around, panicked. To his relief, the toilet, the

tub, the sink with its purple streaks in his bathroom had not budged.

Holding his breath, Toby leaned closer to the glass. By sitting perfectly still, he found he could bring the garden into sharp focus. Now he recognized some of the trees by the cut of their leaves: cherry and oak and linden, walnut and plum. Not since he'd gotten his first pair of glasses in seventh grade had he seen trees that clearly.

The man in the mirror had a lute slung over his shoulder and was picking fruit from a low tree that resembled a date palm. Under the tree spread a deep shadow; the tiny flowers dotting it had been pressed flat, as if someone had recently been sleeping there.

Unicorn. The only thing missing in the mirror was the unicorn, who had not moved from his place beside Toby.

The window in the bathroom was dark.

The mirror, too, was dark.

What a bizarre dream, he thought. How long have I been sitting here? He hated to have time slip away from him without telling him where it was going. The poor beast must be starving. Toby stood up carefully, so as not to disturb him, and tiptoed into the kitchen, poured milk into a saucepan without measuring it, and turned on the stove. Suddenly there rose before him a clear image of Sarah's mother, heating the baby bottle, testing the temperature of the milk on the inside of her wrist. The image filled him with melancholy.

He poured the milk into a cereal bowl, stirred in a spoonful of honey, and carried it into the bathroom.

Under the bathroom sink lay the unicorn, flat and still,

his eyes closed, his head on his hooves. *An island about to be submerged. A lost continent.*

Tk tk tk.

The faucet dripped as steadily as a water clock, unheard until all the other sounds in the room have left it.

He set the bowl on the sink and ran back into the kitchen. The clock over the stove said half past ten.

I can't call her later than eleven, he told himself.

Without looking at the clock, he dialed Betty Belinsky. The phone rang one, two, three, four, five, six. He imagined her asleep on the saggy sofa, exhausted from packing books or hauling them to a place of storage. What if her house was gone? "I will stay calm," said Toby to himself. I will stay on this phone until she answers it.

"Argh," said a sleepy voice.

"Betty?"

"Who is this?" demanded the voice, no longer sleepy.

"It's Toby. Listen, I hate to bother you but the unicorn is sick."

There was a long silence.

"I'll be right over," she said.

Toby started to give her his address but she cut him off.

"I already know where you live," said Betty Belinsky. "I looked you up in the phone book."

When the doorbell rang, he was sitting by the unicorn, stroking its ears. As he raced to open the door, it opened by itself and Betty Belinksy stepped inside. She was wearing a plaid raincoat and a purple rain bonnet and clutching a freshly boxed pizza.

"I asked the cab to stop at Dominick's," she said. "I thought you might be hungry."

"I'm starved," said Toby.

"Where's the unicorn?"

"In the bathroom," answered Toby.

They decided to eat the pizza on the bathroom floor, so they could keep an eye on the unicorn. Toby pulled the last two napkins from a package in the cupboard. As he rummaged through the icebox for a beer, he caught sight of the unicorn's golden collar on a saucer behind the butter.

"Maybe he's missing this," he said and held it up to show Betty, who looked surprised.

"Why did you take it from him?" she asked.

"I thought he'd be more comfortable without it."

"Better give it back," said Betty.

The unicorn had not moved from its spot in front of the mirror. There was something touching about the way his hair thinned into a pale band where the collar had been, and he did not struggle when Toby buckled it into place.

"We're down to the Happy Birthday napkins," said Toby. He opened the pizza box and offered Betty Belinsky the first piece.

"He's lonely," said Betty. "Just like my parakeet. My parakeet used to spend hours looking at herself in the toaster."

"The toaster?" exclaimed Toby.

She nodded, licking her fingers.

"It was a Toastmaster, and I always kept it polished. When I let Henrietta out after breakfast, she liked to sit on the toaster and watch her reflection. She thought it was another parakeet. Just like the unicorn in the mirror—" Betty sucked in her breath. "My God, there *isn't* a unicorn in the mirror!"

The two of them sat huddled on the cold floor. Betty shivered a little. There were two people in the mirror now, the man and a woman. Not a woman you'd call pretty. But attractive, quirky, and full of surprises, like a path twinkling with rain caught in the hoofprints of running deer. Toby admired the woman's hair, tied back with a scarf the color of purple heather. It tumbled dark and shining over her plaid cloak.

Why couldn't I meet someone like her? thought Toby.

Betty leaned forward.

"What are *they* having?"

"Roast chicken and wine," said Toby.

Close to his ear, a man's voice crooned,

> *I care not for these ladies*
> *That must be woo'd and prayed.*
> *Give me kind Amaryllis,*
> *the wanton country maid.*

The unicorn lifted his head.

When did I turn on the radio? thought Toby. I don't even have a radio.

The man in the mirror laid aside his lute. Of course it was he who had sung.

"Please finish the song," begged the woman in the mirror.

"Alas, dear lady, I've forgotten the words," said her companion.

"Nature art disdaineth," sang Betty, and she ran her fingers through the unicorn's mane. "Her beauty is her own."

"You know that song?" asked Toby, astonished.

She nodded without missing a beat.

> *Her when we court and kiss,*
> *She cries, forsooth, let go;*
> *But when we come where comfort is,*
> *She never will say no.*

The man and woman in the mirror were feeding each other chunks of chicken breast.

"Our unicorn is perking up," said Toby. "If he were a cat, he'd be purring."

Betty stopped petting the unicorn.

"The trouble with unicorns is, they can't do anything for you," she muttered. "A horse can carry you. You can put your money on a horse. A dog can protect you. A cat can mouse for you. A parakeet can talk to you. But a unicorn is useless."

"Shhh," said Toby. "You'll hurt his feelings."

"What about *my* feelings? I brought that beast home, I fed him, I talked to him, I gave him my love"—she was almost shouting now—"and all that time he just sat around looking pleased with himself. What has a unicorn ever done for me?"

As if he'd been waiting for this moment, the unicorn seized her sleeve in his mouth and held it for an instant, savoring it.

Then he leapt straight into the mirror.

With a tremendous splash, Betty and the woman in the mirror shattered the dark surface of the pool and sank out of sight.

Toby jumped to his feet and dove in after them.

"What are you doing?" cried the man in the mirror. "I can't swim."

"Neither can I," gasped Toby.

He could not see the unicorn, but a pearly light shot with gold shivered and rippled around the four of them.

I'm dying, he thought. All the nights he'd fretted about losing Sarah, it never dawned on him that she could lose him.

He was floating on the water, which bore him up easily, as if he had left himself behind and become his own reflection.

Betty was paddling toward him. Toby held out his hand to her, and together they clambered over the edge of the pool.

They found themselves standing between the sink and the bathtub. In the mirror, a middle-aged man and a chunky woman were walking away into whatever country was home to the unicorn. Stout in her sweatshirt and jeans the woman in the mirror might have been Eve following Adam out of the garden. You could tell by the way the man walked that his fears and failures weighed heavily on him.

"There but for the grace of God go I," said Toby. He turned to kiss Betty Belinksy, who was laughing and shaking the spring rain out of her shining hair.

PETER S. BEAGLE

⚬⚬⚬

PROFESSOR GOTTESMAN AND THE INDIAN RHINOCEROS

Janet: I said my piece about my personal relationship with **Peter S. Beagle** in the preface to this book; his official bio can be found at the end of this book. Since he (not unsurprisingly) refused to write this introduction to his own story, let me insert here what he wrote for what was originally intended as a coeditor's note for this volume: "Just because my stuff usually turns up on the fantasy and science fiction shelves doesn't mean that I keep up with the field worth a damn. A few years ago, when I was visiting in New York City, my closest old friend and I drifted into the bookstore Forbidden Planet, and found ourselves gaping at serried ranks of books written by nobody we'd ever heard of—and we both grew up on this stuff. I can still hear my friend asking in a hushed and anxious tone, 'Peter, who *are* these people?' I hadn't a clue then, and I haven't much of one now; but some of them can write up a storm . . ."

Peter is correct about the stories in this book. However, what *he* writes is more like the soft murmuring of breezes across the sensibilities of readers from seven to seventy. Regarding his story in this volume, Peter said, "I didn't intend it to, but it came out an homage to Robert Nathan, who was my friend and a wonderful writer." Outside of that, I'm safest if I paraphrase what Peter said about my story: "Anything I might say about 'Professor Gottesman and the Indian Rhinoceros' would at best be taken as seriously biased." All that's left, therefore—and this, at least, I must say—is that "Professor Gottesman" is uniquely, inimitably, Peter S. Beagle. That I love it goes without saying. Now go ahead. Read it. I dare you not to delight in it as much as I did.

Professor Gottesman and the Indian Rhinoceros

PROFESSOR GUSTAVE GOTTESMAN WENT TO A ZOO for the first time when he was thirty-four years old. There is an excellent zoo in Zurich, which was Professor Gottesman's birthplace, and where his sister still lived, but Professor Gottesman had never been there. From an early age he had determined on the study of philosophy as his life's work; and for any true philosopher this world is zoo enough, complete with cages, feeding times, breeding programs, and earnest docents, of which he was wise enough to know that he was one. Thus, the first zoo he ever saw was the one in the middle-sized Midwestern American city where he worked at a middle-sized university, teaching Comparative Philosophy in comparative contentment. He was tall and rather thin, with a round, undistinguished face, a snub nose, a random assortment of sandyish hair, and a pair of very intense and very distinguished brown eyes that always seemed to be looking a little deeper than they meant to, embarrassing the face around them no end. His students and colleagues were quite fond of him, in an indulgent sort of way.

And how did the good Professor Gottesman happen at last to visit a zoo? It came about in this way: His older sister Edith came from Zurich to stay with him for several weeks, and she brought her daughter, his niece Nathalie, along with her. Nathalie was seven, both in years, and in the number of her that there sometimes seemed to be, for the Professor had never been used to children even when he was one. She was a generally pleasant little girl, though, as far as he could tell; so when his sister besought him to spend one of his free afternoons with Nathalie while she went to lunch and a gallery opening with an old friend, the Professor graciously consented. And Nathalie wanted very much to go to the zoo and see tigers.

"So you shall," her uncle announced gallantly. "Just as soon as I find out exactly where the zoo is." He consulted with his best friend, a fat, cheerful, harmonica-playing professor of medieval Italian poetry named Sally Lowry, who had known him long and well enough (she was the only person in the world who called him Gus) to draw an elaborate two-colored map of the route, write out very precise directions beneath it, and make several copies of this document, in case of accidents. Thus equipped, and accompanied by Charles, Nathalie's stuffed bedtime tiger, whom she desired to introduce to his grand cousins, they set off together for the zoo on a gray, cool spring afternoon. Professor Gottesman quoted Thomas Hardy to Nathalie, improvising a German translation for her benefit as he went along.

> *This is the weather the cuckoo likes,*
> *And so do I;*
> *When showers betumble the chestnut spikes,*
> *And nestlings fly.*

"Charles likes it, too," Nathalie said. "It makes his fur feel all sweet."

They reached the zoo without incident, thanks to Professor Lowry's excellent map, and Professor Gottesman bought Nathalie a bag of something sticky, unhealthy, and forbidden, and took her straight off to see the tigers. Their hot, meaty smell and their lightning-colored eyes were a bit too much for him, and so he sat on a bench nearby and watched Nathalie perform the introductions for Charles. When she came back to Professor Gottesman, she told him that Charles had been very well-behaved, as had all the tigers but one, who was rudely indifferent. "He was probably just visiting," she said. "A tourist or something."

The Professor was still marvelling at the amount of contempt one small girl could infuse into the word *tourist*, when he heard a voice, sounding almost at his shoulder, say, "Why, Professor Gottesman—how nice to see you at last." It was a low voice, a bit hoarse, with excellent diction, speaking good Zurich German with a very slight, unplaceable accent.

Professor Gottesman turned quickly, half-expecting to see some old acquaintance from home, whose name he would inevitably have forgotten. Such embarrassments were altogether too common in his gently preoccupied life. His friend Sally Lowry once observed, "We see each other just about every day, Gus, and I'm still not sure you really recognize me. If I wanted to hide from you, I'd just change my hairstyle."

There was no one at all behind him. The only thing he saw was the rutted, muddy rhinoceros yard, for some reason placed directly across from the big cats' cages. The one rhinoceros in residence was standing by the fence, torpidly mumbling a mouthful of moldy-looking hay. It was an Indian rhinoceros, according to the placard on the gate: as big as the Professor's compact car, and the approximate color of old cement. The creaking slabs of its skin smelled of stale urine, and it had only one horn, caked with sticky mud. Flies buzzed around its small, heavy-lidded eyes, which regarded Professor Gottesman with immense, ancient unconcern. But there was no other person in the vicinity who might have addressed him.

Professor Gottesman shook his head, scratched it, shook it again, and turned back to the tigers. But the voice came again. "Professor, it was indeed I who spoke. Come and talk to me, if you please."

No need, surely, to go into Professor Gottesman's reaction: to describe in detail how he gasped, turned pale, and looked wildly around for any corroborative witness. It is worth mentioning, however, that at no time did he bother to splutter the requisite splutter in such cases: "My God, I'm either dreaming, drunk, or crazy." If he was indeed just as classically absent-minded and impractical as everyone who knew him agreed, he was also more of a realist than many of them. This is generally true of philosophers, who tend, as a group, to be on terms of mutual respect with the impossible. Therefore, Professor Gottesman did the only proper thing under the circumstances. He introduced his niece Nathalie to the rhinoceros.

Nathalie, for all her virtues, was not a philosopher, and could not hear the rhinoceros's gracious greeting. She was, however, seven years old, and a well-brought-up seven-year-old has no difficulty with the notion that a rhinoceros—or a goldfish, or a coffee table—might be able to talk; nor in accepting that some people can hear coffee-table speech and some people cannot. She said a polite hello to the rhinoceros, and then became involved in her own conversation with stuffed Charles, who apparently had a good deal to say himself about tigers.

"A mannerly child," the rhinoceros commented. "One sees so few here. Most of them throw things."

His mouth dry, and his voice shaky but contained, Professor Gottesman asked carefully, "Tell me, if you will—can all rhinoceri speak, or only the Indian species?" He wished furiously that he had thought to bring along his notebook.

"I have no idea," the rhinoceros answered him candidly. "I myself, as it happens, am a unicorn."

Professor Gottesman wiped his balding forehead. "Please," he said earnestly. "Please. A rhinoceros, even a rhinoceros that speaks, is as real a creature as I. A unicorn, on the other hand, is a being of pure fantasy, like mermaids, or dragons, or the chimera. I consider very little in this universe as absolutely, indisputably certain, but I would feel so much better if you could see your way to being merely a talking rhinoceros. For my sake, if not your own."

It seemed to the Professor that the rhinoceros chuckled slightly, but it might only have been a ruminant's rumbling stomach. "My Latin designation is *Rhinoceros unicornis*," the great animal remarked. "You may have noticed it on the sign."

Professor Gottesman dismissed the statement as brusquely as he would have if the rhinoceros had delivered it in class. "Yes, yes, yes, and the manatee, which suckles its young erect in the water and so gave rise to the myth of the mermaid, is assigned to the order *sirenia*. Classification is not proof."

"And proof," came the musing response, "is not necessarily truth. You look at me and see a rhinoceros, because I am not white, not graceful, far from beautiful, and my horn is no elegant spiral but a bludgeon of matted hair. But suppose that you had grown up expecting a unicorn to look and behave and smell exactly as I do— would not the rhinoceros then be the legend? Suppose that everything you believed about unicorns—everything except the way they look—were true of me? Consider the possibilities, Professor, while you push the remains of that bun under the gate."

Professor Gottesman found a stick and poked the grimy bit of pastry—about the same shade as the rhinoceros, it was—where the creature could wrap a prehensile upper lip around it. He said, somewhat tentatively, "Very well. The unicorn's horn was supposed to be an infallible guide to detecting poisons."

"The most popular poisons of the Middle Ages and Renaissance," replied the rhinoceros, "were alkaloids. Pour one of those into a goblet made of compressed hair, and see what happens." It belched resoundingly, and Nathalie giggled.

Professor Gottesman, who was always invigorated by a good argument with anyone, whether colleague, student, or rhinoceros, announced, "Isidore of Seville wrote in the seventh century that the unicorn was a cruel beast, that it would seek out elephants and lions to fight with them. Rhinoceri are equally known for their fierce, aggressive nature, which often leads them to attack anything that moves in their shortsighted vision. What have you to say to that?"

"Isidore of Seville," said the rhinoceros thoughtfully, "was a most learned man, much like your estimable self, who never saw a rhinoceros in his life, or an elephant either, being mainly preoccupied with church history and canon law. I believe he did see a lion at some point. If your charming niece is quite done with her snack?"

"She is not," Professor Gottesman answered, "and do not change the subject. If you are indeed a unicorn, what are you doing scavenging dirty buns and candy in this public establishment? It is an article of faith that a unicorn can only be taken by a virgin, in whose innocent embrace the ferocious creature becomes meek and docile. Are you prepared to tell me that you were captured under such circumstances?"

The rhinoceros was silent for some little while

before it spoke again. "I cannot," it said judiciously, "vouch for the sexual history of the gentleman in the baseball cap who fired a tranquilizer dart into my left shoulder. I would, however, like to point out that the young of our species on occasion become trapped in vines and slender branches which entangle their horns—and that the Latin for such branches is *virge*. What Isidore of Seville made of all this . . ." It shrugged, which is difficult for a rhinoceros, and a remarkable thing to see.

"Sophistry," said the Professor, sounding unpleasantly beleaguered even in his own ears. "Casuistry. Semantics. Chop-logic. The fact remains, a rhinoceros is and a unicorn isn't." This last sounds much more impressive in German. "You will excuse me," he went on, "but we have other specimens to visit, do we not, Nathalie?"

"No," Nathalie said. "Charles and I just wanted to see the tigers."

"Well, we have seen the tigers," Professor Gottesman said through his teeth. "And I believe it is beginning to rain, so we will go home now." He took Nathalie's hand firmly and stood up, as that obliging child snuggled Charles firmly under her arm and bobbed a demure European curtsy to the rhinoceros. It bent its head to her, the mud-thick horn almost brushing the ground. Professor Gottesman, mildest of men, snatched her away.

"Good-bye, Professor," came the hoarse, placid voice behind him. "I look forward to our next meeting." The words were somewhat muffled, because Nathalie had tossed the remainder of her sticky snack into the yard as her uncle hustled her off. Professor Gottesman did not turn his head.

Driving home through the rain—which had indeed begun to fall, though very lightly—the Professor began to have an indefinably uneasy feeling that caused him to spend more time peering at the rear-view mirror than in looking properly ahead. Finally he asked Nathalie, "Please, would you and—ah—you and Charles climb into the backseat and see whether we are being followed?"

Nathalie was thrilled. "Like in the spy movies?" She jumped to obey, but reported after a few minutes of crouching on the seat that she could detect nothing out of the ordinary. "I saw a helicopiter," she told him, attempting the English word. "Charles thinks they might be following us that way, but I don't know. Who is spying on us, Uncle Gustave?"

"No one, no one," Professor Gottesman answered. "Never mind, child, I am getting silly in America. It happens, never mind." But a few moments later the curious apprehension was with him again, and Nathalie was happily occupied for the rest of the trip home in scanning the traffic behind them through an imaginary periscope, yipping "It's that one!" from time to time, and being invariably disappointed when another prime suspect turned off down a side street. When they reached Professor Gottesman's house, she sprang out of the car immediately, ignoring her mother's welcome until she had checked under all four fenders for possible homing devices. "Bugs," she explained importantly to the two adults. "That was Charles's idea. Charles would make a good spy, I think."

She ran inside, leaving Edith to raise her fine eyebrows at her brother. Professor Gottesman said heavily, "We had a nice time. Don't ask." And Edith, being a wise older sister, left it at that.

The rest of the visit was enjoyably uneventful. The Professor went to work according to his regular routine, while his sister and his niece explored the city, practiced their English together, and cooked Swiss-German specialties to surprise him when he came home. Nathalie never asked to go to the zoo again—stuffed Charles having lately shown an interest in international intrigue—nor did she ever mention that her uncle had formally introduced her to a rhinoceros and spent part of an afternoon sitting on a bench arguing with it. Professor Gottesman was genuinely sorry when she and Edith left for Zurich, which rather surprised him. He hardly ever missed people, or thought much about anyone who was not actually present.

It rained again on the evening that they went to the airport. Returning alone, the Professor was startled, and a bit disquieted, to see large muddy footprints on his walkway and his front steps. They were, as nearly as he could make out, the marks of a three-toed foot, having a distinct resemblance to the ace of clubs in a deck of cards. The door was locked and bolted, as he had left it, and there was no indication of any attempt to force an entry. Professor Gottesman hesitated, looked quickly around him, and went inside.

The rhinoceros was in the living room, lying peacefully on its side before the artificial fireplace—which was lit—like a very large dog. It opened one eye as he entered and greeted him politely. "Welcome home, Professor. You will excuse me, I hope, if I do not rise?"

Professor Gottesman's legs grew weak under him. He groped blindly for a chair, found it, fell into it, his face white and freezing cold. He managed to ask, "How—how did you get in here?" in a small, faraway voice.

"The same way I got out of the zoo," the rhinoceros answered him. "I would have come sooner, but with your sister and your niece already here, I thought my presence might make things perhaps a little too crowded for you. I do hope their departure went well." It yawned widely and contentedly, showing blunt, fist-sized teeth and a gray-pink tongue like a fish fillet.

"I must telephone the zoo," Professor Gottesman whispered. "Yes, of course, I will call the zoo." But he did not move from the chair.

The rhinoceros shook its head as well as it could in a prone position. "Oh, I wouldn't bother with that, truly. It will only distress them if anyone learns that they have mislaid a creature as large as I am. And they will never believe that I am in your house. Take my word for it, there will be no mention of my having left their custody. I have some experience in these matters." It yawned again and closed its eyes. "Excellent fireplace you have," it murmured drowsily. "I think I shall lie exactly here every night. Yes, I do think so."

And it was asleep, snoring with the rhythmic roar and fading whistle of a fast freight crossing a railroad bridge. Professor Gottesman sat staring in his chair for a long time before he managed to stagger to the telephone in the kitchen.

Sally Lowry came over early the next morning, as she had promised several times before the Professor would let her off the phone. She took one quick look at him as she entered and said briskly, "Well, whatever came to dinner, you look as though it got the bed and you slept on the living room floor."

"I did not sleep at all," Professor Gottesman informed her grimly. "Come with me, please, Sally, and you shall see why."

But the rhinoceros was not in front of the fireplace, where it had still been lying when the Professor came downstairs. He looked around for it increasingly frantic, saying over and over, "It was just here, it has been here all night. Wait, wait, Sally, I will show you. Wait only a moment."

For he had suddenly heard the unmistakable gurgle of water in the pipes overhead. He rushed up the narrow hairpin stairs (his house was, as the real-estate agent had put it, "an old charmer") and burst into his bathroom, blinking through clouds of steam to find the rhinoceros lolling blissfully in the tub, its nose barely above water and its hind legs awkwardly sticking straight up in the air. There were puddles all over the floor.

"Good morning," the rhinoceros greeted Professor Gottesman. "I could wish your facilities a bit larger, but the hot water is splendid, pure luxury. We never had hot baths at the zoo."

"Get out of my tub!" the Professor gabbled, coughing and wiping his face. "You will get out of my tub this instant!"

The rhinoceros remained unruffled. "I am not sure I

can. Not just like that. It's rather a complicated affair."

"Get out exactly the way you got in!" shouted Professor Gottesman. "How did you get up here at all? I never heard you on the stairs."

"I tried not to disturb you," the rhinoceros said meekly. "Unicorns can move very quietly when we need to."

"Out!" the Professor thundered. He had never thundered before, and it made his throat hurt. "Out of my bathtub, out of my house! And clean up that floor before you go!"

He stormed back down the stairs to meet a slightly anxious Sally Lowry waiting at the bottom. "What was all that yelling about?" she wanted to know. "You're absolutely pink—it's sort of sweet, actually. Are you all right?"

"Come up with me," Professor Gottesman demanded. "Come right now." He seized his friend by the wrist and practically dragged her into his bathroom, where there was no sign of the rhinoceros. The tub was empty and dry, the floor was spotlessly clean; the air smelled faintly of tile cleaner. Professor Gottesman stood gaping in the doorway, muttering over and over, "But it was here. It was in the tub."

"What was in the tub?" Sally asked. The Professor took a long, deep breath and turned to face her.

"A rhinoceros," he said. "It says it's a unicorn, but it is nothing but an Indian rhinoceros." Sally's mouth opened, but no sound came out. Professor Gottesman said, "It followed me home."

Fortunately, Sally Lowry was no more concerned

with the usual splutters of denial and disbelief than was the Professor himself. She closed her mouth, caught her own breath, and said, "Well, any rhinoceros that could handle those stairs, wedge itself into that skinny tub of yours, and tidy up afterwards would have to be a unicorn. Obvious. Gus, I don't care what time it is, I think you need a drink."

Professor Gottesman recounted his visit to the zoo with Nathalie, and all that had happened thereafter, while Sally rummaged through his minimally stocked liquor cabinet and mixed what she called a "Lowry Land Mine." It calmed the Professor only somewhat, but it did at least restore his coherency. He said earnestly, "Sally, I don't know how it talks. I do not know how it escaped from the zoo, or found its way here, or how it got into my house and my bathtub, and I am afraid to imagine where it is now. But the creature is an Indian rhinoceros, the sign said so. It is simply not possible—not possible—that it could be a unicorn."

"Sounds like *Harvey*," Sally mused. Professor Gottesman stared at her. "You know, the play about the guy who's buddies with an invisible white rabbit. A big white rabbit."

"But this one is not invisible!" the Professor cried. "People at the zoo, they saw it—Nathalie saw it. It bowed to her, quite courteously."

"Um," Sally said. "Well, I haven't seen it yet, but I live in hope. Meanwhile, you've got a class, and I've got office hours. Want me to make you another Land Mine?"

Professor Gottesman shuddered slightly. "I think

not. We are discussing today how Fichte and von Schelling's work leads us to Hegel, and I need my wits about me. Thank you for coming to my house, Sally. You are a good friend. Perhaps I really am suffering from delusions, after all. I think I would almost prefer it so."

"Not me," Sally said. "I'm getting a unicorn out of this, if it's the last thing I do." She patted his arm. "You're more fun than a barrel of MFA candidates, Gus, and you're also the only gentleman I've ever met. I don't know what I'd do for company around here without you."

Professor Gottesman arrived early for his seminar on "The Heirs of Kant." There was no one in the classroom when he entered, except for the rhinoceros. It had plainly already attempted to sit on one of the chairs, which lay in splinters on the floor. Now it was warily eyeing a ragged hassock near the coffee machine.

"What are you doing here?" Professor Gottesman fairly screamed at it.

"Only auditing," the rhinoceros answered. "I thought it might be rewarding to see you at work. I promise not to say a word."

Professor Gottesman pointed to the door. He had opened his mouth to order the rhinoceros, once and for all, out of his life, when two of his students walked into the room. The Professor closed his mouth, gulped, greeted his students, and ostentatiously began to examine his lecture notes, mumbling professorial mumbles to himself, while the rhinoceros, unnoticed, negotiated a kind of armed truce with the hassock. True to its word, it listened in attentive silence all through the seminar, though Professor Gottesman had an uneasy moment when it seemed about to be drawn into a heated debate over the precise nature of von Schelling's intellectual debt to the von Schlegel brothers. He was so desperately careful not to let the rhinoceros catch his eye that he never noticed until the last student had left that the beast was gone, too. None of the class had even once commented on its presence; except for the shattered chair, there was no indication that it had ever been there.

Professor Gottesman drove slowly home in a disorderly state of mind. On the one hand, he wished devoutly never to see the rhinoceros again; on the other, he could not help wondering exactly when it had left the classroom. "Was it displeased with my summation of the *Ideas for a Philosophy of Nature*?" he said aloud in the car. "Or perhaps it was something I said during the argument about *Die Weltalter*. Granted, I have never been entirely comfortable with that book, but I do not recall saying anything exceptionable." Hearing himself justifying his interpretations to a rhinoceros, he slapped his own cheek very hard and drove the rest of the way with the car radio tuned to the loudest, ugliest music he could find.

The rhinoceros was dozing before the fireplace as before, but lumbered clumsily to a sitting position as soon as he entered the living room. "Bravo, Professor!" it cried in plainly genuine enthusiasm. "You were absolutely splendid. It was an honor to be present at your seminar."

The Professor was furious to realize that he was blushing; yet it was impossible to respond to such praise with an eviction notice. There was nothing for him to do but reply, a trifle stiffly, "Thank you, most gratifying." But the rhinoceros was clearly waiting for something more, and Professor Gottesman was, as his friend Sally had said, a gentleman. He went on, "You are welcome to audit the class again, if you like. We will be considering Rousseau next week, and then proceed through the romantic philosophers to Nietzsche and Schopenhauer."

"With a little time to spare for the American Transcendentalists, I should hope," suggested the rhinoceros. Professor Gottesman, being some distance past surprise, nodded. The rhinoceros said reflectively, "I think I should prefer to hear you on Comte and John Stuart Mill. The romantics always struck me as fundamentally unsound."

This position agreed so much with the Professor's own opinion that he found himself, despite himself, gradually warming toward the rhinoceros. Still formal, he asked, "May I perhaps offer you a drink? Some coffee or tea?"

"Tea would be very nice," the rhinoceros answered, "if you should happen to have a bucket." Professor Gottesman did not, and the rhinoceros told him not to worry about it. It settled back down before the fire, and the Professor drew up a rocking chair. The rhinoceros said, "I must admit, I do wish I could hear you speak on the scholastic philosophers. That's really my period, after all."

"I will be giving such a course next year," the Professor said, a little shyly. "It is to be a series of lectures on medieval Christian thought, beginning with St. Augustine and the Neoplatonists and ending with

William of Occam. Possibly you could attend some of those talks."

The rhinoceros's obvious pleasure at the invitation touched Professor Gottesman surprisingly deeply. Even Sally Lowry, who often dropped in on his classes unannounced, did so, as he knew, out of affection for him, and not from any serious interest in epistemology or the Milesian School. He was beginning to wonder whether there might be a way to permit the rhinoceros to sample the cream sherry he kept aside for company, when the creature added, with a wheezy chuckle, "Of course, Augustine and the rest never did quite come to terms with such pagan survivals as unicorns. The best they could do was to associate us with the Virgin Mary, and to suggest that our horns somehow represented the unity of Christ and his church. Bernard of Trèves even went so far as to identify Christ directly with the unicorn, but it was never a comfortable union. Spiral peg in square hole, so to speak."

Professor Gottesman was no more at ease with the issue than St. Augustine had been. But he was an honest person—only among philosophers is this considered part of the job description—and so he felt it his duty to say, "While I respect your intelligence and your obvious intellectual curiosity, none of this yet persuades me that you are in fact a unicorn. I still must regard you as an exceedingly learned and well-mannered Indian rhinoceros."

The rhinoceros took this in good part, saying, "Well, well, we will agree to disagree on that point for the time being. Although I certainly hope that you will let me know if you should need your drinking water purified." As before, and as so often thereafter, Professor Gottesman could not be completely sure that the rhinoceros was joking. Dismissing the subject, it went on to ask, "But about the Scholastics—do you plan to discuss the later Thomist reformers at all? Saint Cajetan rather dominates the movement, to my mind; if he had any real equals, I'm afraid I can't recall them."

"Ah," said the Professor. They were up until five in the morning, and it was the rhinoceros who dozed off first.

The question of the rhinoceros's leaving Professor Gottesman's house never came up again. It continued to sleep in the living room, for the most part, though on warm summer nights it had a fondness for the young willow tree that had been a Christmas present from Sally. Professor Gottesman never learned whether it was male or female, nor how it nourished its massive, noisy body, nor how it managed for toilet facilities—a reticent man himself, he respected reticence in others. As a houseguest, the rhinoceros's only serious fault was a continuing predilection for hot baths (with Epsom salts, when it could get them.) But it always cleaned up after itself, and was extremely conscientious about not tracking mud into the house; and it can be safely said that none of the Professor's visitors—even the rare ones who spent a night or two under his roof—ever remotely suspected that they were sharing living quarters with a rhinoceros. All in all, it proved to be a most discreet and modest beast.

The Professor had few friends, apart from Sally, and none whom he would have called on in a moment of bewildering crisis, as he had called her. He avoided whatever social or academic gatherings he could reasonably avoid; as a consequence his evenings had generally been lonely ones, though he might not have called them so. Even if he had admitted the term, he would surely have insisted that there was nothing necessarily wrong with loneliness, in and of itself. *"I think,"* he would have said—did often say, in fact, to Sally Lowry. "There are people, you know, for whom thinking is company, thinking is entertainment, parties, dancing even. The others, other people, they absolutely will not believe this."

"You're right," Sally said. "One thing about you, Gus, when you're right you're really right."

Now, however, the Professor could hardly wait for the time of day when, after a cursory dinner (he was an indifferent, impatient eater, and truly tasted little difference between a frozen dish and one that had taken half a day to prepare), he would pour himself a glass of wine and sit down in the living room to debate philosophy with a huge mortar-colored beast that always smelled vaguely incontinent, no matter how many baths it had taken that afternoon. Looking eagerly forward all day to anything was a new experience for him. It appeared to be the same for the rhinoceros.

As the animal had foretold, there was never the slightest suggestion in the papers or on television that the local zoo was missing one of its larger odd-toed ungulates. The Professor went there once or twice in great trepidation, convinced that he would be recognized and accused immediately of conspiracy in the rhinoceros's escape. But nothing of the sort happened. The yard where the rhinoceros had been kept was now occupied by a pair of despondent-looking African elephants; when Professor Gottesman made a timid inquiry of a guard, he was curtly informed that the zoo had never possessed a rhinoceros of any species. "Endangered species," the guard told him. "Too much red tape you have to go through to get one these days. Just not worth the trouble, mean as they are."

Professor Gottesman grew placidly old with the rhinoceros—that is to say, the Professor grew old, while the rhinoceros never changed in any way that he could observe. Granted, he was not the most observant of men, nor the most sensitive to change, except when threatened by it. Nor was he in the least ambitious: promotions and pay raises happened, when they happened, somewhere in the same cloudily benign middle distance as did those departmental meetings that he actually had to sit through. The companionship of the rhinoceros, while increasingly his truest delight, also became as much of a cozily reassuring habit as his classes, his office hours, the occasional dinner and movie or museum excursion with Sally Lowry, and the books on French and German philosophy that he occasionally published through the university press over the years. They were indifferently reviewed, and sold poorly.

"Which is undoubtedly as it should be," Professor Gottesman frequently told Sally when dropping her off at her house, well across town from his own. "I think I am a good teacher—that, yes—but I am decidedly not an original thinker, and I was never much of a writer even in German. It does no harm to say that I am not an exceptional man, Sally. It does not hurt me."

"I don't know what exceptional means to you or anyone else," Sally would answer stubbornly. "To me it means being unique, one of a kind, and that's definitely you, old Gus. I never thought you belonged in this town, or this university, or probably this century. But I'm surely glad you've been here."

Once in a while she might ask him casually how his unicorn was getting on these days. The Professor, who had long since accepted the fact that no one ever saw the rhinoceros unless it chose to be seen, invariably rose to the bait, saying, "It is no more a unicorn than it ever was, Sally, you know that." He would sip his latté in mild indignation, and eventually add, "Well, we will clearly never see eye to eye on the Vienna Circle, or the logical positivists in general—it is a very conservative creature, in some ways. But we did come to a tentative agreement about Bergson, last Thursday it was, so I would have to say that we are going along quite amiably."

Sally rarely pressed him further. Sharp-tongued, solitary, and profoundly irreverent, only with Professor Gottesman did she bother to know when to leave things alone. Most often, she would take out her battered harmonica and play one or another of his favorite tunes— "Sweet Georgia Brown" or "Hurry On Down." He never sang along, but he always hummed and grunted and thumped his bony knees. Once he mentioned diffidently that the rhinoceros appeared to have a peculiar fondness for "Slow Boat to China." Sally pretended not to hear him.

In the appointed fullness of time, the university retired Professor Gottesman in a formal ceremony, attended by, among others, Sally Lowry, his sister Edith, all the way from Zurich, and the rhinoceros—the latter having spent all that day in the bathtub, in anxious preparation. Each of them assured him that he looked immensely distinguished as he was invested with the rank of *emeritus*, which allowed him to lecture as many as four times a year, and to be available to counsel promising graduate students when he chose. In addition, a special chair with his name on it was reserved exclusively for his use at the Faculty Club. He was quite proud of never once having sat in it.

"Strange, I am like a movie star now," he said to the rhinoceros. "You should see. Now I walk across the campus and the students line up, they line up to watch me totter past. I can hear their whispers—'Here he comes!' 'There he goes!' Exactly the same ones they are who used to cut my classes because I bored them so. Completely absurd."

"Enjoy it as your due," the rhinoceros proposed. "You were entitled to their respect then—take pleasure in it now, however misplaced it may seem to you." But the Professor shook his head, smiling wryly.

"Do you know what kind of star I am really like?" he asked. "I am like the old, old star that died so long ago, so far away, that its last light is only reaching our eyes today. They fall in on themselves, you know, those dead stars, they go cold and invisible, even though we think we are seeing them in the night sky. That is just how I would be, if not for you. And for Sally, of course."

In fact, Professor Gottesman found little difficulty in making his peace with age and retirement. His needs were simple, his pension and savings adequate to meet them, and his health as sturdy as generations of Swiss peasant ancestors could make it. For the most part he continued to live as he always had, the one difference being that he now had more time for study, and could stay up as late as he chose arguing about structuralism with the rhinoceros, or listening to Sally Lowry reading her new translation of Cavalcanti or Frescobaldi. At first he attended every conference of philosophers to which he was invited, feeling a certain vague obligation to keep abreast of new thought in his field. This compulsion passed quickly, however, leaving him perfectly satisfied to have as little as possible to do with academic life, except when he needed to use the library. Sally once met him there for lunch to find him feverishly riffling the ten Loeb Classic volumes of Philo Judaeus. "We were debating the concept of the logos last night," he explained to her, "and then the impossible beast rampaged off on a tangent involving Philo's locating the roots of Greek philosophy in the Torah. Forgive me, Sally, but I may be here for a while." Sally lunched alone that day.

The Professor's sister Edith died younger than she should have. He grieved for her, and took much comfort in the fact that Nathalie never failed to visit him when she came to America. The last few times, she had brought a husband and two children with her—the youngest hugging a ragged but indomitable tiger named Charles under his arm. They most often swept him off for the evening; and it was on one such occasion, just after they had brought him home and said their good-byes, and their rented car had rounded the corner, that the mugging occurred.

Professor Gottesman was never quite sure himself about what actually took place. He remembered a light scuffle of footfalls, remembered a savage blow on the side of his head, then another impact as his cheek and forehead hit the ground. There were hands clawing through his pockets, low voices so distorted by obscene viciousness that he lost English completely, becoming for the first time in fifty years a terrified immigrant, once more unable to cry out for help in this new and dreadful country. A faceless figure billowed over him, grabbing his collar, pulling him close, mouthing words he could not understand. It was brandishing something menacingly in its free hand.

Then it vanished abruptly, as though blasted away by the sidewalk-shaking bellow of rage that was Professor Gottesman's last clear memory until he woke in a strange bed, with Sally Lowry, Nathalie, and several policemen bending over him. The next day's newspapers ran the marvelous story of a retired philosophy professor, properly frail and elderly, not only fighting off a pair of brutal muggers but beating them so badly that they had to be hospitalized themselves before they could be arraigned. Sally impishly kept the incident on the front pages for some days by confiding to reporters that Professor Gottesman was a practitioner of a long-forgotten martial-arts discipline, practiced only in ancient Sumer and Babylonia. "Plain childishness," she said apologetically, after the fuss had died down. "Pure self-indulgence. I'm sorry, Gus."

"Do not be," the Professor replied. "If we were to tell them the truth, I would immediately be placed in an institution." He looked sideways at his friend, who smiled and said, "What, about the rhinoceros rescuing you? I'll never tell, I swear. They could pull out my fingernails."

Professor Gottesman said, "Sally, those boys had been *trampled*, practically stamped flat. One of them had been *gored*, I saw him. Do you really think I could have done all that?"

"Remember, I've seen you in your wrath," Sally answered lightly and untruthfully. What she had in fact seen was one of the ace-of-clubs footprints she remembered in crusted mud on the Professor's front steps long ago. She said, "Gus. How old am I?"

The Professor's response was off by a number of years, as it always was. Sally said, "You've frozen me at a certain age, because you don't want me getting any older. Fine, I happen to be the same way about that rhinoceros of yours. There are one or two things I just don't want to know about that damn rhinoceros, Gus. If that's all right with you."

"Yes, Sally," Professor Gottesman answered. "That is all right."

The rhinoceros itself had very little to say about the whole incident. "I chanced to be awake, watching a lecture about Bulgarian icons on the Learning Channel. I heard the noise outside." Beyond that, it sidestepped all questions, pointedly concerning itself only with the

Professor's recuperation from his injuries and shock. In fact, he recovered much faster than might reasonably have been expected from a gentleman of his years. The doctor commented on it.

The occurrence made Professor Gottesman even more of an icon himself on campus; as a direct consequence, he spent even less time there than before, except when the rhinoceros requested a particular book. Nathalie, writing from Zurich, never stopped urging him to take in a housemate, for company and safety, but she would have been utterly dumbfounded if he had accepted her suggestion. "Something looks out for him," she said to her husband. "I always knew that, I couldn't tell you why. Uncle Gustave is *somebody's* dear stuffed Charles."

Sally Lowry did grow old, despite Professor Gottesman's best efforts. The university gave her a retirement ceremony, too, but she never showed up for it. "Too damn depressing," she told Professor Gottesman, as he helped her into her coat for their regular Wednesday walk. "It's all right for you, Gus, you'll be around forever. Me, I drink, I still smoke, I still eat all kinds of stuff they tell me not to eat—I don't even floss, for God's sake. My circulation works like the post office, and even my cholesterol has arthritis. Only reason I've lasted this long is I had this stupid job teaching beautiful, useless stuff to idiots. Now that's it. Now I'm a goner."

"Nonsense, nonsense, Sally," Professor Gottesman assured her vigorously. "You have always told me you are too mean and spiteful to die. I am holding you to this."

"Pickled in vinegar only lasts just so long," Sally said. "One cheery note, anyway—it'll be the heart that goes. Always is, in my family. That's good, I couldn't hack cancer. I'd be a shameless, screaming disgrace, absolutely no dignity at all. I'm really grateful it'll be the heart."

The Professor was very quiet while they walked all the way down to the little local park, and back again. They had reached the apartment complex where she lived, when he suddenly gripped her by the arms, looked straight into her face, and said loudly, "That is the best heart I ever knew, yours. I will not *let* anything happen to that heart."

"Go home, Gus," Sally told him harshly. "Get out of here, go home. Christ, the only sentimental Switzer in the whole world, and I get him. Wouldn't you just know?"

Professor Gottesman actually awoke just before the telephone call came, as sometimes happens. He had dozed off in his favorite chair during a minor intellectual skirmish with the rhinoceros over Spinoza's ethics. The rhinoceros itself was sprawled in its accustomed spot, snoring authoritatively, and the kitchen clock was still striking three when the phone rang. He picked it up slowly. Sally's barely audible voice whispered, "Gus. The heart. Told you." He heard the receiver fall from her hand.

Professor Gottesman had no memory of stumbling coatless out of the house, let alone finding his car parked on the street—he was just suddenly standing by it, his hands trembling so badly as he tried to unlock the door that he dropped his keys into the gutter. How long his frantic fumbling in the darkness went on, he could never say; but at some point he became aware of a deeper darkness over him, and looked up on hands and knees to see the rhinoceros.

"On my back," it said, and no more. The Professor had barely scrambled up its warty, unyielding flanks and heaved himself precariously over the spine his legs could not straddle when there came a surge like the sea under him as the great beast leaped forward. He cried out in terror.

He would have expected, had he had wit enough at the moment to expect anything, that the rhinoceros would move at a ponderous trot, farting and rumbling, gradually building up a certain clumsy momentum. Instead, he felt himself flying, truly flying, as children know flying, flowing with the night sky, melting into the jeweled wind. If the rhinoceros's huge, flat, three-toed feet touched the ground, he never felt it: nothing existed, or ever had existed, but the sky that he was and the bodiless power that he had become—he himself, the once and foolish old Professor Gustave Gottesman, his eyes full of the light of lost stars. He even forgot Sally Lowry, only for a moment, only for the least little time.

Then he was standing in the courtyard before her house, shouting and banging maniacally on the door, pressing every button under his hand. The rhinoceros was nowhere to be seen. The building door finally buzzed open, and the Professor leaped up the stairs like a young man, calling Sally's name. Her own door was unlocked; she often left it so absent-mindedly, no matter how much he scolded her about it. She was in her bed-room, half-wedged between the side of the bed and the night table, with the telephone receiver dangling by her head. Professor Gottesman touched her cheek and felt the fading warmth.

"Ah, Sally," he said. "Sally, my dear." She was very heavy, but somehow it was easy for him to lift her back onto the bed and make a place for her among the books and papers that littered the quilt, as always. He found her harmonica on the floor, and closed her fingers around it. When there was nothing more for him to do, he sat beside her, still holding her hand, until the room began to grow light. At last he said aloud, "No, the sentimental Switzer will not cry, my dear Sally," and picked up the telephone.

The rhinoceros did not return for many days after Sally Lowry's death. Professor Gottesman missed it greatly when he thought about it at all, but it was a strange, confused time. He stayed at home, hardly eating, sleeping on his feet, opening books and closing them. He never answered the telephone, and he never changed his clothes. Sometimes he wandered endlessly upstairs and down through every room in his house; sometimes he stood in one place for an hour or more at a time, staring at nothing. Occasionally the doorbell rang, and worried voices outside called his name. It was late autumn, and then winter, and the house grew cold at night, because he had forgotten to turn on the furnace. Professor Gottesman was perfectly aware of this, and other things, somewhere.

One evening, or perhaps it was early one morning,

he heard the sound of water running in the bathtub upstairs. He remembered the sound, and presently he moved to his living room chair to listen to it better. For the first time in some while, he fell asleep, and woke only when he felt the rhinoceros standing over him. In the darkness he saw it only as a huge, still shadow, but it smelled unmistakably like a rhinoceros that has just had a bath. The Professor said quietly, "I wondered where you had gone."

"We unicorns mourn alone," the rhinoceros replied. "I thought it might be the same for you."

"Ah," Professor Gottesman said. "Yes, most considerate. Thank you."

He said nothing further, but sat staring into the shadow until it appeared to fold gently around him. The rhinoceros said, "We were speaking of Spinoza."

Professor Gottesman did not answer. The rhinoceros went on, "I was very interested in the comparison you drew between Spinoza and Thomas Hobbes. I would enjoy continuing our discussion."

"I do not think I can," the Professor said at last. "I do not think I want to talk anymore."

It seemed to him that the rhinoceros's eyes had become larger and brighter in its own shadow, and its horn a trifle less hulking. But its stomach rumbled as majestically as ever as it said, "In that case, perhaps we should be on our way."

"Where are we going?" Professor Gottesman asked. He was feeling oddly peaceful and disinclined to leave his chair. The rhinoceros moved closer, and for the first time that the Professor could remember its huge, hairy muzzle touched his shoulder, light as a butterfly.

"I have lived in your house for a long time," it said. "We have talked together, days and nights on end, about ways of being in this world, ways of considering it, ways of imagining it as a part of some greater imagining. Now has come the time for silence. Now I think you should come and live with me."

They were outside, on the sidewalk, in the night. Professor Gottesman had forgotten to take his coat, but he was not at all cold. He turned to look back at his house, watching it recede, its lights still burning, like a ship leaving him at his destination. He said to the rhinoceros, "What is your house like?"

"Comfortable," the rhinoceros answered. "In honesty, I would not call the hot water as superbly lavish as yours, but there is rather more room to maneuver. Especially on the stairs."

"You are walking a bit too rapidly for me," said the Professor. "May I climb on your back once more?"

The rhinoceros halted immediately, saying, "By all means, please do excuse me." Professor Gottesman found it notably easier to mount this time, the massive sides having plainly grown somewhat trimmer and smoother during the rhinoceros's absence, and easier to grip with his legs. It started on briskly when he was properly settled, though not at the rapturous pace that had once married the Professor to the night wind. For some while he could hear the clopping of cloven hooves far below him, but then they seemed to fade away. He leaned forward and said into the rhinoceros's pointed silken ear, "I should tell you that I have long since come to the conclusion that you are not after all an Indian rhinoceros, but a hitherto unknown species, somehow misclassified. I hope this will not make a difference in our relationship."

"No difference, good Professor," came the gently laughing answer all around him. "No difference in the world."

CONTRIBUTORS

Michael Armstrong lives in Homer, Alaska, with his wife Jenny Stroyeck, part-owner of the Homer Bookstore. Born in Virginia and raised in Florida, he moved to Alaska in the winter of 1979. He spent his first two Alaskan summers working on archaeological digs in the Arctic, experiences which inspired him to write "Old One-Antler" and *Agviq: The Whale*. He's done all the pre-requisite Alaskan experiences: flown over the Arctic circle, run sled dogs, built his own cabin, chopped wood, carried water, used an outhouse at 20° below, pissed in the Yukon River, faced down a grizzly bear, fished for monster halibut, etc. He has taught creative writing, English, and dog mushing at the University of Alaska. The author of four novels, he has been published in numerous anthologies and *Asimov's* and *The Magazine of Fantasy and Science Fiction*. His most recent work has appeared in *Fiction Quarterly*, with stories upcoming in *Asimov's* and *Not of Woman Born*. He is the SFWA Western Regional Director.

Peter S. Beagle was born in New York City in 1939. He has been a professional free-lance writer since graduating from the University of Pittsburgh in 1959. His novels include *A Fine and Private Place*, *The Last Unicorn*, *The Folk of the Air*, and *The Innkeeper's Song*. When *The Folk of the Air* came out, Don Thompson wrote in the *Denver Post*, "Peter S. Beagle is by no means the most prolific fantasy writer in the business; he's merely the best." His short fiction has appeared in such varied places as *Seventeen*, *Ladies Home Journal*, and *New Worlds of Fantasy*, and his fiction to 1977 was collected in the book *The Fantasy Worlds of Peter S. Beagle*. In 1997, ROC published *Giant Bones*, a series of novellas Peter wrote taking place in the world he created in *The Innkeeper's Song*. 1997 also saw the release of a limited edition collection, *The Rhinoceros Who Quoted Nietzsche and Other Odd Acquaintances* from Tachyon Press.

His film work includes screenplays for Ralph Bakshi's animated film *The Lord of the Rings*, *The Last Unicorn, Dove*, and an episode of *Star Trek: The Next Generation*. More recently he scripted two historical animated features including the award-winning *A Tale of Egypt*. He has also written a stage adaptation of *The Last Unicorn*, and the libretto of an opera, *The Midnight Angel*.

Peter currently lives in Davis, California, with his wife, the Indian writer Padma Hejmadi.

Janet Berliner is the award-winning author of five novels and over thirty short stories. She has edited five anthologies, including two with illusionist David Copperfield, and is in process of completing another with Joyce Carol Oates. In addition, she developed the concept for *The Unicorn Sonata* for her friend Peter Beagle to write. That book is now in development as a film.

Born in South Africa of parents who had escaped the Holocaust in Europe, Janet herself fled her homeland in 1961 under threat of imprisonment for her outspoken criticism of Apartheid. Her novel *Rite of the Dragon*, a political thriller set in South Africa, was banned there.

Her Madagascar Manifesto series—co-authored with George Guthridge and ending with a bang in the Bram Stoker Award–winning *Children of the Dusk*—attacked the question of anti-Semitism by examining the lives of three friends growing up in Germany between the wars. The books follow the characters down a bizarre sideline of alternate history to a small island off the coast of Madagascar where Jewish mysticism, African magic, and Nazi madness collide.

Janet is a member of the Council of the National Writer's Association, joining such past and present members as Jerzy Kosinski and Clive Cussler. She also served as the 1998 president of the Horror Writers Association.

Edward Bryant, though born in White Plains, New York, grew up on a cattle ranch in southeastern Wyoming. He attended a one-room rural school for four years before starting classes in the small town of Wheatland. He attended the University of Wyoming, receiving a B.A. in English in 1957 and an M.A. in the same field a year later.

He began writing professionally in 1968 and has published more than a dozen books, starting with *Among the Dead* in 1973. Some of his titles have included *Cinnabar* (1976), *Phoenix Without Ashes* (with Harlan Ellison, 1975), *Wyoming Sun* (1980), *Particle Theory* (1981), and *Fetish* (1991). *Flirting With Death*, a major collection of his suspense and horror stories, will appear in Autumn 1998. *Strangeness & Charm*, a new, expanded hardback edition of *Particle Theory*, will also appear. Someday.

Bryant's short stories have appeared in all manner of magazines and anthologies, including the prestigious *Norton Book of Science Fiction*. He's won two Nebula Awards, and in 1984 made it onto the map—literally—when he was placed on the Wyoming Literary Map by the Wyoming Association of Teachers of English.

Although a bit of a techno-phobe, he's presently hosting an Internet interview and talk show for Event Horizon, successor to OmniVisions, the electronic version of *Omni Magazine*.

He has worked as a guest lecturer, speaker, and writer-in-residence. He frequently conducts classes and workshops. He occasionally works in film and television, as a writer and as an actor; in 1994, he played the Bard's parody of himself-as-opportunist-writer, Peter Quince, in *Ill Met by Moonlight*, a modern, punk retelling of *A Midsummer Night's Dream*. He has also been a radio talk show host, a substitute motel manager, and a stirrup buckle maker, among other jobs. These days he lives with two Feline-Americans in a century-old house in North Denver along with many, many books. Presently he's working on a feature film script, a start-up comic book, and trying to finish a novel.

P. D. Cacek was born and raised in the sunny climes of California (many, many years ago), but she recently had her belly-button surgically removed and replaced with an "I-❤-Colorado" bumper sticker. Writing "ghostly" tales since the age of five (a fact that had both family and teachers worried), P. D. has, if the Internal Revenue Service is correct, actually been making a living as a free-lance writer for the past ten years.

Still a "ghost" writer by nature, her work has appeared in a number of small press magazines as well as *Pulphouse, Deathrealm, The Urbanite, Bizarre Bazaar, Bizarre Sex and Other Crimes of Passion, 100 Wicked Little Witches, Newer York, Deathport, Grails: Visitations of the Night,* and *Return to the Twilight Zone.* She won the 1996 Bram Stoker Award for her story "Metalica" (*Hotter Blood – Fear The Fever*) and has published a collection of her short stories, *Leavings* (StarsEnd Creations). Her first novel, *Night Prayers*, was recently released from The Design Image Group.

Included in the 11th volume of *The Year's Best Fantasy and Horror*, her short story "Dust Motes" (originally published in *Gothic Ghosts*, edited by Charles Grant and Wendy Webb) also made the 1998 World Fantasy Awards final ballot.

Robert Devereaux's stories and novellas have appeared in numerous periodicals and anthologies as well as being short-listed for the World Fantasy Award. Robert's first two novels, *Deadweight* and *Walking Wounded*, were published by Dell Abyss. His third, *Santa Steps Out: A Fairy Tale for Grown-Ups* (Dark Highway Press), which presents the erotic misadventures of Santa Claus, the Tooth Fairy, and the Easter Bunny, features introductions by David G. Hartwell and Patrick LoBrutto and a full-color cover and interior illustrations by Alan M. Clark.

Robert lives in Fort Collins, Colorado, working as a software engineer by day and letting his imagination run wild by dawn. A lighthearted devotee of the sacred and the sensual in everyday life, Robert has an extensive collegiate theatrical background and a grounding also in choral singing. He loves most types of music but has a special fondness for opera, particularly late Wagner and early Strauss. He accumulates far too many books and CDs and lives in bliss without a TV.

Finally, long an admirer of the deceptive simplicity and visual lyricism of Peter S. Beagle's prose, Robert counts it a signal honor to be included in this anthology.

Marina Fitch's short fiction has appeared in *F&SF, Asimov's, Desire Burn, Tales from Jabba's Palace,* and *Pulp-*

house. Her first novel, *The Seventh Heart*, was published in 1997. *The Border*, her second novel, is due out in January 1999.

She lives in Watsonville, California, with her husband Mark, about a mile from the oak tree where the Virgin Mary appeared a few years ago. She works as a PIP aide—playing with children one-on-one in a playroom filled with toys. Her previous "real" jobs included stints as editor, java jockey, bookstore clerk, secretary, journalist, luthier, busker, and publishing minion. She was once offered a job as a pitcher of Kool-aid, a position which she now regrets turning down. Of her writing she says, "My experiences and my dreams shape my fiction. Who knows what I might have written had I danced in front of Kmart in that Kool-aid suit."

Eric Lustbader was born and raised in New York City. He graduated from Columbia University in 1969. Before becoming the author of such bestselling novels as *The Ninja*, *Angel Eyes*, *Black Blade*, and others, he had a successful career in the music industry. In his fifteen years of work in that field, he wrote about and worked with such artists as Elton John, who later asked Lustbader to write the liner notes for his 1991 box set "To Be Continued . . ." He was also the first person in the United States to predict the success of such stars as Jimi Hendrix, David Bowie, and Santana.

He has also taught in the All-Day Neighborhood School Division of the NYC Public School System, developing curriculum enrichment for third and fourth grade children. He currently lives in Southampton, New York, with his wife Victoria, who works for the Nature Conservancy.

Lisa Mason graduated Phi Beta Kappa from the University of Michigan School of Literature, Sciences, and Arts, and the University of Michigan Law School; she practiced law in Washington, D.C., and San Francisco. Now she lives in the San Francisco Bay area with graphic designer and fine artist, Tom Robinson, and three cats, and writes fiction full-time.

Mason is the author of four novels: *Arachne*, *Cyberweb*, *Summer of Love*, and *The Golden Nineties*. *Summer of Love*

(Bantam Spectra, 1994) is about a far-future time traveler who must return to San Francisco during the summer of 1967 to save the universe. In *The Golden Nineties* (Bantam Spectra, 1995), a time traveler returns to San Francisco during the wild and extravagant 1890s. *Arachne*, *Cyberweb*, and *Spyder*, (William Morrow-AvoNova) are cyberpunk tales set in a future San Francisco.

Her acclaimed short fiction has appeared in numerous publications, including *Omni*, *Full Spectrum*, and *Year's Best Fantasy and Horror*. Most have received Nebula nominations, many have been translated into other languages, and "Tomorrow's Child," (*Omni*, 1989), was optioned for film to Helpern-Meltzer Productions.

William Howard Shetterly was born in Columbia, South Carolina, on August 22, 1955. He has written six novels and a few short stories, comic books, and screenplays. He lives in Los Angeles, California, with his beloved wife, Emma Bull. They have two cats, Chaos and Buddha, the secret masters of the universe. In 1994, he ran for governor of Minnesota on the Grassroots Party ticket, and came in third in a field of six. Among his favorite isms are vegetarianism and Unitarian-Universalism. Prisms are nice, too.

By day, **Susan Shwartz** is a financial writer and editor on Wall Street. By night and in any spare minute she can scrounge, she writes, edits, and reviews fantasy and science fiction. She holds a Ph.D. in English literature from Harvard with a medieval specialization. Her writing ranges from high fantasy to nuts-and-bolts military SF and alternative history.

She has been nominated for the Nebula four times and once each for the Hugo and World Fantasy Award and is now working on her twentieth book. Her most recent anthology, *Sisters in Fantasy (vol. 1)* will be published by New American Library. Her past two novels were *The Grail of Hearts* (Tor) and *Empire of the Eagle* (cowritten with Andre Norton and also published by Tor). Her forthcoming novel is *Shards of the Empire*, a historical fantasy of Byzantium, and will be published by Tor. She has written about sixty pieces of short fiction and published in *The New York Times* and *Vogue*.

Judith Tarr is the author of over twenty novels including the World Fantasy Award nominee *Lord of the Two Lands*, the historical novels *Pillar of Fire*, *Queen of Swords*, and *King and Goddess*, and the acclaimed fantasy trilogy, *The Hound and the Falcon*. Her most recent novels include *White Mare's Daughter* and the forthcoming *The Shepherd Kings*. She has published short stories in *Asimov's, Amazing Stories*, and numerous anthologies, including *After the King*, *Horsefantastic*, and *Alternate Kennedys*.

She holds a doctorate in Medieval Studies from Yale, and degrees from Mount Holyoke College and Cambridge University. She handed in the page proofs for her sixth novel and the final draft of her doctoral dissertation on the same day.

She lives just outside of Tucson, Arizona, where she breeds and trains Lipizzan horses. Her stallion, Pluto Carrma, was born at sunrise in a winter storm, under a comet, no less—and with a huge star on his forehead. There is, to date, no sign of a horn.

Asked why she wrote this story, Judith replied:

> "Very simple. I wrote what I know. I own, or am owned by, a Lipizzan. My friend owns another. We agreed quite some time ago that these are not normal horses. They're a rare breed, one of the rarest in the world. They live long, for horses; they're luminously white; they move with power and grace, and live to dance. And they understand English. They hardly need the horn and the cloven hooves—but since the editors of this anthology asked for both, I took matters to their inevitable conclusion."

Since *Immortal Unicorn*'s initial publication in 1995, Judith has added the following:

> "Life continues to imitate art. As I write this, Pluto Carrma is a yearling. Picture this: coat the color and textured shimmer of Damascus steel. Tail bright silver, flowing almost to the ground. Mane bright silver, but edged with a palm's width of jet black. Then he moves. He touches the ground once in a while, to

prove that he can. Mostly, and effortlessly, he floats.

"As I said, I write what I know."

Lucy Taylor is a full-time writer whose horror fiction has appeared in *Little Deaths*, *Hot Blood 4: Hotter Blood*, *Northern Frights*, *Bizarre Dreams*, *The Mammoth Book of Erotic Horror*, and other anthologies. Her work has also appeared in such publications as *Pulphouse*, *Palace Corbie*, *Cemetery Dance*, *Bizarre Bazaar 92*, and *Passion*. Her collections include *Close to the Bone*, *The Flesh Artist*, *Unnatural Acts and Other Stories*, and most recently *Spree*. Her novel *The Safety of Unknown Cities* was published by Darkside Press in 1995. Her latest novel, *Dancing With Demons*, was published in August 1998 by Obsidian Press. She is currently at work on a novel in White Wolf's Vampire game world.

A former resident of Florida, she lives in the hills outside Boulder, Colorado, with her five cats.

Nancy Willard has published two novels, *Things Invisible To See* and *Sister Water*; a book of essays on writing, *Telling Time: Angels, Ancestors and Stories*; numerous collections of poetry, including *Household Tales of Moon and Water* and *A Visit to William Blake's Inn: Poems for Innocent and Experienced Travelers*. Her most recent book for children is *An Alphabet of Angels*, which she also illustrated. Her work has appeared in *The New Yorker*, *Esquire*, and the O. Henry and Pushcart Prize anthologies.